THE GRAVE

RUSS WATTS

For Karen – this is just the beginning.
May the nightmares keep coming.

PROLOGUE

The year 2185

"Give it up, they're not going to tell you anything," he said wearily. His wrists were sore from the ties, his legs were going numb, and he had been jostled around for hours. The flight had not been smooth; strong winds had buffeted the helicopter and he was thankful his stomach was empty; otherwise, he would have spilled its contents several times over. Like the other prisoners, Franklin Roach's hands were tied behind his back, his legs were bound together and his feet were chained to the floor. He wore a dusty hood over his head. It had been placed there so he could not tell what direction they were going in, or see where they were flying. He knew though.

"I'm not talking to you, bitch," came the muffled reply from the unidentified man next to him.

Roach had no idea who else was on the flight. The last year of his life had been spent in a maximum security prison of which the last six months were in solitary confinement. He preferred the solitude to the constant interrogations though. He had endured many since his arrest three years ago, all to no avail. He had nothing to tell them. Agnew had made sure Roach would not see freedom again.

Sixteen hours ago, before ending up in the uncomfortable seat he now occupied, Roach had been given an injection. Protestations and demands to know what he was being given had been met with silence. He woke up some time later with a filthy hood over his head. From the way the room tilted from side to side, he could tell he was on a ship. He could not see, but the sensation of tilting made it obvious that he was out on an ocean somewhere. He had asked for help, where he was, asked for a lawyer, his wife, anyone, but he had received no answers. Evidently, he was back in solitary. He stayed there for another six hours passing in and out of a restless sleep.

Three hours ago, he had been marched out of the bunk he had been kept in and taken up onto the deck of the ship. His captors never once responded to his questions and when he was taken out into the fresh air, with the smell of the ocean so fresh and powerful, he thought he was going to be thrown overboard. However, with his hands and feet bound, he had been walked up the loading ramp of a Mi-17 helicopter and strapped in. That's when he had finally heard other voices and realised there were other people in the same situation as he was. For the most part, he kept silent and tried to listen to who was around him. He made out three different male voices and two female. Occasionally, a solider would grunt and tell them to shut up, but otherwise, he had no idea of who was surrounding him. The helicopter was transferring them somewhere, but they were being kept in the dark about it, literally.

"I can keep this going all day you know. Where the fuck is my lawyer? Hmm? You can't do this. You can't just move me from my cell without letting my lawyer know first. Answer me. God damn you, answer me!"

The voice that spoke was deep and gruff. Roach guessed it was from a male, probably of African descent, although it was blind guesswork at the moment. The speaker sat to Roach's left.

"They're not going to answer you," Roach said. "If they were going to they would've answered you hours ago, if only to shut you up."

"What do you know? Who are you? Are you one of them? I'll fucking kill you, man, you can't do this. I will fucking murder your family and..."

"Oh shut up, you'll do no such thing. You're a prisoner here as much as I am," said Roach. He had listened to the pleading and the baiting for hours and could take no more. "It doesn't matter what you say or what you do. I assume your hands and feet are bound like mine? True? Nice dark hood over your head so you can't see, right? You might as well sit back and enjoy the ride. If I'm right, then it's nearly over. I think we're descending."

"He's correct." A light female voice with a hint of an accent spoke from opposite the men. "The pressure is levelling out and the engine is slowing, you can tell. Wherever we're going, we're nearly there."

Roach had decided this woman was American too, but not from the South like him. She spoke well, clearly, and surprisingly calm, considering the circumstances. He rolled his head on his shoulders, trying to loosen his muscles. If they were headed where he suspected, it would have been better if they had thrown him overboard. Drowning would be a far better way to die than this.

There was the sound of someone walking toward them and the footsteps stopped directly in front of Roach. "Right, we are almost there. Keep your seatbelts fastened, ladies and gentlemen. Turn off all electronic devices and put your seatback trays into the upright position."

Roach heard laughter from toward the cockpit and then a different voice.

"Don't you get tired of the same joke every time, Warwick?"

"Never. Now shut up and let me do my work, Brooks."

Roach wondered why the men had been quiet for so long. The soldiers had hardly spoken for the whole flight, yet suddenly, they were chatting and laughing just as they were landing. They were using each other's names too. It was as if they suddenly felt free; as if the usual rules of engagement didn't apply.

"As I was saying before Brooks so rudely interrupted me, we are now entering neutral airspace. That means that from now until we get on the ground, which should be in about five minutes, we are effectively in a dead zone; so no radio, no satellites, no sexy phones, and no internet. That means nobody is listening, nobody is watching, and *I* am in charge. If you all listen to me and follow my instructions, then we can get this over with quickly and easily."

"Get *what* over with, Mr Warwick?" asked the female voice opposite Roach. "We've been asking you for the past three or four hours but..."

There was the sound of something being hit, a thud, and then Roach heard the woman sobbing.

"That's *Sergeant* Warwick to you, or Sir, if you prefer. Now let me just say this has been a very pleasant flight today. I personally have managed to have a good nap and I intend to be home in time for the lamb rack this evening. So, no more questions please. I've had to put up with your constant fucking moaning *all* the way here. Sit tight, shut up and all will be explained soon. Now buckle up, people, and we'll have you on the ground in no time."

Roach heard his neighbour protesting and shouting about his civil rights, but surmised that Sergeant Warwick wasn't much interested in anyone's civil rights. The woman was still sobbing and it wasn't hard to guess that she had been struck with something, most likely a gun. Some of the other voices were shouting now. Roach heard two more men from further down the helicopter. One was gibbering away in Spanish and Roach had no idea what that man was saying. The other voice was Southern like his, but he didn't recognise the voice as anyone he knew.

Roach stayed silent and waited for the landing. When it came, it was surprisingly smooth. The winds were much stronger higher up it seemed. It was going to be a relief to get the cuffs and hood off. He hadn't seen daylight for almost twenty four hours now and it was going to be painful when they finally let him see again. What he was going to see was questionable. He had long ago given up hope of seeing his family again. Ever since they had dragged him out of his bed at three a.m. and separated him from his wife, Roach had not seen her or his children. He had never actually been formally charged with anything, but again, he wasn't surprised. He had made some formidable enemies in his work and Agnew was as powerful as they came.

When they had safely landed, he heard the soldiers laughing and talking before they opened up the back of the helicopter. The chains around his ankles were unlocked as hands grabbed him, raised him up, and forced him down the ramp. Even though he wore the hood, he could tell they were in direct sunlight. His feet dragged across a hard surface that felt solid, like asphalt. The hood was sharply pulled off his head, and instantly, he shut his eyes. The sun was square in his eyes and it took a full minute before he could properly adjust to the light. Even then, it was painful and his eyes watered constantly. The air was cool and the sky blue. He had begun to lose track of time, but estimated it to be late afternoon. There were no streetlights or noise from engines or factories nearby. He could not hear any birds. The place they had landed in was lacking that general hum you get from walking down a busy street, and every second that passed, only reinforced his idea as to where they were.

Whilst he waited for his eyes to get used to light again, the soldiers busied themselves and he felt the ties around his wrists being cut. He heard the snips as his fellow prisoners were cut free too, although their legs were still shackled. They would be able to use their hands and shuffle slowly, but though he thought about trying, he was incapable of running. Where would he even run?

The helicopter's blades had stilled and the engine was quiet. Apart from the soldiers working, Roach became aware of another noise. It was like a crowd of people talking in low voices, just murmuring and whispering. It was coming from all directions, but as he looked around through squinted eyes, he could not see a crowd. There were four soldiers ahead of him and one sat in the helicopter's cockpit. They all looked quite relaxed. One was smoking and the others were idly chatting. All were armed to the teeth. The final soldier was silently reading a piece of paper. Roach looked to his left and right. The other prisoners had been lined up alongside him. There were five others: two women and three men. One of the women had a nasty cut on the side of her face and Roach assumed she was the one that Sergeant Warwick struck.

The lone soldier standing in front of the six prisoners slung his automatic weapon over his shoulder and held the piece of paper up. "I am Sergeant Warwick and I'm in charge of this detail. I am hereby legally sworn to read aloud this affidavit, under instruction of Resolution 59, Article 6 of the United Nations Decrees that stipulates that, as the present commanding officer, I am lawfully permitted to advise you that all charges against you have been dropped and you are now free to go. You are hereby released from the custody of the US government. The terms and conditions of your release will further be availed to you upon disembarkation of your transport. Congratulations."

The four soldiers behind Warwick cheered and clapped. Roach looked on in disdain. Prisoners who were released were usually led out through the front gates and given release forms to sign along with a load of other paperwork. He had worked in an office for ten years and never seen bureaucracy take a day off.

There were no legal representatives present here and it did not feel like a release. He looked around him. They had landed on the roof of a building. There was no airport or runway. There were no identifiable features as to their location, just a concrete wall on two sides and a sheer drop on the others. He could see the top of a fence with pointed metal posts and barbed wire running across the top and then nothing. The sunlight was still painful and he wiped the tears with his now free hands. They might have been released from custody, but they were not being given their freedom, not yet.

"So where are we? If we're free, I want to go home. Where is my family?" The woman to Roach's left had so far remained quiet. She had a strong physical presence and although Roach was six feet tall, she stood several inches taller than he did. She was dressed in standard prison uniform, but had striking features; a blunt nose and a thick accent that made Roach think she was not from the US, at least not originally.

"I do not recognise your *power*, Sergeant. I answer to one power only. After God, there is my people and the Ukrainians who voted for me. My name is Dagrzycksa Izliev and I *demand* to see..."

"You can demand all you like darlin', but what you see is what you get," said Warwick. "You see any Ukrainians here, Brooks?"

"Sir! No sir! I don't see God either."

Roach could see Brooks was sitting with the others, smoking and laughing. They were at ease and had obviously gone through this procedure many times before.

"What is this bullshit, man?" A voice from down the line spoke and Roach turned to see who it was. He recognised the voice as the same one that had spent the last three hours next to him on the plane whining.

The man was dressed in standard issue prison uniform, as they all were except for himself. The stranger was dark skinned and had a shaved head. His arms were folded in front of him and he shuffled forward to speak. "You say we're free, but I don't see no ride, man. Where am I? Who the fuck are you? This is whacked."

Warwick laughed and turned to the other soldiers. "Who *I* am is not really very important, besides I already told you that. You,

Mr Jackson, are much more relevant to what is going on here. You know what? I enjoy my job. It has its good days and its bad. On the whole, it's a frigging breeze." Warwick walked back to the helicopter and took a smoke from one of the other soldiers. He leant leaned back against the helicopter and took a couple of drags before continuing. "Mr Jackson, you are a homicidal maniac. Convicted on all counts, I hear. You killed three police officers in Boston before shooting two hostages, one of whom was a pregnant woman. You really think you can get away with that?"

"Whatever, man, I don't have to listen to this." Jackson flicked the solders the middle finger.

"Do you know who else is here, Mr Jackson?" said Warwick calmly.

"I don't give a shit. Just let me go before I kill you. You said I'm free, didn't you? I haven't had a beer in three years,so just let me go, man."

Warwick laughed once more and then flicked the cigarette away. "What do you say, Brooks, shall we fill them in?"

Roach watched as the young soldier stood smartly to attention and saluted. "Sir! Yes, sir!"

"Fine. At ease, Brooks. Mr Jackson look to your left and you will notice you are standing next to a fine chap by the name of Mr Dwight Emmerson. He has been convicted of first-degree murder on six counts. Six *black* people, Mr Jackson. Not just anyone either, but a whole family: mom, pop and the four kiddies. The youngest was only eleven months old. Mr Emmerson is what you would call a *white supremacist*, isn't that right, Dwight?"

The man looked straight ahead and said nothing. Roach could see the tattoos covering his neck and bald head. Both Emmerson and Jackson looked as if they spent their waking hours lifting weights. Roach hoped that if there were any trouble, he would end up on their side. There was no doubt that he was in bad company though, and wondered why he had been put together with these people in particular.

"The man standing beside Dwight is Mr Leone. Originally from Mexico, he spent the last five years building up quite an impressive drug industry in the South West. It's literally impossible to say how many people have died from the fucked up heroine he put onto the streets. In our little playgroup today, we also have a couple of ladies for a change."

The soldiers behind Warwick cheered again, and then wolf-whistled at this. They were acting like schoolchildren on day release. When Warwick turned around to glare at them, they quickly shut up and he went on.

"Min Wang, the woman with a big mouth, is probably best described as...what...a political dissident? She sold state secrets to the Chinese. Ms Izliev is a guest here, courtesy of our friends from Russia. Whatever she's done, I'm sure she deserves to get what's coming to her. Finally, further down the line we have Mr Franklin Roach, something of a superstar. I almost feel like getting my autograph book out."

Roach felt all eyes on him. The prisoners stared at him too and he could feel his face burning red. He knew what was coming next. He also knew there was no point denying it as he had spent the last two years doing just that. The fact he was innocent was irrelevant. Agnew wanted him out of the way and now he had found a way of doing it.

"You're Franklin Roach? The one who did the bombings? I thought you were living it up in Paraguay or someplace. Fuck me," said Emmerson. "I heard you took out twenty nine niggers in one go, that's impressive."

"What did you just say?" said Jackson outraged. "I should beat your white ass right now."

"Settle down, boys," said Warwick, bringing his rifle back around to his front. He walked up to Roach. "Mr Roach here organised the San Francisco bombings of 2180. Probably pushed the button himself, for all we know. You would have read about it all over the news I'm sure. You're in special company today. This here is enemy number one."

"I don't get it," said Min. "You say you're releasing us, but why? Murderers, terrorists, and racists? I don't care who these people are, they're nothing to do with me. Where are we? Explain what exactly is going on, *Sergeant*."

Warwick walked to face the group, and with a salacious smile, looked them up and down. "Anyone? Anyone at all?"

"I know," said Roach. "I *think* I know where we are."

"Where?" said Izliev. She looked at him scornfully, unaware that he had nothing to do with the bombings and the deaths of eighty-five people. She had seen the news the same as everyone else. Roach was a terrorist and a cold-blooded murderer.

"The Grave," said Roach quietly. He felt disconsolate. They had won. Agnew had beaten him. The world had been fed a pack of lies and they had bought it all. Roach was going to die and he knew it.

"What's The Grave?" asked Emmerson.

"Read a fucking book, you redneck, racist retard," retorted Jackson.

Emmerson swung a punch at Jackson and the two men fell in a heap, punching and hitting each other as they rolled about on the roof. With their feet tied, neither of the men could stand up to fight properly. Warwick unleashed a volley of bullets into the air above them and the fighting immediately ceased. Both men scrambled to their feet, knuckles bruised and noses bloodied.

"All right, party's over," said Warwick. "Let's get on with this. You are now officially on American soil. Over there to my left is a ladder. Sort of. You must exit these premises using the ladder until you reach the other side of the perimeter fencing. Once you reach the other side, you are free. Any questions?"

"You're joking, right?" asked Izliev. She jutted out her prominent jaw and took a small step forward. "I'm not going anywhere with these people."

Since the gunfire, the murmuring Roach heard earlier had grown in volume and he now knew where it was coming from. It was all around them, just out of sight. It was coming from below them, surrounding them on all sides. There was nowhere to run to. He knew the ladder would almost certainly not lead to freedom.

"The Grave? This is a joke. Where are your superiors?" asked Min.

"No way, man, no way you can do this," said Jackson.

Roach could sense the panic building in the prisoners. They knew what it meant to be here and why they were here. Freedom was not waiting for them on the other side of the fence, only death. Roach could see Dwight looking confused and scared. He didn't know what this place was. At that moment, Roach noticed the other man, the one who had until now kept quiet. He was elderly and small, not like the other men. Warwick had ignored him when listing their names.

"Sergeant Warwick," said the man clearing his throat. "If I may?"

"What is it, Quentin?"

Quentin turned to face the prisoners. "You're not being freed. Far from it, you're expected to die here. I've been working with the authorities trying to find a cure for them. Until about a year ago anyway, then it all changed. I found out what's really going on here. This place is..."

"All right, Quentin, that'll do," said Warwick. He took a step toward the man.

"Fuck you, Warwick, I know all about you," said Quentin.

Roach was surprised. The man looked so small and frail, yet he spoke with determination and fierceness. He was glaring at the sergeant now and Warwick almost stepped back. Roach looked around and could see the ladder they had been told to cross. It was perched perilously on the edge of the rooftop and went across the yard with the other end resting on top of the tall fence. A fallen tree was leaning against the fence on the outside, no doubt conveniently placed for them to make their escape to 'freedom.' Beyond the beech trees, he could not see. What was below the ladder, the things making the moaning sounds, was too terrifying for Roach to contemplate. Perhaps, this Quentin would be able to help them. He seemed to know what was going on.

"What's out there?" asked Emmerson. "What's with this place?" The man might have the muscled body of a weightlifter, but he had the look of a man who knew he was about to be in some serious shit, thought Roach.

"If we take a step onto that ladder, we are dead," continued Quentin. "The Deathless live here. They have this island all to themselves. I, for one, am not going out there. If the dead don't kill you, the infection will. Sergeant Warwick, I demand you take us back this instance. A lifetime in prison would be preferable to being condemned to The Grave." Quentin began shuffling forward toward the helicopter.

"Hey if he's going, I want out too." Jackson began shuffling forward too.

Roach stayed where he was. He watched as Sergeant Warwick raised his gun and pointed it squarely at Quentin.

"Freeze, now!" shouted Warwick, but Quentin kept moving closer to the soldiers and the helicopter.

Roach watched as the other soldiers got up, realising events were getting out of hand. He heard Warwick tell Quentin to stop, and then gunfire shattered the peace. Quentin's body exploded as a barrage of bullets smashed through his body, sending his blood all over the rooftop. The man crumpled to the ground, dead. Min screamed as Emmerson and Jackson dropped to the ground, shielding themselves from the gunfire. Roach instinctively ducked, but was too shocked to react. He heard Izliev next to him begin crying and Leone muttering in Spanish. When Warwick stopped firing, there was near silence again. All Roach could hear was the murmuring from below. It was definitely louder now and he could hear thumping noises and bangs as the Deathless tried to climb the building.

"Jesus Christ," said Brooks.

"If you lazy fuckers had been paying attention, we could be halfway back by now. He would've exposed us and you know it. We've got our orders. Pick up his body and get rid of it. Now!" screamed Warwick.

Brooks and Springman reluctantly picked up Quentin's bloody body and dragged it to the edge of the roof where they dumped it over the edge. Roach felt sick. He knew that if they didn't leave now, Warwick was likely to shoot them all where they stood. He put his hands up. "Warwick, I'll go. I'll go first. Just give us a fighting chance. Okay? How about these leg braces, eh?"

Warwick motioned for another of the soldiers to go over to Roach and his legs were finally unshackled. Warwick kept his gun aimed at the prisoners the whole time, as did the others behind him now, alert for any more trouble.

Roach walked slowly to the ladder. "Min, Jackson, everyone; you should follow me. I don't think we have much choice here."

As he got closer to the ladder, he heard the others being released and their leg braces collected. The roof began to plateau and then he saw them. Below the roof, trapped in the yard by the fence on all sides, were hundreds of them. There were men, women and children, all pushing and shoving each other, all moaning and baring their teeth. Hands and feet banged on the walls, picking at the masonry, punching the bricks as if they could make the whole building fall down. Roach was terrified, but he felt pity too. These poor people that were before him; they had not deserved this. The infection had taken them and they had been abandoned here on The Grave. They no longer thought or acted like the living because they were dead. The terrible poison that man had created to save them from death had only hastened them toward it.

Roach reached the ladder and knelt down. He put his hands firmly on the rails and shuffled onto it with his knees supporting him on the rungs. He reasoned it must be about fifteen feet to the fence. He quietly said a prayer and looked down through the ladder. The dead were reaching up for him, jumping, scrabbling over one another, and fighting each other to get to him. If they made it, he would be eaten alive. He began to crawl forward carefully and hoped he could make it past the Deathless.

ONE
Four years later

"Sorry I'm late," said Suzy as she skipped down the steps and into the office of Dr Kelly Munroe. "New York traffic, what can I say?" she said holding her hands up.

"Don't worry, Suzy, it's only the single most important event in the museum's year," said Kelly without looking up. "It's not like the President's wife is attending or anything."

Kelly was sat behind her desk analysing some new data on her laptop. She was wearing a stylish Desigual Selva dress that Suzy had picked out for her earlier in the week. Her short brunette hair showed off her neckline well and she had applied just a touch of make-up. She was far more at home studying or out there in the field than hobnobbing, but this was an important fundraiser and a lot of high profile people were going to be there.

"I know, I know, I'm sorry. You look great by the way." Suzy burst into the office, a bundle of energy, and sank into a chair. She pulled off her sneakers and pulled a pair of black heels out that matched her dress. "You really think she'll be here? I heard she's into the arts, mostly opera, ballet, stuff like that. Are you going to tap her up? Imagine if the freaking President was on the board. We'd never have to do a fundraiser ever again. So what do you think?"

Kelly dragged her eyes away from the screen to see Suzy twirling around her office in a little black dress. It showed off her slim figure perfectly and Kelly couldn't help but smile. She had taken Suzy on a year ago and she had proven herself an excellent assistant. There was no doubt she loved the New York lifestyle, but she worked as hard as she partied and was very reliable.

"Very nice," said Kelly. She turned off her laptop and glanced at the time. She would have to go and start mingling now. "You sure you're wearing that for the museum's benefit and no one else?"

Suzy picked up her bag and straightened down her strawberry blonde hair. "I don't know what you mean. I'm here to meet the First Lady. No one else is going to get a look in, period."

"Of course, Suzy," said Kelly as she picked up her handbag. She flicked the lights off and together, they left her office and began walking back up the stairs to the main hall. "I think Will Forrest will be here tonight. His flight landed a couple of hours ago, so I asked him if he would make an appearance. He *is* one of our best researchers."

"I don't know why you're telling me that," said Suzy as they continued up the stairs. She looked at Kelly and couldn't help but grin. Kelly winked back at her and they said no more.

The American Museum of Natural History was buzzing. On the steps outside, photographers waited anxiously, and men in dark suits stood either side of a red carpet. Various dignitaries and celebrities had been entering the museum for the last hour. The majority had made their way through to the Guggenheim Hall where waiters served champagne and hors d'oeuvres. All the directors and employees of the museum were present, talking up the next expedition and exhibits planned in the year ahead.

Kelly, as Associate Director, was due to give a speech in an hour. It was not her favourite part of the job, but she understood its importance to both her own career and the future of the museum. She spent a lot of the year travelling and as much time as possible in her office studying and planning for the next trip. She had asked Suzy to pick out a dress for her to wear because she didn't have time herself. It had been a year since she had last worn one and hoped it would be another until the next occasion.

As Kelly and Suzy entered the Hall of Ocean Life, they spied a familiar face. Breaking away from the group of men he had been chatting with, Professor Rasmus came over to them immediately. He had worked at the museum for nearly forty years, which was far longer than anyone else had. What he didn't know wasn't worth knowing and Kelly made sure he was well looked after. He would be retiring in a few years and the upcoming trip was to be his last. Kelly wanted to make sure it was a worthwhile venture and that he would enjoy it.

"Ladies, you look beautiful," he said beaming as he gave them both a quick kiss.

"Rasmus, I've never seen you look so smart," said Suzy. "Oh hang on, I don't mean that you're usually, you know, well..."

"Relax dear; you need a glass of champagne." Rasmus reached over to a passing waiter and grabbed a couple of glasses. He handed one to Kelly and one to Suzy.

"She's just nervous," said Kelly. "We have a VIP here tonight, don't you know."

"The First Lady? Why of course. Suzy, you must just not think about it. Relax and be yourself, my girl." Rasmus smiled at Suzy who was blushing.

"Actually I think she is hoping Will Forrest is going to make an appearance." Kelly looked at Suzy, trying to make her blush even more.

"All right, you guys, can it. I swear it's like being back at school here sometimes. Look, I am a professional. I am here to work and help the museum. Whoever is here is here and whoever is not is not." Suzy knocked back her champagne and handed the empty glass to Kelly. "Now if you'll excuse me, I have people to see and work to do." Suzy winked at Kelly, gave Rasmus a peck on the cheek, and then waltzed off in the direction of the main hall where a chamber orchestra was playing.

"So you all set for tomorrow? You must be looking forward to it immensely. Bags packed? Any last minute hitches?" Rasmus scratched at his white beard, thinking he should really trim it before the flight.

"Absolutely, you know me, I love it. I have everything planned and organised down to the last, so there had better not be any last minute hitches. If you jinx me, Rasmus, you're in for it. I don't know whose bright idea it was to book a flight for eight o'clock in the morning, the day after the museum fundraiser. There are going to be some sore heads on the flight tomorrow." Kelly sipped her champagne. She was purposefully making herself drink it slowly. She would need a clear head for the speech later and she didn't want to make a fool of herself in front of the First Lady and five hundred people.

"I have to thank you, Kelly. I thought I had been on my last field trip, but this one is just so exciting. I can't wait to get stuck in. I was talking to Tricia earlier and she said there would be ten of us going. I knew of you and Suzy and of course, Tricia and myself. Josef rang me yesterday to say he and Wilfred were going to meet us in LA and pick up the flight there. Who else are we bringing along to the freezing depths of the Antarctic?"

"Well I've managed to get National Geographic on board. It's a bit last minute, but they're sending a reporter, Mark Osborn. He's one of their best photographers and journalists. They haven't done a piece on the Antarctic Tundra for a while, so it's a good opportunity for them. The museum will get a fair bit of coverage out of it too. He's going to document what we're doing out there and will probably do some interviews with you guys too so talk us up. Let him see the research we're doing; this is a really good chance for some publicity for the museum."

"Good work, Kelly, I'm sure he'll be a fine addition to the team. So who else?" asked Rasmus.

"Brian Hadley. Everyone calls him Tug. Don't call him by his real name or you'll be in for it. He hates being called Brian. He's an English guy and I've worked with him a couple of times. Officially, he is the 'Executive Administrator' of our trip. Unofficially - he's the dogsbody. He'll be doing the heavy lifting, carrying the gear, sorting out the equipment, cooking our meals, and tucking us in at night. If you need anything, you come to him or me. Our last guest is a bit of a surprise: Claire Bishop."

"I don't believe I know her. Where is she from? Not another journalist, I hope. I think one is plenty, don't you?" said Rasmus.

"Actually, we've been running a competition in the schools and colleges in the area for the last few months. You know, trying to get the kids interested in geology and science, rather than basketball and baseball for a change. We have a wonderful young girl from Philadelphia. She's showing real promise and the museum is paying for her to come along. I'm going to get her involved with what we're doing, so it's *not* a free holiday. Hopefully, if it works out, we might even offer her a scholarship. I'm going to be announcing it in my speech shortly."

"Well, well, well," said Rasmus scratching his beard furiously. "I must say you are going to have your work cut out for you, my dear: a reporter, a school girl, an old man like me pestering you every five minutes and our two budding lovebirds. It's certainly going to be an interesting trip."

"I'll say." Kelly took Rasmus by the arm and they began walking toward the main hall where everyone was congregating. They said hello as they passed various colleagues and acquaintances. Kelly saw Tricia as she entered the Guggenheim Hall and waved. Tricia waved back and mouthed 'good luck' to her as she passed.

Once inside the hall, Kelly was taken aback at how splendidly they had made the place look. Instead of the quiet museum she knew, the hall was now full of colour, life and laughter. Huge sweeping curtains had been raised with the museum's logo displayed on each side. Helium filled balloons bobbed around the ceiling and she saw attentive waiters skirting amongst the guests with platters of food and drink. Kelly felt proud. Every year, it seemed to get better and better. Her father would have loved to see the museum today.

The sound of the orchestra was almost drowned out by the chatter and conversations going on. Kelly spied Suzy in a corner of the room discreetly fixing her dress behind a glass case full of stuffed birds. She left Rasmus and went on over to Suzy.

"How's it going?"

"Wonderful," said Suzy straightening up. "I saw Tricia on the way in. She's looking good. Has she lost some weight?"

"Yeah, she's on some new diet. Don't ask me. We both know whatever she loses, she'll put straight back on. Shit, how much of a bitch do I sound like? Anyway, have you seen Will yet? I was rather hoping he would be here so I could introduce him to..."

"Did someone mention my name?"

Will put a hand on Kelly's shoulder and she shrieked in surprise. Nobody noticed over the noise of the room and she greeted Will with a bear hug. He was wearing a tuxedo, like most men at the fundraiser, and he looked fresh and clean. He was a little over six feet tall and at twenty-nine, still had a shockingly full head of hair.

"Will, you made it!"

"Wouldn't miss it for the world," he said as Kelly released him. "I got home, unpacked, packed again, and here I am. I've gotta say, this tie is not my thing." Will fiddled with it, trying to loosen the button beneath the tie. "Feels like I can't breathe in the damn thing."

"Let me," said Suzy. Will stood still as Suzy laced her fingers behind his collar and loosened his tie. She kept her eyes focused on his neck, knowing he was looking at her.

"How you doin' Suzy Q?" said Will, giving her a kiss on the cheek as she stepped back. He ran his fingers around his collar, pleased he could breathe more easily now. He had christened her Suzy Q shortly after meeting her. He had a passion for old rock music, very old, and Suzy reminded him of Suzy Quatro. They looked completely different, but there was a certain confidence, a swagger about them, that they both shared. He didn't know if Suzy had figured it out yet, but she certainly hadn't picked up on it.

"See, you just needed a woman's touch," said Kelly, amused.

"Good to see you, Will, it's been a while," said Suzy. She couldn't help but admire him. He certainly knew how to wear a suit and with a good shave, he smarted up well. She was more used to seeing him in combat boots and trek shirts. Like Kelly, he spent most of his time travelling and avoided office functions when possible. He had itchy feet; that was how Kelly put it.

"Too long," said Will. "I just got back from the GC."

"The where now?" said Suzy.

"Grand Canyon. Sorry, I forgot. You New Yorkers don't go further than the Hudson, do you."

"Smart ass." Suzy shook her head and laughed.

"Look I've got to get moving. The First Lady will be here any moment. I'd better get out there and put on my best smile. How do I look?" Kelly patted her hair and struck a pose for Will to see her new dress.

"Great," said Will. "Knock 'em dead."

Kelly left and Will took a Snickers bar out of his pocket. He unwrapped it and took a huge bite.

"Holy cow, Will. What are you doing?" said Suzy in a firm but quiet voice. She looked around conspiratorially, but nobody had noticed them.

"Oh sorry," said Will. He held the bar out to her. "You want some?"

"No, thank you. That's not what I...never mind." Suzy stared at him amazed as he shrugged his shoulders and continued eating.

"What? I'm hungry," he said between mouthfuls as he shoved the empty wrapper back into his pocket.

Suzy wanted him to tell him off, and say he was embarrassing her, but all she could do was think how much she wanted to kiss him.

Will brushed the chocolate crumbs from his lips and took Suzy's hand. "Come on, let's go."

"Where?" Suzy felt a flush of excitement and grasped his hand in hers.

"The Yankees, where do you think? The First Lady just arrived, see?"

Will pointed and Suzy saw Kelly walking alongside the First Lady. She wore a sparkling deep blue dress and she was flanked on either side by men wearing dark suits. They were not museum staff or waiters.

Will led Suzy through the throng of people who were all clamouring to see the new arrival. There had been some doubt and gossip as to whether she would show up, but now she was here, the excitement level in the room went up another notch. Will tried gently to push past the A-listers and celebrities toward Kelly, but as he got closer, the crowd became thicker.

"Let's wait here," he said stopping by a sarcophagus.

"Why here? Kelly said we'd get to meet her. I'm sure if we explain who we are, we'll be able to get closer." Suzy pressed herself back against the display, resting on Will's arm.

"I'm sure we will, but we'll also piss off everyone we push past to get there. And they've got deep pockets," he whispered in Suzy's ear. "Kelly will have to go straight past here to get to the podium, so the President's wife will be right by her side. In about sixty seconds, she should be right here."

As they waited to meet the guest of honour, Will turned to Suzy. "I've actually been meaning to catch up with you. I'm sorry it's been a while."

"What do you mean?" asked Suzy innocently.

Will struggled to find the right words and hesitated before he spoke. "Truthfully, I wanted to call you, I really did. It's just that

I've been so busy with work. I had a great time with you and I...um..."

"Will Forrest, lost for words? I don't believe it," said Suzy. She could see him labouring to think of the right thing to say and decided to put him out of his misery. She wanted to talk to him too, but he had to be the one to bring it up first. "Look, Will, I had a nice time too. You don't have to explain anything or apologise. You're busy, I'm busy, that's the way it is. You're an honorary New Yorker now, so suck it up."

"You can take the boy out of Wisconsin, but..." Will realised he was still holding Suzy's hand, so he consciously let go. "You look damn good tonight, Suzy."

"Thanks. Does that mean you're going to buy me a drink later?"

Will's face gave away his inner thoughts and Suzy laughed. "Oh come on, I'm not the shy type. I grew up in Brooklyn with two brothers for heaven's sake. So you wanna get a drink after?"

"You know, I've dated a few women in my time, Suzy Q, but none like you."

"I'll take that as a compliment. One day, maybe you'll tell me why you keep calling me Suzy Q. Now shut up, here's Kelly."

They waited as the people in front of them were moved along by the security men. The First Lady was only feet away now and still talking with Kelly. A man wearing mirrored shades and a jet black suit suddenly put a hand on Suzy's shoulder. He had a gun discreetly holstered inside his jacket and short-cropped blond hair.

"Ma'am, if you'll just move along please, over there."

"Oh no, it's okay. I'm with the museum. Kelly Munroe is..."

"*Now,* please, ma'am," said the man trying to shove Suzy behind the display case.

"Hey, pal, you heard her, there's no need for that," said Will, putting his hand on the security guard. The blond haired man removed his shades and looked at Will with a fierce gaze. "Sir, this is not the time. Move or be moved."

Will was not for backing down and the men locked eyes. Just when Suzy thought Will was about to throw a punch, Kelly caught her eye.

"Suzy, Will, this is Mrs Richard, the First Lady."

"An honour to meet you," said Suzy, beaming.

Will nodded. "A pleasure."

"Mr White, get out of the way. These people are here for a good time and they're not doing any harm," said the President's wife sternly.

The blond haired man let go of Will and shuffled backward allowing a clear path for the First Lady. As he did so, his eyes never left Will.

"Kelly was telling me that you are her top man, Mr Forrest. You're leading a team on this expedition tomorrow, I believe?"

Now it was Will's turn to blush and Suzy enjoyed seeing him squirm. "Yes, yes, well not leading, really. I guess I'm doing my part for the...well, you know, there are a few of us going. It's going to be...fun."

"Fun? I hope you get a lot more out of it than that, Mr Forrest," said the First Lady, "Kelly was telling me that you have a lot of work to do. For what I'm contributing, I hope we're going to get a lot more out of this little trip south than *fun*?"

"Absolutely," said Suzy, unable to watch Will flounder any longer. The First Lady was clearly teasing him. When it came to research or finding new exhibits for the museum, Will was second to none. When it came to formal situations, expressing emotions or public speaking, he needed a lot of work. "We're hoping that the newly discovered plant life and nematodes within the Antarctic ice shelf could lead to numerous scientific advances. There's a lot of research we need to do to develop some of the ideas we have. Seeing it first hand is invaluable. Lake Vostok has been relatively untouched since it was mapped, but we've drilled down and already found an abundance of bacteria that we haven't even been able to chart yet. There are species of algae that..."

"Thank you, Suzy," said Kelly interjecting before the President's wife died of boredom. "I can fill you in with some of the more specific details later, if you wish, Mrs Richard. Right now, I'll take you to your table. I believe dinner is about to be served."

"Excellent. Oh, and Kelly, call me Sophie, please."

Kelly led the First Lady away and Will let out a sigh of relief. "Shall we get that drink now?"

"Oh, Will, you are hopeless."

"I don't know how you do it. I just felt so...nervous. Put me in an underground excavation or throw me out of a plane and I'm fine. Make me do a presentation in front of a room full of people and I crumble."

"I told you, I grew up in Brooklyn with two brothers."

Will grinned. "Kinda explains a lot."

"Don't get smart again, Mr Forrest. Or should I just call you the '*top man.*' Are you sure you even want to be seen with me? I mean, am I worthy of hanging out with the '*top man?*'" asked Suzy mockingly.

"Ah, Will, you made it, excellent." Rasmus appeared from behind the sarcophagus with a glass of red wine in hand.

"Rasmus, you old dog, how're you keeping?" Will shook Rasmus' hand vigorously.

"When you get to my age, dear boy, you'll know not to ask those sorts of questions anymore. So how did you get on with *Mrs Richard?*"

"Well, we had to get past her guard dogs first. One of them was getting a bit too heavy with Suzy. However, once we got past him, she seemed quite nice. I mean, I died a death, but Suzy here made a good impression. Well, actually, I don't know about *good*, but she certainly won't be forgotten."

Suzy hit Will on the arm and he pretended to be hurt. "She was fine, Rasmus. She's a nice lady and she looked *so* cute in that dress."

"I don't know how he managed to snare her, I really don't," said Rasmus. "Richard Agnew is a mean son of a bitch."

Suzy and Will were taken aback. Rasmus was always the gentlemen, even under pressure. They had never heard him swear or say a bad word about anyone before.

"The President? You probably shouldn't be saying stuff like that out loud here. The walls have ears," said Will.

"And guns," said Suzy remembering Mr White, the blond haired man from earlier.

"I wouldn't trust that man if my life depended on it," said Rasmus. His face was set in a frown and he looked angry. "Sophie

Agnew is the nicest woman you could hope to meet, I agree with you there, but her husband? Don't get me started on him."

Suzy was eager to change the topic. "Let's go eat. Will, can you find our table please? Rasmus, come on, let's just enjoy tonight. We're up early tomorrow so you might want to ease off on the red wine."

"You're right, of course." Rasmus handed his glass to Will. "Lead on, dear boy. Tomorrow is the start of an adventure. It's not without danger, so forgive me if I indulge in a glass or two of Shiraz. It seems the budget has well and truly been blown. We must be in prestigious company tonight."

As they walked toward the dining area where the tables had been laid out, Suzy quietly asked Will, "What does he mean danger? He's not going to pop a hip, is he?"

"Ha, no," said Will. "It's quite safe. This is your first trip, isn't it?"

"My first with the museum, yes. I had a few field trips back when I was at University. Spring break doesn't really count, does it?"

Will smirked at her joke. "He's talking about getting there. Once we reach base camp, we'll be fine. Cold, but fine. The most dangerous part of the expedition is getting there, but you needn't worry about that. We'll be fine. Kelly has sourced the best pilots for us. Just stick by me, you'll be okay."

They reached their table and sat down just as applause broke out. President Agnew's wife watched on as Kelly stepped up to begin her welcoming speech and the lights dimmed. It would be the last time Kelly gave a speech at the museum.

TWO

Dr Kelly Munroe swallowed the last of the mints Rasmus had given her and felt her ears 'pop' as they adjusted to the pressure. No matter how often she flew, she still could not get used to it. Taking off wasn't so bad. The landing is what aggravated her sinuses more. It was going to be a long flight and she settled in. She had brought some old copies of the museum's regular monthly journal with her to kill the time and settled on one from October 2154, twenty years before Kelly had started working for the museum herself.

She opened the journal and flicked through the pages, glancing at the headlines until she found something she wanted to read. It was a piece written by her father, Cedric Munroe, who had worked at the museum until his heart attack when she was twelve. She had fought hard all her life to be able to live up to her father and she had recently been awarded the post of Associate Director, the same title her father had carried before his death. He had articles in every journal, but the one she happened upon now seemed most apt.

They were en route from New York to LA where they were going to pick up Dr Josef Jahn, a freelancer who specialised in biogenetics, and Wilfred Kravern, an expert in Antarctic geology, who was cutting short his vacation to join them. Kelly had booked business class seats months ago to ensure they all got there as rested as possible. Last night had been a tumultuous affair and she had ended up not getting to bed until well after midnight. She stretched out and reclined her seat as the lights dimmed. Looking around, she could see Will, Suzy and Rasmus already asleep. Tricia and Claire were behind her, lost in a movie, whilst Mark in front was deeply involved in a thick paperback. Tug was staring out the window, holding a glass of water and swirling the ice around. The flight was due into LA late in the evening and they were then due to catch a connecting flight to Jakarta before onto American Samoa. From there she had organised a small charter to their final destination, Scott Base in Antarctica.

Kelly was tired. She yawned, but refused to sleep yet. She wanted to read this article first. Rasmus and Tug had mentioned something about the route they were taking and she wanted to know more. She had heard of The Grave and she was keen to learn more about the history of the island. She had a scattered knowledge of it, but it was a secret the world tried to keep quiet about. History lessons were brief. Quietly, she was equally eager to see how her father had reported on it.

'THE CULTURE OF DEATH'
A report by Cedric Munroe, Ph.D.

'We live in a time of fear. When they grew in number, they were given many names: The Broken Ones, The Perished, The Chosen, God's People; even The Devil's People. The name that stuck was the one simply that summed them up most accurately: The Deathless.

They divided opinion starkly and still do. It is only four years since our world changed forever with the advent of this new race. The fact they are a man-made race is either a cause for celebration or a curse. The only agreement the governments of the world have managed to reach is that these people were dangerous; *are still dangerous*. These men and women (or perhaps 'creatures,' depending on your point of view) are now protected and in the last few years have all been transported to a remote island where they are safely monitored and contained. We are told we are completely safe. Animals and birds can carry the disease, however, that infects these people, so the island has been cut off from the outside world by land, air and ocean equally.

Originally, the ruling party of this island attempted to slow the progress of this deadly infection. At first, they killed them. Towns were bombed and destroyed. When that failed, they isolated them. Small towns were covered by glass domes that spanned dozens of kilometres, huge bubbles over the land that wrapped the towns in a kind of protective bubble-wrap. The domes failed though and the outbreak continued. The domes were doomed to failure from the start; the materials and resources available meant isolation was impossible. The cost was too great and the Deathless were far enough spread that closing off one town was pointless. Rats and mice easily found their way out under the domes. It was decided to stop and simply build huge barricaded fences around the island instead.

Huge fences have now been erected all along the island's coastline and there is a strong military presence surveying and monitoring the country. It is an isolated country, one naturally protected by its mountains and oceans. Any birds flying in, out or through airspace close to The Grave would be shot down by the ever-watching military around the coastline. That was another reason New Zealand was chosen as the new land for the Deathless; most of its birds were flightless and the country did not have the mass migrations and flocks so prone to warmer countries. Te Ika-a-Maui was closed down and shut off. Te Waipounamu was abandoned. It was too close to be safe enough to inhabit and so it too was protected like Te Ika-a-Maui with its huge fences and UN ships guarding the waters.

For years, the country was known as Aotearoa. Then white men settled it and renamed it New Zealand. The country had to be given a new name, one more appropriate to its new standing in the world and one that would serve as a warning to anyone crazy enough to try to go there. So it was chosen as the place for the new race, the Deathless, to live. It is called The Grave.

There was worldwide condemnation and approval in equal measure, of course, but ultimately someone had to pay the price, and unfortunately, it was the Kiwis. The Deathless were to be put on that island and kept quarantined from the rest of the world. It had abundant life, both vegetable and animal, and it was easy to protect from terrorists. Around five million New Zealanders were forcibly relocated; some to Asia, some to Europe and many to the US. Remember, Australia had been destroyed by this point, so there was no close brother to take them in. Australia - a dead land, devoid of life, and contaminated by the disease - was almost chosen as the new home for the Deathless, but its barren, dry land and powerful heat was deemed cruel and inappropriate by the liberals. If we weren't going to kill the new race, then we had to put them on a land that would at least give them a chance to 'live.' This was spoken of without any irony.

Any inhabitants of the infected countries were deemed infected and killed. There was mass genocide, civil war, and rioting. Europe and parts of Asia escaped unscathed, as did North America. The sub-equatorial regions suffered the worst. Australia was decimated and genocide took place on a scale unheard of before. The Caribbean islands were wiped off the map with a tactical nuclear strike by the US who had been taking in countless boatloads of thousands of refugees. That was when, finally, the UN stepped in. Genocide could not be tolerated any longer, they said. Some observers raised a good question: why was it tolerated at all?

So where did the Deathless come from? Were they clones, aliens, some wicked little present from Mother Nature, or a scientific quirk from some previously undiscovered creature that had hitherto remained dormant at the bottom of the Mariana Trench? No, unwittingly it was human intervention. With the best of intentions, man has nearly obliterated himself. Again. The Enola Gay still flies around the globe, dropping these little gifts from time to time.

There was a massive drought problem in many parts of the world and it was only increasing as the years went by. Between 2130 and 2150, it was conservatively estimated that as many as ten million people died due to a lack of access to clean water: too many. A solution to this water famine was to create artificial water using the new genetic science that was shaping medical advances at that time. Electrolyte particles were allied to a new chemical substance created in 2149, commonly referred to as 'Aqua-Gene 119.' The resulting fusion led to a substance that had 99% of the properties of water. It looked like water, tasted like water, and yes, it even *felt* like water. It was far cheaper than desalinisation or mass migration. The only issue was that it wasn't actual water. Pumping the human body full of chemicals has never been a good idea.

It was decided to press ahead though. Only five years ago, millions were dying and so Aqua-Gene 119 was given the go-ahead, rushed through the testing phases, and distributed worldwide. In the driest areas, lakes and reservoirs were pumped full of the new wonder chemical. Three days is all it took to wipe out Australia forever. The African continent fell next. The central and western areas died out and much of the rest of the continent descended into war and chaos. Any survivors who had consumed the water had three days to live. That was the incubation period for the disease. It could gestate in the human intestinal tract without even being detected. It would then erupt like a volcano that had been tightly shut up for a thousand years.

The main problem with the infected is that they cannot die, which is to say, they are already dead. And you cannot kill something that is already dead. You can nuke them certainly; obliterate them, turns their atoms inside out and wipe their very existence from the surface of the Earth. However, guns, knives, and bombs are all useless. You can chop off an arm, but they will keep fighting you. You can blow off their legs, but they will crawl on their bloody stumps to get to you. You can even take off a head, and its jaws will keep biting. With the infection, the human body became an organism designed to kill. Stopping it was achieved only by total annihilation. That is why there was so much death, and something had to be done. Corpses were walking the Earth.

So here we are today. The end result of man's interference with the natural order of things is The Grave. If you want to try taking a positive out of killing nearly fifty per cent of the earth's population, I suppose you could say it meant four billion less mouths to feed. That certainly alleviated the problem of the food mountain and the millions starving in the Third World. Unemployment was non-existent afterwards. The world had bankrupted itself, but humankind had been saved.

A small country at the bottom of the world, thousands of miles away from the nearest living human being and cut off by vast oceans, became the new home for almost two million walking dead people. Most were dumped in Te Ika-a-Maui. The lower part of the country, Te Waipounamu, was mostly left alone, deemed unsafe for human inhabitation and too dangerous for the Deathless. Around the borders of the whole country, a peacekeeping unit was established. There is a permanent naval base with a flotilla of around fifty ships patrolling the water to make sure nobody gets in or out. Beaches were laid with mines and trip wires, and three billion miles of barbed wire were laid out along New Zealand's borders where its once green land had met the oceans.

The fences and soldiers are still there to keep people out. Naturally, some demanded to see their loved ones. Some wanted to kill them. Some just wanted to see what all the fuss was about. After a few incursions, nobody tried again. Lethal force is mandatory for anyone trying to enter or leave the islands. No questions are asked. No warning shots are fired. Anyone foolish enough to try to get to The Grave is executed immediately. The world cannot risk the infection getting out again. One scratch or bite from the infected is enough to turn you into one of them very, *very* quickly. A scratch or a bite allows the infection direct access into the bloodstream and the infected person has approximately thirty seconds before they die and reanimate. However, by ingesting Aqua-Gene 119 through contaminated food or water, it takes the human body between two to three days to turn: for some reason the infection lays dormant before causing death and reanimation. A drop of water, just one drop, is all it takes. There is no current method to detect if a person is infected or not, and it is not known why the death and reanimation process is so much longer. There is much work to be done on realising the damage this does to the human body.

If anyone from that island escaped and contaminated a water supply in the Northern hemisphere, the results would be catastrophic. It was sheer luck that five years earlier, the US had erected the 500 meter wall between itself and Mexico, otherwise North America would not be here today.'

Kelly was horrified. She had only a cursory knowledge of The Grave. It was marked on every map in every schoolroom in America and it was referred to as another country, although it had no flag. On the globe in her office, it was just two small, black triangles that she paid no attention to. To think that people had been dumped there like trash made her feel sick. And this had happened in her father's lifetime? She struggled to imagine how horrible it must have been at that time. New York had its problems, crimes and poverty, but this was a whole new level. She looked over at Rasmus who was still asleep. She was worried that their flight path was taking them too close to the island, but surely, the pilots would account for that. The airspace would be closed and the military probably wouldn't let them get within a hundred miles. Intrigued, she read on.

'The inhabitants of The Grave have been studied, but no one can agree exactly what they are. Once infected by Aqua-Gene 119, the body begins to die. Sufferers reported feeling as if they had the flu; that is until their final moments. Several subjects were monitored until the practise was deemed cruel. What we do know is that the heart withers away. It turns black, and at the last moment, contracts quickly and implodes. Those final few moments are torturous agony for anyone infected. A few seconds later though and the dead body will reanimate. Any semblance of a soul or humanity, of personality or character, is all gone; they are moving yet they are clinically dead. There are those who say that if the body is moving, then there must be something of the person still alive. No. If the heart no longer beats, then it is no longer keeping the human body alive. If blood is no longer pumping around the body and the lungs are no longer inflating or deflating with air, then that person is no longer...well, a person. Whatever impulses and functions are operating within the body is perhaps a part of the decomposition process. Make no mistake; the Deathless are a race of people certainly, but they are not living human beings. We are dealing here with dead bodies that move around *as if they are living*. Perhaps the infection makes them act like humans so they can move amongst us and hunt us down. Perhaps it is simply a motor-neurone action, started by the infection once the body has died, and thereby enabling the body capable of seeking out food sources in order to replenish itself. Tests were briefly carried out on those subjects and the neural pathways in the brain showed no indication of life. So how do they move? How do they use their senses to find prey? All attempts at communication with the test subjects failed. They were, and still are, a mystery: a dead end.

The Deathless effectively are rotting bodies and they can ingest only raw meat. They also take in water, preferably *infected* water it seems. The Aqua-Gene 119 chemical is like a drug to them. They cannot defecate or urinate, so it was surmised that whilst they appear dead on the outside, they are getting enough nutrients and minerals from the raw meat and water to sustain their bodies. The more they eat, the less they rot. Experts have testified that this infection almost acts like a retardation; reducing the mental power of anyone infected by Aqua-Gene 119. Instead of evolving, they are devolving. The Deathless are more akin to a prehistoric caveman, a primordial state of being, than a modern, civil human being. They show no sign of intellect or reasoning. They grunt and groan, but can't communicate with living humans. They live with a constant need to eat. Raw meat of any kind is palatable to them, yet they cannot stomach anything else. They do not eat their own kind for their meat is already putrid, rotten and maggot-infested. Living humans are ideal.

Therefore, these people now live in a forbidden zone where access is for highly ranked military officers only on official duties and a brave consort of scientists. They actually live on the island, buried away deep in a hidden bunker, surrounded by an impenetrable barrier, working desperately on a cure; trying to find something that will reverse the process and bring these diseased dead souls back to a more modern human state. The hope and aim is for one day to reintegrate these people back into society. I suspect it is too late for that. Nevertheless, a cure should be found. We cannot throw our arms up in the air and say, 'Oh well, life goes on.' For many millions, it never will again.

These scientists are living in terrible danger, but their work is so important to the future of the world that they are willing to put their lives on the line. Such is the secrecy and security put around them that we might never learn the names of these people. Whoever they are, I salute them. Reliable sources have informed me that a helicopter frequently lands on the rooftop of this secretive complex and offloads supplies: boxes and crates of food, clean water, and essential equipment for the scientists. Indications are that they are quite safe. The US Embassy is believed to be the access point for this bunker. It is secure, well maintained, and able to withstand any terrorist attack. Wherever they are, God bless you. Our nation respects and believes in you.

The Grave has been left unchecked for three years now and the ecology of the country will start to change and evolve. Without cultivation, wildlife will grow and the vegetation will flourish. We may see a very radical change to the land. Much of Te Ika-a-Maui has already begun to revert to its more natural, tropical vegetation that existed before, if reports are to be believed. Animal life, I'm sure will spread its wings far and wide. The sheep and cattle, so vital to men living there before, will die out. They are too domesticated to survive in the wild. Cattle's stomachs will explode and nearly all bovine life will die within days or weeks of being abandoned. Some sheep might still roam free, but the majority will be dead by the time I write this report. Thirty million sheep carcasses will provide enough meat for the Deathless to live on for months if not years. Infected lakes and water supplies will mean they can live much longer than humans can. For how long, nobody truly knows yet.

As for the homes and houses, the shops and restaurants, the cottages and power plants of this once proud nation, well they are all deserted now. The Deathless have no care or consideration for shelter. They have no need for sleep or rest. The land is but a shell, a pit to bury our dead and our secrets. Our children will be ashamed when they learn of what we have done to the world. Should we teach them everything? What, I wonder, should I tell my beautiful only child, my daughter who is barely six weeks old? We find ourselves at a crossroads. Our enemies are everywhere, terrorists are lurking in every town, and we destroy some of the most incredible places on Earth. You reap what you sow and humankind has planted the permanent seeds of death. That is the legacy of The Grave.'

Kelly let the magazine fall to her lap and closed her eyes as a shiver ran over her. She couldn't read anymore. Her father had been a brilliant scholar and his photo still hung in the Great Hall at the museum, alongside all the other directors. Hers would be up there one day too. How had he coped? With what the world must have gone through, he had still gone ahead and raised a family. Kelly had not married, not found anyone special, or had a serious relationship. She had just read an article about how the world almost ended, and all she could think about was her father. Was she so selfish, so intemperate and self-absorbed? Was that why she was still alone?

Somebody brushed past Kelly on their way to the bathroom and the jolt roused Kelly. She slid the magazine into the pocket in front of her and dimmed the light. She needed to sleep. It had been a busy few months and it had all built to a head last night. She needed rest for the expedition. When they arrived, they would be straight into work and she had to look after everyone. It was going to be a hectic few weeks.

She closed her eyes and remembered the gala last night. The First Lady, Sophie, had proven to be a very warm person and enjoyable company. Her minders had kept in the background apart from the brief altercation with Will and Suzy. Kelly smiled. She had noticed they had both taken off before the end of the evening and wondered if they had spent much time last night resting for the trip or divulging in other extra-curricular activities that were not on the museum's regular agenda. She forced her mind back to what lay ahead.

For Kelly, the chance of first hand research excited her. If she spent more than six months in her office back in New York, it was considered a long stay. She organised special field expeditions and usually managed to get herself a place on them too. The museum hadn't led a trip to the Antarctic for five years, so it was only natural that she should lead it. At thirty five years of age, she had dedicated her life to the museum and enjoyed the trips away from New York. She had no partner and no long-term boyfriend. Even the potted plants in her lounge were plastic so she could take off at a moment's notice and not worry about leaving her Upper East Side apartment.

The plane continued west and everyone on board relaxed and slept peacefully. The sun was chasing them and the flight was smooth and stress-free as the jumbo flew above the flat, white clouds. Josef Jahn and Wilfred Kraven were on route to LAX to join their colleagues and friends. They had worked together previously and knew each other well. Both were looking forward to working with Rasmus again too. Over the last thirty or so years, they had shared as much beer together as they had research. Though Josef and Wilfred had both missed out on the fundraiser, they knew they would be well represented. The First Lady had given Kelly assurances that the museum would be well looked after and a sizeable donation was on its way.

Kelly found her inquisitive nature getting the best of her, so she slid the journal out of the seatback pocket. She just wanted to read some more about The Grave. Sleep could come later.

* * *

Sophie Agnew had spent the night at the Hilton after the fundraiser and then travelled back to Washington the next day with her security detail. Back at the White House later in the day, she managed to find her husband in between meetings.

"How was it?" asked Richard Agnew, greeting his wife in their private chambers.

"Well, they were hoping the President of the United States would show up, but I guess you were busy, hmm?" Sophie embraced her husband and ran her hands through his dark hair. "What was so busy that Richard Agnew couldn't spend the evening with his wife?"

"You know how it is, Sophie. I said I probably wouldn't make it. How did you get on? Did White look after you?" Agnew squeezed the bridge of his nose together with his forefingers; trying to alleviate some of the pressure, he could feel building.

"It was a great evening, shame you missed out. Maybe next year? Kelly is really taking the place in the right direction."

Agnew frowned.

"Kelly Munroe, you remember her? From the museum? You – we – are sending her a big cheque tomorrow," said Sophie.

"Oh sure, fine. And White?"

"Why? I know he's your favourite, but he's been looking after me for what – six, seven months? He could do with loosening up a bit, but he's no trouble. I can handle him."

Agnew sat down in an armchair and rifled through some papers. "What with the G25 coming up and this damn conflict in the Yemen escalating, I barely had time to sneeze last night. I spent an hour on the phone with Senator Collins. Jeez, what an old woman. He needs putting right."

"I'm sure you can take care of him," said Sophie as she changed. She had a couple of hours before her next engagement and wanted to freshen up. She had stripped down to her underwear and paused. "What else is it?" She noticed her husband was flicking through the papers in his hands, but not really looking at them, or her. "Another of your migraines?"

"Hmm? Oh, sorry, it's just we've got the ten year anniversary coming up and Collins was banging on about what we're going to do: memorial services, ceremonies, media events, blah, blah, blah. As if I don't have enough to do without that old gasbag in my ear every five minutes."

"Darling, you need to relax," said Sophie. She checked to be sure that the bedroom door was locked and then walked over to her husband.

Agnew heard the door click and looked up. Sophie had slipped off her bra and had her thumbs tucked into her panties. She was still svelte and being on her feet all day helped maintain her healthy figure. She was looking at him with those come-and-get-me eyes she usually reserved for special occasions.

"It's been a while, Richard. I've got a bit of spare time before I have to go out again. You don't have to rush off do you?"

He looked at his wife approaching him and then gathered up the papers. He looked at his watch and stood up. "Actually, I've got to go meet Verity. She's giving us an update in the Oval office in a few minutes. We need to see what those Arabs have done now. I tell you, trying to keep on top of them is..."

"Shhh," said Sophie, putting a finger to her husband's lips. "You should just get on top of me," she whispered. Sophie traced her fingers across his lips and chin, and then reached up to kiss him. Her tongue sought to open his mouth, but he pushed her away.

"No, I'm busy Sophie, this isn't the time." Agnew marched over to the door and unlocked it.

"Richard, darling," said Sophie as she went over to her husband. She nuzzled against his neck, her cold nose making his warm neck tingle. She wrapped an arm around his waist and pressed her breasts up close to him. "I can help with your headaches, you know? A little stress relief..."

"No." Agnew pushed her and Sophie stumbled backward, falling onto the bed. He pointed his finger at her as she lay there, confusion drawn across her face, anger etched across his.

Sophie drew the covers around her naked body. "Richard, I love you, how can..."

"Fuck you, Sophie," said Agnew angrily. "You think this is easy? You think it's all fancy dinners and pretty dresses, parties and cocktails? You have no idea what I'm dealing with. Get dressed and start acting your age. You're not sixteen anymore. I'll see you later."

Agnew left Sophie with tears forming in her eyes on the bed and slammed the door behind him as he left. He stormed down the corridor, ignoring the men stationed outside his private room, and went directly to the Oval office. White was standing guard outside it and Agnew gave him a cursory nod as he went in. The room was quiet and empty. The curtains were drawn and the room was dark and soothing. A table lamp illuminated the room gently, enabling him to see what he needed to without having to look too hard. He needed a break.

Agnew threw the papers he was carrying onto a chair and sat down in front of his huge mahogany desk. Aside from the lamp and an intercom, the desk was clear and he ran his fingers along the cool surface. He let out a sigh and pinched the frame of his nose. Ten years ago, this had all been a lot easier. With the anniversary coming up, it was going to open up a lot of fresh wounds and raise more questions. The liberals would probably want another damn inquiry, just as they did every year. The survivors would want more explanations and he could expect more recriminations from the media. He had to rule the country now with an iron fist, not a velvet glove. It was being soft that had led to these types of problems in the first place. He did not intend to give up power now he was here, but that did not make it any easier. Sophie was just another headache he had to endure. His advisors constantly reminded him that the people would never vote for a single man. The President had to be a family man, honest, truthful, kind and caring. He would smooth things over with her later, but right now, he needed to forget everything and relax. A migraine was definitely threatening to erupt and he needed something to take his mind of the job, just for a little while.

Agnew pressed the intercom button. "White? Send in Verity Dawson and make sure we're not disturbed for the next hour. *By anyone*. I mean it. Unless an alien lands on the White House lawn, it is imperative we are not interrupted. Understood?"

"Yes sir," was the quiet reply. The intercom went silent and Agnew could feel himself loosening up already. He sat in his chair, waiting patiently. He made a mental note to speak to White about Senator Collins later. The man was making too many noises, causing too much kerfuffle about the upcoming anniversary. He had forgotten whose side he was on. A sharp reminder was in order. White could see to it. Agnew knew he could rely on him.

Three short knocks on the door broke his train of thought and the door opened. Verity Dawson, twenty five years old, a graduate of Stanford and now Senior Publicity advisor to the President, entered the room. She shut the door behind her and turned the lock.

"I don't believe our meeting is for another hour Mr President." Verity walked slowly into the centre of the room. She was not fazed by the low level light or lack of people in the room. She knew exactly what she was doing.

Agnew smiled. Verity was wearing a smart black suit and white blouse. She had her blonde hair bunched up as usual, tied at the back. Her natural brunette roots were just starting to show through. There was something about blondes that he just couldn't resist. Agnew pulled at his tie. "Take your clothes off. Now."

Verity stood in the centre of the room and slowly unbuttoned her blouse. She cast off her jacket and shirt, exposing her firm breasts, cupped in a pure white bra. Then she undid her skirt and let it fall to the floor where she stood. All the time she was undressing, she stared at him, not speaking or making any sound.

Agnew had removed his tie and he was in the process of taking his shirt off. He came from around the desk and walked up to her.

Verity licked her lips and ran her hands down his chest. She smiled wickedly and in the dimness of the room, she caught the glint in Agnew's eyes. "Just don't leave any marks this time," she said.

THREE

The small Dornier 228 drifted on the air current, jolted sharply in an air pocket, and then settled down to continue toward its destination. Its occupants settled down in their seats unaware of the danger thirty two thousand feet below them. They were cruising in a small but comfortable propeller plane, which had been chartered, organised and paid for many months ago by the American Museum of Natural History. The twelve men and women on board, excluding the two pilots, all worked for the museum in some capacity and had been picked up from American Samoa earlier in the day. They were on route to Scott Base, station FY3902-XX1 in the Antarctic, where they intended to spend the next three weeks observing and exploring the rapidly declining ice shelf. There were reports of new growths on the shelf and a host of interesting new specimens had been excavated already. They were all excited to be in on the possible new discoveries.

For Tricia Willis, it was her first field trip in nearly six years. She was fifteen years Kelly's senior, but worked under her at the museum. Unlike Kelly, she disliked field trips and she had managed to avoid them for the last four years. New York was home and her last trip was only to the Rockies, so she didn't even class it as a real trip, if it wasn't a different time-zone, it didn't count. Her office was next to Kelly's in the basement and she adored working there. She had swept through Philadelphia State and spent a year at a private research clinic before joining Kelly as an assistant. She knew being of African descent had raised a few eyebrows, but Kelly had never brought it up and had employed her for her skills, nothing else. Tricia lived on her own too, besides her cat, and despite being much older than Kelly, looked up to her. Tricia absorbed herself in her work, often stayed late, and appreciated the fact that she could use work as an excuse not to go out. Kelly on the other hand was a buzz of activity, never able to sit still for more than five minutes.

Tricia drew her jacket up to her chin. When they had boarded the plane it had been hot, but Will had been right. There were no blankets or heating on board, and now it was quite cold. Where they were going was even colder and as soon as they landed, they needed to be rugged up and ready. She had her bag packed with essentials and the new gloves and scarves she had bought in the Macy's sale on the empty seat next to her.

"This rust bucket is bloody freezing," said Tricia to herself. She had tried to convince Kelly that she didn't need to go, but she knew when she was going to lose an argument and this had been one of those occasions. She was pleased Will had come along too. He was a reassuring presence. He had given her good advice back at the airport and she intended to gain every ounce of knowledge she could from him while he was around. She was sure that the second they got back to New York next month, he would be off straight away. Josef and Wilfred were sitting a little way behind her. She met Wilfred a few times before and they got on well. Wilfred had studied the site they were going to and was going to be invaluable. She did not know Josef very well, but if Wilfred and Rasmus trusted him, then she trusted him. When she thought about it, there wasn't really anyone at the museum she didn't get on with. It was like being part of a family. There were no rivalries or idiots there. Everyone just wanted what was best for the museum.

The plane hit a patch of turbulence and the plane jolted from side to side. Tricia clasped her jacket tighter. She wasn't afraid of flying, but it felt as if they were travelling in nothing more solid than a paper plane.

"Any drink service on this flight, Suzy? I could do with a Gin and Tonic. Many more of those air pockets and I might just crap myself," said Tricia.

Suzy leaned over the aisle. "After last night, how can you even think about drinking? No, nothing until we reach the base. Should be another four or five hours yet."

"Great," said Tricia. "Shame we couldn't stay on the flight from JFK all the way, huh?"

"You got that right," said Suzy setting back in her chair. She was not looking forward to the next few hours. She had only flown a couple of times before today and had not particularly enjoyed either experience. She stretched her legs out and tried not to think about how they were flying thirty thousand feet up in the air, probably doing three hundred miles per hour in a tiny metal can filled with enough gasoline to blow Queens off the map.

She stretched and pointed her toes under the seat in front, then pulled her dress, which had ridden up during the flight, down over her knees. She probably should have worn something more practical, but she liked to show off her long slim legs. In twenty years, she knew she would probably be as wide as she was tall, like Tricia, but right now, she was fit, healthy, and sexy and saw no reason to hide it. She was a museum director's assistant, but that didn't make her a nerd or force her to wear slacks and cardigans all day. Her breasts hadn't gone south yet and her sense of adventure was still strong. She kept a coat under her seat for when it got really cold, but her thermals were in the overhead locker and they would stay there until they landed.

Suzy had moved up to New York from Denver with her parents as a child and she had landed her dream job almost straight out of university. Kelly kept her very busy, always flying off around the country or overseas, so her diary was constantly full and changing. Suzy had to look after Tricia too and somehow she seemed to have become the help, constantly running after them both, running errands and making coffee. She put up with it because she knew if she bided her time she could work her way up the chain. She had majored in ecology and was trying to get sponsorship from Kelly for a PhD. Unluckily for her, Suzy was doing such a good job of being her EA, Kelly had no intention of letting her go anytime soon.

Suzy looked across to the window. Will was in the window seat and had drawn the shade down so that the sunlight only came in half way, streaking across his face below his nose. The seats didn't move much, yet had had gotten his to recline slightly and had his eyes closed. Being practical, he had insisted on putting his winter gear on as soon as they boarded. He even wore his boots on the flight and she could see a half-eaten Snickers sticking out of his pocket.

"How's it going, Will? Asleep yet?" Suzy prodded him and he grunted.

"Are you kidding me?" he said opening his eyes. "With this turbulence? I'm trying and failing. The pilot's must have trained on the rollercoaster at Coney Island."

Suzy giggled. She wasn't quite sure of Will yet. He had joined the museum only a year ago, but had proved to be something of a star pupil as far as Kelly was concerned. Half of his time, he spent giving guided tours around the museum. He knew everything there was to know about the museum and its exhibits, from the Akeley hall to the Saurischian dinosaur fossils, and he loved showing the museum off to anyone who cared. The other half of his time, he was employed to find new artefacts and exhibits, which meant he was often using up the museum's air miles. He had proven himself to be very adept at securing important items for the museum already. He and Suzy had shared a very brief date last month and at the end of the night, he had given her a kiss before leaving. It had been a short one, but his lips had lingered long enough for her to know that he was interested. Since the, he had been so busy travelling, in and out of the office, that they had not had a chance to catch up. Last night had promised much, but delivered little. Ultimately, fate had taken him away from her. They had left together with the intention of finishing their first date only for Will to have to rush off. His mother was ill and Suzy had insisted he go. So the coffee date had been postponed yet again. She didn't know what was wrong with Will's mother, but when she asked about it, he clammed up or changed the subject, so she gathered it must be serious.

The plane dropped abruptly and everyone gasped. This time, the bouncing was more prolonged and Suzy grabbed Will's arm. The overhead lockers rattled with their contents and the aeroplane threw its passengers about violently for a minute before settling down. Will drew the shade up and peered outside, squinting. He could see the ground beneath them. There was the edge of land, a coastline far below, and he guessed where they were. This was the part of the journey he wished they could just fast forward. The sun was so bright he had to draw the shade again.

"Sorry," said Suzy withdrawing her hand. "I'm not a very good flyer." She looked at his lined face. For someone so young, and with such a wild head of hair, he was already showing a lot of life on his face. Laughter lines creased around his blue eyes and when he looked at her, she could almost feel the years on his rippled forehead. He didn't look old, but for twenty nine he looked well worn; weathered was how he put it. She'd told him he was grizzled, and she'd meant it in a good way. Too many men she had dated in New York were slimmer than she was and wore as much make-up. Real men were hard to find.

Will looked at Suzy; her face frowned with concern. "I'm sure it's nothing to worry about," he said. "If I had a dollar for every time my plane was caught up in turbulence I could've retired by now."

There were two short pings and the seatbelt sign above them lit up. Will clicked his belt together and noticed Suzy had not even undone hers. He could hear Tricia struggling with hers, trying to stretch it across her ample stomach. Nobody sat next to her.

Kelly had kept the seat free, knowing it would only cause problems if she tried to sit anyone next to Tricia. Kelly had also purposefully seated Suzy and Will next to each other. She might be single, but she wasn't stupid.

"How does he do it?" Suzy asked Will.

"Who?" said Will still looking at her eyes. He didn't trust himself not to let his gaze drift down her body and forced himself to maintain eye contact. Why she had chosen to wear such a sexy dress on a trip like this was beyond him; a down jacket and cargo pants would've been far more suitable. Not that he was complaining. He had taken to Suzy as soon as they'd met. It was unfortunate he travelled so much as he really wanted to spend more time with her.

"Professor Rasmus. Look, he's sleeping like a lion that's just eaten a whole gazelle. How does he do it? Lucky old man." Suzy sat straight back in her seat and tried to forget the bumping and bouncing of the aircraft.

"Easy," said Will. "He took two Diazepam tablets before we got on. I saw him knock them back with a cold one before we boarded. He knows what he's doing. He'll sleep right through it 'til we get there. I'm afraid the air currents can get pretty strong around here. You might want to try to sleep. It's not going to get any smoother, Suzy."

Professor Rasmus was snoring soundly. He was in the chair one up and over the aisle from them, and his head was lolling back on the neck rest. At sixty-one, he was the most experienced of the group and worked freelance for the museum. He liked to think of himself as semi-retired. The truth was he couldn't stay away. His wife implored him every day to take a back seat, relax and let the younger ones pick up the strain. He enjoyed it too much though. The thrill of finding new species, exploring places he had not been to before. He had not been to Antarctica for twenty years so there was no way he was going to miss this one. In fact, he was the only one on the plane who had been before. That was a key factor in Kelly taking him along. This would be his last trip, he had promised her. Kelly had reminded him that he had been saying that for the last five years. With Will and Suzy along now, it was a bit like 'out with the old and in with the new.'

A journal fell to the floor from Rasmus' lap and a hand reached down to pick it up. Claire folded the journal up and tucked it into the seat pocket in front of her. At eighteen, she was the baby of the group. She had won a place on the trip as part of a statewide competition run jointly by National Geographic and the museum. She had never been so excited about anything in her life, yet right now, she wished she had taken one of the pills the Professor had offered her. She didn't mind flying, but all the bumping around was making her feel queasy. She tried to concentrate on her phone again. It was set to flight mode and she was drafting an email to her mother back in New Jersey.

'Oh, Mom, you would not believe what the flight from JFK was like. We got business class *all* the way to Los Angeles. It was so nice and much better than this crappy plane. I know, I know, I'm not complaining. If this turbulence doesn't calm down though I think I'm going to throw up. My stomach feels like it's been turned inside out. Anyway, where was I? Oh yeah, so from there we flew onto Jakarta and had a very brief stop overnight. We didn't get to go out or anything. By the time we landed, we just went to bed and we were up at 5am this morning. We caught another flight to American Samoa and then finally this flight. We're on our way to the base now. It is going to be *totally* amazing. I am going to take *so* many pictures and I'm going to send them to you all the time. I assume you can get reception in the Antarctic right? I can't wait until we land!

Shoot, I just heard Suzy say it's going to be another four or five hours yet. I'm being jostled about in my seat and wishing I had taken one of the sleeping pills Rasmus had offered me. He looks like he's out for the count. Do you remember him? We met at the gala function last night. He was the old guy with the beard. You know, I said he looked like Santa? Well he is super nice. He's a bit like Granddad, always looking out for me. I swear he has a never-ending supply of mints in his jacket pocket. You remember Kelly and Tricia too, don't you? They're kind of in charge but I think everyone just does what the Professor says really.

So I forgot to tell you who else is here. I'm sitting next to Tug. He's like the guide. He's here to cook and clean and look after everyone and carry the heavy bags. He's okay and he's also fast asleep right now. Seriously, men! Oh, but Mom, there's this other guy on our trip, Will. He's so cute. But don't worry he's way too old for me and I think he has the hots for Suzy anyway, Kelly's assistant.

Then there's Mark. He seems quite nice, but he's quiet so I haven't spoken to him much. He's a photographer for National Geographic. He keeps himself to himself. There's a couple of older guys from the museum too, Wilfred and Josef. It's so funny, they're both so old and they're like brothers, but they're not! They bicker and squabble like little boys, but they're as old as Dad. I haven't had much to do with them really. They're always reading or talking about stuff so I don't want to disturb them. Suzy and Rasmus tend to look out for me the most. Suzy is *so* cool and beautiful and she even has her own apartment in New York. Oh Mom, this trip is going to be amazing, I'm going to learn so much. I'll totally email you every day. Okay, gotta go now, this plane ride is making me feel sick. Love you, Claire x x x'

Claire saved the email to send when they landed and put her phone in her pocket. She unclasped her seatbelt and carefully stood up. The plane was still jumping up and down so she took each step slowly as she made her way down the aircraft to the toilets at the back. She passed Wilfred and Josef who were animatedly discussing something in the museum's Bulletin. Claire smiled as she passed them. Mark had his camera hanging around his neck as always and was lost in a book. Claire discreetly tried to see what he was reading but all she could see was the author's name, Jules Verne.

Claire spent a few uncomfortable minutes in the bathroom, as the turbulence only seemed to get worse. On her way back up to her seat, she paused by Suzy.

"Hi, Claire, you feeling all right? You don't look too good." Suzy's face clearly showed her worry for Claire who was looking distinctly off-colour. Her forehead was clammy with sweat.

"Yeah, it's just this flight. It's like being on a roller coaster that never stops. Is this normal, Mr Forrest?" asked Claire.

"Well, Claire," he said, raising the window shade once more, "for starters, you can call me Will. I told you, I'm only Mr Forrest to my accountant and my priest, and you don't fit into either of those categories."

"Ignore him, Claire, he thinks he's funny but he's not," said Suzy, digging an elbow into Will's ribs.

"As for the turbulence," Will said chuckling, "Well, yeah it's pretty normal for this part of the world. Why don't you..."

The plane suddenly lurched to one side and Claire tumbled backwards, falling into the aisle. There was a huge bang and the cabin was filled with shouts and screams. The plane was still tilted at an angle and some of the overhead lockers came open, spilling their contents out and showering the passengers with their bags.

"What the hell is going on?" shouted Kelly as a laptop whistled past her ear.

Suzy undid her belt and leant down to help Claire. The young girl had a cut on her head, but it didn't look too bad or deep, only superficial. There was blood on her face and Suzy helped Claire up into the nearest available seat.

The aeroplane was still leaning to the side and in all the commotion, Rasmus had woken up to find his luggage at his feet. The sleeping pills had not been enough to let him sleep through this. His bag was wet and his files would be ruined; duty free had probably not been the best idea. Most of the important files were in the cargo hold, thankfully. He undid his seatbelt and stood up.

"I've pressed the call button. If the co-pilot can come, he will," said Professor Rasmus getting up. He stood in the aisle and stared down toward the back of the small plane. He had awoken with a startle and was running his hand through his white beard. He saw frightened faces staring back at him. "I would suggest everyone stay seated and buckled up. Suzy, Claire, quickly now."

"I think the pilots are busy," said Will dragging Suzy back into her seat. She was consoling Claire through the gap in the seats and Will clicked her belt back in.

As the Professor stood in the aisle, Tug began shouting. "Why are we flying like this? Why aren't we straightening up? Fuck me, I didn't sign up to..."

"Be quiet, Tug," said Will seeing how scared Suzy and Claire were. He loosened his seatbelt and turned around to Kelly. "You think we should go up there? Perhaps the pilots can tell us what's going on."

"I think we should stay where we are for now, Will. Rasmus is right, the safest place we can be right now is in our seats. They'll have us straightened out in a jiffy. I think..." Kelly screamed.

There was a huge roaring noise and the plane hit another air pocket, this time dropping a few hundred feet in only a second. Rasmus was catapulted into the air and thrown against the roof of the cabin. He crashed down onto the floor, unconscious. Tricia screamed and Claire began sobbing.

"Will!" shouted Suzy. It seemed as if she was pointing right at him. Her face was filled with horror and he turned round to see what she was pointing at. Through his window, he could see flames coming from the propeller. The fire was being sucked into the wing and over it, flowing down smoothly before flickering out into the blue sky. The plane was now at such an angle that Will could only see sky. He could tell they were heading down, and fast. The turbulence was increasing again and it felt as if the plane was being torn apart. It was as if every bolt and joint in the plane were slowly being unscrewed. If the pilots didn't shut down the propeller, it would burn out and Will knew the fuel was stored in the wing.

"Mark, help me," demanded Will, getting out of his seat. He began to clamber over Suzy.

"Will, what are you doing? Sit down!" said Suzy. Her tears had caused her mascara to run down her face, and he wanted to grab her and hold her. Rasmus needed help though. If they left him like that, he could be thrown around the cabin and suffer worse injuries than he no doubt already had.

Mark ran his hands over his short blond hair and unclasped his belt. Instinctively, he flung his camera around his neck, letting the strap hang over his thin shoulders. No matter what, he never left it behind. Mark advanced cautiously up the aisle, holding onto both seats as he did so. The plane was descending at such an angle that it was difficult to walk. As he passed Claire, he put a hand on her shoulder and squeezed. "Don't worry, Claire, it'll be fine."

She looked at him briefly as he carried on up the plane beyond Tricia and Suzy to where Will was trying to pick up Rasmus. Claire touched her mobile phone in her pocket and wondered if she could call her mother now. You could get reception most places so why not up in a plane? Then she remembered how the signals could interfere with the plane's controls and decided against it. The situation was already bad and she didn't want to risk making it any worse.

Will and Mark managed to scoop Rasmus up and put him back in his seat. He had a nasty looking cut on his head and the blood had trickled through his white hair. The bright red blood made his beard look like he had dribbled ketchup down it. With Rasmus strapped back into his seat, Will cautiously approached the cockpit door. The plane was still lurching down and to the left. There was no sign of it being pulled up. Will glanced out the windows on the left side of the plane and could almost feel his heart skip a beat. Through the window, he could see only land. The ocean, the coastline, the sky were all gone. He could see nothing but brown dirt mountains, which were much too close for comfort and only getting closer. There was no way that they were thirty thousand feet up in the air now. Will estimated they were barely half that and clearly still going down. The plane was screaming under the pressure of the rapid descent and it would be a miracle if it didn't break up. Will turned to the cockpit door and pounded on it with his fists.

"Hey, what's going on? You okay in there?" he shouted.

Mark joined him, shouting through the door to the pilots. "Open up. What's going on?"

The two men braced themselves against the cabin walls as the plane began to right itself. They stopped shouting and waited for a response. For a moment, there was no reply. All they could hear was the metal on the plane as it tried to sustain the pressure it was being placed under. The small craft was not designed to suffer such stress for prolonged periods and they were all worried. Will looked out the right hand windows. The fire had gone, but so had the propeller. He didn't know if it had been sheared off by the descent or the fire, but either way, it was not good.

"What the fuck is happening? For Christ's sake, this is ridiculous." Tug undid his seatbelt and stood up. He was wearing a tight black T-shirt that showed off his muscles and he was angry. His face was red and his eyes bloodshot. "I didn't fly halfway round the world to get killed in a bloody backwater jet plane driven by some two-bit trainee. Let me at those bloody pilots. Who the hell do they…"

There was another bang and the plane began to nosedive again. Instantly, Will and Mark were thrown forward against the cockpit door and Tug forced himself back down into his seat. Flames erupted from the plane's other propeller and the plane rattled and rolled as if it were trying to battle a giant monster.

Will heard shouts from the cockpit, but the pilots weren't talking in English and he couldn't understand them. He pushed Mark away and they sank back into front row seats ahead of Rasmus.

"Everyone okay back there? I mean is anyone hurt?" asked Will clipping his belt in. He turned around to look down the plane. Through the left side windows, he could see only clear blue sky and through the right nothing but crimson fire and black smoke. His friends and colleagues were silent, but their faces told him everything he needed to know. He could hear crying coming from some of the women and Josef was asking how Rasmus was. Rasmus, however, was not answering.

Tricia and Claire were white, their eyes closed tight. Tricia was praying as her parents had taught her to as a child, hoping God would hear her this time. Tug had already adopted the brace position, obviously expecting the worst and not waiting to be told. Rasmus was still out cold. Wilfred was looking around the plane nervously, his eyes wide and alert, darting about the plane as if looking for an escape. Kelly was sat upright, her back straight and her eyes focused dead ahead. As he looked around, Will met her gaze and they both nodded to one another. He knew she would not collapse under duress and she knew she could rely on him if the worst happened. When his eyes found Suzy's, his heart skipped a beat.

She was crying and holding onto the armrest beside her with a vice-like grip. He wished he were sitting back with her now, holding her and comforting her, but to get up again would be suicidal. He could do nothing now but wait and hope the pilots regained some sort of control. The plane was being thrown around like a leaf in a hurricane. They were being jolted from left to right and up and down, with no apparent control. Suzy's eyes locked onto Will's and he tried to send her reassuring thoughts. She seemed so fragile in that moment. A tough New Yorker reduced to crying like a little girl.

There was another bang and the plane exploded into a cloud of smoke and fire. The cockpit door blew apart and icy cold wind rushed into the cabin, snatching their breaths out of them. From his seat at the front of the plane, Will saw the co-pilot thrown forward and then sucked straight out into the sky, flying into nothingness. The man was ripped out of his seat in a second, the side window no longer there. Will heard his body bounce off the hull and there was a faint scream; Will never saw the man again.

Through eyes that were being forced shut by the high velocity wind rushing at them, Will saw that the front of the plane was now a mess. The control panel looked dead and the remaining pilot was wrestling with the controls. Their steep descent was levelling out. God knows how, but the pilot seemed to be getting them under control. With the cockpit door gone, the plane's contents were being sucked out into the sky as they plummeted down toward the ground. Bags, briefcases, papers, books and jackets all rushed passed Will on their way out of the plane. He thanked God that he had stayed in his seat and not decided to get up and head for Suzy.

If he had, he would've been sucked out along with the now dead co-pilot.

The plane was still descending and the ground was rushing up to meet them quickly. It would be over in a few seconds. Will could see the fields beneath them and then up ahead a thick jungle of trees. With the angle they were coming in at, they might just be able to glide in at a level where they could land, although he doubted it. Even if they did, the impact would probably rip the plane apart. He had flown across central Africa in a two-seater, he had hang-glided from Table Mountain, and he'd been dragged through the Amazon upside down when his canoe had capsized; this however was his scariest ride yet. Seeing the verdant green fields so close below and trees approaching, Will held his breath and prepared for the inevitable impact that would lead to their inevitable deaths. Up ahead, he saw buildings, houses and gardens. There were cars in the streets below, close enough to see now. He had no idea how the pilot was even keeping them in the air. They surely had to have lost both engines by now. Somehow, they were still flying. Was the pilot trying to land on the road below them?

Will was not too proud to admit he was petrified. If they were lucky, they would die immediately. That would almost be preferable to surviving the crash landing. Kelly, Rasmus, Josef and Wilfred almost certainly knew where they were headed now. He didn't know if Suzy, Mark or Tricia did, and Tug and Claire very likely had little idea. His worst fears were coming true. As the plane careered down, there was no time to think about the ground rushing up to meet them. Will didn't even notice the small figures below following the plane's trajectory. The Grave was about to welcome its newest residents.

FOUR

A droplet of blood splashed into a pool of rainwater at the dead man's feet. He let go of the recently killed lamb and reached upward with both of his dumb, numb hands. A strange noise was filling the air and he scanned around for the source. A tearing, grinding noise had shattered the peaceful valley and the dead man was confused. Whilst he had no rational thought, he was aware that such a noise was unusual in the same way a mosquito becomes disorientated and bewildered when confronted by a thunderstorm. A large shape flew above the corpse's head, heading south and leaving a blazing trail of smoke behind it. Small shiny objects were falling from the shiny oblong thing as it fragmented and sprinkled pieces of charred metal over the valley floor. As the shape passed overhead, low in the sky, the dead man reached his bony arms up to touch it. With no sense of depth, the dead man's fingers kept reaching for it even though it could not possibly reach the aircraft.

A crack rang out, snapping through the air and echoing across the valley, bouncing off the hills like a gunshot. The dead man did not jump, duck, curse, or react in any way. Through blurry bloodshot eyes, the dead man saw more things fall from the sky. Unrecognisable things fell, raining down through the trees ahead and crashing into the earth with loud bangs and thuds. No more than ten feet in front of the corpse, a man landed on the ground, flattening the long grass and leaving a small crater in the soil. Gravity sucked the body into the sodden earth with enough impact that it sent vibrations through the ground and the walking corpse stumbled. The body that had fallen from the sky was horribly mutilated, limbs broken and smashed. It had ceased to look like a man once it had impacted upon the ground.

The walking corpse could smell the fresh blood and the raw meat. Instantly, it fell upon the grizzly pile of flesh that used to be Nonu, the aeroplane's co-pilot, and it began devouring the warm, succulent meat. More walking corpses appeared, drawn at first by the noise from the sky, but then to the strange new food that fell from above.

When the pilot had been consumed, only a hollow in the ground and a scattering of bloody clothing even signified he had been there at all. The many dead had ingested virtually his whole body: hair, blood, tissue and bone. The burning plane had left behind a smoky trail in the evening sky, a sweet burning smell from the spent aviation fuel, and so the Deathless took flight. More joined them as they marched through the valley across green lush fields and through the small forest ahead. Pieces of the doomed plane were strewn across the valley, but it was only the prospect of flesh that drew interest and curiosity from the dead. Rarely were they interrupted from their scavenging and feasting. The forest floor was alive as animals and birds scurried away from the approaching death. Rabbits buried deep into their hollows, mice and voles scuttled into riverbeds and the Kakapos and Kiwis hurried quietly to hide in their nests. All through the forest, the birdsong and mating calls of spring ceased. The animals had learnt to sense when danger was near and how to avoid it, mostly.

Not all were quick on their feet and successful. A young woman, ageless, thin and dead, grabbed a skink as it tried to run. She shoved it into her mouth as it wriggled and squirmed, unable to escape her grasp. Her teeth crunched through its bones and tore its flesh as she ate it alive. Nothing was left of the creature within a minute and the dead woman carried on, following the flock in search of more. Their hunger was insatiable and their existence pitiful, though they were pitiless themselves. Men, women, children and infected animals existed only in that place with one intention, to consume flesh and to eat the living.

The Deathless did not consider their position on Earth as consequential, for they did not consider anything. The bodies of the dead moved and walked, occasionally summoning up the energy to what could be described as a jog, but little more. Muscles had long since wasted away and they had no need for speed in the same way that they had no need for sleep or rest. They desired no material things, nor suffered from pride. They had no need for procreation or love, no maternal or paternal instincts, and had no knowledge of their neighbour. The corpse walking next to them was as pointless as the moon rising or the sun setting. It could rain or snow and they would not take shelter. The fiery summer sun could burn the land and fry their skin, but they would not attempt to find shade. They simply existed, their senses attuned to one goal: a never-ending search for food. Usually, they hunted alone, although occasionally they sensed a migration such as this one. When a flock of them moved, it signified a food source ahead and so they joined the others in the same direction. There was no hive mind or sense of togetherness and certainly no willingness to share or feeling of brotherhood as they walked. A Pilot fish will live beside and follow a shark through the oceans, not because of any kind of kinship or kindred connection with the shark, but because it knows, it can sustain itself if it stays close and find a constant source of food.

For so long now, many of them had lost their clothing to the elements and time. The seams had split and the cotton had torn, and many of the dead were half-naked. They did not care, as they did not know they were naked. Breasts hung low and limp, and putrid flesh sloped off the older ones. The dead children ignored the bare flesh on display. Male and female, black and white, they were all oblivious to their nudity. Their skin was discoloured and damaged; there was no longing, embarrassment or self-awareness. The walking corpses simply carried on every day, roaming wherever they wished across the land. If they caught an arm or a leg on a spiky bush, they would simply tear the limb off and continue. If they fell and broke an ankle or a bone, they felt no pain or suffering. If they could walk, they walked. If they could no longer walk, they would drag themselves along on their hands. If they could no longer drag themselves anywhere, they would wait for food to come to them. They could not die and so would lie still for weeks, months, years, until an inquisitive animal would foolishly get too close and then snap! Rotten black teeth would seize upon the hapless creature and drink down the blood from the animal's still pumping heart. It didn't matter if the meat was stringy or fatty, it was all the Deathless wanted. It was a curse they would never be rid of. And any creature in their path would be eaten. Those not killed instantly, any creature that might escape with just a wound from the dead would not last long. A bite or a scratch meant irreversible infection and an eternity of oblivious death. Once bitten, an animal would turn within a few seconds.

The heart would implode causing agony and then it would be all over. They would return as one of the dead.

The Deathless followed the trail of smoke and destruction through the forest toward the crash site. They were like moths flocking to a flame and nothing would stop them. A burnt path led them through charred ground and past trees with broken limbs to the edge of the city. The plane had skimmed the tops of the trees and ended up in the town of Judgeford. Grass gradually gave way to gravel and toppled trees conceded ground to crumbling houses as the dead marched on in their search for the fresh meat that fell from the sky.

The domes that had hastily been erected over some of the smaller towns had long since cracked and fallen. There was nothing to stop the plane's catastrophic descent and so it had smashed through the town before finally coming to rest.

The Deathless now controlled this land. Millions of them had been shipped there from all over the globe, a shunned race that were both feared and despised equally. Some of these people, these dead beings, were now on their way to Judgeford. They did not know the town's name or need to. All they knew was that was where they needed to get to, because that was where food was.

* * *

Will staggered from the plane and sank to the ground. Blood poured from a cut on his cheek and he held his hand to it trying to stem the bleeding. He felt dizzy and spaced out, as if he had been inside a centrifuge on full speed before being abruptly spat out. He looked up and saw a row of houses, small low buildings and fences. The plane had come to rest in a residential street. Evidently, the pilot had attempted to land between the houses and had at least partly succeeded.

Looking back at where they had come from, he saw a trail of destruction. Several cars and vans were flipped over and deep cracks in the road had been gouged out where the plane had landed. A couple of cars were burning. Will felt a hand on his shoulder and looked up to see Tricia looming over him. Tears streaked her face.

"Can you help me? We can't get Wilfred out."

Tricia went back toward the plane and Will stood to follow her. The plane had been split in two, its fragile body breaking up on impact with the ground. The wings had sheared off and the sides of the plane had been peeled back, exposing the destroyed interior and ragged seats. Debris littered the area around the hull of the plane. In places, Will could see all the way through it to the buildings on the other side of the road. He looked at the empty row of seats inside and then saw the body lying on the ground at his feet: Josef.

Will knelt down and examined his colleague. His first impression was that Josef was dead. His clothes were untarnished and his face calm and clean, yet he lay perfectly still. Will put his hand against Josef's neck and felt for a pulse. It was strong. Will felt relief wash over him and was grateful that his friend wasn't dead. Will shook Josef gently at first, then stronger, willing him to wake up. Josef began to stir and Will called out his name over and over. Finally, Josef sat up.

"What happened?" asked Josef rubbing his head.

"I don't know, we just...I don't know." Will left Josef and headed toward the plane. He had to know what had happened to everyone else. Between the plane coming down and a minute ago, he had a blank. Tricia was with Tug trying to free Wilfred. His seat had been thrown forward into the one in front of him and it had jammed itself. Wilfred could wriggle his arms and legs, but there was no space to squeeze out. Will didn't even need to get into the plane to help. He just stood outside and helped Tug, who was pulling at Wilfred's seat. Tricia was holding Wilfred's hand, trying to reassure him. He was saying nothing and looked very pale.

"Come on, you bastard," screamed Tug as he pulled at the back of the seat.

Tug was sweating and Will noticed a few cuts and scrapes, but no serious injuries, apparently. Together, they pulled and Wilfred's seat began to move. Slowly it began to inch backwards and eventually Wilfred was able to clamber out. He almost fell out of the plane and collapsed into Tricia's arms.

'My God, my God," was all he said as he sat there on the ground with Tricia holding him.

Tug jumped down and handed Will a rucksack. "Here, we're going to need this, mate. Take it over there to the will you? Glad to see you're back with us."

Will took the pack from Tug and walked slowly in the direction Tug had nodded. He felt like he was experiencing everything through a bubble; it was as if he was standing just beside his own body, watching what was going on. Memories started to pop back into his head. The plane had crashed into a village or small town. He remembered the trees giving way to houses and then...then he remembered waking up on the plane, still in his seat. Mark had been shouting at him, but he hadn't heard a word. He touched his head and recalled that he had scrambled out of the plane with Mark. Claire and Kelly had already been out of the plane before he had collapsed. He must have passed out. He recalled seeing Tricia and a moment ago, Josef. Had he seen Suzy? He couldn't think. Where was she?

Will saw Kelly sitting on a low stone wall in front of a decrepit cottage and hurried over to her. His mind was now firing on all cylinders and he dropped the bag at her feet.

"Are you okay? Where is she? Where's Suzy?"

Before Kelly could answer, he heard the reply.

"I'm here, Will, I'm fine."

Suzy appeared from behind him and he grabbed her, thanking God silently that she was alive. He held her out and looked her up and down. Her legs were already showing some nasty bruises and dirt streaked across her face, but she was looking up at him with bright, lively eyes.

"Are you okay?" she asked him tenderly.

"I think so. How are you? Is everyone all right?" Will kept a tight hold of Suzy's hand and turned to Kelly. She was holding a piece of cloth to the back of her head and grimacing.

"It's a god damned miracle, if you ask me," said Kelly. She felt like someone had taken a hammer to the back of her head and she took a quick glance at the bloodied cloth before reapplying it to the back of her head. She needed to keep pressure on, let the wound heal and the blood clot. "Now that Wilfred is out, everyone is off the plane. I think Claire might have broken her arm, but apart from that, it appears we've suffered nothing more than cuts and bruises. Rasmus is wrapping her arm up now. He is remarkably fine, all things considered. Just a bump on his head, but otherwise...fine. Thank God, you got Josef up. I was just about to go over there myself but...Mark helped me off the plane. I think something whacked me when we landed. I don't know, I was out of it for a while. Mark's been trying to figure out where we are."

"Holy cow," said Suzy under her breath. "Here, let me see that." She took the cloth from Kelly and examined the back of her head, parting the hair so she could see the cut. "You might have a concussion, you know. You're going to have to take it easy."

Kelly pressed the cloth back on her head and winced. The bleeding was stopping, but Suzy was right. Who knew how seriously injured they were really. They had taken a good beating when the plane had come down and could have untold injuries. She was going to have to watch the others for symptoms of concussion or internal injuries. The ones you couldn't see were the most dangerous. She knew Suzy was right and she should be taking it easy, but that wasn't really an option now. She was responsible for these people and she was going to have to try getting help quickly.

"What about the pilot?" asked Will. "I saw the co-pilot, he...when the plane was going down...he couldn't have made it. But I'd like to thank the pilot. He did well to get us down. If it wasn't for him we'd all be dead right now." Will looked around for the pilot.

"Sorry, mate, that's not going to happen." Tug dropped a couple of bags at Will's feet. "He didn't make it either. Impact tore him right out of his seat and cut him in half."

"Fuck," said Kelly.

They were quiet then. The pilot's death hit them. More than that, they had crashed and both pilots were dead. They all realised they were on their own now with no plane and no pilots.

"We need to make a move. The plane is not safe. I don't know how long it'll take for the fuel to catch fire, maybe never in this weather, but there's fuel all over the place and we shouldn't hang around to find out." Tug was putting on a jacket he had rescued from the plane.

Will realised it was raining. He hadn't even noticed before. It was a small rain shower, just a drizzle. Will looked up at the sky, which was dark and bleak. Suddenly, he began to think practically again. He forgot the dead pilot and the pain in his head. He realised Tug had been doing just that too, thinking practically; fetching bags and items from the plane whilst he could. Tug had a short, abrasive manner, but Will respected him for thinking logically when everyone else was panicking. He looked at his watch, but it was broken, the hands permanently stuck at five thirty one.

"What's the time?" Will asked, knowing it must be late. The sky was dark and not just because of the rain clouds. The air was cold and the night would not be far away. Will picked up a bag and slung it over his shoulder.

"Nearly six," said Tug. "Time to move. Suzy, put this on, you're going to get cold." He handed her a jacket he had pulled from a rucksack and she quickly pulled it on over her dress. "Kelly, think you can carry this?"

Kelly took the final bag from Tug and nodded. "Where are we going to go, Tug? Why do we need to move? We should stay close by. They'll be looking for us. Planes don't just disappear; there'll be search parties looking for us already. Won't there?"

Tug shook his head. "The best way to stay alive in a situation like this is to find shelter. We need to stay dry and warm. We can't sit around here waiting to be rescued. It could be hours away, maybe longer. What if it's days? We need to find shelter and quickly. It's going to be dark soon."

"That's not all," said Will. He turned around and shouted to the others. "Tricia, Wilfred, Josef, we're leaving. Are you okay to walk?"

They gave him the thumbs up and Josef went to help Wilfred to his feet. Wilfred was still pale and quiet, but there were no apparent injuries. Rasmus was walking over with Claire who had her left arm wrapped up in a shirt they had found in someone's luggage.

"So what do you suggest, Tug? Try one of these houses? See if we can find somewhere to stay for the night?" Suzy noticeably shivered as she spoke and was keen to leave. The sight of the smouldering plane only made her feel more frightened.

"Somewhere close by, yes. Any of these houses should be fine. Then when the A-team turn up we won't be far away and we can be out of here." Tug looked down the street and spied a two-storey building that looked in good repair. He marched off toward it purposefully.

As everyone followed him, Will thought that Tug had it almost right, but there was something risky about his plan. "Tug, slow down. I'm not sure we should stay here, not so close anyway."

"Why not?" Tug continued walking away.

"Because *they're* probably here. If not already, then they won't be far away. They would've noticed us, the crash, the noise...we should try to get away from this place. Hide."

"Hide? Is he mad? We need to be found, not hiding." Claire looked up at Rasmus who chose to ignore her. He knew what Will was getting at.

"What are you on about, mate? I know where we are, I'm not stupid." Tug snorted and turned down a path to the house he wanted to check out. "The things you're talking about are a load of bollocks. They're dead. There ain't been fuck all on this island for years and *they* are long gone. What did they live on, the fresh air? Give me a break."

Will was concerned that Tug's bravado might lead them into further trouble and hurried to catch up. He had to calm Tug down. There was logic to his thinking and he was right, they did need to get out of the cold rain. However, staying so close to the crash site might not be a good idea and Tug seemed to have made his mind up. "Please, Tug, just slow down. We need to talk about this."

Tug stopped at the front door. The house was dark and the windows showed no sign of movement inside. The drapes had rotted away and the rooms inside were bare and dusty. The rain still fell from the darkening sky and Tug wiped the water from his face. "Look, Will, I'm not going to argue with you. You do what you do, and I'll stay out of the way. If we ever get to the bloody Antarctic, you can be in charge. But right now, you need to listen to me. Talking is not what's needed now, it's action. I am here for one reason only, and that is to look after all of you. That is exactly what I'm doing. Yes, the situation has changed, but my job hasn't." Tug put his hand on the front door.

"Maybe you should just hang on, Tug?" said Mark. He had been up and down the street looking for signs of life, but the village was deserted. He had taken some photos of the crash site and then seen the others all headed for this house. "You don't know what's behind that door? What if you open it up and they're inside, just waiting to pounce?"

Mark was standing with the rest of the group in the front yard, surrounding Will and Tug. He had no interest in stoking the embers of the argument that seemed to be brewing. Will might be right though. They had just cheated death and Mark didn't fancy heading into another dangerous situation. He was a journalist, not a fighter or an explorer. Compared to Tug, he looked spindly and weak and he felt exhausted.

"What are they on about?" asked Claire. She pulled at Rasmus' sleeve. "Who's here? Where are we?"

Rasmus was stroking his beard as he looked down at her. He knew they were in terrible danger, but didn't know how to break it to the girl. "The residents of this island, Claire, are not friendly. They're...look, I'm sure it'll be fine. Best to keep quiet, Claire. I'll fill you in later." Rasmus held his breath as Tug pushed on the front door and it opened an inch.

"Tug, don't. Please," Will brushed the rain from his eyes and asked Tug quietly. He was concerned that even their raised voices might be enough to draw *them* out. They couldn't afford to get into a pissing contest now. Tug was doing what he thought was the best thing for all of them. He didn't know that he might be leading them into peril.

"We're going in. It'll be fine. Come on." Tug pushed the door harder and it swung open.

Will looked through the doorway into the darkness and hoped they were alone. After surviving the plane crash, he doubted any of them, Tug included had the strength to fight off the Deathless.

Tug stepped over the threshold and entered the house.

FIVE

Tug stepped into the dark hallway of the house and waited. He listened for sounds, anything that might suggest they weren't alone. He waited ten seconds and counted slowly to twenty. The cold house remained dark and quiet. Tug turned around where Will was stood nervously in the doorway.

"Told you it's safe. There's nothing here. They're a myth, Will, a legend like sodding Bigfoot or the yeti. They were real once, years ago, but they're dead now. Come on. Just watch your step, yeah? These floorboards are probably damp and rotten, so be careful."

Surprised, yet happy that the house was empty, Will followed Tug and signalled for the others to follow him. As they all trooped inside, Will caught up with Tug. He had gone ahead into the kitchen and was rummaging through the drawers.

"Tug, you got lucky, but next time, what if something is behind the door. You know what the Deathless are? The clue's in the name. We don't know how long they can live. They could very well be coming here right now." Even in the darkness, Will could see Tug was paying him little attention.

"Live? Ha, that's a good one, Will. Frankly, I doubt there are any around, and dead people don't *live*, they just exist, the same way a worm does when it's been cut in half. They should've been destroyed years ago. All we need to do now is focus on surviving until the rescue comes. We need warmth, shelter, food; every minute we waste talking about this is a minute closer to not surviving this bloody place."

Kelly and Suzy joined them in the kitchen and the others followed. Chairs scraped on the kitchen floor as Tricia, Wilfred, Josef and Claire sat down.

Mark was fiddling with the camera around his neck, adjusting it for the low-level light conditions. He hadn't prepared for this, but he knew a good photographer should be ready for any event and he didn't intend to go home empty-handed. He had taken a couple of snaps of the plane crash and wanted to get as much as he could from this strange place.

"Where are we?" said Josef. "What are we going to do now, Kelly?" His hands were shaking with fear and he tried to hide the tremble in his voice.

"I think that's up for debate," said Rasmus. "Ideally, I would say we need medical attention. I'm worried about all of us. I've strapped up Claire's arm as best I can, but I'm no doctor. I'm pretty sure the wrist is broken. And look at Wilfred; he's as white as a ghost."

Wilfred tried to speak. "I'll be fine," he rasped. He tried to speak again, but he began coughing and Tricia took his hand. Wilfred tried to hide it, but they all saw the blood he coughed up on the kitchen table. What they couldn't see was the punctured lung beneath his broken rib cage.

"Hang in there, Wilfred," said Josef. "Tug, do you think we can find a hospital or something around here? Maybe even a doctor's surgery that might have some supplies we could use?"

"It's not likely," said Tug frowning at Wilfred. "By the looks of it, we are in a very small town and even if there was a hospital around, any supplies would've been cleaned out years back along with the inhabitants of this poxy hole."

"So what, we sit here and wait? For what? For how long?" asked Tricia.

"Actually, no," said Tug. "I was looking for some matches so we could start a fire and try to dry out our damp clothes. I haven't found any so we should look in the rest of the house. Once we get some warmth in us, we can decide what we want to do. If we stay like this we'll all end up with hypothermia."

Josef got up and headed for the doorway. He wanted to help and Wilfred looked terrible. "I'll go look. There was another door in the hallway. Old houses like this used to have wooden fires so there may be some in there."

"I'll go upstairs and look," said Kelly.

"Me too," said Suzy. "I'll check out the bathroom too. Maybe we'll get lucky and find some medicine or bandages, you never know."

Rasmus got up too. "I'll come with you, Josef. It does seem safe here, Will."

"Good man, Rasmus," said Tug. "Right then, let's..."

"Hang on, hang on, I think you're all forgetting something," said Will exasperated. "I don't know if you're all trying to ignore what's just happened, but we have landed, *crash-landed*, on a land without humans. There is no electricity, water, power, no phone lines or radio. We don't know if rescue is even coming. This is The Grave. *The Grave.* There is a reason nobody is allowed on or off this island. We don't know what is out there. We should not be running around now or splitting up. Hell, for all we know, they could be right outside."

"Can someone please tell me what the hell is going on?" Claire shoved her chair back and it flew into the sideboard. "Please, I don't know what you're talking about. I just want to go home." She began crying and Suzy pulled her into her body. Claire's sobs were stifled by Suzy's shoulder.

There was silence in the room for a moment before everyone started talking at once. Will and Tug began arguing about whether to stay or run. Rasmus was trying to talk to Claire whilst Suzy tried to protect her and was telling Rasmus in no uncertain terms to leave her alone. Tricia and Mark were trying to get Will and Tug to calm down whilst Wilfred slowly sank into unconsciousness.

Nobody saw Josef sneak out into the hallway that they had just come through. He wanted to leave the arguing to the others, and went to find matches. By the time they were through, he could have started a fire and then they would all be feeling a lot better. He couldn't just stand by idly whilst Wilfred was suffering.

"All right, all right, enough," shouted Kelly. "Enough!"

Silence descended upon the room once more and Kelly held her hands to her head. "Listen, we are all tired and scared, I know. My head is killing me. But arguing amongst ourselves is solving nothing. I'm not one to put my foot down very often, but I'm doing it right now. *I* am in charge. I am responsible for all of you. I know you all have your own ideas and thoughts, and yes, Tug, we do need to get warm and safe. And yes, Will, I agree, it's probably not safe to stay here. But ultimately, whatever happens I will have the final say. If anything happens to any of you, then I will be the once facing the music when we get home. More than that, if anything happens to any of you, it will be on *my* conscience. I don't want that. I don't want to spend the rest of my life wishing we had been trying to help each other when all we did was argue and stuff things up."

Kelly lowered her voice. She had gotten everyone's attention. She hated playing the authority card, but she had to get control of the situation before it spun away from her and someone got into trouble.

"Will, no more talk of not being rescued, okay? Planes do not disappear. This is not the Bermuda Triangle. Someone, somewhere, will already be looking for us. Tug, calm down. I appreciate what you are doing, but the truth is that nobody knows for sure where we are or what is on this island. Maybe the Deathless are all gone, I hope so. But maybe they aren't. I'm sorry, Claire, but they are not pleasant people and we need to avoid them at all costs. So for now, we must be extra careful. Rasmus, can you please go with Josef, I don't want him going off on his own and...shit, where is he?"

"Josef?" Rasmus peered down the hallway, but there was no sign of him. "Josef?" he called out again, louder. A chill ran down Rasmus' spine.

Kelly stiffened up. Josef should have answered by now. "Mark, would you mind going with Rasmus to get Josef back. We can't afford for anyone to go wandering off on their own."

Mark followed Rasmus into the hallway. The front door was still open and the rain was still pouring down. If anything, it had gotten stronger. The secondary door they had seen was ajar, and Rasmus guessed Josef had just gone ahead without them once the arguing had started.

"Josef?" Rasmus pushed the door open and entered the room. The living room was deserted. The air smelled foul and the leather suite was covered in a grey fungus. Mould adorned the ceiling in huge patches, brown and yellow clouds mushrooming out in all directions. The wallpaper was peeling off and in places, it exposed the crumbling plaster underneath. Rasmus didn't want to spend any more time in this house than he had to, but he felt compelled to go on. Josef had still not answered him and Rasmus was getting worried now. He walked across the room to another door. This one was ajar too and Rasmus pulled it open with Mark behind him.

The room beyond was similar to the one they had just crossed, except the floor had caved in. The old floorboards that had stood for decades had finally given way, succumbing to the weather and old age. The wet evening's dull light trickled in through a square window and Rasmus looked down through the decayed floorboards. He could see the faint outline of Josef's body lying in the cellar below. The air was still and Rasmus gasped. Judging from the angle at which they now lay, Josef's legs must have broken and he had probably been knocked out instantly. He had not even had time to call out for help. Rasmus and Mark had been going slowly in their search for him, but Josef had walked straight into the dark room without thinking to check first and had fallen.

Mark could not see past Rasmus in the doorway and wondered why they had stopped. "What's going on? What is it?" he hissed.

Rasmus was about to break the news to him when he saw movement in the cellar. It was so dark he hadn't noticed at first, but a figure was crouching over Josef. At the sound of Mark's voice, the figure turned around and looked directly up at Rasmus. Suddenly Rasmus forgot the bump on his head, the crash and the expedition. Sheer panic overcame him and he froze.

"Mark," he whispered, "do you have a light on your camera?"

"No, but Tug probably has one. What is it?"

"Can you go get it please? Keep your voice down and for God's sake, don't let anyone else come back here. Just you, okay?"

Mark left Rasmus alone as he went to find a light, puzzled as to why Rasmus was acting so oddly.

Rasmus' eyes were slowly getting accustomed to the gloom and he could make out that the figure was quite small. It was hunched over Josef, obscuring his face. Rasmus could hear faint crunching sounds and slopping noises as if the figure was eating something. Rasmus suspected what it was, but couldn't bring himself to say it out loud. He didn't want to think about it, but he had to know for sure. He jumped as he felt a hand on his shoulder.

"Here," said Mark handing him a small pocket torch. "It's all Tug had. Now tell me, what can you see? Is it Josef?" Mark gently squeezed into the doorway beside Rasmus so he could see too.

Rasmus flicked the torch on and shone the beam down into the hole. The weak light illuminated Josef's feet and legs. Rasmus moved the torch slowly upward exposing Josef's chest. A thin, bare arm lay on his chest and the hand was covered in blood. It was obvious that the arm was not Josef's.

Rasmus' hands were shaking so much that the light was unsteady and flickering as he moved it further up Josef's body. The dead child looked up suddenly as the light fell upon his face. Dead, pale eyes looked up at Rasmus and Mark. The child must have been about eight or nine when it had died. It wore loose ragged clothes over its thin body and it snarled into the torch light. The child's face was covered in blood and as it stood up, they could see Josef's neck had been torn open. His eyes were glazed over and it was clear he was dead.

After falling down into the cellar, the child, who had been trapped down there, pounced immediately, ripping Josef's throat out before he had time to regain consciousness or shout for help.

Moving the torch up further, Rasmus could see Josef's head had cracked open when he had fallen. His brains lay pooled out over the floor in a sickening creamy white puddle looking like curdled milk. Small bloody handprints covered Josef's face, and Rasmus guessed the child had eaten some of the brains, pulling them from Josef's broken skull. Perhaps that was why Josef still lay dead on the ground and had not reanimated; he had cracked his skull and broken at least one of his legs when he had fallen into the deadly cellar.

"Oh fuck," said Mark backing away. "Oh fuck," he said again.

The child in the cellar reached up toward Mark and Rasmus, bloody hands straining for them, but he was too far away. Rasmus watched as the child's teeth snapped uselessly, pieces of Josef's stringy neck still caught in the child's jaws. A gooey grey lump fell from the child's mouth and plopped onto the dusty ground. Rasmus recognised it; it was unmistakably a piece of Josef's brain tissue and he gagged.

Rasmus swallowed down the bile that was threatening to erupt from his churning stomach. He flicked the torch off and turned to face Mark.

"We need to leave. Now."

In the kitchen, Suzy and Will were trying to wake Wilfred who had fallen unconscious. Kelly was still holding onto Claire whilst Tug and Tricia were searching for anything useful in the pantry.

Mark burst into the room, swiftly followed by Rasmus. "Time to go," said Mark urgently.

"What's happened? Where's Josef?" said Will. He could tell from the wild look in Mark's eyes that it was bad. Rasmus was avoiding eye contact with anyone and looking down at the ground.

Mark shook his head. "He's...he's not...we need to leave. Just listen to me, everyone, this house is not safe. There's no time to..."

He stopped as a crashing sound came from above them. Something, or someone, had fallen to the floor and there were loud scrabbling sounds above them, as if a thousand rats were trying to claw their way through the ceiling to get down to the kitchen.

"Fuck this, I'm outta here," said Mark.

Without further discussion, everyone poured out of the house, racing after Mark and Rasmus.

Tug and Will were last as they carried Wilfred between them. He was still unconscious and they hadn't been able to raise him. Everyone had congregated on the pathway to the house, unsure of where to go.

"Rasmus, where's Josef?" asked Kelly.

Rasmus had turned almost as white as his beard. "He's dead. They're here. The Deathless. They're in the house. I saw one. A child was...it had killed him and..."

"They're not just in the house," said Suzy. "Look."

Suzy pointed down the road, past the wreckage of the plane. There were a dozen figures on the road, heading straight for them. More were joining them, ambling into the street from the trees and hedges at the roadside. There were men and women of all shapes and sizes. Some were naked, some were clothed, but all of them were dead. They made a yearning, moaning sound as they approached and some were faster than others were. The fastest of the pack, a stout woman with her belly slit open, had already made it to the plane and was advancing upon the group rapidly.

Tug dropped Wilfred and Will just managed to catch him before he hit the tarmac.

"This way," shouted Tug, running away from the dead and not waiting for anyone else.

The others ran after him, not knowing where he was heading, just knowing it was away from the throng of the dead. Will tried to pick up Wilfred on his own, but he was struggling. Suzy stopped and ran back to help him.

"Will, hurry up please, they're getting close," she said, trying to help him lift Wilfred.

"I'm trying, but..." Will and Suzy together managed to get Wilfred between them and began after the others who were by now far ahead.

Suzy cast a look over her shoulder and screamed, "Will, we're not going to make it."

Will looked back and saw that the dead woman at the front had almost caught up with them. There was no way they were going to outrun the Deathless while carrying Wilfred as well.

Will lowered Wilfred to the floor and knelt over him. "We're going to have to leave him, Suzy." He was furious with himself for letting his guard drop. He should have forced Tug to listen. Maybe they would have found somewhere safe instead of wasting time in that house. He was right. The Deathless had found them, drawn by the plane and the noise. Now he had to choose. Stay here and fight to protect Wilfred, or run and get Suzy away.

"But...but..." Suzy looked at Will and then back at the woman who was only ten feet away now. Suzy could smell the rotting stench of decayed flesh and stepped back.

"Oh, Will." Sheer terror gripped Suzy and the dead body was almost upon her.

Will stood, took Suzy's hand, and they ran. Will looked back to see if they were getting further away from the woman and was relieved to see they were. However, it was only because the woman had stopped at Wilfred's prostrate body. Will had hoped that if Wilfred stayed unconscious the Deathless might not notice him. He'd hoped they would run past and perhaps they would be able to circle back around and get Wilfred when the road was clear. However, the dead had found him and there would be no going back for him.

The stout woman fell upon Wilfred and took a chunk out of his arm. Wilfred's eyes shot open and he let out a deep roar as another of the dead fell upon him. An old man, bald and sallow-skinned, collapsed on top of Wilfred and began biting at his face. Another and another fell upon him and soon Wilfred's cries were stopped. Will turned away, unable to watch, knowing he couldn't save his friend. With Wilfred's body hidden under a pile of writhing corpses, many of the dead ignored him and continued giving chase to Suzy and Will.

"Over here!"

Will saw Kelly waving frantically at them from around a corner and he led Suzy to where Kelly stood waiting for them.

"Where are the others?" said Will out of breath.

"Over there, come on. I wanted to make sure you'd find us. Wilfred?"

Will shook his head and Kelly nodded in understanding. Then she took off, running up the winding hill that led out of the town centre. Will and Suzy were hot on her heels as they ran, occasionally looking back to see that the dead were slowly getting left behind. The road twisted and turned as it meandered uphill and Will saw a signpost beneath a large oak tree.

'Thank you for visiting Judgeford.

Please drive safely.

Haere ra.'

As they rounded a corner, they stopped running. The others were all on the roadside, exhausted, waiting for Kelly, Will and Suzy to catch up. The evening was rapidly turning into night and the only light in the countryside came from the moon above. Rainclouds still darted about the sky and the pale half-moon jumped in and out of view skittishly, disappearing just as quickly as it appeared.

"We have to keep moving," said Tug leaning over a gatepost. "They won't stop."

Rasmus tried to answer, but was shattered and couldn't summon the energy to talk back.

"What about over there?" said Mark. "That post you're leaning on is part of a fence. It looks like the start of a driveway. It must lead somewhere, maybe someone's home. There are so many trees though I can't see the house and that means *they* won't see it either. If we're quick enough, maybe we can hide out there for a while?"

"You want to go back inside another house?" said Suzy doubled over. She was fit and healthy, but running up hill was not something she had planned to do tonight. Her knees felt like jelly and she could only imagine how bad Rasmus felt. Not only was he over sixty, he had just seen his two old friends killed.

"We can't stay out here," said Will. "He's right. They won't stop."

"If they don't get us, the cold and the rain will. We won't make it 'til morning," Tug said, pushing open the gate. He realised that Mark was right. There was a rough, dirt track leading into a secluded copse. If they were lucky, there might be shelter somewhere on the other side. If not, it was going to be a very long night.

"Everyone, move it," said Kelly. "Down the path, now. Tug, shut that gate behind you. Everyone keep quiet. If we're lucky we might just get out of sight before they catch up."

Nobody spoke another word as they marched down the driveway. It was little more than a mud track littered with leaves and fallen branches. Twigs cracked sharply underfoot and all of them kept their senses alert, listening out for the dead that were somewhere behind them. The trees on either side of the track became thicker and hid them from the road as they walked on. They turned a bend and the driveway opened out into a large gravel yard. Tall hedges stood staunchly around it and an enormous farmhouse confronted them.

The building was newly built of brick and mortar, and looked much more solid and dryer than the cottages back at Judgeford. The windows were dark and the curtains drawn. There was no sign of light or life inside and no smoke came from the chimney. The front door was closed and Will half expected a farmer to come out with a shotgun, warning them off his property. Nobody came from the house though and the group stood in front of it with trepidation. They all wanted to go inside, out of the rain that was seeping through their clothes and soaking their skin, yet they were afraid. After what they had seen in Judgeford, they were sceptical about the safety of another house.

Will approached the wooden front door and tried the handle. It was stiff, but it turned and the door evidently wasn't locked. He knocked quietly on the door and waited. He couldn't hear anything and turned to the others in the darkness.

"I'm going in. Wait here. I'll skirt around the house as fast as I can, upstairs and down. If I'm not back in five minutes...don't wait for me, just move on." Will pushed the door open and disappeared inside, flashing out of sight like a ghost.

As they waited outside in the yard, nobody spoke. Suzy listened as the rain fell on the gravel and the trees around them. She had tuned the rest of them out. When Will had gone inside the farmhouse, she had thought that someone should offer to go with him; that *she* should have gone with him. But nobody had spoken up. They had let him go in alone and she felt both guilty and relieved. He had sacrificed Wilfred to save himself and her. Now here he was again, putting himself in danger for the sake of others. She needed to thank him, tell him she was grateful he was here with her. What if he didn't come out of the house though? Two minutes had already passed and there was no sign of him. Despite the cold temperature and her drenched clothes, she was sweating. A tough upbringing in Brooklyn had been nothing compared to this.

Suddenly Suzy heard a series of low-pitched screeches and looked about for the source of the noise. It didn't sound like the Deathless and if it had been a person they would've heard the footsteps on the gravel. It sounded more like a parrot.

"It's probably a Kakapo," said Rasmus. "Nothing to worry about, my dear. It's a nocturnal bird that was nearly brought to extinction. I'm not sure I have it right though. Josef would know." Rasmus trailed off, remembering his old friend. Did his body still lie half-eaten in that cold cellar, or had the child consumed him? What if by disturbing the child, Josef's body had time to reanimate? Rasmus felt queasy and tried to put the thought out of his head. Surely, that was not possible. It was hard to rid his mind of the image though; Josef's mangled dead body lying there so still.

The front door opened and Suzy flinched as a hand appeared on the frame. A second later, Will appeared.

"It's safe. There's no one here."

Will held the door open and one by one, they filed in. As Suzy passed him, she looked at his eyes, trying to see if he was all right. She wanted him to talk to him, to check how he was feeling, but he didn't see her. He was lost in thought, his blue eyes scanning the yard for trouble and the dead. Suzy carried on deeper into the house, following Kelly who was leading the way.

At the end, Tug stepped into the house, the last of the group to enter. Will put a hand against the opposite wall and blocked his path. Tug looked at him slowly.

"What?" Tug looked at Will defiantly.

Will stared back. "Thanks for your help back there, Tug."

Tug smiled and shrugged. "You're not going to make me feel guilty about Wilfred. He was checking out anyway and he would only slow us down. You did the right thing, letting him go. It's all about survival now, mate."

"Survival? What about looking out for each other? What about your ethics, your morals? Who's next, eh, Tug? You going to cut us all loose if it means saving your own skin?"

"Probably," nodded Tug. He gripped Will's arm and he relinquished, letting Tug inside. "So should you. I'm not here to make enemies, Will. This is a survival test now, pure and simple." Tug walked into the house. "And shut the door."

Will slammed the front door and closed the latch. It wouldn't hold up against many if the Deathless found them, but it would give them some time to find another way out. Will rested with his back against the door for a moment. He didn't want to join the rest while he was still angry. He had been ready to pound Tug into the ground, but he knew he was only half-angry with Tug. He was angry with himself as much. He had left Wilfred to die. He hadn't even thought about Josef. He had only thought about how he and Suzy were going to get out of there. If they were going to get through this ordeal, he was going to have to stay sharp. Tug had proven adept at handling the situation so far, but Will didn't trust him. There was no doubt that if it came to it, Tug would put himself before anyone else on this failed expedition. Will wondered how he would react if put into a tight corner. Would he let Kelly or Rasmus die to save himself? Would he let Tricia or Claire die? Suzy?

The house was cold and Will shivered. Further in the house, he could hear talking and he saw a flicker of light from down the long hallway. Tug had probably started a fire already. Will looked through the peephole in the front door and saw nothing in the yard. There was a brisk breeze picking up, throwing rubbish and leaves around, but there was nothing to suggest they had been followed. He hoped that was true. They needed the rest. He seriously doubted they would be found now.

Will walked briskly down the dark hallway to join the others, struggling to comprehend that they might have to find their own way off the island; a task that may well prove to be impossible.

SIX

There was a small fire going in the fireplace and every chair in the room was taken. Tug had found some dry matches on the mantelpiece and started the fire quickly. The solid house had avoided becoming a trap for the damp and the rooms were mostly dry. Luckily, that meant the objects in them weren't too damaged either and the shelves of books in the sitting room had proven to be very useful kindling. Once Tug had started the fire going, the others had rapidly joined him in trying to dry out.

Tricia, Mark and Rasmus were sitting on a comfortable beige sofa together, while Kelly was helping Claire take her wet jacket off. Claire's wrist was throbbing, but she didn't want to complain and kept quiet about it. Suzy and Tug were crouched on the floor with their hands outstretched and wrinkled fingers slowly thawing out. The temperature of the room was slowly lifting and Will walked in.

"You don't think the smoke will be a problem, Tug?" asked Kelly as she got Claire unwrapped.

Tug shook his head. "On a dark night like this, with the wind as it is, it won't get noticed. We've got good cover around the house with those trees, so I reckon we're good."

Kelly dragged a small chair closer to the fire and insisted that Claire sit on it. "Take your shoes off too," said Kelly. "Everyone, actually. We need to get as dry as possible. If you get the onset of trench foot it's going to be a big problem."

"What's that?" asked Claire.

"It's when your feet start to rot," said Tug. "They smell bad at first, and then the skin goes bad. You'll get blisters and sores which get infected. Eventually, you'll get gangrene and they have to amputate. So do what she says and get dried out."

As they all took off their boots and shoes, Will checked the thick, mauve curtains. They were double-lined and shielded the room from the yard well. He was worried the light of the fire might attract the dead, but he doubted the fire would even be noticeable if they were right in the front yard. As far as he could tell, the Deathless were back on the road, or in Judgeford well away from this temporary haven. He dragged a chair closer to the fire and sat down. Wearily, he took of his boots. He wrung his socks out and slumped back in the chair.

Kelly sighed as she unzipped her knee length boots. "So, what now? We need to figure a way off this island."

Rasmus cleared his throat. "Before you start, Kelly, may I ask for everyone's attention?"

Kelly nodded as he stood. Rasmus looked around the room. "I just want to say how thankful I am that all of you, who I consider my friends, are alive. Unfortunately, not all of us who came on this trip are still with us. Both our pilots are dead and so are two of our dear colleagues. I knew Josef Jahn for thirty something years and Wilfred not much less than that. They were good men. I don't know how I will face their families when we get back to New York, but I will, somehow. They deserve to be remembered. I hope we can all agree that when we get back, we should hold a memorial service for them. I think the museum would be willing to arrange something, wouldn't you, Kelly?"

"Absolutely," said Kelly. She had been thinking about it already. They weren't going to be able to retrieve their colleagues' bodies, but she had no intention of letting them be forgotten.

"Now to the matter at hand," said Tug, cutting Rasmus short before he could continue his speech. Tug had not known Josef or Wilfred and as much as he felt bad about their passing, he had to keep the group focussed on the future. If he let them drift into melancholy or wallow in pity, they were doomed. Apathy and attitude could be dangerous in life threatening situations like this. If he let them, they would drag him down with them. Tug knew, just *knew*, that he was going to get off this island alive.

"I think in the short term that we need to use what we have at hand," said Kelly. "We have two bags with us. What have we got, Tug?"

After all his efforts at salvaging their essentials from the plane wreck, in the rush to escape the attack at Judgeford they had only managed to bring two backpacks with them. Tug grabbed them and poured the contents out over the floor in the centre of the room. He briefly rifled through them, but it did not take long to look through the bags' meagre contents.

"We've got half a dozen power bars, a bottle of perfume, a basic first aid kit and a pen knife here. I don't know whose bag this is, but we have a couple of paperbacks, a pair of gloves and a couple of sweaters. All in all, not much. We're going to have to ration what food we have." Tug looked around at the disconsolate group. "First of all, we need dry clothes. I suggest we have a hunt upstairs in the bedroom and hope the owners didn't have a chance to take everything with them."

Mark stood up. "I'll go look," he announced.

"Wait!" said Kelly sharply before Mark had even put his hand on the door. "Before anyone else wanders off on their own we need a few ground rules. Firstly, nobody goes *anywhere* on their own. Even if you need the bathroom, take a buddy. It's far too risky to be on your own. Secondly, nobody goes outside unnecessarily. If we're going to start exploring this house we need to make sure we keep ourselves secure. Curtains and blinds must be drawn at all times. No lights, other than this fire. No loud noises or shouting. That means no arguing, boys."

Will and Tug looked at each other sheepishly and said nothing.

"My only other rule is that we stick together. We're going to figure this mess out. I intend to get us home, no matter what. I don't want to lose any more of you. Right, speech over," said Kelly.

Rasmus joined Mark at the door. "I'll go up with you, Mark. We'll bring down what we can."

"Take care," said Tricia. As they left, she leant forward, eager to feel the warmth of the fire. "So how are the rescue teams going to find us? Is there some sort of tracking thing on the plane? What if they see the crash and when they don't see us there think we all died along with the pilots? Should we go back and wait there tomorrow?"

Tug snorted. "Back there? Unless you want to be breakfast, then I would not advise that, darling."

Will wanted to wipe the smug expression from Tug's face, but kept his emotions in check. "I hate to say it, but rescue might not be coming. We can't rely on it at least, so we have to come up with a plan out of here ourselves."

"Why do you think that?" said Suzy staring into the fire. "The museum isn't going to forget us and what about the airline? They've lost their plane and two pilots."

"You know where we are," said Kelly. "The stark reality is that we are in serious trouble. The Grave is a forbidden zone. There's no access permitted to anyone and if they think we crashed here, we may as well accept it now - the chances of our being found are slim. Even if they look for us, even *if* they think we're still alive, they might not let us off the island. This place is contaminated. The Aqua-Gene is everywhere. Everything on this island is a potential contaminant and just by being here, we are considered just as dangerous."

Claire could feel her stomach tensing as they spoke. She was beginning to piece together exactly where they were and what was going on. She needed to know more though and stayed silent as the others spoke. She noticed Tricia wasn't saying much either, probably because she was terrified.

"Look, it doesn't matter what's out there really. It could be grizzly bears or pirates. At the end of the day, we have to be smart about this," said Tug. "We need to figure out a way off this island and we need to do it fast. Those power bars will give us some energy for tomorrow morning, but then we are going to struggle to find food. Nobody's lived on this island for years so we're not likely to find much food left. Water either."

"He's right," said Rasmus. "It's not just the bodies we have to be careful about. Other than fresh rainwater, all water has to be considered contaminated. Tins and pre-packed food are probably fine, but anything organic is too risky. Mind you, anything in a tin or a packet is likely to be long out of date. Even animals must be considered dangerous. If they appear normal then there's no danger as it means they've found a fresh water supply. But approach anything with care. Josef, God rest his soul, rushed ahead without thinking. I remember we..."

"Yeah, thanks, Rasmus." Tug cleared his throat. The old man had his shit together, but if he got back onto the subject of his old friends, they were going to be there all night. "We also need to defend ourselves. We were caught with our pants down back there and some of us paid the price. If we're going outside, and honestly

I don't think we have much choice, then we need to be able to fight those bastards off. I ain't taking one of those things on with my bare hands. You should listen to me. *Then* you might stand a chance. I'm experienced at dealing with survival situations. I've been in a few scrapes before and I've always gotten through them. I can deal with the dead."

"So you admit they're real now then, Tug?" said Will. "I'm sure you said earlier that they were a myth, a legend, didn't you?"

"So I was wrong, so what? I deal with facts, plain and simple. I know what we're dealing with now." Tug kept his back to Will as he spoke.

"And Josef and Wilfred are gone because of it. I'm sure their families will be fine once they know you have all the *facts* now." Will's irritation with Tug was rising every second and it was hard to keep his anger under control. What Will had at first perceived as rational thinking from Tug had just been self-preservation.

"It wasn't me who fed Wilfred to the dead to save his own neck, *mate*." Tug turned and eyeballed Will.

"You are a real piece, you know that?" said Suzy to Tug. She could see the fire in Will's eyes and wanted to calm them both down. "Look, what's done is done," she said. "There's no use pointing fingers now, Tug."

"Well you would say that, you're fucking him, aren't you?"

Will could take no more and launched himself at Tug, striking him as they collapsed on the floor together. Will had the upper hand and rolled on top of Tug, beating him as Tug tried to protect himself. He managed to land a good right hook on Tug's jaw and Will took great pleasure in giving Tug a bloody nose.

Claire jumped back onto the sofa beside Tricia as Kelly and Suzy pulled Will off. Kelly stood between them as the two men threatened and cursed at each other.

"For heaven's sake, what did I just say? Stop it now or I will throw you both outside!" shouted Kelly.

Tug wiped his face and fresh blood stained his sleeve. He sneered at Will. "You're an idiot. You're going to die here, Will. I'm going to live through this. I'm going back home, no matter what."

"Jesus, Tug, just stop it." Kelly left Suzy to take care of Will and approached Tug. The flickering flames of the fire flashed in her eyes as she reprimanded him. "You'd better get your head straight, Tug, or by God I will leave you here. You are getting paid to take care of us. If you're not up to the job, then say so now. If you've got a problem with Will then tough, grow up. I am not having any member of my team jeopardise the rest of the group. From now on, you do exactly as I say, or you're on your own. I am in charge. Are we clear?"

Kelly stood with her face inches away from Tug's. He tried to stare her down, but eventually he looked away.

"All right, all right, whatever," Tug said wiping his nose again. The blood in his nose had clotted and he could feel his jaw aching where Will had punched him.

"Christ almighty." Kelly rubbed her forehead. The pain was throbbing back in and she really just wanted to curl up in front of the fire and sleep. "Right, Tug, I want to you go into the kitchen and find some pots and dishes. Take whatever you can that will fill with water. The rain is clean and we need to collect as much as we can. Take what you find outside and leave it in the yard. Hopefully by morning we will have enough to drink and even take with us. Tricia, do you think you could help him? I don't want anyone out there alone."

Tug looked at Kelly and just nodded. He knew it made good sense to collect water, but hated that she was right. "I don't need a chaperone. I'll be fine out there. If I see anything, I'll be back inside in a heartbeat, don't worry."

"Okay, thank you," Kelly said giving Tug a pat on the shoulder as he left. "Right then," Kelly said as she whirled round to face Will. "Don't think you're getting let off the hook either, Mr Forrest."

Suzy knew he was in for it and inched herself away towards the sofa. Claire and Tricia looked petrified and Suzy tried to give them a warming smile.

"No matter how much he winds you up, I expect better of you, Will. I've never seen you act like that. I know this is a fucked up situation, but we have to try to get on. If we end up fighting one another, we're won't get anywhere, certainly not home. Poor Josef and Wilfred will never be going home. Please, Will? I need you with me on this." Kelly was calming down and knew Tug had provoked Will. Still, she had to take control and stamp out any problems immediately.

Will gave Kelly a hug and quietly apologised in her ear. "I'm sorry, Kelly. I'm sorry I couldn't save Wilfred."

As he pulled away, Kelly saw Will's eyes and knew Tug had hit a nerve. It hadn't been Will's fault that Wilfred got left behind. She was about to say something to him when Will spoke first.

"I'm sorry about all that, everyone. I was just a bit...out of my head, you know?"

Everyone looked back at him and said nothing. He could see Claire and Tricia were scared. Suzy was looking at him with sympathy. He was expecting her to give him a blasting too for going off the handle the way he had. Her eyes were kind though and he only felt worse, his guilt about Wilfred resurfacing when he looked at her.

Kelly drew her breath and let out a long sigh. "Okay, we stay here tonight. I want everyone to double up and find somewhere safe to bed down. Tricia, can you please stay with Claire. I'll bunk in with Suzy, Rasmus can keep an eye on Tug, and Will, you can share with Mark. Is that okay with everyone? I expect there must be at least four bedrooms in a house this size?" She looked at Will and he nodded. Nobody answered her so she continued. "We'll leave at sunrise. Tricia and Claire, I've got a job for you. Have a look around, quietly, and see if you can find anything we could use for weapons. There might be some knives in the kitchen? I don't know, just have a look please. Suzy, you're in charge of our bags and rations. Can you tidy it up please and bag everything up. We might need to leave in a hurry so we'd best be prepared."

Suzy began gathering up the pile that Tug had built whilst Tricia led Claire out of the room. Kelly sat down on one of the vacant chairs beside the fire. She picked up a book and ripped the pages out, throwing them onto the fire.

Will knelt down beside Suzy and helped her pick up their belongings. "How're you doing?" he asked her.

"So-so." Suzy looked up at Kelly and signalled for Will to do the same. They both saw Kelly sitting with her head in her hands.

She had finished destroying the book and she was just sitting quietly, looking into the fire. Suzy zipped up the bags and motioned for Will to follow her out of the room.

"What is it?" asked Will once they were out in the dark, cold hallway.

"We need to keep an eye on her. She banged her head real bad in the crash. I'm worried that she might have concussion. If she's feeling sick, she probably isn't going to tell us. You know what she's like."

"Yeah. She acts like a tough bitch, but she's putting it on half the time. She feels responsible for us. I'll keep an eye on her."

Will put his hands in his pockets and to his surprise, found a portion of a Snickers bar he hadn't finished. He brushed fluff off it and offered it to Suzy.

"Um, thanks, but I'll pass. You have it. There's barely a mouthful left anyway." Suzy smiled as Will devoured it in one go. He was still a bit of a mystery to her. Sometimes he was incredibly tough and masculine, other times he just looked cute, like now, as if he was still a boy. She could picture him as a young boy, running around his parent's Wisconsin farm, and it made her feel comforted, warm, thinking of him like that. How he had been back there with Tug was not the real Will. She vowed to herself that when they got back to New York she would buy him a bucketful of Snickers.

"If you're sure," said Will. The chocolate bar was gone in five seconds and he shoved the empty wrapper back into his pocket. "Look, what Tug said about..."

"Forget it," said Suzy shivering. "He's an idiot. He's just as scared as you and me. Come on, let's go up and see what Rasmus and Mark have found. My clothes are so wet it's a struggle to warm up."

They wandered upstairs, checking in all the rooms. There were five bedrooms in total, and two bathrooms. They were all cold and dark, but in good repair. The doors and windows had been kept shut, and no vermin had apparently found their way in so the bedclothes were still intact and clean. Eventually, they found Mark and Rasmus in one of the bedrooms.

"We were just coming back down. There's a surprisingly good amount of decent clothes actually. Look at this." Rasmus held up his arms and turned around, showing off the tweed jacket he had found. "Dry socks too. Even a few boots."

"How about you, Mark?" asked Suzy, picking up some of the clothes they had stockpiled on the bed. She could see he had thrown on a brown chequered shirt that was easily a size too big for him.

"Yeah, not too bad. I'd say a big family lived here once. There are men and women's clothes, and a good spread of sizes. Everyone should be able to find something. As long as you like tweed." Mark rolled his eyes and Suzy and Will laughed.

"*Especially* if you like tweed," said Rasmus proudly, failing to notice Mark's sarcasm and holding up a tweed flannel shirt.

They rifled through the clothes and found some things they could wear. They filled the men in on what had happened downstairs and what the plan was. They told them of how Kelly wanted them to sleep in the house tonight and make a move first thing in the morning, how Claire and Tricia were looking for things they could carry, and how there would be no supper tonight as they were saving their only food for the morning.

"I feel for Claire, I really do," said Rasmus. "Poor thing must be wondering what is going on. I'll bet she's missing her mother terribly." Rasmus was looking through the curtains at Tug outside in the yard. He had placed several dishes and saucepans of varying sizes around. There was no question that he would get a decent amount of water collected by morning.

"I'll look in on her before we turn in," said Suzy. "Look, we'd better get this stuff downstairs. Everyone's feeling the cold. We should get down to the fire, dry out, and figure out where we are actually going tomorrow."

Down in the sitting room, everybody found some dry clothing to put on and tried to warm up as best they could. There were many grumbling, empty stomachs, but nobody complained. They knew they had little choice in the matter and would have to wait. As they sat around drying out, Claire and Tricia showed what they had found in the kitchen. They had managed to pick out two large carving knives, but little else. They had brought some smaller knives that they all agreed would be little use in a fight with one of the dead. Tug had noticed a small shed in the side garden when he had been outside, and suggested they check it out quickly in the morning. If it contained gardening tools, then shovels and pitchforks would be very handy. He ignored Will and avoided looking at him. Will reciprocated, and Kelly was thankful the animosity had been forgotten.

Rasmus wrapped Claire's wrist again in fresh bandages they had found upstairs. The bathroom had turned up plenty of useful drugs and medication: headaches tablets, sleeping pills, plasters, creams and bandages. Mark had brought them down, and after Kelly had popped a couple of pills dry, packed them into their two solitary bags. They all agreed that, despite their desire and nerves, it would be dangerous to take sleeping pills. They would need to remain alert and awake, ready to leave at a moment's notice.

They all chatted for a while, reminiscing about Josef and Wilfred, remembering their former colleagues. Rasmus told them a story they hadn't heard, about a convention he had attended with Josef some ten years ago in Milwaukee. It had involved several glasses of scotch, a mix-up of room keys, and some grovelling apologies to the hotel manager the next morning. Rasmus told them he still hadn't gotten over the hangover from that night and the mood in the room lightened.

Eventually, the conversation headed to more serious matters. It was universally agreed that rescue was unlikely. They discussed the Deathless and Claire realised with every passing minute that they were in terrible danger. Her wrist still ached, but the pain had numbed and Suzy had let her take two paracetamol. She didn't have much to contribute to the discussion about how to get off the island. She had not even been aware of its existence until a few hours ago.

"Look, we've basically got three options," said Kelly. "One, we wait here for rescue. I think we've all decided that is not going to happen. Secondly, we head for the coast. It's not far away; the coast never is on this island. We head west and hope we get there quickly. I know we can't get past the fences and borders, but if we get spotted then we may get picked up. They patrol and monitor these waters regularly so I think that's the quickest way home."

"And the third option?" asked Suzy. "If the coast is the quickest way home, then let's just do it."

Tug shook his head. "It's the quickest, yes, but it's also risky. What do you think the border patrol does when it sees someone walking across the beach to their fences? I can tell you right now, they would be shot down, assumed to be one of the Deathless. Even if we go out there, making a lot of noise and waving a white flag, there's no guarantee we'd get picked up. What if they think we're infected? We'd be shot down the same as the dead."

"So option three," said Kelly. "The plane came down over the north of the country on Te Ika-a-Maui."

"So? What does it matter where we crashed?" asked Mark. "It's not like we can head to the airport for a lift back to New York. Every inch of this damn place is a death-trap."

"True," replied Rasmus. "But I believe we came down quite close to what was the once the capital city. If that's the case, then we may just have gotten lucky."

"Lucky? That's a good one," said Tricia. "It's like winning the lottery and losing your ticket before you collect on it, isn't it? We might as well have crashed into the ocean."

"Actually, that's a good point," said Will. "If we're near the old capital then we're near the research base."

Will drifted off in his own thoughts and Rasmus picked up the conversation. "The Deathless were thrown on this island, but they weren't completely left alone. There's a scientific base in the city where they are working safely, trying to find a cure for the disease; to find some way of repairing the bad job we did years ago. If we can get to that base, we'll find help. There'll be people who can help us with food, water, and shelter. The people working there will have satellites, telephone lines, radios, I don't know - something anyway that will help get us off this island."

"So what's the catch?" Suzy looked at Will who was still lost in thought.

"The catch is that we have to get into the city." Kelly almost wished she hadn't thought of it. Getting to their only way off the island was going to lead them right into the heart of the country. "Where do you think the majority of the dead like to hang out? The city is going to be full of them. What we saw back there is nothing. I don't know if we can make it. Perhaps the coast is our best bet. Shit, it's like being caught between the devil and the deep, blue sea. We should vote. If we're going to do this, we need to be fully in on this all together. I want a show of hands, please." She waited a moment and then asked them. "So who's for heading to the coast?"

The room was silent as Kelly counted the hands. It was going to be a close call. "Now, who is for the city?"

Kelly stood up. "That's that then. Let's get some sleep everyone. Tomorrow morning, we're heading for the coast and getting off this island."

SEVEN

"How is she holding up?" Suzy was talking to Tricia whilst Claire used the bathroom.

"Not too bad, all things considered. She's obviously in pain from her wrist. She's not saying much either. I don't know if that's a good thing or bad." Tricia climbed into bed.

Her room had two single beds and it was covered in dust. It looked as if it might have been a guest room. The wardrobes were empty and everything in the room had been laid out like a hotel. It was immaculate and the owners must have left in a hurry. She half expected to find a mint on her pillow when she got into bed.

"Well, at least I know she's in good hands, Tricia." Suzy walked across to the window and peeked out of the curtains. The yard was empty.

"I think we're okay for tonight," said Tricia. "I'm going to say my prayers. We need Him now more than ever. I can't help but think that tomorrow..."

"Don't," said Suzy tucking her hands into her pockets for warmth. "Just don't think about it. If you do, you'll not sleep. I can't even begin to think about today. What if..."

Claire came back into the room and quickly clambered into her bed. "What if what?" she said

"Nothing, honey," said Suzy. She crossed the cold room and leant over Claire, giving her a kiss on the forehead. "How's your arm, feeling any better?"

In the dark, Claire gave Suzy a shrug. "Sort of. I'm trying not to think about it anymore. Rasmus has strapped it up good and tight. Besides, when I start thinking about what's happened, I forget all about the pain anyway."

"Well, Tricia here is the best. You need anything you just holler," said Suzy as she softly walked to the door.

"You betcha," said Tricia. "Goodnight, Suzy."

Suzy left them alone and headed across the hallway to her room. She hesitated and then turned around. She wanted to make sure Will and Mark were okay. Kelly had already gone to bed and fallen asleep almost straight away. She was probably exhausted.

Suzy knew Kelly was trying to keep it together, not just physically, but mentally trying to stay strong for the sake of the group. She passed by the room where Rasmus and Tug were staying and hoped that Rasmus would cope with his bunkmate. Rasmus seemed to be coping well, considering he had just lost two of his old friends. Tug was a handful and she hoped he would give Rasmus some space. Suzy knocked on Will's door and went in.

"Hey, Suzy, what's up?" said Mark. He was sitting cross-legged on top of the bed, looking at his camera. "I'm just looking at the photographs I've gotten. I can review them, edit them, and even email them straight to my editor from this baby. Well, I could if there was any service around here."

"There's some grim stuff on there. He's got a good eye, that's for sure," said Will who was perched on the edge of the double bed next to Mark.

Suzy went over and sat down next to Will and looked at the view-screen on Mark's camera. She saw a picture of Judgeford. She saw the wreckage of the plane and marvelled once again how they had managed to walk away from it. Mark flicked onto the next picture. The photo was taken from a strange angle and she realised Mark must've taken it when they were running. Looking closer, she could see herself and Will bending over Wilfred's body. In the background, she counted at least twenty of the dead. She looked away. "That's horrible."

"Reality is," he said. Mark turned the camera off. "Look, I don't intend to publish these, not ones like that at least. But all I do is capture what I see. I'm not going to apologise for what I do. They say every picture tells a story, right? Well this is my story now. This place: The Grave. This is a chance nobody has *ever* had before. Probably never will again. I have to record as much as I can. When we get home, the world is going to want to know what we saw, what we experienced and how we lived through it."

"You think we're going to live through this?" asked Suzy, still unable to look at the camera. All she could see now was Wilfred's body as they ran away, leaving him to the clutches of the Deathless.

"We have to," said Will. "We can't give up now. There's so much to tell, so much to do. I need to get home."

Will trailed off again. Suzy waited for him to speak, but he said nothing.

"I'll be back in five," said Mark getting up, putting his camera on the bedside table. "Bathroom break. Then I might hit the hay. See ya, Suzy."

Mark closed the door behind him and Suzy didn't even realise when Will put his arm around her. She was still thinking about Wilfred.

"I know, I can't get him out of my head either," said Will. "We won't forget him, but we have to move on. We have to focus on the future, Suzy, or we're never going to get out of here. Do you think Tug is grieving right now? I'll bet he's sound asleep. He's a pain in the neck, but he has one thing correct. We have to think about how we're going to survive this."

Suzy let out a long sigh and looked at Will in the dark, cold room. His face was troubled and his brow furrowed. In the dark of the room, he looked more handsome than ever. She wiped her red eyes and suddenly felt like crying. She knew she was on the verge, but Will was right. There was no time to grieve. She had to get home.

"Why did our plane crash, Will? Seriously, I am so pissed off. Some tiny thing probably, some little bolt or nut that wasn't screwed in quite right. Some engineer who didn't spot the metal fatigue or..." Suzy sighed. "Whatever. It doesn't matter now. I miss my family. I only see them occasionally. You know what it's like in New York. There's always something that keeps me busy and stops me getting home as much as I'd like."

Will smiled and Suzy's lips trembled. She really didn't want to cry in front of him, but she began thinking about her brothers and how she might not see them again.

"We'll make it. I know it. Suzy Q, as tough as old boots, right?" Will licked his lips. Sometimes Suzy seemed a lot more fragile than she let on. Will wanted to let her in. He found it difficult to open up, but he felt at ease with Suzy. "I told you my mom was sick, but I didn't tell you how sick. She's in St. Luke's. They tell me she's got a few weeks at most. I sure would like the chance to see her one last time."

Will looked at Suzy and leant forward to embrace her. He swept his arms around her and pulled her into his body. His hand sank into her soft blonde hair and they kissed, softly and tenderly. Suzy's lips were salty from the tears she had been unable to hold back. They knew the kiss could not lead any further, but it felt good at that moment in time. The despair and tension was forgotten in that brief moment. It felt good to know they weren't going through this alone. Their lips parted and they lingered there together, their foreheads gently resting on each other's.

Mark swept the door open and came striding into the room.

Suzy jumped up off the bed quickly and brushed past him. "Oh, hey, Mark, I was just leaving."

Will watched, bemused, as Suzy almost ran out of the room.

"You okay, buddy?" said Mark slipping beneath the bed covers, making sure his camera was within arm's reach.

"Yeah, yeah, fine," said Will. He couldn't expect too much of Suzy now, not with what was going on. He just hoped that she didn't think he was taking advantage of her. Somehow, being with Suzy just felt right. He shrugged off her speedy exit, kicked his shoes off and got beneath the duvet. "No funny business now, Mark, you hear?"

Mark let out a short laugh. "Sorry darling, you're not my type. You just keep to your side of the bed, and I'll see you in the morning."

They lay there in silence, waiting for sleep to take them. It took a long time though. Will's mind would not rest. He thought about his mother and about how she was coping without him. He thought about the journey they were going to undertake tomorrow and the inherent risks involved. He thought about Suzy too. When they got back to New York, he was going to put himself first for once and take her out on the date he kept promising her.

The night was restless for all of them. Sleep came sporadically. Some dreamt of home before nightmares interrupted them; visions of the dead, of Josef and Wilfred lying cold and dead, and of the plane crash. Even Tug slept fitfully, tossing and turning all night.

Eventually, Suzy was awoken by Kelly moving around the room. The curtains were still drawn, but there was a sliver of sunlight coming over the top of them. "Is it morning already?" She could see Kelly dressed and swallowing something. "More paracetamol?" said Suzy throwing back the bed covers and exposing herself to the frigid air.

Kelly threw her head back and swallowed. "You caught me. It's a bitch without water too."

Suzy quickly dressed and was grateful they had dry clothes. She had found a blue shirt and some old jeans that were a little baggy on her, but were certainly better than the wet dress she wore yesterday. She pulled on a pair of thick socks and then reluctantly her slip-on black shoes. She wished she had worn something more practical now. "How's the head?"

"Sore, but I'll live. Sorry, I didn't mean to wake you. I just heard some noise downstairs and thought I should check it out."

"Noise?" said Suzy alarmed.

"Don't worry," said Kelly seeing the shock on Suzy's face. "I heard Will and Mark's voices so it's nothing untoward. I haven't dared look outside yet. I should guess it's time for us to make a move though. You all right?"

Suzy just nodded and followed Kelly out of the room. In the hallway, a dim patch of sunlight lit up the wooden floor from a skylight overhead. The bedroom doors were all open and it seemed they were the last up. They made their way downstairs and Suzy began to hear the voices again. It was impossible to hear what was being said though as there was a banging noise too. They headed for the kitchen where the sounds were coming from.

Upon entering the room, it was clear what the banging was. Tug and Mark were pulling up floorboards and Will was hammering at them with a pickaxe. Rasmus and Tricia were filling empty plastic bottles with water from saucepans whilst Claire held the two backpacks open for them.

"Morning all," said Kelly. "Looks like I missed the memo."

She was greeted by a chorus of cheerful voices, much to her surprise. "Up at last, sleepyhead," said Will. "Hi, Suzy."

Suzy made a beeline for Rasmus. "You should've woken us. Here, let me help." She held a small bottle steady whilst Rasmus carefully poured the rainwater in.

"Oh we've not been up long, my dear. Tug here was up hard at work whilst we were snoring. He went and found those tools in the garden shed so we could tear up some floorboards."

"Okay, firstly, Tug, you should *not* be going out on your own, it's not safe," said Kelly exasperated already. "Secondly, why? What are we doing with the floor?"

Tug rested a floorboard against the wall and leant back against the counter, wiping sweat from his face. "We need something to defend ourselves with out there. I found one shovel and one pickaxe out there. With the kitchen knives we found that's four weapons, at best, we've got. There's eight of us, Kelly. We need more. These floorboards are perfect. They're strong, solid and will be useful for smashing against anyone or anything that attacks us."

"It's true," said Will. "Here, Tug, this is the last one." He handed a board to Tug who stacked it up against the others. "How's the water situation?"

"Not bad, it must've rained a fair bit last night," said Tricia as she screwed the top on an old coke bottle now full of rainwater. "We've managed to fill a few bottles. We can carry these easily enough between us. There's a cooking pot on the side there that we can't use, we've run out of bottles. I'd say we might as well drink it now."

"Right, let's get sorted," said Tug pulling up a chair to the kitchen table, winking at Claire as he did so. He scattered the food on the table around him. "We've got ten power bars in total. One each and two spare."

Claire put the two spares into one of the bags. "Should we eat it now? I'm starving."

"Up to you. Personally, I'm going to have half of mine now and the rest later. I don't think we can expect to get to the coast much before evening so you might want to ration yourself. Unless we get picked up straight away, it could be a long day," answered Tug, peeling off the wrapper to his bar.

Everyone grabbed a bar and began eating. Rasmus scooped water from the pot into mugs and handed them around. A few minutes later and the food and water were gone.

Tug got up and began checking through the cupboards and drawers, pulling them open and slamming them shut again, when he found them empty. He ignored the conversation and instead focused on what he did best: surviving. He knew they were in a desperate situation and rather than waste time talking about it, he preferred to keep himself busy. He was looking for food, weapons, anything that would be useful in the next few hours or days they were going to be stuck here. So far, he had come across very little of use. Any food had long since perished or been taken. The power had obviously been turned off long ago, but the fridge had not been emptied and he didn't need to open the door to know what was inside; green mould had sprouted from the cracks around the door and the smell was putrid. Whatever vegetables or perishable food had been in there had had years to decay and rot.

"So how do we do this?" said Suzy. "I mean, literally, how do we even know the best direction to head?"

"Follow the road for now." Will put one of the backpacks on and picked up the pickaxe. "By the way, I'll take this. It's heavy and I can manage it. Tug or Mark, do you want to take the other pack?"

Tug gave up his search for anything more useful and quickly grabbed the other pack, slinging it over his shoulders. "Back the way we came, back to the road and then head west. Follow the sun. We'll stick to the road as long as we can. We'll have to play it by ear, see how it goes. If we run into trouble we'll try to go around."

Kelly picked up one of the rough floorboards. It was fairly heavy, but not so much that it could not be carried easily. If she had to defend herself, it would make a substantial weapon. "I'll take lead with Tug. I want Rasmus behind me with Tricia and Claire. Will, Mark, I want you two at the back, please. Anyone got a problem with that?"

Nobody spoke. Suzy cast a glance at Will, but he was examining the pickaxe. She picked up a wooden board. It was roughly four feet long and she knew if she struck someone with it, they would know about it. She also hoped she would not have to use it.

"Right, grab your gear, let's go. Once we're outside we keep quiet until we're in the clear. We don't know where those things went last night, so be careful. If you see something, let me know." Kelly didn't wait for an answer and marched to the front door.

Outside in the yard, the air was crisp and cool. The power bar Kelly had eaten had settled her stomach, but she already regretted eating it all. It had been so good though that she hadn't been able to resist the whole thing. As she made her way across the yard, she looked and listened for signs of the dead. The air was perfectly still and she heard no sounds other than her own breathing and the footsteps of everyone behind her. As she walked down the driveway back to the road, she began to feel tense. Very little was known about the Deathless. What if they were lying in wait? What if they had regrouped and now instead of a handful there were a hundred, a thousand, or more? As she walked, she looked into the bushes and the trees, trying to spot anything unusual. Was there a pair of feet under that gorse bush? Had she seen eyes watching her from over the crest of that hill? A small rabbit darted out in front of her and she let out a shriek. It raced off into the undergrowth, immediately disappearing out of sight.

"Don't let your nerves get the better of you," said Tug as he walked up beside her. "Don't be worried about what you can't see, just what you can. Okay?"

"Yeah," she replied, trying to sound confident. Not only had she made herself look a fool, she had risked them all by screaming like that. She gripped the wooden board in her hand and continued down the driveway, letting Tug take the lead.

At the junction to the roadway, there was no sign of them. The dead had left having either found food elsewhere or having lost sight of their prey last night. Yawning, Tug lead the way up the hill, following the road as it wound its way amongst the green hills of The Grave. The sky was clear and it looked as though all of last night's rainclouds had blown away. Will, the last one out, shut the gate to the farmhouse driveway quietly, and then jogged to catch up to Mark.

"You think we're going in the right direction?" Will asked him.

Mark raised his eyebrows. "You mean do I think we can trust him? He's got an attitude, but yeah, I think we can follow him. If there's one thing I know about him, it's that he wants off this island. Right now, he's probably our safest bet."

Mark held up his camera and took a quick shot of a house as they walked by. One side had collapsed and exposed the ramshackle interior. The outer brickwork had crumbled away exposing the inner struts and joists. Surrounding the house were overgrown roses of all colours and bright flowers, making the dark house look even more striking.

"I hope you get to do something with those photos of yours, Mark," said Will as he waited for Mark to finish.

"I will. I haven't shirked a story yet and I'm not going to start now. It's pretty amazing actually. Look at that place, all the colour and life. I thought...well I don't know what I thought exactly, but I didn't expect this place to be so *vivid* and full of life."

"I need some of what you're on," said Will, incredulous. "I don't see what you do. That house is just dead. This whole place is utterly devoid of life. It's like looking at one of those old sepia photographs. You know, all brown and tinted colours? I guess you probably think they're cool, but I just see an emptiness, like it's a memory of life. It's not the real thing. There's no life here, just death."

Mark chuckled. "You've spent too long in New York. I don't think you know how to live without that constant buzz. It's a rush all right, but sometimes you've got to get away from it all."

"And a vacation in The Grave is your recommendation?" Now it was Will's turn to chuckle.

"Well, it's peaceful. You're never going to get stuck in a traffic jam. And the beaches are deserted," joked Mark.

The two men laughed and talked, all the while keeping their voices low. It seemed as though the dead from last night had truly gone though. It didn't feel like there was anyone around. The area had seemed deadly ominous last night in the cold, dark evening. Now that the sun was up and they were on their way, it felt different.

Mark was optimistic for the first time since the crash. Tug would find a path to the coast and surely, it wouldn't take long before they were seen. A boat ride and a plane would see them safely back on American soil in no time.

Will was concerned, but he said nothing else. Mark had his little project to keep his mind occupied and that was good. Will supposed that everyone did. His mind kept switching between his mother and Suzy. Tricia and Claire were supporting each other and Kelly was still trying to be team leader, taking care of everyone. Rasmus wanted to get back to the museum so he could honour his friends and Tug had himself to think about. If they had nothing else, the desolation of this place would wear them down. Will felt as if The Grave was not just devoid of life, but of hope. How could anyone survive a place like this? He shuddered and concentrated on what Mark was saying.

"Tug's stopped. We'd better see what's going on."

They had been walking for about half an hour, all the while keeping their wits about them. No dead bodies had approached them, and they had managed to follow the road for a few miles before they'd needed to stop.

"What is it?" said Will as they joined the others.

"It seems we're approaching some more houses. You can see down the road that there's a cluster of buildings. We'd better be careful," said Kelly. "There's no point looking in those places for help, we won't find any. We should keep on and pass straight through."

"Should we go around?" asked Suzy. "What if those...things are hiding inside?"

Will tucked his hands into his pockets. The morning was cold and he was lucky he had been wearing his overcoat when the plane crashed. It had dried out overnight and the fleece-lined pockets were comforting. "Best to stick to the road," he said. "In theory there's no reason why any of them should be hiding inside the houses - there's nothing to hide from. If anything, they're more likely to be out in the open looking for food."

At the mention of food, Rasmus' stomach growled audibly. Will felt his turn too, but refused to let it distract him. They were unlikely to get much food soon and he had enough experience to know to eat small amounts slowly. Rasmus had wolfed down his ration so quickly this morning that it had barely touched the sides.

"We'll be much faster if we stick to the roads," said Tug. He began to walk up the road, striding out purposefully. "We'll only get slowed down in the fields and the long grass. Best follow me and keep to firm ground."

Will and Kelly took off immediately, with Rasmus moaning under his breath about his hunger, but reluctantly following. Tricia was retying her laces and Mark was adjusting his camera strap so it hung loosely around his neck.

"You all right, Claire?" asked Suzy putting an arm around the young girl as they followed behind Will and Kelly.

"Yeah, I'm fine." Claire smiled, but it was clearly forced and she was not fine. Suzy left her arm on Claire's shoulder as they walked together.

"Try not to worry too much, okay? These guys have been in some serious scrapes, they'll get us through this. Will and Kelly have been all over the world so they know what they're doing. Tug's an asshole, but he won't take us anywhere dangerous. And Rasmus, hell he knows everything about everything. Plus you've got me." Suzy squeezed Claire's arm and then let her go. If she mothered her too much, she sensed Claire was liable to start crying. Suzy remembered last night and how she had started crying with Will before they had kissed. She bit her lip and focussed on Claire.

"You really think those houses are empty?" Claire looked nervously at the road ahead. Since leaving the farmhouse, they had kept to the road. It seemed to lead in the direction they wanted to go, so they decided to follow it for as long as they could. After leaving the farm, they had not seen or heard anything; no birds or animals, nothing living or dead, and no towns or villages either. The road now however was lined with about a dozen houses on either side. In the middle was a small shop. The village, if you could call it that, was deserted. The houses were like giant tombs just waiting to open up and spill death out into the road. Windows and doors were broken, open and rotting; the very air smelt of damp.

"Come on, let's go," said Suzy taking Claire's hand.

The eight figures walked through the morning air, treading quietly. Clouds were forming in the sky and Suzy hoped the rain was not returning. The sunshine was becoming weaker and the drains had become blocked with fallen leaves and branches. They frequently had to avoid stepping in pools of murky water.

Up ahead, Rasmus was showing no fear and confidently marching through the row of houses. He looked from side to side occasionally, but saw no reason to panic. He had decided he couldn't leave everything to Kelly. Tug might have the experience of being out in the 'thick of it', but he didn't know these people. Rasmus decided he needed to step up and help lead his friends out of this desolate place. He was scared, but he could not show it. The young girl, Claire, particularly, would be looking up to him and expecting someone more experienced and knowledgeable to lead them home. They had not asked him to lead, yet somehow he felt like he should. There was no reason why he couldn't assume the role. He knew they did not have much time so he tried to hurry the others along as much as he could. There was precious little untainted food and water available to them so the better time they made, the more likely they would be to make it off the island alive.

"Hurry up now, let's crack on shall we?" called Rasmus. "I believe we are at the top of the hill. Around the bend I'm sure we will find the coastline in view."

Tug shook his head. Rasmus was being too loud, too cocky; it was likely to lead them all into trouble. Tug stepped up the pace to catch up. He was going to have to get Rasmus back into line.

Rasmus bent down to examine something on the side of the road; a purple flower sprouting from a crack in the pavement. On another day, in another time, The Grave might have made for a fascinating study. With the land untouched for so many years, nature was changing the landscape, quite literally, and the flora and fauna with it. Beyond the row of houses, Rasmus could see a huge hill covered in yellow gorse, an unwelcome remnant of the Pakeha, and a spiky row of native cabbage trees towering into the sky. The hill cast a shadow over the land; a dark veil as if it wanted to hide the lifeless land from view.

Looking in the front yard of the house closest by, he saw Totorowhiti and a red Matipo that had grown to at least ten feet tall and just as wide. Whilst he had not yet seen any sign of animal life himself he was sure that it was there. So many of the birds and creatures of this land had been nocturnal before it had been renamed, and they were unlikely to have changed now. Since the influx of the dead, they had probably become more afraid of man, more timid, and better at hiding. Rasmus continued onward, feeling his mood lightened and his body full of vigour. His mind had suddenly clicked that he was in a wondrous place, dangerous yes, but really quite a magnificent place that promised so much to a scientist like him.

"Come now, my dears, almost there," Rasmus called out.

Will and Kelly trudged not far behind Rasmus content to let him lead the way for now and there was a mutual trust in each other's ability to find a way out. Will kept looking behind to make sure everyone else was keeping pace. Suzy and Claire were close and Tug was just ahead of them. The particular line that Kelly had asked for at the farmhouse had disintegrated. Tricia was now at the rear and Mark close behind her. Will saw Mark fiddling with his camera, but he knew full well that there was nothing wrong with it. Mark had been in enough situations to not need to prepare for action. His camera was always on, and Will suspected that Mark had hung back purposefully, so as to put the women in the middle of the group and himself deliberately at the back.

Assured they were safe enough, Will walked on and wondered if Rasmus was right. Beyond the top of the hill, he believed the plains would open out and they would be on course to reach the coast. If the clouds kept away, they would be able to see the coastline. Will pushed his hands further into his pockets, feeling the warmth of his body slowly sapping away. The air was still very cold and they had not had anything hot to eat or drink.

Rasmus, Tug, Will and Kelly had gotten through the row of houses safely and nothing had jumped out at them or attacked them. Suzy and Claire were almost clear and Tricia was ahead of Mark, who having seen the red Matipo that Rasmus had done a few minutes ago, had stopped to take a photograph. The shrub had entwined itself with a trail of white roses and the colours struck him as quite beautiful amid all the gloom of the ghost town. As he paused to admire the overgrown garden, a bright yellow ball rolled slowly toward Mark. He reached down as it neared him, picked it up and crushed the soft ball into his palm. Turning it around, he saw a smiley face had been crudely drawn onto it with a thick, black marker. The ball had rolled out of the doorway from the house one up from him, and as the others were still walking away, he tried to see why the ball had appeared now. Something must have caused it to move; a rat, a bird, or a gust of wind maybe. Perhaps it had just been dislodged by one of the others and they hadn't even realised it.

Mark peered at the doorway the ball seemed to have come from. The house was dark and impenetrable. Beyond the swinging wooden door, there was just an icy blackness, as if the heart of the house had been ripped out. Mark could hear the rusty hinges creaking and the faint footsteps of his friends as they walked on ahead of him. They had passed through the row of houses without trouble and the little grey building beside him was the last cottage of the row.

He began to walk after the others, spying Rasmus at the front of the group now very close to the top of the hill. If one of the dead were in that house, he did not want to wait around for it. The hill they were walking up was quite short and in a moment, they would be out of sight of whatever might be in that house. Mark felt nervous about being so exposed in the street like this and a feeling of dread settled over him, sinking into his stomach uneasily.

Mark took one last quick look at the smiley face and then dropped the ball on the ground. It bounced away and ended up in the gutter where it bobbed along a stream of dirty rainwater. Mark watched the ball drift away and then turned his back on it and the row of houses. Suddenly, he wanted to be far away from here, the striking colours of the garden long forgotten. The group seemed so far away now; Rasmus, Will and Kelly were standing at the top of the road, just before it curved out of sight. Claire and Suzy were far away too and Tug and Tricia were in shouting distance, but he didn't want to risk calling out. Mark felt a spatter of rain on his face and looked up. Almost from nowhere, a dark grey cloud had appeared and the heavens opened. The thick cloud hid the sun, and the village was enveloped by the shade of the cloud. Great drops of rain began splashing their way down Mark's body and he quickly snapped the cover over his camera. Looking up, he realised that suddenly the others were barely visible through the deluge.

The rain increased in strength as Mark attempted to catch up with Tricia. He heard the swinging rusty hinges in the doorway behind him stop and then there was a bang as the front door to the little grey cottage crashed out of its frame and hit the ground. Mark whirled around and saw two figures emerge from the dark house. Two dead men stumbled out, their unblinking eyes focused on Mark. Mark froze in shock. The dead stood only a few feet away from him. The Deathless were here.

EIGHT

"Hey, move it!" shouted Mark as he rapidly caught up with Tricia. He had taken flight when the first dead man reached for him and only just managed to avoid being grabbed. Mark was now sprinting up the road.

"What's wrong with..." Tricia pulled back the hood of her jacket and through the rain she saw Mark running toward her. Behind him were others; people she didn't recognize.

Tricia began running and screaming at the same time. She splashed through a huge puddle and then tripped over a fallen branch, slipping onto her side. The knife she had been carrying flew out of her grasp and dropped into a storm drain far out of reach. Mark dropped to his knees to help Tricia up and turned around quickly to see how much time they had. One of the two men was slow, stumbling slowly along the road, whilst the other man was close: very close. He had pale skin, almost translucent, and he made urgent, throaty, grunting noises as he jogged toward them. His clothes were no more than rags over his gaunt body and the dead man ran between the raindrops like a ghost.

Mark hauled Tricia up to her feet and he shouted at her to run. He knew there was no way they would outrun it, so he braced himself, flinging his camera onto his back. He wished he had carried a weapon as Tug had suggested. He had thought he wouldn't need one and it would only get in the way of his camera. He was regretting that decision now.

As Tricia ran screaming for help, the dead man advanced. Mark swivelled on the spot quickly and grabbed the dead man's arms as they lunged for him. Mark spun the man around and twisted the arms backwards. One broke instantly, the brittle bones unable to keep fused together. The dead man hit the ground and Mark jumped onto the man's back to stop him getting back up. He knelt over the dead man, pinning the body to the road as it thrashed beneath him. The dead body wriggled like a worm, unable to turn over as Mark sat on top of it, calling for help. He grabbed the man's arms and pinned them to the tarmac, all the while struggling to keep the man from striking him as he bucked beneath him.

Tug skidded to a halt beside Mark. "Looks like you've got a slippery one there, mate," he said as he withdrew a large knife from his backpack.

"Just hurry up and do something, will you I can't hold it for long," hissed Mark. He was worried that the man was so frail that his arms would break clean off and then Mark would not be able to hold him down any longer.

"All right, all right, steady on, mate."

Mark watched as Tug left to take care of the second figure. Tug quickly thrust his knife into the dead man's skull through an eye socket, and the figure crumpled to the ground. Tug ran back to Mark and knelt down on the road before him. He held the knife over the dead man's head. Tug clasped both hands around the handle and waited for the man's head to still.

"Whenever you're ready, Tug. Sometime today would be nice." Mark felt the dead man beneath him squirming and almost felt sorry for him. How long had he been in that house? A week, a year, or five years? Had that house been the man's home once, a home he had shared with a wife and children? What had he done to deserve dying like this?

Tug struck the knife into the man's fragile skull and embedded the blade into the dead man's brain. The knife went in, right up to the hilt, and instantly the man stopped moving. The arms that Mark held flopped down and he let them go.

Mark breathed out a sigh of relief. "Is he dead?"

Tug yanked the knife out and wiped the blade on his jeans. He stood and kicked the dead body. "Yep." Tug turned and walked away, leaving Mark to get up and follow.

As Mark joined the others, he found Tricia sobbing beside Kelly. "Jesus, that was close."

"There's no more is there? Was that it? Are we being followed?" Claire was almost hyperventilating and Suzy tried to calm her down.

"Did you get bitten, Mark?" asked Tug, his hands still holding the knife.

Mark shook his head. "No, thank God. I think that was it."

"I'm sorry," said Rasmus, "I hope that wasn't my fault. I didn't mean to usurp you, Tug. I was just trying to hurry you all along, you know. I thought it best to get us going, to..."

"Talking. Chatting. Stopping to take sodding pictures. Do you lot think you're out for a fucking picnic?" Tug tucked the knife back into his pack and raised a muscled arm. He pointed west. "That's what you wanted to see, isn't it, Rasmus? Is this what you were shouting about? Was it worth it? Nearly getting us all killed?"

They all looked to where Tug was pointing. Rasmus had been right after all. The coast was very much in view now, although they were a long way off. The road they were on followed the hill down to the coast, winding its way through grass fields dotted with farmhouses. Between them and the coast though, at the base of the hill, was a large town. They could see endless houses and buildings, shops and factories. Getting to the coast was not going to be as easy as they had hoped it would be.

Rasmus' eyes darted about from one person to another. "Yes, but...I'm sorry, I just thought..."

"Well, old man don't, okay? I'll do the thinking from now on," said Tug.

"All right, Tug, you've made your point," said Kelly. "The main thing is we're all okay. Right, Mark? Tricia?"

The raincloud was blowing away and the deluge had turned into a mere drizzle. The sun was threatening to disappear altogether though, only peeking out occasionally between the growing bands of clouds above.

"For now, we stick to the plan," said Kelly. "We're going down there to see if we can find a way to the coastline. We are going to take it slowly. If anyone falls over or gets stuck, we wait and stick together. This weather is going to make the road slippery. If we come across anymore houses, we go around them from now on. Once we get to the bottom of the hill, we'll follow the road as much as we can. Tug and I will be at the front, no excuses. Tug's right, this is not a Sunday school outing. Keep your heads together; it's going to be a long day."

It had taken them over an hour to reach the summit of the hill and Tug estimated it would take them at least as long to get to the bottom. Assuming they did not encounter any more of the dead, they may make the base by noon. The difficulty then would be getting through the town. The chances of it being deserted were slim. Tug felt frustrated, but he couldn't go ahead and leave them. Not yet.

As they walked, their dry clothes slowly became wet again. The sky turned darker and the rain stronger. Minute by minute, they were drenched and so they began to talk, only in whispers this time, too fearful of talking out loud and waking the dead. Rasmus was afraid of incurring Tug's wrath again and kept his voice low and soft.

"Do you want me to take a look at your wrist, my dear?" he asked Claire. He noticed she looked tired, understandably, but if anything, even paler than yesterday. She was probably in a lot of discomfort, but she was not saying anything about it.

"No thanks, Rasmus, it's fine," she said. She coughed and put her hand over her mouth to stifle the noise. "I'm just scared," Claire blurted out. "I'm scared of touching anything in case it's infected, scared of closing my eyes and when I do, scared of opening them again. I'm hungry, but I can't eat. I'm thirsty, but I'm too scared to drink anything. I want to get out of here, but every step I take, it feels like we're just getting closer to death, to them, the Deathless."

Rasmus offered reassurances, but she clammed up and kept her head down, refusing to talk any more. As Claire kept walking, Rasmus fell back to walk in line with Will and Mark. "I'm concerned about Claire. Mentally, she's very fragile right now. Her wrist is broken for sure, but I wonder if there's something else. She doesn't look well."

"Have you looked in a mirror lately? None of us do." Will had thought the pickaxe would be useful and had wanted to carry it knowing it was heavy. He was now finding it a burden and it weighed him down. He refused to leave it behind though. He had seen how Tug had dispatched the dead man who had attacked Mark. If more came, they would need more than knives.

"I won't be sad to see the back of this island. It's horrible. It's not just the dead. The whole place is just ruined. I never knew it before the Deathless, but it probably was a beautiful country. Look around you now. There's death everywhere. The houses are malignant, the air stagnant...it gives me the creeps."

"Come now, Will," said Rasmus. "Just look at the vista below you." He pointed to a gap in the hills that gave them a glimpse of the ocean. "There's such a depth of foliage on the tress and an amazing variety of plant life. In the short time we've been here, I've seen Dactylanthus, rare ferns, Rimu, Matipo and things I could never see growing back home. Such healthy growth is amazing, especially here. If man were here, I doubt those trees would be. It's only natural for us to expand and grow, to multiply, to want to colonise where we live, but it's usually at the expense of the natural habitat. Do you see that plant over there? That's Clianthus puniceus."

Mark looked unimpressed as he ambled beside them. He had little intention of joining in the conversation, but liked listening to Rasmus and Will. He felt comforted too, knowing they were so close by, literally, and able to talk so easily. The incident with the dead man back there had left him shaken.

"Sorry, Kaka beak to you and me," said Rasmus. "Those scarlet flowers have probably not been seen in this country for a *decade*, yet here it is sitting at the side of the road. Who knows how many more are growing now their habitat is left untouched."

Mark took a photo of the flower as they moved on.

"You can see it how you want, but I prefer to be more pragmatic." Will yawned, feeling exhausted. Last night's sleep had not been restful. "You say life is flourishing here since man left. I say it's dying. That Kaka flower, those trees – they're only here because so many died. Millions, Rasmus, *millions*. They're not symbolic of life to me - they're just symbols of death."

"I see, I see," said Rasmus. "Look, I'm not a tree-hugger, don't get me wrong. I'm on mankind's side. What has happened, what *is* happening, is just terrible. But I can't believe we have lost so much for nothing to come of it."

"I guess we just see things differently."

Mark sneezed and pinched his nose. "Bloody hay fever," he muttered, wiping his nose on his jacket.

Will laughed. "See, Rasmus, not everyone is as happy as you are to be spending so much time in nature."

"You know the Aqua-Gene didn't hinder vegetation or organic growth in any kind of weed, plant or tree," said Rasmus. "It only affects living beings, humans and animals. Look at this place. Everywhere we look, every branch we step on, and every blade of grass we crush has probably been touched by the Aqua-Gene. It's in the soil, rivers, and fruit hanging from the trees. Yet if anything, the flora on this land is growing extraordinarily well. I saw some lemons back there that were twice their normal size. I remember some research done a long time ago on the effect it had on crops. Wheat and corn grew dramatically. They can grow perfectly well when cultivated by the Aqua-Gene. There's life all around us."

"It's just a shame all those crops and fruits you talk about Rasmus are useless." Mark took a photograph of a huge fern that was eleven feet tall. Its fronds offered them momentary respite from the rain.

"I hope those scientists are getting somewhere with their research," said Will. "Imagine if we could harvest the Aqua-Gene. Imagine if it had actually worked. The people on this island wouldn't be after our skin for starters. If all those millions of people were still alive today..."

"Then we'd have a different problem," interrupted Rasmus. "We'd still not have enough food and water to go around. Millions would die of starvation or the diseases associated with lack of access to clean water. We bled the planet dry."

"It's not the millions you talk about I'm so worried about," said Mark. "We don't have access to water, do we? I mean it's all around us, but it's tainted. We have to assume everything here is contaminated. One drop and we've got a death sentence. Apples, berries, whole fields of edible food and yet we can't eat a mouthful. How long would we have if we did? A day or two? Jesus, I'm scared to pick my nose in case my hands have touched anything and picked up the infection."

"If you get bitten or scratched by them, or if one of the dead gets their hands on you, you'll soon know about it." Will hunched his shoulders, trying to keep out the rain. "What is it, twenty, thirty seconds? You're lucky you got away, Mark. If they had bitten you anywhere, you would have been in agony for a few seconds and then death. After that...just more death. It doesn't bear thinking about."

They walked on in silence for a while. Mark noticed more of the plants and trees that Rasmus had pointed out. They were quite different to the ones he sat under in Central Park on his free days. He was pleased he had kept his camera on him during the flight. He had thought of stowing it in his luggage, but didn't trust the airlines not to lose his gear, as had happened when he had visited the Galapagos Islands once. His boss hadn't let him forget the cost of shipping out a new camera and so Mark hadn't made that mistake again. He had taken so many pictures so far that he could probably release a book. Not all of them would be suitable for publication though. He remembered the dead man who had attacked him earlier, the pictures he had taken of the crash site where Wilfred laid dead and the photo of the Deathless as they had advanced upon them yesterday. As far as Mark was concerned, this whole country was a death trap and the sooner they got out the better. Will was right; this place was evil. Either the Deathless or the land would kill them all given the opportunity.

Rasmus had his reasons for finding this place so fascinating, but Mark wasn't so convinced it was all scientific. It might be a bluff; just a ruse so they would think he wasn't scared. If you spent your time thinking about the biology of the plant life and the exotic plants around them, it would undoubtedly take your mind off the fact there were dead people running around trying to eat them. He could see why so many people looked up to Rasmus though. He looked old, but he exuded an inner strength that belied his years. Mark wondered how Rasmus would cope when he finally retired. He seemed to enjoy imparting his knowledge and never came across as patronizing or 'school-teacherly' that so many did.

A stark line of fir trees sat atop the hill ahead of them. The trees were stiff and immobile, their branches unbending in the wind. The rain battered their tall, solid trunks, but they stood firm, like a line of soldiers standing to attention. The sky was dim and gloomy matching the atmosphere and the road was curving around yet another bend.

The constant drizzle was cold and numbing, but it wasn't what was making Claire shiver. Up ahead nobody spoke. The only sound was of the rainwater as it hit the concrete, splashing off their hoods and jackets before trickling down into small running streams at the side of the road. Claire touched her phone in her pocket. She knew it was useless here, but she found it reassuring. She had tried many times to get a signal. Every time though was a failure. Now, as she walked, she just gently touched the buttons and traced her fingers around its metallic edge. It reminded her of home. It was all she had now to link her to her family who were back home in New York wondering where she was and why she hadn't contacted them. She should've been at the base now helping Kelly and settling in for her first scientific expedition. Instead, she had a broken wrist and a bleak future. Her mother had always told her to 'look on the bright side.' Whenever she had struggled at school or had boy trouble she had remembered that. She could picture her mother right now when she had said it. Claire had been eight and a bully at school had taken her milk carton. It seemed ridiculous now, but she had gone home crying. Her dad had told her to fight back, but her mother had consoled her and told her, 'Look on the bright side. When you got home, you've got me and you father. We love you. That bully is probably going home miserable to a family that can't afford to buy milk cartons. She's not happy. Karma, Claire - what goes around comes around.'

Claire found herself welling up as she thought about home. She took her phone out of her pocket and checked the screen once more. The signal was still dead. Her battery was weak too. She hoped she would be able to ring or email her mother before it died too. Claire looked up into the rain. The sky above looked as dark as it had when she'd woken up.

The descent was slow, even slower than when they had been going uphill. The rain was making the road very slippery and at times, it got quite steep. They had to pass several houses as they descended and when they could not go around, they crept by, quite literally, for fear of arousing what might be inside.

As they walked on, the sky finally began to clear once again. The clouds were dispersing and the sun was shining, poking its head through the wispy clouds like a scared baby. They followed the road and it levelled out. A feral cat darted across the road and Tug stopped, surprised. He watched, as it stayed hidden in the long grass. The cat watched them carefully and Tug waited for the others to catch him up.

"It'll be good when we get down," said Rasmus. "My legs are not used to all this exercise. My left knee is killing me. I'm certainly beginning to feel my age."

"I think we all are," said Kelly. "I'm just pleased that the rain has stopped. Seriously, what's with this weather? I suppose it's that indecisive spring pattern of sunshine and showers."

"Huh, look at that. Looks like your exercise is not finished yet, Rasmus." Suzy pointed ahead of them and Rasmus saw the huge, gnarled oak tree that was blocking their path. Its mammoth trunk completely blocked the road. It had been split in two and the bark was charred and burnt.

"Probably hit by lightning," said Rasmus approaching the fallen tree. He examined the branches that were sticking out in all directions. At the base, the tree's roots had been unearthed from the ground and were rotten and damp. The branches were stark and devoid of leaves. "It'll be difficult climbing over the poor fella. One slip and it's a painful landing. We should go round."

Tug watched as the cat disappeared into the undergrowth. Rasmus began heading for the exposed massive roots and Kelly followed, signalling for the others to join them. She noticed that either side of the road were other tall trees, but not oaks or elms. With their silvery bark, they looked more like eucalyptus trees. She hadn't seen anything like them so far and they looked out of place against all the other greenery around. The grass was different too. On the hillsides, it was thick and overgrown, covered in weeds and gorse. Here it was long and unkempt, although few weeds grew. Almost hidden by a thick bush, she noticed the distinct façade of a building. The glass doors had been broken, and the outer walls were thick with grime, but the sign above the door was clear.

"Hey, I think we're by a golf course," she announced.

"Well, I'd love to stop for a round, but I didn't bring my clubs," said Will. He joined Kelly at the roadside, watching Suzy and Claire walk lightly through the grass, as if they were scared to walk on it. "You think there's anything worth stopping for in there?"

There was an old transit van parked in the driveway and the metal had rusted away so it looked as if it were painted a light brown. Will had thought for a moment that they could take it and drive away, but of course, the battery would be dead. Even if they were lucky enough to find a vehicle with keys in it and a tank of petrol, the body would've rusted so much it probably wouldn't even hold together if they got in. They would be lucky to find any solar powered vehicles around. They had not been made in over ten years now since the world's resources were put towards dealing with the Deathless. The production of many luxury items such as solar powered cars, high-end clothing and mobiles had long been abandoned.

"Might be some food or something in there?" Kelly said it half as a statement and half as a question. She knew it was going to take a long time to reach the coast and was worried they hadn't enough to eat to keep them going.

Tug briskly walked past. "Keep moving." He didn't give the others a glance. He noticed Rasmus bending down at the tree roots and wanted to shout at them. Why were they even thinking of stopping? Rasmus was too busy admiring the island's vegetation and the others were easily distracted too. They needed to keep moving. Who knew when the Deathless would catch up with them. If they thought they were going to stroll out of this, they were wrong.

"We should keep going. It looks deserted. It just looks horrible and cold and...empty." Suzy tugged on Will's sleeve and he trudged back onto the road behind her.

"Come on, Rasmus," said Kelly, leaving. "Whatever you've found will have to wait for another day."

Rasmus was examining the base of the tree. The sun was now shining brilliantly and steam was rising from the damp ground. A family of possums had made a drey in the tree's tangled roots and the remains of one of the young were curled up in the nest. A few scraps of flesh and tissue still stuck to its bones and Rasmus was poking at the body with a short stick he had broken off the tree. "Uh-huh," was all he said as Kelly departed.

Claire hurried to join up with Suzy as Mark and Tricia approached. Mark took some snaps of the clubhouse and the bones of the baby possum. He couldn't understand Rasmus' fascination with the place and so he hurried to catch up with Will and Kelly, wanting to talk to them more about The Grave. He needed some background information to go with his photographs.

Tricia knelt down beside Rasmus, taking the rare opportunity to rest. The most exercise she normally did was walking to the hotdog cart outside work at lunchtime. "Having fun, Rasmus?"

"Mmm, yes, I was just inspecting the remains of this poor creature. It's quite unusual. It's clearly an infant. You can see from the bone structure and the jaw. Here, see where the teeth haven't fully formed? Yet it is really quite large for a newborn. If I was to guess, I would say it was an adult, yet it clearly never reached maturity. I was also trying to establish if it died of natural causes or if the presence of the Aqua-Gene in this tree might have had something to do with it." With the stick, he continued poking at arm's length around the bones.

Tricia was exhausted. She watched Rasmus working and wanted a rest so she let Rasmus talk. "How so?"

Rasmus kept his back to her as he spoke, crouching down in front of the old drey. "Well, it's entirely natural to suppose this possum died of natural causes. Nature has not yet eschewed the ideal of 'natural selection,' or 'survival of the fittest' and all that. But by the looks of this tree, it's been dead a long time, perhaps long before the lightning strike brought it down. I was wondering if the possum might have eaten something nearby which caused it to turn."

"Surely, it would have reanimated if that were the case. If it had, you wouldn't be poking around in its bones right now, would you?" Tricia turned her nose up as a thick dollop of blood trickled from the possum's mouth.

"Absolutely. But see how the skull is crushed? All the other bones are intact. I wonder if its family somehow knew it was turning and killed it. If so, did they do it out of protection for themselves or some kind of pity for the diseased creature? Some sort of euthanasia possibly. It really is truly fascina..."

Rasmus jumped back as a shrill scream pierced the still dewy air. As he scrambled up, he knocked Tricia over onto the wet grass. He pulled her up and they looked down the road in the direction of the scream. The others were running, waving their arms above their heads. There was a clang as Will's pickaxe struck the ground. He had swung it at an approaching Deathless and it had smashed through a head with ease. Unfortunately, it had slipped from Will's grip when he had swung it, and it had fallen behind more of the Deathless. There was no way to retrieve it. The others were trying to fend off their attackers with the old floorboards, but against an army this size, it was like swatting flies with a matchstick.

Tricia brushed herself down, wiping the dirt from her clothes. "What the hell…"

Rasmus grabbed her arm. "Oh dear. Oh my dear, we had better run I think."

From all sides of the road they came. Dozens and dozens of dead bodies, spilling from the hillside and up from the road ahead. They poured onto the road, chasing after Tug, Will, Mark, Suzy, Kelly and Claire. There were men and women, many naked, all in various states of decay. Their diseased bodies and rotten legs were carrying them as fast as possible. A terrifying moaning filled the air and Rasmus heard Will and Tug shouting at them to move.

Tricia turned around and screamed. The outstretched arms of a dead child clawed at her dress. She grabbed Rasmus' arm and they ran.

NINE

Rasmus and Tricia ran away from the fallen tree, evading the clutches of the Deathless. Rasmus couldn't believe how many there were or how they had appeared so quickly. Yet again, they had gotten complacent and allowed themselves to be snuck up on. He kept hold of Tricia and headed straight to the doorway of the dark clubhouse in front of them. Maybe they could escape in there and give the dead the slip, perhaps hide out or barricade themselves in. A lone Deathless figure stumbled through the doorway and swayed into the grass outside. The body had been dead for years. Its skin had fallen away and its muscles had withered and shrunk so it looked like little more than a walking skeleton. A knife was embedded in the shoulder of the bony corpse, the blade wedged in its collarbone.

Tricia screamed when she saw it appear. "Rasmus, we can't, we have to get out of here!" She tore herself loose from his grip and headed past the rusted old transit van into the dense trees beyond.

"Tricia, wait! Come back!" Rasmus watched as Tricia disappeared into the thick foliage and he hesitated. Should he follow her or try for the clubhouse? He whirled around and saw the others still running too. There were so many of the dead surrounding him on all sides, he had no choice. He couldn't wait for help. He knew deep down that he couldn't leave her. He had to get Tricia back.

Kelly and Suzy were swinging wildly as they ran, their broken floorboards connecting with arms and heads. Tug slashed with knives in both of his hands, lopping off fingers and stabbing at any of the dead within reach. Too often, a hand would grab hold of his shirt and he would shove it away, praying he hadn't been scratched. Mark kept his head down and tried to run through the crowd, weaving in and out, as teeth tried to bite him. Will had grabbed Claire and forced her to run. Her broken wrist banged against her body with every step, but she pushed the pain to the back of her mind. Everywhere she looked, she saw her imminent death, the haggard old women and decaying bodies of men, the broken yellow teeth gnashing and grinding only inches away and the children who were so much quicker than the adults, their spritely feet keeping pace with her.

"Rasmus! Tricia!" Will watched as they both disappeared into the trees behind the van. If they went too deep, they would get lost. Out here, there were no markers or signposts. If they got disorientated, they might not find the others again.

There was no response to his calls though and Will tried to think where they could run next. He noticed the skeletal figure standing unsteadily in the doorway of the clubhouse and decided it was their best bet. He hoped there were no more inside and charged ahead.

"Follow me," he shouted, dragging Claire along behind him. Beside the oak tree, there was a fallen branch on the ground and he scooped it up. Immediately, he had to use it, bashing on the head of the dead child who had nearly bitten Tricia. Will winced as he struck the child's head and sent the poor wretch reeling. As they neared the doorway, the skeletal figure reached out and took an unsteady foot forward. Will rammed into it and together they flew into the clubhouse.

He heard Claire scream in the darkness and the hands of the dead figure groping at him, pulling at his hair and clothes. Will managed to push it away and brought the branch down on its head, cracking the skull open. Still, the dead creature tried to get up and Will struck again and again, finally caving in the skull until the creature lay on the floor twitching. Will jumped on the figure, smashing the bones until it lay completely still.

Suzy and Kelly joined him in the room. Mark followed them and Tug stumbled in as another of the dead fell in behind him, its arms thrashing around blindly as it saw so many people. Tug thrust his knife into the man's head and the dead man fell onto the ground.

"We have to keep moving," said Tug in the gloom. He twisted the knife in the man's skull, making sure it wasn't going to get back up.

The room was very dark and the only light came from the open doorway and another door at the back of the room. There were some wooden tables and benches to one side and a counter from where food had been served back when the clubhouse had been full of happy golfers. To one side of the room was a bar still fully stocked with bottles of spirits and a huge menu on the wall behind it with the dinner menu clearly still displayed. Despite the darkness, Tug could tell there were no more of the dead inside. If they stayed there for long, he knew there soon would be.

"Those mother fuckers," said Tug between breaths. "We hadn't left them behind. When we lost them last night, they must have kept going. They went past the farmhouse and they were probably still searching for us. They actually got ahead of us. We just ran right into them. I'm such an idiot. I should've thought of it."

"Where now?" asked Kelly. "We can't go back out there. We can't outrun all of them." She had collapsed down onto one of the benches. She still held a floorboard in her hand, sticky and wet with blood.

"This way," said Will, walking toward the back door. "We'll see if we can find a way around them. We don't have many options."

As if to reinforce the point, a dead woman appeared in the doorway behind him. She was dressed in jeans and a blue lace top. Her hair was bunched up in a ponytail and if it hadn't been for her lower jaw missing, she would've passed as normal. Her pale, thin arms reached out and she took a step forward before tripping over the dead man in the doorway.

The woman got up quickly and headed for Mark who was closest. He was struck by the woman's features. Her blue eyes and shiny hair made her look almost beautiful. Blood and grime dripped from her broken jaw and Mark's first reaction was to lift his camera up to capture her face forever. As his fingers slipped around the lens, a plank of wood connected with the woman's face and she fell back once again, her teeth scattering over the floor. Tug swung again and scalped her, sending the top of her head flying back against the wall.

Mark let his camera drop and felt guilty. "Thanks."

"I suggest you lot stop fannying around and follow Will," said Tug. He marched to the back door where Will was waiting. The others quickly followed Tug.

Will stepped out into the back area of the golf club rooms. A low rope surrounded the garden area that had long since become overgrown with weeds and flowers. There was a tin storeroom, but Will could see it had been ransacked and the room was empty. There was an ice cream shack to his right and another building with a low roof and some rusted golf clubs outside. He was tempted to lead them into the other building and hide out until the dead thinned out enough to escape. Then he saw what was nothing short of a miracle.

"I see it," said Tug before Will had even pointed it out. Tug took a step toward the buggy and Will put an arm out to block his way. Tug remembered the farmhouse from last night, and how Will stopped him from entering. "Now is not the time to resume our argument, mate," said Tug.

"I'm not going to argue with you, Tug," said Will. "But we can't go without Rasmus and Tricia. We need to find them first."

"Are you kidding me? Who knows where those two daft sods have gone. They shouldn't have been pissing around and gotten separated from us."

"What is that?" asked Kelly.

"It's a golf buggy," said Will. "Solar powered. It'll be a squeeze to get everyone on, but we could do it. Keep your fingers crossed, but that could be our way out of here."

Kelly looked at the buggy. It would offer very little protection from the horde of dead. There were no doors or windows. It had a metal framework and a roof made of solar panels. There were four seats in total, including the drivers. The wheels had not perished and she began to believe it might just be the best way past the Deathless. "And you think it'll still work?"

"Don't see why not," said Tug, eager to get going. "Those solar panels look intact to me and it's not shaded by anything close by. Someone conveniently left it right out in the open so it should be charged up and ready to go. The sun's been out for a little while so it should have some juice in it. Not much, but enough to get away from here. We should make a move now while we can."

"What about Tricia?" said Suzy.

"And Rasmus?" said Claire rubbing her bandages. Her wrist was throbbing again after all the running and the bone had not yet had time to heal. "We can't leave them."

"Like fuck we can't." Tug pushed past Will and strode over to the buggy.

"Tug, get back here," hissed Kelly. "Tug!"

He ignored her and kept walking, reaching the buggy in only a few seconds. He could hear the wailing of the dead close by and got into the driver's seat. He pressed the start button and the engine pulsed into life. It was quiet, smooth and started instantly. He turned to the others. "Coming?"

"Fucking asshole," cursed Will. He heard crashes and bangs coming from inside the clubhouse. He heard clumsy footsteps from behind them. They had no time to waste. "Everyone get over there and get on."

Mark and Claire ran over and got into the back seats.

"I'm not leaving them," said Kelly.

"Me neither," said Suzy. "They wouldn't leave us."

"Kelly, get over there and get Tug to do a circuit of the building. He can do that much for us at least. It'll give us a few minutes to find them. Suzy, you stick by me. We're going to get them."

Kelly ran over and Will watched her talking to Tug. He was shaking his head in obvious disagreement. Kelly was pointing at him animatedly and Tug began to look uncomfortable. Will had only been on the receiving end of one of Kelly's outbursts a couple of times and they weren't pleasant. Tug slowly nodded and Kelly got in beside him. A moment later and the buggy took off.

"Right," said Will. "We have to make this fast, Suzy Q. Tug will give us a few minutes, no more. We have to shout like hell and hope Tricia and Rasmus hear us. If they're too far gone, I'm afraid we don't have much choice."

"No. I'm not going anywhere without them. Kelly was right. We stick together. That's the only way we'll make it through this."

Will grabbed Suzy's shoulders and looked into her light blue eyes. She proudly looked back at him and he knew she was trying to dig her heels in on this one. He wanted her to. He wanted her to be right and for them to wait for Rasmus and Tricia. He desperately wanted to prove Tug wrong, but he couldn't. Not this time. He was aware that every second they stood there was another second for the dead to catch up with them. "Suzy, if we stick together this time, we die. We all die. Rasmus and Tricia have one chance. Shout as loud as you can. It doesn't matter if the dead hear us; they know we're here already anyway. Scream for them, scream as loud as you can for Rasmus and Tricia.

"Now, I'm going to grab one of those golf clubs and head into the treeline they disappeared into. You should get a club too, because you might need it. I'm going to find them and I'll meet you back here in a minute. You are *not* going to die on this island, Suzy."

Will did not give her a chance to respond. He gave her a kiss and then ran off before she could respond. He plucked one of the rusted golf clubs up and ran toward the thick treeline out of Suzy's sight.

Suzy felt queasy. Her head was spinning. She had only a moment before the dead would be on her. Will had left her, Tug had driven the others around the other side of the building, and she suddenly realised she was alone. She sprinted over to the prone golf bag and took a club out. She knew nothing about golf, but the club was heavy in her hands and had a thick solid end. The rust didn't matter; it was still sturdy enough to beat the crap out of any Deathless that came her way.

"Rasmus! Tricia!" Suzy shouted as loud as she could, calling their names out over and over. "Where are you? We're leaving, guys, come on. Rasmus! Tricia!"

The dead stumbled from the clubhouse and headed straight for Suzy. She looked around for Will, but he was nowhere to be seen. There was no sign of the buggy either and she wondered if Tug had abandoned them. Surely, Kelly wouldn't let him?

Suzy swung her club as one of the Deathless advanced upon her. A young man, both arms missing, was careering toward her menacingly. Suzy struck the man on the side of the head and he fell away into the long grass. The whole left hand side of his face caved in, yet he got back up. Suzy swung again and the man's face exploded. Bloody tissue and small bones showered the ground at her feet. There was no time to react though as the next one appeared.

"Will, where are you?" Suzy swung again and again. She hit one, two, three, four or more, all the time smashing in jaws and skulls, sending pieces of decayed brain into the air and spraying the ground with rotten meat and broken teeth. Blood splattered her clothes and pooled at her feet. Every time she struck one of the dead, she wanted to give in, just let go and sink to her knees. She knew it would be over quickly, but something inside drove her on.

Her arms were beginning to ache when she heard the faint approach of the buggy's engine. She called out for Rasmus and Tricia once again and then felt arms grab her waist from behind. Suzy screamed and the hands held onto her tightly. She tried to pull away, but they held onto her and she wished she didn't have to die alone like this. She waited for the inevitable teeth to sink into her neck, bracing for the pain that was coming any second.

"It's me," said Will. "Get on, quickly."

Tug pulled the buggy up beside her and Suzy jumped on beside him, sitting next to Kelly in the front seat. She kept the club in her hands, ready to strike at the dead who were still close. She turned around to glare at Will for giving her such a fright. When she saw Tricia though she stopped. Will was gently sliding her into a seat at the back. She was dazed and confused. Her face was covered in small red scratches and her hair was dishevelled, covered in petals and blossom. Claire and Mark wedged themselves in beside her and Will.

"Move it," demanded Will.

Tug had barely stopped to let them get on and he put his foot down without hesitation. The buggy could reach speeds of up to fifty Ks, although he was going much slower right now. He drove it over the long grass, struggling to keep it level. The buggy found it hard to gain traction on the overgrown course and Tug had to pull hard on the wheel to make it respond to him.

"Where's Rasmus?" asked Suzy.

Tricia stared back at Suzy blankly. Then her eyes dropped and Tricia clasped her hands in her lap.

Will opened his mouth to speak and then closed it again. He wiped sweat from his forehead and then spoke in a low voice.

"No time. We couldn't...just move it, Tug."

They drove past the dead, zigzagging past them and avoiding the decapitated limbs. Tug got them back onto the road and soon they were headed downhill. Some of the Deathless tried to follow, but they couldn't keep up with the cart. Nobody spoke as they drove. They did not slow down for anything. Occasionally, a body would appear in front of them, but Tug always managed to drive around it.

Suzy let go of her club as they drove and it bounced onto the road. She wasn't aware she had even dropped it. How could Rasmus be gone, just like that? What had happened to them? Were they going back for him? From the look on Will and Tricia's faces, she didn't think so. Had Rasmus gotten himself lost in the woods, or worse?

They passed a large house and Kelly asked if anyone was injured or needed to stop. Nobody answered and so Tug kept driving. He didn't say so, but the cart was running out of power. It had been for the last few minutes. Only gravity kept them going. The road was curving downward and he hoped it would get them to the bottom. He noticed the clouds were back and it would take a lot more than a few rays of sun to get them going again.

Eventually the road levelled out and the buggy came to a stop. On the left was the hill they had come down from, and to the right was a steep bank that led down to the sea. There was an inlet and on the other side, another road leading around more houses and higher hills. They had lost sight of the town they had seen earlier. Tug jumped out and tightened the straps on his backpack.

"Whoa, hold on, Tug, what's happened. Is that it?" Kelly jumped out of the cart as the others followed suit.

"Yep. What did you expect? We ran out of power ten minutes ago. I've been coasting the last mile. We're on foot from here. So let's get going eh? If we get a move on we might make the coast by sundown." Tug looked up at the sky. "I think there's a storm coming too. We shouldn't be outside any longer than we have to be."

"Sorry, but I need a minute," said Suzy. She got out of the cart and headed over to the bank, looking out across the water. "What happened to Rasmus? Why are we not going back for him?" She looked around the group and no one answered her. Infuriated, she marched up to Tricia and slapped her hard across the cheek. "Where the fuck is he?" demanded Suzy. She lifted her hand to slap Tricia again and Tricia recoiled. "What did you do?"

Will took Suzy's arm. "He's gone, Suzy. If he's lucky maybe he'll find a way down to us. But..."

"No. I don't believe it. I don't..." Suzy collapsed into Will sobbing. She buried her face in his chest and let her tears soak his shirt. She let him hold her and felt no shame in it.

Tricia held her cool palm against her stinking cheek. "I'm sorry, Suzy. We tried to get away from them, but they followed us into the woods. He was there beside me one minute and then he was gone. I saw a couple of the Deathless around him and he was shouting. I tried to call for help, but then he was gone. I was lost and if it hadn't have been for Will, I wouldn't have made it out of there. Like Will says, maybe he made it? Maybe..." Tricia didn't really believe what she was saying. She wanted to think Rasmus might make it, but she also knew how thick the bushes and undergrowth had gotten. She had fought her way through a thorn bush and just when she thought she was going to get stuck, Will had found her. The barbs and spiky branches had scratched her face as Will had dragged her out, but she didn't care.

Kelly looked down at her hands and saw they were trembling. The adrenalin was still pumping. She looked and saw Claire sat on the back of the cart with tears rolling down her face. Mark looked like he was struggling to hold it together too. "Tug, we need a break. You might not know us very well, but what's happening here is...we're losing our friends. You're right, absolutely, we should keep going. But look at us. You can go off on your own if you want, but right now, we need a break. We'll walk west and try to find somewhere safe to rest for a bit. If you want to carry on without us, just do it. I'm not going to stop you anymore."

Tug looked at Kelly and considered his options. He felt bad about Rasmus, but he wasn't prepared to give up now. He probably could make it on his own. He needn't feel bad about going on alone. Kelly had basically just given him permission to do it. Still, could he leave them? Suzy and Claire were still sobbing. Will was shattered and even Kelly looked drained. Tug contemplated if he would be better off alone or if there was safety in numbers.

"I'll find us some place safe to rest up," said Tug. There were plenty of houses scattered on the road ahead. "Stay here. I'll come get you all in a couple of minutes when I've found somewhere."

Kelly smiled. As Tug walked away, she wanted to thank him. She forgot how maddening and pig headed he was. She turned to Will and tears filled her eyes when she saw him holding Suzy. What had happened to Rasmus?

* * *

Puce fronds brushed over his face and Rasmus trod cautiously. The bush that sprouted from the earth was ten feet tall at least and its tapered stems came to a sharp tip. He had already cut his hands on the bushes getting this far and his palms were stinging from the cold air cutting at him. The trunk was black, wet and slippery from the giant slugs and snails that slithered around it. A frothy foaming pool of black water ran around it to the left before gurgling under a rock out of sight. The way behind the huge bush was hidden by the forest.

Rasmus had unwittingly run away from the golf course and the road, stumbling through the trees only to find himself deeper in the forest. If he had gone the other way, he would have found himself back on the road and able to meet up with the others Instead, he was lost.

The ground was sodden and mossy, and each step almost caused him to slip. He parted the branches and leaves to find the water was not just disappearing under a rock, but in fact a huge rock face. A smooth granite surface shot up into the air at least thirty feet and shale and boulders had piled up at the bottom. There was no way he could back track through the forest he had just come. What had started out as a few trees had soon become thicker with no end in sight. The canopy above blocked out the sun and all he could hear now was the sound of his own laboured breathing. It had been exhausting, pushing through the thick vines and overgrown bushes and his cut arms, hands and legs were the painful result. He had managed to evade the Deathless so far and he knew going back would be suicide. There were dozens of them out there looking for him now in the thick scrub he was lost in. He had to press on and find another way back to the clubhouse where the others would surely be waiting for him.

Rasmus stared up at the rock face. It was impossible to climb up. Even if he had been twenty years younger, it would have been impossible for him. Leafy trees obscured his view to the side, but it looked like the rock face continued for a while. He sank to his knees and let the bloody, dirty water collect around his legs and soak into his clothing. Tears welled up in his eyes and he felt like giving up. It was too hard. Getting out of here was literally impossible. Even if he somehow managed to climb over the rocks, then what? It must be a good day's trek to the coast. How many of the dead were out there waiting for him? Without food and water, he would only get weaker. He could barely walk as it was. He refused to call out for help and put Tricia in danger. If she were found because of him, he could not bear having her death on his conscience.

A noise from the forest jolted him back into the present. There was a rustling sound coming from the direction he had come from. It might be a wild pig or a bird, but he wasn't sure. The noise was getting louder and it began to sound more like something was running and crashing through the bushes toward him; something too big to be a boar. Rasmus looked around, but there was nothing to defend himself with. Could he fight off another of the Deathless with his bare hands? He looked at his palms, criss-crossed with lacerations. The noise grew louder and suddenly the instinct to live kicked in. He looked at the water swirling around his feet and his eyes followed it to the rock. Where it entered underneath the sheer cliff was a gap of about two feet, no more, and Rasmus had an idea.

He sprinted toward it, splashing through the stream and hoping he would make it in time. At the opening to the underground stream, he dropped quickly and pushed himself low to the rough ground. He dug his hands into the crumbling stones and pebbles of the shallow riverbed and crawled along it into the blackness under the rock. The crashing noises behind him were very loud now and he prayed that the dead would not see him or be able to follow him inside.

As Rasmus slunk under the rock, drenching himself in the cold water, he continued to pull himself further into the dark cave. When he was inside, he reached up above his head and his hand touched nothing. Evidently, the cave had opened up. He turned and slowly stood up. Inside the cavern was pitch black and the only light came from the small opening through which he had just crawled. He stood completely still, listening to the noise on the other side of the rock. Feet suddenly dashed through the outside stream and Rasmus clenched his fists, hoping whoever was out there wouldn't find his hiding place. From the grunting and moaning, he could tell it was nobody living. He heard splashes and the sound of twigs snapping. They were looking for him. How long would it be before they noticed the opening under the rock? He knew the dead would not stop. There were so many out there, it was only a matter of time before they smelt him or heard his wheezing. He decided he was going to have to go further into the cave system and hope there was an exit. The river had to flow somewhere. Maybe he could just push through and come out the other side of the rocks.

Rasmus got down on his knees and began pulling himself forward again on all fours, away from the stream's entrance. The water was icy cold and it actually dulled the pain in his hands. He was aware that he was trembling; a mixture of fear from being caught and from what might lie ahead. As he went on further away from the opening, the light dimmed and soon it was completely dark. The footsteps outside echoed around the vast cavern, but they were getting fainter. As he reached out his hand to grasp the next rock to pull forward, it plunged into nothing but a deep pool of water and he retracted it immediately. If the river ran into a deeper pool, he could find himself swimming in the dark. Rasmus stopped and felt again, reaching out his hand slowly, trying to find the riverbed. He found nothing to get purchase on though, and he began to panic. He turned around to go back toward the opening and as he did so, the stony riverbed beneath him gave way. He was swept under the water as he fell into the deeper, fast flowing water. Frantically, he tried to swim to the top and he gasped for air as his head broke the surface. The current was pushing him along in the dark but he could not see a thing. His eyes darted around uselessly.

There was not even the faintest chink of light in this underground tomb. He was drawing in quicker and quicker breaths as he gasped for air. He tried to tread water and stretched his arms out, hoping to find a rock or something to grab hold of. He needed to stop himself from being dragged further into the underground river. Above the water's surface though, he felt nothing but icy cool air. The raging water echoed around the dark caves. The rushing sound of the river reverberated wildly, confusing his senses so he could barely tell up from down. He couldn't hear the footsteps of the dead anymore and began to panic.

Rasmus let out a yelp of pain as his knee banged into a sharp rock. Then he let out a scream as his left ankle suddenly wedged between two underwater rocks and it snapped. He immediately knew his ankle was broken. With his left leg trapped and the current growing stronger, he was pulled under the water again. He opened his eyes and the water stung instantly. The cave was drenched in blackness and he could see nothing. He pulled at his leg, but it was stuck fast. The rushing water pulled him down and he sucked in a mouthful of air before the current dragged him under once more. His ankle was crushed and the more he pulled on it, the more painful it got. As his head bobbed above the surface, he spluttered and coughed. He took a mouthful of water and retched. His breathing got quicker and quicker as he realised he was not getting out of this.

"Help. Help!" Rasmus called out, hoping someone might hear him. Tricia could go to hell. If it wasn't for her, he wouldn't be in this mess. He didn't care if the Deathless heard him. He didn't have the energy to keep going like this for long. The water was numbing his feet and hands already. The force of the underground river was overwhelming and he slipped beneath the surface. Taking in a huge gulp of air, he frantically began punching at the rocks that held his broken ankle trapped tight. The rocks could not be shifted though.

He began to panic as each time he resurfaced, he struggled to breathe. Was the level of the river rising or was he imagining it? He felt like his whole body was on fire. He thrashed his arms around trying to find something to take hold of; a branch, the wall of the cave, anything to hold himself up – but there was nothing.

"Help, help!" He called out over and over, pleading, hoping, and praying someone would hear him. "Don't leave me!" Rasmus began sobbing, choking as the water washed over his head. His tears flowed out into the infected water surrounding him and he hated the world in that moment. He knew he had been left to die. He had been abandoned and in all likelihood was infected too.

Rasmus managed to keep himself alive for almost half an hour before he finally succumbed to the water. The Deathless did not hear his pleas for help or anguished cries for clemency. They never did find him. Nobody heard him crying for his wife. His friends and colleagues were now safely at the bottom of the hill, well away from him and unable to hear his weeping and yelling.

Other than a flash of memories as he died, he never saw his wife again. His prayers went unanswered as the rising tide of the river killed him. With all the rainwater flowing into the cave system, the level of the river was creeping ever upward. He was stuck in an underground cave system that went on for miles. Soon, the cave would be completely submerged.

Finally, Rasmus took one last breath and ducked beneath the surface. The first mouthful of water he took in burnt his throat and lungs. His body convulsed and his heart hammered away faster than ever in his life, trying to give him the last surge of adrenalin to escape. The second mouthful of water caused his body to begin shutting down and he drowned. His old lungs filled with water; his throat and mouth tried to suck in air, but it was impossible. The dark cave kept his body there, never to be buried, forever to be entombed in the icy cavern. His body would reanimate soon, but it was a mere shell; just the physical reminder of the man he had once been. Rasmus was dead.

TEN

Tug had found a small cottage over the road from where the golf buggy had lost power and he just as quickly found it was deserted. It was well hidden from the road with its green painted plasterboard well camouflaged by the massive Rimu trees and ferns surrounding it. Hoheria plants and tangled vines covered the cottage's gateway and Tug had easily broken inside. The lock on the front door had given way easily as the wooden frame had rotted over the years it had stood there. The house was small and only had one bedroom, a tiny kitchen and sitting room. He had fetched the others over and they had sunken into a grieving stupor once inside. Rain began to lash at the dirty windows and Tug busied himself checking their packs. He took the one off his back and emptied the one Suzy had been carrying. He handed around some water and waited for the others to rest. He was beginning to get a headache, so he took out his half of uneaten power bar. He took one bite and then stopped.

"Here," he said offering it to Suzy. "You should eat something."

She took it from him and nibbled on it slowly. The bar was flavourless and gritty, but it helped to settle her stomach. Since they had left the farmhouse earlier, it had not stopped churning.

Will mouthed a thank you to him as Tug walked away. Will looked at his watch, but it was still five thirty one. He had forgotten it had stopped when the plane had crashed. He looked over at Tug who was repacking their gear. Will wondered how he could do it. How could he just put everything to one side and carry on like that? Will gave Suzy a squeeze and then went over to see Kelly and Claire.

"How are you holding up?" he asked them both.

"I can't believe he's gone," said Kelly. She dabbed at her eyes with a tissue. "This was going to be his last big trip you know. One last hurrah before his retirement." Her voice wavered and she stopped to clear her throat. "Do you think he might make it?"

Will shook his head. "No. The Deathless were everywhere. It's really just luck I got Tricia out. I heard her calling for help, but

I didn't hear from Rasmus. I called out for him, but I think he was too far in to hear me." He looked at Claire. She was pale and sniffing. Her nose was red and the skin around her nostrils and eyes seemed flaky. "How are you, Claire?" He wanted to tell her she looked terrible, but caught himself before he did.

She shrugged. "I feel like I'm coming down with the flu. I'm all bunged up and my head feels like it's full of bricks. My chest is hot and it's hard to catch my breath sometimes."

"It's probably the damp," said Tug. He came over and put a dry blanket around her shoulders. "The rain, the cold, and the lack of a decent meal...it's not surprising really. Here, make sure you drink as much water as you can." He offered her some of the bottled rainwater he had collected from the farmhouse and she gratefully drank it down. "We're running low on water and it's pissing down outside so I'm going out to see if I can collect some more. Guess I was right about that storm coming in." Tug went outside and shut the door behind him.

Claire sneezed and rubbed her head. "I feel like death."

"We should pray together." Tricia sat upright. She had never forced her beliefs onto anyone her whole life, but she couldn't sit idly by while her friends died. "It'll help, truly it will. I can lead us if you like. I think now is a good time. Merciful Lord, we ask that you..."

"Whoa, hold on there, Tricia. I'm not sure now is the time. You can pray to an imaginary deity if you like, but count me out." Mark folded his arms. He had been taught plenty about religion and seen a lot of missionary work in Africa. But he was not a believer, and had no intention of joining a prayer group now.

"He's right, Tricia," said Kelly wearily. "I don't think we're all comfortable with this. No one is stopping you doing what you want, but we need some downtime right now. Rasmus is gone. I just want a few minutes of quiet. Please."

Tricia indignantly raised her eyebrows. "Well, I didn't mean any offence. Fine. I just thought it might help." Her ample frame leant back and the springs in the sofa creaked.

"How can you believe in something so intangible anyway?" Mark asked. "As a scientist, I thought you only dealt with facts and figures. How can you believe in God? How can you reconcile those two aspects of your life?"

"I don't have to, Mark, you do." Tricia sighed. She had been questioned about the very same thing by her mother a few times. "I can believe in whatever I like because I have faith. My work doesn't rule my life. I find the work we do at the museum fascinating and I'm very good at it. But you need some sort of spiritual guidance in your life. You can't ignore that side of yourself or you're just another lost soul. You should explore some of Jesus' teachings, Mark, and open yourself up. You never know what you might realise and learn. His Kingdom is always ready for you."

"And if I don't, I'm going to hell?" Mark laughed. "Oh come on, Tricia..."

"Enough!" shouted Kelly. "Enough. All right? Save your theological discussions for another time. Just everyone shut up for five fucking minutes and let me think, would you?"

The room descended quickly into an uncomfortable silence. Mark wanted to apologise. He hadn't meant to goad Tricia like that. He thought it best if he kept quiet though. Kelly's tone was clear and he didn't want to upset her.

They waited, deep in their own thoughts and prayers, whether to a real God or not, listening to the rain lashing the outside of the cottage. Nobody even gave a thought to helping Tug. It was as if he was their guide, still an outsider, and whilst they accepted his help, they had not fully accepted him into their group yet.

Suzy broke the silence a few minutes after Kelly's outburst. She abruptly stood up and pointed up into a far corner of the room. "Holy cow, what is *that*?"

All eyes turned to the dark corner of the room and Claire let out a small cry as she tucked herself back into the sofa. A table nestled in the corner of the room adorned with pottery figurines. Above it on the wall was a huge insect. It was at least a foot in length and its spindly brown legs were slowly inching it up the damp wallpaper. It crawled slowly into the dark corner of the room, its mandibles twitching, looking for food. It was so big they could see the thing's black eyes, and its hideous body was thick and rippled. It paused in its trek to the corner as if to let everyone admire it.

"I think it's a Weta," said Kelly getting up for a closer look. "I've never seen one so big though."

"It's disgusting." Suzy realised she was still pointing at it and quickly withdrew her arm, as if the creature might suddenly take flight and jump on her.

"It's amazing," said Will approaching it.

"You're not going to...oh no." Suzy recoiled as Will knelt on the trestle table and reached up, scooping the giant Weta into his hands carefully. The spiny hind legs dug into his wrists but he didn't care. Suzy could see the light in his eyes as he handled the insect and remembered again why Kelly had employed him. As his blue eyes sparkled, she also remembered why she had kissed him.

"Amazing," said Will again examining the insect. He turned it over and looked up and down. "It's pregnant too."

Its mandibles began to bite into his skin and he carefully placed it back on the table. It scurried into the crevice of the wall and down to the floor where it could hide in the shadows.

Kelly smiled ruefully at Will. "I guess she's just looking to get home."

"Aren't we all," said Mark putting his camera away. The photos of Will with the Weta would make good contrast to some of the more destructive or negative photos he had taken. It was evidence of life on this deadly island.

Just then, Tug came crashing back into the house, followed by buckets of rain and wind. He shook off his coat and placed a bucket of clear water in the middle of the room. "Found this outside. It's clean. We can all fill our bottles with the rainwater."

With the insect forgotten, one by one they did so, and Kelly helped Claire with hers. She unwrapped the bandage around Claire's wrist and Kelly wrapped it back up tightly. The skin was bruised and yellow. Claire kept wiping her nose on her jacket, sniffing and wheezing.

"Here, take these," said Kelly handing her some paracetamol. The packet was empty now, but it looked like Claire needed them more than most. Once Claire had swallowed them, Kelly went on over to Tricia. Kelly sat down beside her and asked how she was feeling.

"Oh, Kelly, I don't know anymore. I didn't mean to. I didn't know what to do. They were everywhere. I didn't ask Rasmus to come with me, I just..." Tricia welled up. "I know it's my fault he's gone. What was I thinking..." She trailed off, unable to talk. Salty tears trickled down her face and stung her wounds.

"What's done is done," was all Kelly could say. She knew she should put an arm around her. She knew what she was supposed to do, how she should be comforting Tricia and reassuring her, telling her it wasn't her fault. But actually, she felt like it was kind of Tricia's fault. If she hadn't run off like that then maybe Rasmus would still be here. He would be cajoling them into getting along, helping Claire and talking about the landscape and the interesting wildlife. He would have loved to see that Weta. Kelly knew he was dead. Why should Tricia be here and not him? Kelly felt sorrow that Rasmus wasn't around anymore, but also anger. She was annoyed with Tricia. What did she expect, sympathy? Kelly sighed and stood up. "All you can do now, Tricia, is pray for His help and forgiveness." Kelly didn't elaborate on what she meant, but the implication was clear and Tricia didn't respond.

Tug shook off his wet coat. He had heard Kelly and Tricia and he knew the guilt Tricia must be feeling. It wasn't her fault, it was just this place. What was happening to them was out of anyone's control now. He sipped some of the cold, fresh water as the others did the same.

Will could not believe Rasmus was gone, but he had to drag them out of this place. If they sat around absorbed in pity and grief, they would get nowhere. They would also get colder and weaker. They had to make the coast today. He knew his mother would be okay for now. He had made sure her friends would be around whilst he was on this expedition, but he wanted to be back in New York. What if they didn't make it to the coast, or worse didn't make it off the island? Josef, Wilfred and Rasmus were dead. How many more of them would die here? He needed to get home. He needed to see his mother again, to make sure she passed with comfort. He didn't like to think of her alone, without him. Since his father had passed a few years back, they had been forced to sell the farm. Will was her only son and they had gotten close again in recent years. Will stood up and walked to the centre of the room.

"We should move soon," he said. "Who knows how long this rain will last. We can't sit around waiting for the sun to come out again. It'll take hours before the cart recharges so we're on foot. Like Tug says, the sooner we get going, the sooner we get there."

"I was thinking about something," said Mark. "We're pretty close already. I mean the water is right there. We just have to find a boat and take it through the bays until we hit the open sea. Then one of the patrols is bound to spot us. It'd be much quicker than walking wouldn't it?"

"That's not a bad idea," said Will. "A place like this there's a good chance we might find a small sailboat or a yacht or something. It would shave a few hours off our day."

"I'm not so sure," said Kelly quietly.

Everyone looked at her. The idea of finding a quicker way off the island had lifted all their spirits.

"The waters are patrolled and monitored yes, but the people on this land are not supposed to leave. Birds, animals, you name it; *nothing* is supposed to leave. There are nets around the coast, a bit like shark nets to stop any of the dead accidentally getting into the water and then washing out to sea. You wouldn't want one of them washing up on Venice boardwalk."

"So what, who cares about the nets, a boat would get past them easily," said Mark, annoyed that Kelly was putting a downer on his idea already. He had admired her stoicism and the way she was handling everything. However, it seemed like she was shooting him down before he'd even had a chance.

"And the mines? All the beaches, every inch of coastline, has been planted with landmines. You take one step onto the sand and you're likely to end up in a thousand pieces," countered Kelly. "They thought of everything."

"So there's a way around them, isn't there? We find a boat that's still tied up to a jetty or a private dock and we don't have to set foot on a beach. Easy." Mark couldn't understand why Kelly seemed so set against it. It was as if she wanted to drag it out, wanted to spend the day miserable and tired. Did she want to die here, in this cold, damp cottage?

"And the mines in the water? The ones you can't see and would blow our boat up, killing all of us? What about the automatic guns that are stationed at random points along the bays and inlets? They are triggered by movement and we don't know where they are. This island is quarantined for good reason. Getting on or off is meant to be impossible. If it was that easy to jump in a boat and sail away, think how many would've done the opposite and sailed in here." Kelly looked at Mark and it pained her to see him looking so dejected. She had to be realistic about their situation though, and if that meant offending someone, so be it.

"Why would anyone want to come here?" asked Suzy.

"How many people are there out there who have lost someone to this? How many people want to see their husband or wife, their children again? How many terrorists know that if they could get just one drop of infection off this island, they could take out any target they wanted: any town or city, or even country? I can give you a hundred reasons as to why someone would want to come here. Unfortunately, that means we are up against it now in getting off." Kelly cleared her throat. "So for now, we stick to the plan. If we can get to the coast and find a clearing, maybe we will be spotted. We can light a fire, jump up and down, hell, I don't know, anything to get their attention. We wait to be picked up."

"Right, let's move. Gather your shit up, we're..." Will stopped, interrupted by a small but sharp bang. The floor of the old cottage began to tremble and then it was joined by the walls and the roof. Soon, everything inside the house was shaking and they struggled to stay on their feet.

"What the hell is happening?" screamed Claire.

The cottage continued to shake and things began falling from shelves in the kitchen. A large, framed picture of a smiling family hanging on the wall swung wildly from left to right until it finally flew off the wall and smashed on the floor beside Mark. It felt like the whole house was crumbling around them. The walls and floor were still vibrating, but it ended as suddenly as it had begun.

Suzy cried as a piece of plaster narrowly missed her head and she looked around the room. Everyone was crouched down on the floor, holding onto one another. Being the closest one to her, she had grabbed Tug's hand without even realising it and let it go. The rain and wind continued unabated outside, but the cottage was now returned to silence. "Holy cow, what was that?" said Suzy.

"Another plane didn't crash, did it?" whispered Tricia.

Kelly was now tired, angry and scared. "For Christ's sake, Tricia, don't be an idiot, it was an earthquake." As soon as she said it, she regretted it. She didn't need Tricia asking dumb questions. Kelly knew she shouldn't have snapped, but it was all getting too much.

Tricia was too shocked to reply. She fumbled around with her water bottle and got up, preparing to go outside.

Will broke the awkward silence. "Look, don't panic. Quakes and tremors are not unusual in this part of the world. We're right above some major fault lines right now. Look, if everyone is okay we should just make a move. Tug, you know which way to go?"

"Follow me." Tug opened the door and instantly the pouring rain began flooding in. He walked out head first into the storm without looking back. He was glad to be leaving the cottage behind. Another quake like that and it was liable to come crashing down on their heads.

The group trudged behind Tug as he walked down the road. Everyone was wary, monitoring the treeline and the hills for the dead, but they thankfully saw none. They had been shaken by the earthquake and with Rasmus absent, it felt like time was conspiring against them, colluding with the island to keep them there.

Mark looked around through the rain at the scenery. On the left side of the road was the hillside, dotted with houses, driveways and cars. On the right, a short, steep bank leading to the water. Every now and again, they would pass by a warning sign advising that mines and fences were being put in place, trespassing was forbidden and all access was denied without military supervision. He couldn't tell if there were mines in the beaches or the water, but he didn't want to chance it finding out. He knew Kelly had been right back there, he was just frustrated at their slow progress.

The rain was incessant. It came from the sky in huge drops, buckets of it soaking through every layer of clothing they wore. As they walked, their feet squelched in sodden shoes and shaking off the rain from their jackets was pointless. As the sky continued to darken with the clouds only thickening, lunchtime passed and their hunger grew. They had nothing to eat anymore and only sips of water to quell the churning of their stomachs. Gradually, the landscape changed and they got nearer to the town they had seen earlier in the day. Jagged lines scarred the hillside where vehicles had crashed and fires had swept through, melting roads and bringing down houses. The decimation was everywhere. They crossed a motorway, avoiding the crashed vehicles.

Will looked inside some of the cars, but through the barrage of rain, it was difficult to tell if they were empty. If one of the Deathless were trapped inside, there would be nothing to gain from opening up one of the cars. He also looked out for any solar powered cars, but he saw none. They were very few and far between anyway. He knew solar power worked for smaller vehicles, like golf carts, but lacked the power to drive roadworthy cars. Will noticed too, as Tug lead them through wide streets, that many buildings in this town were destroyed. They were not just ransacked or looted, but literally destroyed. As far as he could tell, they had been bombed or burnt out by fire. It was like walking through the ruins of a warzone.

As they wearily followed Tug, Will decided to speak to Suzy. He noticed her looking around in awe at the remnants of shops and homes. "I seem to remember they bombed quite a few places at the start of the outbreak. Once the Deathless took hold of a town, they tried to seal it off and burn it. This must be one of those unlucky places."

"So many," said Suzy in wonder. "There are just so many places they destroyed. All those homes devastated, all those shops and offices - didn't they try to save them? Was this really the best way?"

"I guess back then, it was. Anything that survived the fire was just luck. Who's to say we would handle it any differently now? Imagine if this Aqua-Gene got into the water supply back home. Imagine the carnage. Do you think Uncle Sam would think twice about taking down Manhattan if it meant saving the rest of the country?"

"Don't even joke about it," said Suzy seriously. "If this shit got home… Screw that."

"It won't," said Will. "I'm sure once we get rescued we'll have to undergo quite a strict quarantining process. They won't let us waltz back into New York without checking us out first."

"But we're okay, aren't we? I mean, we're not infected, we can't be. We haven't touched or drunk anything." Suzy spoke fast, worried that she may somehow be contaminated, doubts breaking into her mind. So many 'what ifs' ran through her brain.

"Suzy Q, we're fine," said Will putting a hand on her shoulder for reassurance. "Like you said, we've been careful. We'd know if we were sick. I can tell from looking at you that you're okay. You still look hot to me, don't worry." Will winked at her.

Suzy laughed. "Now you're hitting me with the pick-up lines? You sure know how to pick your timing, Will Forrest."

Will laughed. He didn't care much now for social conventions. There was a real possibility that he and Suzy might not get that date he had planned and he wanted her to know how he felt. Before he could say anything, Suzy asked him the question she had wanted to since they'd met.

"What's with the Suzy Q business? Am I supposed to get that?"

Will chuckled. "That? It's just that you remind me of someone. You like rock music?"

"Now and again. I'm more of an R&B girl, but who are you talking about? I don't know of any group called Suzy Q."

"Not a group. Suzy Quatro. One of the great pioneers of rock. No? Devil Gate Drive? 48 Crash? Nothing..?"

Suzy looked at Will blankly and shrugged. "Has she released anything lately?"

"Er, no, she's been dead for about 150 years. I guess I like my music old school."

"Will, there's old and there's *old*. Well, as long as she was cool, I guess that's okay. When we get back to New York you'll have to play some of her music for me."

"Absolutely. You can come round to mine, we'll have that drink I keep promising you and I'll chuck on the vinyl. It sounds much better than digital. I'll even cook us a good meal."

It was Suzy's turn to laugh. "If it involves Snickers, maybe I'll cook."

They continued talking and flirting for a while. It felt good to talk about the future, their homes back in New York and their plans. It took their mind off their present circumstances. They were both eagerly looking forward to getting back home to see each other as much as their families.

They came across the shell of a house on the side of the road and paused by it. The roof was gone and the walls were charred. One side of the building had collapsed and exposed its interior. It must have been an old furniture warehouse as it was full of beds and dining tables, lounge suites and recliners, all moth-eaten and weatherworn. Most had been fire damaged too.

Tug stood beside Kelly and looked at the burnt out shell facing them as Mark took some photographs. They had all been walking through the storm for a couple of hours and they were exhausted. As much as he hated to admit it, Tug needed to rest up for five minutes too. "It could be several miles until we reach anywhere else. I can't see anything ahead that's going to be any better and we could do with getting out of the rain for a few minutes. This place is probably a good choice. There's not likely to be anything hiding and the area seems deserted. What do you say?"

"Yeah, fine, now's good." Kelly let Tug head into the abandoned warehouse and made sure everyone followed closely. "All right, everyone inside, we're going to take five minutes here. A quick stop and then we're on our way again."

Inside, they soon all found a place to sit. The furniture was old and broken, but still better than the cold hard ground. They drank some of the water they were carrying and wished they had food. The rain lashed at the building and came through the open roof above. They heard it trickling down the pipes and walls, the constant dripping outside on the tarmac was a reminder they were only being offered a very brief respite.

"We should've stayed by the plane and waited for rescue. They're picking us off one by one." Tricia sat on a leather recliner with her head back, eyes closed. "How do we know those things aren't still following us?"

"We couldn't have stayed there," says Will. "The dead were all around us. We had to leave the plane or we'd all be dead by now."

"He's right," said Tug, "You stay still for long on this island, you're dead meat."

"Can we stop talking about it please?" Claire stood up and walked over to the outer wall. The gutter was broken and water was gushing down the cracked plaster. She held her bottle underneath the torrent of fresh water and let the bottle refill. As she stood there, she suddenly felt faint. She dropped the half-full bottle to the ground and clutched her head. The room was beginning to fade behind a circle of grey spots that danced in her vision.

As she sank to the floor, Will grabbed her and caught her just in time. Kelly and Mark jumped up to help him set her down on a sofa.

"No, no..." muttered Claire. Figures swam before her eyes, the voices faded away into a white noise, and she collapsed into unconsciousness.

ELEVEN

"What's wrong with her?" asked Mark concerned. "She looks worse. It can't just be from her wrist."

Kelly looked her over. It was true, Claire did look worse. Her face was drawn and if anything, she was even paler. Beneath her eyes, the skin was turning a faint red, as if she had been crying and rubbing her eyes too much. Her nose was blocked and she was drawing short breaths through her open mouth. Kelly held her hand. Claire's skin was icy cold and so Kelly put a hand on her forehead; it was hot.

"She's got a fever," said Kelly. "She's stressed out and feeling the effects of this place. She needs a decent hot meal and some antibiotics. She said she felt ill earlier, like she was getting a cold. We need to keep her warm and hope she can sweat it out."

Will looked around for a blanket or anything extra they could use for warmth. There was little of use so he picked up the best looking cushion cover he could see and unzipped the foam interior. He draped the brown suede cover around Claire's shoulders.

"I'll look after her," said Suzy. "I won't let her out of my sight from now on. Don't want her lagging behind or passing out and hitting her head on the ground."

"Thanks, Suzy." Kelly let Suzy take over and she sank into a chair beside Mark whilst Suzy began comforting Claire, trying to wake her up.

Tug took Claire's good idea and began topping up his bottle with the fresh, clean rainwater too. "Despite what's happened, I think our luck may have turned, you know. The hills were crawling with those things, but we haven't come across a single one since we got down to the town." Tug screwed the cap back on his bottle and stood looking out into the street. "If we keep clear of them, we should get a good run to the coast."

"Actually, I noticed a lot of the buildings here are all destroyed. A lot of them seem to be burnt. It's not like back in Judgeford. Maybe that's got something to do with it," said Mark flicking his camera viewfinder on.

"Perhaps the bombs did their job," said Will. "Perhaps we really are the only people here capable of standing. I hope so."

"Why are they here? I mean on this island? How come they're not dead?" asked Suzy. Claire was beginning to stir and come round.

"Because they're dead," Tug said, intentionally patronising her. He turned to face the inside of the building. "The Deathless don't die, they can't. So it seems. Well, I guess I've taken a few out, but really, they'll be here forever, I should think."

"You know, they should have perished by logical thinking." Will went and stood behind the sofa that Kelly and Mark were sitting on. Mark was looking through the photographs he had taken and Will was interested in seeing what else he had captured since the farmhouse. "We don't fully understand them, true, but they've had no food source that we know of. A few sheep maybe, the small animal population that survives here on The Grave, but that wouldn't be enough to keep them going. So why are they here? What is sustaining them? Their bodies should have disintegrated and fallen apart."

"Maybe they found another food source?" said Tug, his hands on his hips. The rain gushed behind him and filled the street. Small rivers were forming and running through the town, swamping the roads and pavements.

"Maybe they're like magic and don't have to eat to keep going," said Tricia. "They were never properly studied as you say."

Tug snorted and waved away Tricia's comments dismissively. "We need to find the scientist's base further south to get any real answers. The speed you lot are moving at, it's a good job we didn't decide to head in their direction, it'd take us weeks. I guess they would know though if you want some real answers. They certainly should by now, since they've been at it for years now."

Will leant over the sofa as Mark slowly flicked through images he had captured. Will found the variety and intensity captured, both frightening and fascinating in equal measure. He saw the Deathless pouring from the hills, bloodthirsty faces snapping at the camera, bright coloured flowers growing amid decayed buildings and the ramshackle homes. Then there was one of him cradling the pregnant Weta. Maybe Rasmus had a point; life always seemed to find a way.

Mark continued scanning his images until he was stopped. "Wait," said Will as Mark was about to press to move onto the next image.

"What is it?" Marks studied the picture to see what had captured Will's attention. It looked horrific yet ordinary. He had taken it as they were driving away on the golf cart. Several of the Deathless were loping after them, and a couple of them were lying over something on the ground.

Kelly leant over and drew in a sharp breath as she saw what Will had seen. "There, you see those two on the ground." She pointed a delicate finger at the screen.

"Yeah, they look like they're eating something," said Mark. He still hadn't seen what they had and wasn't sure he wanted to.

"They're eating something all right," said Will. "But it's not one of us, is it? We know it's not Rasmus, he was nowhere near us."

"So...so who is it?" Mark zoomed in on the hideous image, reluctant to go too far, but inquisitive about what was under those two dead things.

"One of their own would be my guess," said Kelly. "Jesus. If they've turned cannibal that would go some way to explaining their longevity. I mean, perhaps they find other Deathless who aren't as...decayed, and feast on them; a bit like in the wild. There are some animals, crocodiles for example, who will eat their own. It's not unheard of. It's quite natural in a way. If the Deathless are doing the same then they're going to be around a hell of a lot longer than we are."

"There's nothing natural about them. They don't obey the laws of the universe like you and me. You know, we really do need to get going," said Tug. He rolled his head on his shoulders, flexing all his tendons and muscles.

"Maybe they're just thinning out the competition. Kill off the weaker ones so there's more food for the stronger ones?" Will stood and stretched, his neck making cracking sounds as he extended it. He chose to ignore Tug. Hunching over the sofa had not been comfortable. Neither had looking at the vivid images Mark had taken.

"Whales can go several months without eating and a crocodile over a year. Who knows what these things can do." Kelly looked away from the screen too, unable to look at it anymore. The Deathless had been covered in gore. Red muscle and tissue had been torn from the body and thrown all around them. The contrast to the bright and deep greens of the trees and bushes next to them only served to heighten the image's power.

"They're not things, they're people," said Suzy. "Their biology is the same as ours."

Claire had recovered and taken some sips of water from Suzy. She sat listening to the morbid conversation, feeling lightheaded and so not really taking anything in, just happy to hear life around her. Her life in New York now seemed like a dream and her mother only a vague memory.

"The Deathless are black, white, Asian, African, European; a mixture of the whole world. These unfortunate people were castigated by the whole world. They were brought here from all over the globe, wherever they were not wanted." Suzy paused. "Maybe it would've been better to exterminate them all."

"An extermination on that scale? That's up to God, not man." Mark turned his camera's viewfinder off. "Tricia knows more about it than I do, but there are things we shouldn't go messing with."

"Perhaps we should start thinking of them as something else then, looking for answers elsewhere? God created many things and science does not have all the answers," said Tricia. She remembered her old Bible classes at Sunday school and the sermons she regularly enjoyed on a Sunday; the values they had taught her held strong. Despite her scientific brain, she still believed in a higher power. On the road, she had prayed to Him silently, hoping He would hear her and send a message soon, ideally in the form of a large ship headed for New York.

"God didn't create the Deathless," Will shook his head. "Man did. It was tinkering with science that got us into this mess. It was well intentioned, true, but we got in over our heads and look what happened. As much as we'd like to think we have all the answers we don't. I doubt if..."

"For fuck's sake, you lot are having a fucking wet dream over this place, aren't you?" Tug kicked a brass pipe on the floor and it clanged into the road, echoing loudly around the furniture store. "I see five minutes has turned into ten. How much longer do you want to sit around debating this bullshit? I've had it with you. I'm off. If you care to join me, I'll see you at the coast where I'll be sipping on a nice cold one waiting for you."

"Tug wait!" Kelly jumped up out of the sofa. She could see the anger and frustration on his face. She knew they needed him. Whilst he was not part of the museum staff, he had still helped them this far. He had a logical way of thinking about things. He was far more grounded than Tricia and more focussed than Mark. Kelly couldn't rely solely on Will and Suzy to help her with Claire. She needed Tug.

Standing just under the edge of the building's wall, Tug picked up the backpack and slung it on before taking a step outside into the pouring rain. "No. I've had enough of this bollocks. I'm outta here."

Tug stepped out into the street and from behind the wall of the adjacent building came a tall man. It staggered a few feet through the puddles of rain, his approach hidden behind the wall of water drenching Tug.

Kelly watched in horror as, almost in slow motion, she saw the tall, dead man, take hold of Tug and sink his teeth into Tug's neck. She could see Tug trying to free the knife from his pocket, but it was too late.

Tug collapsed to the ground and the Deathless fell on top of him. Bright spurts of blood were flying through the air, mingling with the rainwater that puddled around him. Tug died quite quickly, his arms flopping uselessly at his side as his life drained away. It had all happened so quickly that he had not had time to react.

Kelly frantically tried to run to Tug to help him, but Will held her back. "Let me go!" she screamed, but Will held onto her tightly. She struggled and kicked, but he refused to let her go and held her in a bear-grip from behind.

"Wait!" Will barked. "We don't know how many more are out there. It's too late for Tug now. He's gone." Will felt the guilt rising again. Wilfred, Rasmus, and now Tug. Should he let Kelly go? Should he run out there to help? He looked at the man feasting on Tug. No, he wasn't going to feel guilty this time. Tug had gone out there unprepared, letting his emotions cloud his judgement. This time, Tug had no one to blame but himself. Will had thought that if only one of them survived the island, it would've been Tug.

Another figure appeared in the street. Will strained to see, but couldn't make out any features. The figure walked slowly toward Tug and then stopped. It looked down briefly and then looked through the curtain of rain into the furniture warehouse. It began shambling forward, its arms reaching out. The figure bent over Tug stood too and followed its compatriot. A low moan reached Will's ears and the grey figures increased their speed.

"Okay, time to move, now," said Will urgently. He released Kelly who instantly turned around and glared at him. They hadn't the time to discuss the finer points of Tug's demise now and Will set his eyes firmly back at Kelly's. "*Now.*"

"Oh God." Mark pointed outside at the figures emerging from the rain. There were three headed for them and more behind.

"Oh fuck," said Suzy, grabbing Claire's limp hand and forcing her to stand. She could see Tug's lifeless body staggering to its feet, the Deathless now ignoring him. His face was a mangled mess; scraps of flesh hung in shreds and dark, black blood oozed from his mouth. "Claire, keep up with me, honey." Suzy was worried that Claire might pass out again, but there was no way she would leave her behind. She couldn't do that again. She knew she couldn't leave anyone behind again.

"Let's hope this place has a back door," Will said quietly as he led them through the warehouse, winding his way between the scattered furniture.

At the far end of the building, there was a metal door. Will glanced behind him as he tried the handle. Mark, Tricia, Kelly, Suzy and Claire were right behind him. Past them inside the building were two of the Deathless and a newly reanimated Tug. He would probably be leading the hunt. His body was still strong; his muscles had not weakened by time and his senses were still attuned. He knew exactly where the others were and Will knew Tug would catch them soon if they didn't hurry.

Will shoved the door open and was surprised to find himself back outside in an alley. He had assumed the door led into an office or staffroom of some sort, but the alley would do just fine. He looked left and right. Both ends led back out into the streets they had just been walking on and there were none of the Deathless in sight. There was a large graffiti covered wall opposite with a lone rusty door implanted into a recess, which was probably the back entrance to another warehouse. Will tried it, but the handle refused to budge. He pushed and pulled, but there was no movement. It was still locked. Perhaps it was for the best, he thought. It would probably only lead them into another building where they would be cornered.

"This way." Will held the warehouse door open as the others filed through, out into the alley in silence. He wondered if he should try and put Tug out of his misery. He was an asshole, but he didn't deserve to spend the rest of time wandering The Grave. Will watched as Mark and Tricia walked past looking like they were in shock; Kelly just looked furious.

As Suzy pushed Claire past him, she pulled the door shut thereby forcing Will out into the alley. "Don't even think of being a hero now, Will."

Kelly led the way down the alleyway, which stretched barely ten feet wide and thirty feet long. "Where did they come fr...oh shit." She stopped and held her arms out so the others wouldn't go beyond where she was standing. At the end of the alleyway, there was now four of the Deathless: four scrawny women, utterly naked, their bodies rotten and filled with a lust for raw meat, staggered down the alleyway. Behind them, Kelly saw more. Though the rain still fell from the dark sky above, she could make out the undeniable figures of death in the gloom.

Kelly felt nausea rise in her belly. She turned around. "We have to go back. Go the other way. Go, go, go!" She literally pushed Mark and Tricia around who came face to face with Will.

"We can't. Look." Will pointed down the other end of the alleyway where more of the Deathless were congregating.

Just then, the door from which they had just left the furniture warehouse began rattling in its frame. The Deathless were banging on it from the other side.

"Fuck, how long will that hold?" said Mark. "Screw that idiot Tug. I am not fucking dying like this." He spied a dumpster and jumped up to look inside. It was empty. "Damn it." He crouched down onto his belly and dragged a piece of drainpipe out. It was about ten feet long and he tipped it up to empty out the rainwater. It was difficult to hold its entire length and he used both hands to wield it in front of him like a baton. "Let's...fuck it." The wet, dirty piping slipped from his grasp and it clattered to the ground.

"What are we going to do, Will?" Suzy looked up at him and again he was struck by her beautiful face.

Her skin was soaked and Will couldn't tell where her tears ended and the rain started. Her face was imploring him for help, but he didn't know where to start. Stand and fight their way through the Deathless seemed to be their only option. Yet he knew that one scratch, one bite, was enough to kill them. They wouldn't make it. After all, they had been through they were going to die out here in a dirty alley; him and his friends would be eaten alive. He would never see his mother again. She wouldn't understand what had happened to him and he hoped nobody would ever tell her. She didn't need to know. He would never get to know Suzy as he wanted to. He knew she wanted him as badly as he wanted her, but it was never going to happen now.

He looked at Claire. She seemed unfazed by any of it. Her eyes were vacant and her face showed no recognition of the situation they were in. It was probably a good thing she was out of it. She shouldn't be subjected to die like this, ripped apart at the hands of a monster, miles away from home, without having lived life.

Mark was trying to hold the piping again. Good on him, Will thought, going out like a fighter. Mark would put up a struggle; there was no doubt. Mark might not have the build of a fighter, but he sure had the attitude of one when he was cornered.

Will saw that Tricia had sunk to her knees and she was rocking back and forth. Her eyes were closed and her lips were moving, reciting some childhood prayer to a God she wasn't sure she believed in anymore.

Kelly looked back at Will. For once, she was lost. Will could see the defeat in her eyes and couldn't bring himself to look back at her. He turned his gaze to his shoes. It was better not to fight it. Let them do their worst. There was no way out now and no getting home. He knew he couldn't fight them off with his bare hands. He had let everyone down.

Three short, sharp metallic knocks rang out and Will didn't take notice of them at first. They sounded again and disturbed his thoughts. They were clearly not random or natural sounds. It was someone deliberately making them. He looked up into Suzy's open face, her desperate tears still evident, her question unanswered. He looked over her at the Deathless approaching who were now barely fifteen feet away. Nobody in the alley was making the sounds. Puzzled, he turned to the door in the wall opposite. The rusty door he had tried when they had first run out here, the door that had been locked; it was now open.

From the shadows within, an arm beckoned them in. There was no mistaking it for one of the dead. The hand was firm and waving. If it had been attached to a corpse, they would have seen the rest of the body by now. Will watched as the arm continued to beckon them. There was no voice, no calling or shouting, just a lone arm, drawing them in through the now open door.

"That way," shouted Will, and he pushed Suzy toward the door. He had no choice; they *all* had no choice. They had to accept this bizarre help, this strange open doorway that offered them their only shot at survival.

Too shocked to do anything else or think what may be behind the opening door, Suzy ran into the shadows, swiftly followed by Claire, Will, Mark and Kelly. She paused, ready to slam the door shut when she realised Tricia was still kneeling in the alley with her eyes closed in prayer. Suzy saw and smelt the advancing Deathless, the putrid moving corpses only feet away from her. "Tricia, hurry the fuck up," she shouted. "Tricia!"

Suzy watched as Tricia opened her eyes slowly and looked up into the face of snapping jaws closing in on her. Tricia let out a yelp and bounced up quickly, punching the dead man in the stomach. It tottered backward momentarily giving Tricia vital seconds to escape its clutches. She bounded for the door and hurried through just as it began to swing shut.

A metallic boom echoed around the warehouse as the door shut behind them. Terrible moaning came from behind it as the Deathless tried to follow, unable to break down the solid, thick door.

"Where are we?"

"Who's there?"

"I can't see."

"Will? Kelly?"

Their voices called out in the darkness. There was not a glimmer of light anywhere, not a window nor a crack in any part of the structure they had entered. Had they just jumped from the frying pan into the fire?

TWELVE

"Everyone, calm down. Just calm down for a second." Will's voice rang out above everyone else's. He was trying to let his eyes get used to the dark. He had rushed inside and found nothing to hold onto. His boots found the surface solid, yet gritty, and he guessed they might be in some sort of manufacturing plant. It was cold and other than their voices, and the scuffling sounds of the dead from outside, he heard no other sounds at all. He knew if they started walking around in the dark, someone was liable to fall and hurt themselves.

"Will," said Kelly, "where the hell are we?"

Before he could answer, another booming sound echoed around the dark room, and Will heard metal grating against metal, as if something was being pulled back sharply. He wondered if whoever had let them in had changed their mind and was unlocking the door again.

A low beam of light suddenly illuminated their way. A full sixty yards away, another door had opened. The faint light shone enough for Will to see that they were in another warehouse of sorts, full of rusting metal girders and trolleys. It was deserted though and it seemed they had no option but to follow the light.

"Let's go find out." Will followed the narrow angle of light and the group followed him.

Kelly scurried to catch up with him. "What is this?" she whispered. Despite their apparent secure surroundings, she was reluctant to speak too loudly. She didn't know how safe they would be in here, or for how long.

"I don't know," came Will's honest reply. He shielded his eyes as they closed in on the open door. "But whoever let us in here must be on our side. They could've left us out there to die, but they didn't. So we'll play nice, for now."

Will stepped through the doorway and a barrage of smells and sights hit him. They were inside some sort of shopping mall. The light that had seemed so bright in the previous room now seemed incredibly dull. The source was natural sunlight, coming from a glass dome above them. The mall was two storeys high, and all around him were shops and cafes, bookshops, clothing stores, fast food chains and gifts shops, designer boutiques, jewellery counters and ATMs. Will had doubted he would ever see such things again. He certainly hadn't expected to see them here. The riot of colour seemed at odds with the world they had just come from. Outside was dreary and dull, lifeless and moribund. Inside, scattered throughout the mall's floors, he saw brightly coloured clothes, books, papers and defunct electronic devices everywhere.

After his eyes got used to the sights, he noticed the smell. It was bad. The air purveyed a sense of decay and had a fetid odour, yet it was not of death. The Deathless had a certain smell about them, like rotten meat combined with sewage. In here, it was a mixture of putrefied food and what he could only relate to as BO.

"Holy cow..." was all Suzy could manage to stutter out as she joined them inside the mall. She let go of Claire's hand, assured they were safely away from danger. She saw Will and Kelly looking around in wonder and Mark had already begun snapping away. Suzy watched as Tricia bent down to pick up a magazine.

"'World Soccer Special,' July 2186. Wow, this is three years old." Tricia let it fall back to the dirty floor, uninterested as ever in anything remotely sports related.

"I can't say as I've read that issue yet," muttered Mark.

The door latched behind them and they all whirled around, startled by the strange voice. They had almost forgotten their mysterious saviour and they were astonished to see a man locking the door and dragging a heavy wooden bench in front of it.

Claire let out a shriek and jumped behind Suzy. The man was short and thin, his face gaunt and pale, but he was dressed immaculately. He wore a dark suit over a crinkled, white collared shirt, which was open at the neck. He would have looked like the perfect businessman, if it wasn't for his emaciated frame and the yellow and black striped sneakers he wore. His head was smooth and stubbly, his chin the same. Brown inquisitive eyes poked out from beneath a set of wire-rimmed glasses.

He turned around to look at the bedraggled group of people he had just let in. "Sorry about the cloak and dagger stuff. I'm Roach."

* * *

"Mr Roach, I'm Will, this is Kelly. We..." Will ceased the introductions as he saw he had abruptly lost the interest of Roach. The man's eyes were suddenly looking up at the ceiling and he had cocked his head to one side. Will looked up, but saw nothing that might be of interest.

"They're coming, follow me," said Roach. He sprang away down the littered mall, jumping over the mess. He paused twenty feet away and turned. "Come on, come on," he said hurriedly.

Kelly looked at Will with raised eyebrows and shrugged. "Might as well, we can't go back outside." She tentatively began the hike through the mountains of rubbish toward Roach.

Suzy took Claire's hand as they followed Kelly. "Come on, honey, let's go."

"What does he mean, they're coming? The Deathless?" asked Mark as he joined Will. He noticed Tricia stumbling through the rubbish after Suzy and felt both happy and worried that he was at the back of the group again. The last time he had done that, he had nearly not gotten away from those things.

"I'm not sure. Something's a little odd here," said Will.

"You think he's..."

Will stopped and looked up at the dome. Rain was still pelting against the weathered glass, but now something else, a new noise that added to the clattering din of the rain. An engine? Is that what Roach had heard?

Will couldn't see anything and continued the slow walk with Mark. With his eyes now focussed on not stepping in something organic or slippery, he didn't see the helicopter that brushed the sky overhead. It only appeared for a moment, but it would've caused a commotion if any of them had seen or heard it as Roach had.

Roach led them up a silent escalator and into another furniture showroom. This one was in far better condition than the one they had sheltered in earlier, where Tug had lost his life. They were now in the front showroom in the mall and it had not been exposed to the elements so all the goods inside were still in an almost perfect state. Roach pulled up a leather chair on castors and invited them all to sit down wherever they pleased. There were beds and sofas close by and they all sat obediently, both amused and bemused by the little man.

"Sorry to rush you, but out of sight, out of mind. It's best not to be too...*visible* around here." Roach spun around on his chair doing a full rotation. "So, please, who are you all? Clearly, you didn't intend to be here, but somehow I don't think you're from Agnew. Eco-warriors perhaps? Journalists? Hmmm. How on earth did you get here?" Roach spun around again, smiling. "Sorry if I'm a little excitable, but I haven't had a visitor in what...two, three years now? More I expect. None of the breathing variety anyway, ha ha!"

Suzy and Claire were huddled together on a two-seater suite and Will thought they looked far more scared than they should be. This Roach was quite the character and his odd manner was confusing them all. They seemed safe enough for now and Will wanted the others to feel safe too. If he could calm Roach down, it would benefit them all.

"We er...we weren't really expecting to find anyone alive to be honest, Mr Roach," Will said. "Our plane crashed yesterday on our way to the Antarctic. Us ending up here was, is, just a horrible accident. We crashed up in the hills and have slowly been making our way west. We were hoping to get to the coast by the end of the day. Tug was...well, we were hoping to make it there and find a way off this island and get picked up by the military or something. A boat, a plane..."

Roach shook his head. "No, no, no, out of the question. The Antarctic you say. Then you must be scientists, right? From where?"

Will was shocked by Roach's question. "New York, the American Museum of Natural History. But that's pretty irrelevant now. We need to..."

"Yes, yes, of course. Look, forgive my blunt manner, but you look terrible. All of you, honestly, you look just terrible." Roach jumped out of his chair and fished around noisily in the desk drawers behind him. He pulled out a handful of chocolate bars and began handing them out. "It's all I can offer you for now. I was saving them for a special occasion and this seems appropriate. Your need is greater than mine, it would appear."

Kelly had so many questions she wanted to ask this odd man. Who was he and why was he living on The Grave? How? Why had he answered so vehemently that the coast was not an option? She kept picturing Tug in the street, his throat being torn out. Then his body getting up and walking toward her... "Mr Roach, we're tired and we've lost friends of ours. There were more of us on the plane but...thank you..."

Roach handed her a Mars bar. It had expired a year ago, but she gratefully took it.

"...but how did you know we were here? Where are we? Who..?" Kelly un-wrapped the bar and savoured the sweet taste. The chocolate had gone white and brittle, but it was still the first food she'd eaten since waking.

"You really are lost, aren't you." Roach looked at them kindly. "I'm sorry for your loss. I can hardly believe any of you are here. If you crashed up in the hills then you are lucky to be alive. The hills up there are crawling with them."

"And here, in the town? Are we safe?" asked Suzy. She was rubbing Claire's cold hands, trying to generate some friction to get her circulation going. She glanced over at Will who was in raptures. Roach had randomly given him a Snickers and Suzy had to stifle her laugh.

"Well yes, and no. In here with me, you are quite, quite safe. This town was left to die and the houses burnt. The mall here survived relatively unscathed. The southern side has collapsed, but there's literally no way through the rubble. Trust me, I've checked. The rest of the building is completely locked down. They must have locked up and left. The only way in or out is the alley where I found you. I have the key in my pocket and they won't get in. You can relax. I've been living here for many years and they can't get in." Roach had sat back down on his chair, but kept still now as he talked. His eyes cast furtively around the room, as if he was examining them all, scrutinising his unexpected guests.

"Did you say years?" asked Mark. "How many?" He casually lifted his camera and took a photograph of Roach.

"Well it's hard to be sure. I spent some time in prison before they dropped me off here, so...about four in all. Yes, well three definitely. I stopped counting the days after a while. They don't matter much anymore."

Will whistled through his teeth. "And you've been here the whole time?"

"Mostly." Roach closed his eyes and hung his head for a moment.

Roach failed to say anything more on the subject and Tricia whispered in Kelly's ear. "Do you think we should leave? Should we keep going for the coast?"

Kelly looked around the room and shook Tug's image from her head. She was tired. Will and Mark looked shattered too. She knew if she asked them they would carry on, but did she need to? Suzy was drawn and pale, Claire was but a shadow of her former self, and they were all cold and wet. Without Tug, would they even go in the right direction? She also had to think about this Roach – would he want to come with them?

"Mr Roach," said Kelly standing up, "if this place is as safe as you suggest, can I please ask for your help on all our behalf? We all want to get home as quickly as possible, but that said - we also need to rest. It's getting late in the day and we're cold...our clothes are soaked and we haven't had anything decent to eat in the last two days. After everything we've been through, I think we could do with a good night's sleep. What we've seen out there today was horrific. Our friends Tug, Rasmus..." Kelly swallowed down her grief and carried on. "Perhaps even some more food if you have it please? Do you think we could stay here, just for now, and talk to you some more about how we get off this island?"

All eyes turned to Roach who got up and left his chair spinning and creaking as it circled around. He walked over to Kelly and held out his hand, which she shook. "What kind of a man would I be if I kicked you out onto the streets? I can imagine what you've been going through. I've lost people myself."

Kelly couldn't help but shed a tear as she shook Roach's warm hand. He was a little erratic and thin, but he seemed genuinely nice. It was only those wiry spectacles he wore that made him seem so shifty. Up close, his eyes were soft and suggested he had a caring soul behind that eccentric exterior. If he had indeed been a prisoner here for years there was no surprising he was acting a bit strange. She collected herself, refusing to break down completely, even though every fibre of her being wanted to.

"Listen," said Roach facing everyone, "it's getting late and if you are all in agreement, I will show you around my home so you can feel a little safer. I have some food and you can see I have plenty of spare beds. Follow me, and please introduce yourselves. Then perhaps later I will tell you a little about myself."

Will got up and shook Roach's hand too. This queer man had saved them earlier, and had not hesitated to help them now. It did feel good to get out of the rain and if Roach had spent years inside this old mall, it must be very safe. Will felt reassured and confident that they were not in any immediate danger. He began introducing everyone and Roach made a point of remembering their names.

They decided they would follow Roach through the centre with the exception of Claire. She was exhausted and her headache was worsening, so she stayed behind and tucked herself into one of the beds. Will promised he would bring food and clean clothes back for her.

On the upper level of the mall, Roach stopped outside a department store. "You look completely soaked through, the lot of you. You'll find everything you need in here. Luckily, the store was well stocked and there are both men's and women's clothes. Down the back, you'll find the shoe department. I suggest you find some comfortable walking shoes. You never know when you're going to need to run."

It dawned on Will that Roach had survived here, apparently alone, and had made good use of his surroundings. It explained his unusual footwear, but it made perfect sense. There were a million questions he wanted to ask Roach, but only one occurred to him before he joined the others inside. "What's with the mess on the floors? Was it like this when you got here?"

Roach looked around the mall and laughed. "No, no, it's all my own handiwork. I think I did quite a good job of it."

Will lifted his foot and picked a fifty dollar bill off that was stuck to his sole. "Because…"

"It's kind of an early warning system. If the dead ever miraculously found a way in here, I would hate them to be able to sneak up on me. So I figured the best thing I could do was spread as much junk and garbage around as I could. Keep the floors as difficult to walk though as possible. Nobody's ever gotten in, but if they did, I would hear them coming and it would give me my chance to get out of here with my brains intact." Roach tapped the side of his head and smiled.

"Fair enough," said Will, walking into the department store, giving Roach an appreciative nod as he left. He screwed up the fifty-dollar bill and threw it back onto the floor. "Guess I don't need that in here. We'll see you in five."

Roach pointed out all the exit doors as they walked through the mall. The doors were all locked so they were pointless, but he wanted everyone to feel safe. He knew how hard it was to achieve the peace of mind required to sleep and relax decently in such trying circumstances.

They had all found dry clothing and comfortable shoes, so he was now taking them to the food court where large floor to ceiling windows still stood intact overlooking the streets below.

Tricia pressed her face close against the glass. "Look at them, they're everywhere."

"At the moment, yes. They would have gotten excited by all the commotion you caused earlier," said Roach. He walked away from the window. He had seen this scene too many times now to want to take much notice.

"How are we going to get out of here?" Suzy couldn't see a single road, pavement or street that wasn't swarming with the Deathless.

"Search me," said Kelly. She turned to Will. "But we will, right? I don't want to spend any longer in here than we have to."

Roach appeared from a back kitchen with two trays of food. "It's not much I'm afraid. I have to be careful with my rations. I've got some vegetables growing on the roof, but there's not much at this time of year. So I hope you like tinned food." He placed the two trays on a table and the others sat down with him.

Will read the labels as he ate. There was tuna, chickpeas, tomatoes and even strawberries. "How did you come by all this? It can't have been here, surely?" He looked around at the fast food stores, knowing that they wouldn't have served any of what they were eating. "And if you scavenged all this from the homes around town, you must have an invisibility cloak or something to get past all of the Deathless out there."

Roach smiled, watching them eat. "There's a supermarket downstairs. The shelves were well stocked. Out the back in their storeroom, there were boxes and boxes just piled up. It's lasted me a long time. I managed to find access to the roof where I've gotten quite the garden growing. Plenty of buckets and tubs were in the mall that I could use, so I dragged them up there and found some compost in the supermarket too. They had seeds for all sorts of vegetables. It's been no picnic and I have a strict regime of how much I can eat, but it's gotten me this far. There are plenty of fresh fruits growing out there, apples, lemons, mandarins...but they're tainted. So much of the land has been contaminated now by the Deathless, you don't know what's safe to eat and drink or not. It's far too risky. I'm sure you are well aware of the dangers too. Unless you are confident you have a pure water source, you shouldn't drink anything either. You haven't consumed anything since you landed have you?"

"No, just a couple of power bars we brought with us, and what little rainwater we managed to collect. Are you sure you can spare this?" said Suzy swallowing down a spoonful of cold baked beans. She didn't think anything had tasted as delicious.

"Of course, of course. I've kept a couple of tins back for your friend, Claire. We should probably be getting back to her. I don't want her to worry. She looked quite pale. Is she sick?"

"The flu," said Suzy pushing her chair back as she got up. The scraping sound grated on even her nerves. "She just needs a good rest in the dry and a good feed. Say, is there a pharmacy in here? Maybe I can get her some medication. I'll try to find some antiseptic and antibiotics. At the very least, we could do with some aspirin."

"Sure," said Roach. "I'll show you on the way back."

They all stood up, the tins now empty. Roach held two more in his hand, and Will carried a bundle of clothes.

"I might just stay here for a bit, if that's okay?" Mark hung back, toying with the camera strap that hung around his neck. "I want to get some good shots of all this and the windows here are presenting me with a great lookout. The light will be gone soon, so I won't be long."

"I'll stay with you," said Kelly. "I still think there's safety in numbers. We'll catch up with you."

Roach took Will, Suzy and Tricia back to Claire via a chemist's shop, leaving Kelly alone with Mark in the food court.

"You didn't have to, you know," said Mark adjusting the lens for the low light.

"I know, you're a big boy, you can look after yourself." Kelly joined him at the window. "After what happened to Tug, I'm reluctant to let anyone be on their own. I know we left Claire, but she's sound asleep, so nothing is going to happen to her. She needs the rest too, poor thing. It'll do her good to give her some peace and quiet for a while."

Mark was trying to photograph the Deathless, but through a rain-streaked window, he was not getting very many clear shots. He wondered if he could get Roach to take him up to the roof in the morning.

"Look at that," he said, pointing at an old woman down below them.

The dead woman was pawing at the door to the mall below. Her jaws worked tirelessly, pressing up against the steel barricade that had held her out for years.

"How long do you think she'll keep that up, days, months...years? Do they have any concept of time?" asked Mark.

"I don't think they have any idea. I think they're nothing like who they once were. Most people believe when you die the soul moves on, right? Heaven, hell, rebirth or whatever you think. These dead that we see now are just vessels for the infection. The Aqua-Gene hasn't kept them alive, it has killed them. The infected bodies, kill. The soul has long since left these poor sods."

"Jesus, look at that," said Mark, pointing to a bank's doorway across the road. He zoomed in to take a photograph and then lowered his camera.

He was pointing to a crumpled body, curled up in the doorway. There was no way of knowing how long it had lain there. The arms and legs were slight, the bones pronounced and skin mottled green and black. The figure was motionless apart from its hands, which kept grabbing at the door, trying to haul its useless carcass up. The belly was swollen and Mark wondered if it had been pregnant. Just then, the guts of the dead body gave up their secrets and spilled out the bloody and festering contents all over the road. A bloody fissure erupted in the side of the belly and the extended gaseous gut burst open, a slushy pile of white, writhing maggots spewing out and trickling onto the pavement. Mark looked away before he vomited up the contents of his own guts over the floor.

"Fascinating," said Kelly quietly.

"Really? *That's* what you think? Fascinating?" Mark sat down, unable to look out at the horror anymore. His camera had caught enough.

"Do you know why flies congregate around dead bodies, Mark?" Kelly continued staring at the body in the doorway. She couldn't tell if it had been male or female, but it was irrelevant now. "The flies know that a deceased human being is basically a perfect tool for them. A corpse presents the perfect conditions for them to breed. They lay eggs, which hatch as maggots and consume the flesh. Usually, you will find Calliphoridae in large numbers around a corpse. Sorry, that's a blow-fly to you. You also find the Sarcophagidae, which eat the flesh, but don't lay their young inside. This all aids the decomposition of the body. A dead human is really a wonderful factory for flies to produce their offspring."

Mark let out a long sigh. "Thanks for the lesson, Kelly. I'm not sure I needed to know that, but thanks anyway. I'll be sure to credit you in my book when we get back. If you ask me, they should've been put down ages ago. What's the point of letting them 'live' like this?"

"Just because they're different to us, why should they be exterminated? They no longer function like humans, but they live, move and scurry about their business like an ant. The UN decided they had a right to exist like every other animal on this planet. Would you go out of your way to stomp on an ant hill?"

Mark snorted. "If the ants wanted to eat me, then yes. All day long."

"Great white sharks want to eat you too, but we don't kill them, do we? The dead are doing all they know to do, just like the ants and the sharks of this world. Look, African militia are dangerous. You of all people should know that, Mark. To some people, the Muslims are dangerous. To others, it's Christians, Westerners, the Arabs...I could go on. You have to draw a line somewhere. What does it mean, Mark? All of this?"

"That we're all going to hell." Mark turned away from the window and the conversation.

Kelly watched as hundreds of Deathless swamped the rain soaked streets around the mall. They had converged around the walls and doors, but as Roach had said, there was no way in. She wondered how long they would remain there, trying to find that elusive opening. Was Mark right? Would they stay for days, months, or longer? The thought of spending years in here frightened her. All of a sudden, her desk back at the museum wasn't such a bad idea. She spent most of her working time rushing around and moving from place to place. All she wanted to do now was to go home and stay there. Better to live alone in a cramped New York loft than die amongst the dead, cowering on The Grave amongst the Deathless.

"Let's get back to the others, eh?" Mark had sensed Kelly's sombre mood and the light was failing anyway. He wanted to catch up with Roach and the others to find out how they were going to get home. He had a big story to tell, and was getting sick of the sight of rain and walking corpses.

He was finding himself drawn to Kelly in a way he hadn't expected too. In many ways, she was completely different from him. He also knew that if you spent long enough in someone's company you were liable to end up either loving or hating them. With Kelly, he hadn't quite figured out which way he was going to go. Having never been in a serious relationship, the last thing he wanted was to fall now. Mark knew he was on the verge of a major story. Back in New York, there would be a lot of work to do. An image of the bloated maggot-ridden carcass sprang back into his mind and he forgot about everything else. To think that death and disease were so close. He let out a long breath.

"Let's bust a move," he said getting up.

As Kelly turned to leave, the empty tin cans from dinner fell off the table and rolled noisily on the floor. Pots and pans clanged together loudly in the kitchens and then the floor began trembling. The whole building rocked gently from side to side, at first weakly, then growing stronger until she had to grab a table to stand. Another earthquake was not what they needed now. Kelly wondered if the structure of the building would hold and keep out the Deathless as the floor beneath her feet suddenly buckled. Kelly screamed.

THIRTEEN

Kelly was about to tell Mark they should duck under one of the tables, when the swaying and shaking abruptly stopped as quickly as it had started. It ebbed away like a gentle wave flowing out into the ocean and she looked at Mark.

"Another earthquake, right?" Mark's knuckles were white and his fingers slow to release his grip on the back of a chair.

Kelly nodded. "I would say the one we felt earlier was quite big; somewhere around four to five on the Richter scale. You often get quite large aftershocks after one like that, so it's not going to be uncommon for us to feel some more. This island is centred over several tectonic plates and has a lot of seismic activity. I just hope these are not a precursor to anything bigger. We have enough to handle without anything else fucking with us." She looked down at the food court's tiled floor. Several of them had buckled, but she was grateful there was no further damage. Falling through the floor was not on her to do list.

"Amen to that. Let's get back to the others. I wonder if Roach got any beer from that supermarket he mentioned, I could do with a drink."

Mark and Kelly left the food court with the Deathless still outside.

"Why were they left here like this?" Mark asked Kelly as they walked. "They're a protected species, right? Like the panda?"

"Well, because something is unsightly or dangerous, does that mean we should kill it? We didn't wipe out crocodiles, red-backs or snakes, did we? If anything, man nurtured them, protected them from danger. We let nature take its course. The Deathless are here on this planet and are more than a snake or an insect, they're us. They used to be just like you and me. We can't deny our past or where is our future? Based on lies and deception? If the Deathless were just brushed under the carpet we risk repeating the same problems again."

Mark kicked a stack of newspapers out of their way as they slowly went back to the others. "But what's the point of keeping them alive? If you ask me, they should be exterminated. If you have an unsightly growth on your body, you have it removed."

Kelly had no answer and left Mark's comments hanging in the air. He made a good point, but she couldn't yet agree with him. As they walked back, his hand accidentally brushed hers and for a moment, she thought he was going to take hold of it. She felt a flush of excitement and then realised how inappropriate it would be to think of Mark as anything other than a colleague. The night was closing in and with a full stomach, she was ready for a rest. If she could only get a decent night's sleep, maybe she could start thinking clearly again.

* * *

"You're looking a bit better, Claire," said Kelly, making her way over to the bed and sitting down beside her.

"Yeah, I feel better, thanks." Claire had put on the dry clothes Will had brought back for her and managed to eat one tin of sliced apricots. She had stuffed a couple of pillows behind her head and was sitting up listening to the others. She still felt drained, but she was calmer now. Everyone had taken such good care of her that she was starting to feel better, even optimistic about getting home tomorrow. She had tried her mobile once more when she had awoken, but there was no reception so she'd given up on the notion of sending her mother a message.

"Did you feel the earthquake?" she asked Kelly. "My bed was shaking. It didn't seem quite as scary as before though. I'm glad Mum's not here, because she wouldn't like it. She won't even go on the rollercoaster at Coney Island."

Kelly patted Claire's knee through the floral duvet. "Yeah, we felt it; just another exciting aspect of being on this strange island, honey." Kelly gave Claire a kiss on her forehead. It was hot, but it looked like her fever had run its course. A little colour was back in her cheeks and a rosy patch beneath both eyes that accentuated her slender cheekbones. She was going to be a good looking woman soon. Kelly was impressed at how well Claire was handling the situation.

Kelly got up and sat down on an empty bed next to Claire's. Everyone had found somewhere to sleep for the night, and they were lying either on it, or in Suzy and Tricia's case, in it already. Roach's bed had been obvious surrounded as it was by various bottles, books, and piles of clothes. She scanned around the room and it looked like everyone was still fully dressed.

"So we need to get a plan together for tomorrow." Kelly sat on the top of the bed and thought about taking off her new jumper. The mall was quite cool though and the bed sheets cold, so like the others, she decided to stay in her clothes. They were fresh and clean anyway. "I guess we try to head to the coast as we were. We're very close."

Will sat up, ruffling his hair. "We could..."

"No." Roach's voice cut Will short. "No, you can't do that."

"Why? Once the people monitoring this place see us, they'll send a chopper or a boat to pick us up," said Will. "Won't they?"

"You think I didn't try that already? You think I haven't already exhausted every possible way of getting off this island? I haven't been here for years, living in squalor and losing my mind, and not thought about escape. If all it took was a stroll down to the beach, I wouldn't be talking to you now, would I?" Roach spoke vehemently and everyone listened. He had their full attention now. "There's really only one way off The Grave and you have a slim, *slim* chance of making it. My chances are non-existent."

"What do you mean?" Suzy had propped herself up on her elbows so she could see Roach clearly.

"Well, the coast is a no-go zone. Mines, booby-traps, automatic guns, miles and miles of barbed wire...even if you somehow made it past those, you'd be taken out before you got off the island. They don't want anyone or anything getting away. It's called The Grave for good reason."

"So assuming that is true, how do we get out?" Will didn't doubt Roach, but he wanted to push him. They needed the full story if they were to survive.

"Well, you need to get down to the capital. Ex-capital, since I'm not sure there officially is one anymore. It's not far though; you can fairly easily make it in a day on foot. The dead are spread pretty thin between here and there. There's not much for them to snack on so they tend to stay away from the highway. Of course, once you get there, the real fun begins. I'd estimate there's approximately half a million Deathless in the city, give or take."

Roach heard a few gasps around the room and paused for them to take in what he'd said. He could see Claire's eyes drooping. "Do you really want me to tell you?"

"Yes, of course. You know this place better than we do," Will urged Roach on. He didn't seem to need much encouragement though. "So you mean we get to the scientist's base in the city, right? They'll help us. They'll have communications with the outside world. We had thought about that option."

Roach laughed uncontrollably. He had to put his hand over his mouth to stop and when he did so, he felt embarrassed. They were looking at him as if he were a madman. "I'm sorry, it's just...I'd better explain. There is no base there or anywhere. There are no scientists. Wow, so Agnew has managed to keep the lie still going? Kudos for the effort."

"Of course, there's a base," said Kelly. "If I remember correctly, it was believed to have been set up beneath the U.S. Embassy because that was one of the strongest buildings in the city. We know all about the research they're doing there, the men working around the clock to find a cure, the brilliant team of..."

Roach began laughing again, but stopped himself quickly. He didn't want to offend these people. "Sorry, but you are gravely wrong. Pun intended. You've been fed a pack of lies; the whole world has. That bastard, Agnew."

"Who's this Agnew you keep mentioning?" said Tricia. "You don't mean...the President?"

"That's exactly who," said Roach bitterly. Instantly, his eyes were alight, the coals in his mind stoked and his blood pumping. "I'll tell you my story. I'll tell you the truth and then you'll know why I've been left marooned here like some warped Robinson Crusoe. I should be dead, and as far as Agnew and the world is concerned, I am, but he made a powerful enemy when he picked on me. I don't give up easily."

"I think you'd better start from the beginning," encouraged Will.

Roach did as he was asked and started with a brief summary of who he was. "Franklin Roach, father to Bobby and husband to

Stella. Lord knows what's happened to my family. I can only pray they are safe and well back home. I haven't seen them in years. I was the U.S. Senator of the State of California back in the 80s. I was elected way back in 2176. Agnew was already vice-president by then of course and he didn't like me one bit. The feeling was mutual, the slimy son of a bitch. I had five good, but testing years. You all know what happened in 2180 of course."

"The San Francisco bombings," said Kelly.

She wasn't there, but Kelly remembered the news. It was the biggest terrorist atrocity committed on U.S. soil since the Trade Centre attacks way back in 2001. The Golden Gate Bridge had been blown up. Two powerful bombs exploded simultaneously on one of the pillars, strong enough to destroy it, and along with it, the entire bridge. It had collapsed into the harbour killing ninety-six people instantly with another seven from their injuries dying later in the hospital. The casualty rate was considered low, but the cost and high profile nature of the attacks certainly got the world's attention. It had even cost the President at the time his job, with Agnew taking over. "So you're *the* Franklin Roach?"

"Guilty. But that is the *only* thing I am guilty of. I had nothing do with that attack at all. The stuff the media came out with afterwards was incredible. It was all fed to them by Agnew. I had dirt on him and he wanted me out of the way. I don't want to dredge it all up again, but I was sentenced without trial."

"That's right. I remember you disappeared shortly after you were accused. You were said to have gone to South America somewhere wasn't it? I remember vaguely you were supposed to have sought asylum there, but you fell off the radar."

"You have a good memory, Kelly. Paraguay I think it was that I was supposed to be living in. I've never set foot in South America. They locked me up and threw away the key. I spent two and a half years in prison. No lawyer, no trial, no telephone calls, nothing; I don't even know which prison I was in, but I doubt it was in America. They interrogated me now and again. I think that was something for them to do, rather than to get anything out of me. Agnew knew I had nothing to do with the Golden Gate.

"Anyway, about four years ago, after a long stint in solitary without any hint of what was happening, they dragged me out of my cell and brought me here."

"Why would they do that? Why would President Agnew do that?" Kelly was astounded. She could tell from the faces of her friends that they were amazed too. Roach's story was incredible, yet he was convincing and he seemed to be telling the truth. "The Grave is off limits, a protected island monitored by the UN and the US military. You're telling me they dumped you here? Alone? What about the research base?"

Roach held up his hands in a defensive posture, his palms outspread. "I know, I know, it must seem unbelievable to you. But I have nothing to hide, no reason to lie to you. If you don't believe me, then you can be on your way and forget all about me. But if you want to live and get home, you're going to need to listen to me.

"You see, I was brought here on a U.S. military helicopter. There were five others with me then. We were all handcuffed and blindfolded so we had no idea where we were being taken. Once we found out of course...we were dropped on top of the US Embassy in the old capital of this island, about six miles south of here. I've seen them come and go on an almost daily basis since. They bring convicts, murderers, political dissidents – anyone they need to get rid of. There is no research base. There is no one looking for a cure for this thing, because there isn't one. This is an island of death and a very handy one for those in power. They drop you off here and know you're gone for good. Nobody can leave. You're expected to die here. Nobody is going to come looking for you. Nobody is going to find your body washing up on the banks of the Hudson with a bullet in your head. No journalist is ever going to expose the truth, because anyone who comes here is on a one-way ticket.

"I managed to get out of the embassy with one other person; Min Wang. She was innocent like me, but the Chinese needed her to disappear so she wound up on The Grave. Everyone else in our group was slaughtered within minutes of the soldiers leaving us. They just laughed and joked as if we were dogs. They shot Quentin because he was threatening to expose them. The others never made it out of the embassy. They fell to their deaths into the crowd of Deathless they had waiting for us. Izliev refused to go. I watched as the motherfucker Warwick pushed her over the edge. The Deathless were on top of her instantly. Min and I could only watch helplessly as they ripped her to pieces.

"So Min and I ran. We managed to avoid the Deathless for a few days by hiding out in a nearby apartment block. We saw the chopper come and go, but knew there was no point in trying to get back with them. They would shoot us on sight. So we bunkered down and lived on scraps until we were forced to go out looking for water. It was a fluke really that we made it this far. We got lucky. All the Deathless were concentrated around the embassy so the highway from the city to here was deserted. We never saw another living soul. It wasn't easy. I've had to put down several of those things. It never gets any easier.

"This mall became our home. We had plenty of food and water, apart from the summers when it can get dicey. But it tends to rain a lot in this country so I guess we got lucky there too. We were like brother and sister. We knew there was no way back to our old lives and we came to depend on each other. Min was such an intelligent woman. She opened my eyes to a lot of things, but as the days became weeks, she struggled to adapt. This place is really just another prison. She couldn't face the prospect of living here forever, constantly on the lookout for the dead. I found a couple of guns in an SUV one day, but it wasn't enough to reassure her.

"In the end, she died of desperation. She refused to believe they wouldn't rescue her if she signalled for help. She went down to the coast and I followed her. I tried to stop her. I protested all the way, but it was useless. She had made her mind up. We found a quiet cove and she took a small rowboat out. I refused to go. I couldn't do it. She said that once she got home, she would send help for me. She got past the wire and the mines, but...they just shot her down. They tore the boat apart with her in it. I never saw her again. I was a coward. I should've done more to stop her."

They gave Roach time to compose himself. It had obviously been painful talking about it and he had broken down whilst talking about losing Min. Eventually, they questioned Roach further, probing him for answers and explanations. He was able to satisfy everything they threw at him. Finally, they began to realise he was telling the truth. Stunning though it was, it also explained why they had not seen or heard any sign of rescue. They were doomed to this island too.

"As for finding a cure, well that's a crock of shit. There is no cure. There never was and never will be. There are no scientists, not anymore. There were at first, but they were soon shut down. This place is a quick fix. Agnew can get together with his buddies, and anyone posing a problem is parachuted in here never to be seen of again. There's no mess to clean up afterwards. Agnew just feeds the media a story about how so-and-so is safely locked away in prison or has disappeared as fugitives, never to be seen again, and no one asks any difficult questions. Very handy. Agnew has got a lot of explaining to do.

"I must make sure this story gets out. What's happening here is wrong. This place was supposed to be a final resting place for the poor souls who will never know true death. Instead, Agnew's turned it into a bear-pit; a place to bury his problems where the living are fed to the dead." Roach pulled the covers up to his neck, indicating he had said enough.

Will noticed Claire and Tricia had fallen asleep whilst Mark and Kelly had slunk down beneath the covers, their eyes drooping. It had been a chilling story, one that would take them a while to fully process. Will needed to know one more thing before he could sleep and scurried out of bed over to Roach.

"Hey, Roach, just in case anything did get in here, do you have any weapons? Anything at all?"

Roach bent down and lifted up a black jacket exposing two hand pistols. "Fully loaded," he said, covering the guns back up. "Just in case."

Will nodded curtly and went back to his bed. He glanced over at Suzy who met his gaze.

"Good night," she mouthed to him, drawing the covers up to her chin. She shut her eyes and attempted to sleep.

"Night," Will mouthed back. He lay down and looked at Suzy a while before closing his eyes. She looked so sweet and peaceful. If what Roach had said was all true, and Will certainly believed it to be, then it was going to be even harder getting off The Grave than they thought. He tried to sleep and ignore the burning questions in his mind. How would they get to the embassy, how would they convince the soldiers to take them home, and how could he protect everyone when he had failed to protect Wilfred, Rasmus and Tug? Will hadn't forgotten than Josef was still out there, his body forever entombed in that cold house.

The night was quiet, but they slept restlessly, turning constantly, waking at every slight sound and fearful they had been discovered. Like everyone in the store that night, Will slept badly, worried about what tomorrow would bring.

* * *

Just after five the next morning, another quake shook the building. It caused a small jolt in the building and only Mark woke. He clung to his bed as the tremor passed and looked around. A little light came into the store from the open doorway to the mall and he could see everyone was asleep. Good for them, he thought, get it while you can. Mark had dreamt of Josef curled up in the cellar, the dead boy eating him. Sometimes he would replace Josef in his dreams and find the boy leering over him, ready to take a chunk out of his neck. He had been unable to stop the dreams coming, as if Josef was haunting him; reprimanding him for not helping.

Unable to sleep any longer, Mark got up, pulled on his free new sneakers, and decided to head out into the mall so he could use the bathroom. The regular bathrooms had long stopped working, but Roach had showed them an outlet pipe he used. It was an old air-conditioning duct that had collapsed along with the south side of the mall. Handily for Roach, the top end was sticking out into the mall whilst the lower end deposited its contents somewhere deep within the building's rubble.

On his way back to the others, Mark peered into a bank. It had been designed as open-plan and he could see all the way to the back. The tills were open, the desks upturned and chairs askew. Thousands and thousands of dollars littered the floor. Banknotes of various colours gave the floor an expensive looking rainbow carpet and he picked a note up. It was a green twenty dollar bill and he thought about taking it. It was useless now, just a memento of the trip really, a reminder of what this place used to be, a reminder of how the world was before the Deathless. Then he remembered that anything could be infected and hastily cast it aside where it fluttered to the floor soundlessly. What if someone had been infected and handled that note? Could you get infected that way? Was it like a germ that spread from one thing to another until it passed onto you? He didn't think so, but wiped his hands on his jeans nonetheless, and decided his photos were enough. He didn't need anything else to remind him of this place.

Mark casually sauntered back toward the furniture store. There was no real rush. They were safe and they had certainly needed the break. He looked up at the glass dome in the centre of the mall and noticed the rain had stopped. It actually might be a nice day; the sky was a light blue and the grey clouds of yesterday had gone. Yes, today was going to be a good day, he could tell. They had found help, shelter, food and water. New York all of a sudden didn't seem so far away. If they got picked up tonight, he could be sending his editor some shots tomorrow. Mark smiled to himself; things were looking up.

He reached the store and stopped in the doorway. He had heard a faint coughing and looked around to see who else was up. He saw Claire sat up in bed and he froze in horror. The hairs on the back of his neck bristled and he involuntarily shivered. Her duvet was covered in bright red blood and he watched her coughing again. She raised her hands to her mouth and blood flew through her fingers like water pouring through a sluice gate. Claire took in a lungful of air and spluttered again, showering her bed with more blood.

"Kelly, wake up! Wake up, it's Claire!" She was the first person Mark thought to wake. Her bed was closest and she would know what to do. He had no real first aid knowledge, nor knew much about Claire's history. For all he knew, she was glycaemic or allergic to certain medications. He admonished himself for not talking to her more. If he was going to report on this story, he should've spent more time talking with the others and a little less time behind the camera. He raced over as Kelly sat bolt upright, awoken by Mark's shouting.

Kelly looked at Claire and gasped in horror at the sight of the poor girl, so pale and white. "Claire, what…" As Claire's body heaved and racked with her uncontrollable coughing, Kelly thought that it was all over for her; that Claire was going to cough up a lung or something. She rubbed Claire's back and soothed her, telling her to calm down and that she would take care of her.

"I didn't mean to," Claire said painfully. She clutched her heaving chest. "Back at the farmhouse on that first night? I didn't even think about it. Oh God, why me? Before we went to bed, I had a drink of water from the bathroom tap. It was just habit. It tasted bad and I spat it out, but not before I'd swallowed a bit. Do you think it was polluted? Do you think…" Claire screwed up her face as pain wracked her body. She could not talk any more. Kelly kept rubbing her back, trying to calm Claire down.

By now, everyone was awake and alert. They had heard the shouting and everyone rushed to Claire's bedside. Even Roach had come over to investigate.

"Will, you don't think…" Suzy felt like her heart was going to burst through her chest. She couldn't believe Claire was going to die, not like this. It couldn't be real.

Will didn't know what to do. He grabbed Suzy's arm. "Suzy, what medicine did you give her last night?"

"Just a couple of paracetamol, nothing much. It can't be that, can it?" Suzy felt dizzy. Claire looked awful. Her hair was a straggly mess that clung to her sweaty forehead. Her skin was pale and the amount of blood on the bedspread was unreal. Surely, there had to be another explanation. "She was feeling better…she only had a cold, right?" Suzy looked up to Will for reassurance, but found none.

Will looked at Claire forlornly, feeling helpless. Claire was obviously in a lot of pain. He saw Claire brush her hands through her hair and a thick, matted clump of hair came away. Will watched on astonished as Suzy and everyone else just faded into the background.

Claire put her hands on her chest. "It feels like…having… heart…attack." She stuttered the words out between gritted teeth.

Kelly was trembling and she lost her grip on Claire who was writhing around, making it impossible to help her. Kelly tried to wipe the sweat from Claire's forehead. The skin was slimy and her pores were beginning to seep blood. Kelly withdrew her bloodied hand and wiped it on her side. "I know, honey. I'm here for you. It'll be okay, it'll be okay."

Suddenly, Claire sat bolt upright in the bed, her eyes bulging from their sockets. She cried tears of blood and then let out a blood-curdling scream. "Argh!"

Claire's scream echoed through the whole of the mall. She twisted in agony as if possessed by a demon and began ripping at her nightshirt, pulling it apart and scratching at her chest. The buttons popped as she pulled it apart, not caring that she was exposing herself. Claire tried to scream again, but could not make a sound. Blood spewed from her throat and she began convulsing. Her face turned to Kelly before her eyes rolled back in her head.

Kelly knew Claire was dying in absolute agony. She had drunk water infected with Aqua-Gene 119. She would never get home or see her mother and father again. Oh God, why like this, thought Kelly, why Claire? She was so young. Kelly had never imagined it would be like this. She knew a bite from the infected would turn you almost instantly, but this? This was horrible and she couldn't bear to watch.

Claire's fingers continued to dig into her soft breasts, ripping open her flesh as she tried to get to her black heart as it contracted and stopped pumping blood around her body. She scratched at her skin furiously, tearing away one of her nipples in the process, opening up the mottled skin there with her fingernails.

Kelly scrambled back on the floor as Claire spat out sticky, black blood and dark phlegm dribbled down her chin. Kelly felt guilty as she backed away, but she knew she couldn't afford to get any on her.

Claire's body slumped back in the bed. Her body had stopped moving completely and the silence that replaced her screams was as haunting as her death throes. A lingering foulness purveyed the air. The blanket of death had settled over the group again and they had been powerless to stop it. They had realised too late, what was happening. Claire was dead and another one of their group had left them.

There were sniffles and sobs around the bed as the reality of Claire's death sunk in. Mark stepped back, feeling ashamed, not feeling like he deserved to be around her now. If only he had noticed when he'd woken, perhaps he could have helped her, or at least warned the others that she was so sick. Tricia and Kelly were crying, Suzy too, her arms around Will.

They stared at Claire's lifeless body, too shocked to accept she was gone. Claire was dead.

A single click broke the silence and Roach stepped up to the foot of Claire's bed. "Move back, Kelly," he said raising the pistol. He pointed it straight at Claire's lifeless body.

Kelly jumped up, infuriated. "What the hell are you doing? Put that down."

"You know I can't. You heard her. She's infected. I'm sorry for you, sorry for her. She was so young, but we only have seconds here. Please, Kelly, move out of the way." Roach stood firm, holding his pistol in both hands. He tried to focus on Claire's head, but Kelly was in the way.

"No. We don't know for sure what happened. She was sick. It could be anything." Kelly sought for explanations, tried to think of something she could bargain Roach down with, but she was out of ideas. Roach was probably right, but he couldn't shoot Claire, not like this in front of all of them.

"You've got five seconds. Claire's already dead. I'm just making sure her body doesn't..." Roach looked Kelly in the eye and he knew she wasn't going to back down. He also knew he was right. Any moment now and it would be too late. He stepped forward. He *had* to do it.

Claire's lifeless body twitched and then suddenly she sat upright. The blood stained sheets fell from her shoulders. A quiet moan escaped her lips and rested in the silent air before it registered amongst the others in the room. Her blank face looked slowly around and settled on the nearest person: Kelly.

As Claire's hands stretched out, Roach roared and pushed Kelly aside. He fired the gun twice, putting two bullets in quick succession into Claire's mangled chest. In pushing Kelly away, he had lost his footing and not been able to get a clean head shot.

"Move!" he shouted, as Claire swung her legs out of bed, and she reached out for Roach. The bullets had not slowed her. They had torn through her dead body like paper.

Screams erupted in the store as Claire stumbled from her bed. The sheets wrapped around her gangly legs and she fell to the floor just as Roach fired again. His shot scraped her shoulder and whistled past Mark who was running for the exit.

"Where the fuck did she go?" shouted Roach as he jumped back and positioned himself behind an office chair. One bite, one scratch; that was all it took. He had lived here for years and in one night, he had lost it all. He had to take care of this quickly before it got out of hand.

"I can't see her," shouted Will, running to help Kelly up. He dragged her back behind a sofa where Suzy was cowering. He didn't want Claire shot, but he knew Roach was their only hope right now.

"What do we do?" said Kelly breathlessly.

Will peered above the sofa and looked around. He saw Mark standing by the exit. He saw Roach trailing his gun around the room, also looking for Claire. It occurred to him that he couldn't see Tricia. He bent back down. "Right, pull your boots on quickly, we have to get out of here. Any of you see where Tricia went?"

Claire had spotted her when she had stumbled to the floor. When Claire had passed, Tricia had not believed she would come back. Therefore, when Claire had sat up in the bed, clearly dead, Tricia had still refused to believe what she was seeing. She needed a moment to think, to rationalise what she was witnessing. As the chaos started, Tricia crouched down beneath the bed she had slept in last night and prayed. She ignored the crying and the gunshots, and prayed to God for Claire's soul, for help in delivering her into heaven, and for the safety of all of them. She prayed for every unfortunate being on this island that would never be able to rest. She prayed that she would make it home, to the familiarity of her own bedroom with its scented vanilla candles and simple furnishings. She prayed that one day, she would be back at the museum, helping Kelly with those late night shifts, diving deeper and deeper into the work she so loved. Please God, please, we need you now more than ever.

Then she felt the sting of the bite, as Claire's sharp teeth dug into her shoulder.

Tricia screamed in pain as Claire took a huge chunk of flesh and muscle from her shoulder. She tried to stand, but Claire had already wrapped her arms around Tricia's large frame and there was no escape. Those teeth powered down again, biting Tricia's shoulder, her neck, her arm, her hands and her face. The screaming finally stopped when Tricia fell unconscious. Claire had dragged herself on the floor to Tricia, unwittingly never giving Roach the chance to put her down.

Claire suddenly saw movement and dropped Tricia's lifeless body. She saw Mark standing in the doorway who was desperately trying to signal to the others where the escape route was, waving his camera above his head. Claire stood up and then a shot rang out, this time entering her bloody neck and showering the desk beside her with fresh gore. Unperturbed, Claire turned to see where the shot had come from and saw the bald head of Roach close by. She started shuffling toward him with Tricia's blood pouring from her mouth and dribbling down her bare torso.

"Roach, forget it, get out of there," shouted Will. He pushed Kelly and Suzy upward and over to Mark. He had seen Claire get up and heard Tricia's dying screams. They had to leave before things got any worse. He couldn't believe in the space of only four minutes that both Claire and Tricia had died.

"Roach!" he shouted again, hesitating as the women ran out of the store. He saw Roach firing wildly, missing Claire altogether. The gun barrel clicked empty and Claire was almost on top of him. "Forget it, just move!"

Finally, Roach looked up at Will and accepted his castle had been breached. There was no way of getting to his other gun or belongings now. He was going to have to leave everything behind. He pushed the swivel chair into Claire and skirted around the outside of the store, brushing past Will on his way out.

"Will, hurry!" Suzy clung onto Kelly, watching as Claire shuffled about and started heading for Will. Roach was too quick for her and almost out of the store entirely.

"Coming!" shouted Will as he grabbed his sneakers. He didn't want to make the long journey to the embassy barefoot. Claire was out of reach and he knew he would be long gone before her dead body navigated its way through the maze of beds, suites and desks to him.

Suzy watched as Will winked at her, jogging past the beds to join them. She watched as he stopped and glanced down. He let out a short cry of pain and kicked at something. Had he caught his trousers on something? Had he knocked his shins into one of the corners of the heavy wooden desks? "Will, come on, hurry up!" She saw him kick out again, twice, and then he seemed to wobble. It was as if he were drunk.

Will looked down at his watch: five thirty one. Ashen faced, he looked up at Suzy and his eyes widened. 'Suzy Q...' he mouthed silently. He raised his hand up as if to wave and then dropped it again.

Suzy's face went from confusion to disbelief to horror. Will looked as if he was going to pass out. Blood began to dribble from his mouth and he stumbled forward a few more feet before collapsing over onto the floor. Suzy watched as Tricia's reanimated body surfaced from behind the bed and staggered to its feet. Tricia was soaked in her own warm blood and her mouth was chewing on a lump of grisly, hairy skin. Suzy didn't need to see the bite marks on Will's ankle, nor the gaping hole Tricia had left above his fibula; she knew he was gone.

FOURTEEN

"No, no, no," said Suzy quietly as she went to go to Will's aid. It wasn't going to end like this. She had it wrong. Will was fine. He was just...

Mark grabbed Suzy just in time to stop her from running toward a certain death and he held her back. "We have to go, Suzy, we have to..." Shivers ran up and down his spine as he too saw Claire advancing upon Will. It was too late for him now. Tricia had apparently forgotten all about Will, and Mark saw her heading for the doorway. Suzy's screams had caught her attention.

A fountain of blood flew up into the air from Will's motionless body. A moment later, his body jerked and went into spasms. With Claire unable to get to him to feast, his dead body began to stir. He put his hands on a desk and pulled himself upward. Will unsteadily got to his feet and stood stock still, staring at Suzy. Claire caught up with him and bumped into his body, but ignored him and carried on to the others.

"Will! Will!" screamed Suzy. She was distraught and tears blurred her vision. She tried to fight Mark off, but he held onto her fiercely. "No, please God, no..."

Suzy began to collapse into Mark's embrace as she saw Will's dead body stagger toward her, his arms outstretched, his face tight and characterless, and all traces of affection and life gone. He had been bitten, infected, and killed. Then his body had risen again. It had taken almost thirty seconds in all, yet it had seemed to happen in the blink of an eye. Only a moment ago, she had been talking to him. Surely, he was joking.

Suzy felt Mark pulling her away. She didn't know what was happening. Tears were stinging her eyes and she couldn't hear what Mark was saying. Her feet tripped over books and clothes. Where was Will? Why had he left her? Why had he not looked after her? Mark's hands were cold. She wanted Will's hands and arms around her, and his lips on hers.

Suzy's mind raced, trying to piece it all together. Where was he? Dead? No! He can't be. Will, where are you? Why have you left me? Dead? Dead. Undead.

Kelly threw last night's meagre meal up over the floor of the shopping mall and blindly took Roach's hand. She didn't know where he was leading her, just that it was away from the carnage and the horror unfolding around her. She stumbled through the rubbish, tripping over empty boxes and numerous magazines, food cartons and clothes, while the plaintive moaning of her dead friends receded. She had no concept of time or the amount of time she had followed him. Only when the air grew colder did she look up to find they were down in the empty warehouse they had passed through last night. They had arrived there so quickly. Everything was a blur. Everything was fucked up. Roach was dangling a key chain in front of her. She wiped the tears from her eyes and concentrated on what he was saying. His face was set in a grimace.

"I'm going to say this for the last time. You have to decide *now* what you want to do. I can take us out of here, far away, to the city if you like, anywhere really. Or we can stay here – but we have to take care of your friends if you want to stay." Roach pulled a backpack out from behind a pillar that was hanging on a hook and took a gun out. He zipped the bag back up and clicked the safety off the gun.

"I kept it here in case of emergency. Thank God I did. Kelly, we have a narrow window of opportunity here. Now, what's it to be?"

Kelly couldn't decide. She heard sobbing to her left and looked at Suzy who was being cradled by Mark. He too had tears in his eyes. "Roach, I...I..."

"*Now, Kelly*. You have to decide." Roach had one hand on his gun, and another on the door handle that led outside into the alley.

"What about them? The dead...outside?" she muttered. "There's too many. We won't..."

Roach slowly shook his head. "They're gone. They never hang around long if there's nothing to eat. Something else would've gotten their attention by now. We can get past the stragglers."

Kelly winced. Now it felt like she was having a heart attack. She bent double and threw up again. There was no food to come out, just bile and bitter saliva. She dry retched and literally shook her head, spitting onto the grimy floor. Roach was right; she had to deal with this. She couldn't afford to fall apart now.

Roach continued, ignoring the smell of vomit and fear that pervaded the air he breathed. He had seen and smelt far worse on The Grave. "A noise elsewhere, a bird or a possum, anything, anything that gets their attention will draw them away. I've seen it countless times. There'll be a few for sure, some of the slower ones, but we can get past them if you want to go. If you want to stay here then..." Roach looked at her impatiently. "Well?"

Kelly looked at Mark and Suzy. They were silent now. Suzy had gone into a state of shock. Kelly didn't want to make this decision, but she had to. It was her responsibility. The full weight of the gravity of the situation hit her. They could run now, try to escape, and leave Claire, Tricia and Will's dead bodies forever wandering the empty corridors of the shopping mall. Alternatively, they could go back. Stock up and stay hidden in safety, away from whatever was outside. She had no doubt that this time, Roach would not miss. Now they were away from the confusion and chaos, he could take them down. All three would then be truly dead. She couldn't picture it though. Her friends were dead and gone. What kind of a choice was it to go back and put bullets in their heads, or to leave their soulless bodies marooned in a dirty shopping mall for eternity?

"We go. You take us to the embassy. We go, now." Kelly couldn't find a valid reason to go back. Why stay here any longer? Claire, Tricia and Will were already dead. Why stay and prolong the agony? Why not just go now? It was early and they could make the embassy in the daylight. She wanted to get home. She didn't care about the museum anymore, the expedition, or her home. She cared about the friends and colleagues she'd lost. She cared about someone paying for what had happened to them. She cared enough to want to live, and for the truth of The Grave to come out.

Who had called it that, The Grave? Were they being witty or clever? This place wasn't a grave. A grave was a quiet place of mourning, a place where you honoured the dead. This place, this horrible ruined cesspit was nothing but a stinking cancerous island of death; damn it to hell. Kelly felt the anger inside her welling up, overtaking the grief and demanding something to be done. They - she - had wasted too much time and lost too much.

It wasn't about her anymore. Kelly Munroe, Associate Director of the American Museum of Natural History, quit. She quit feeling second best, trying to prove her worth. She decided that right now, all that was over. Looking for love, looking for promotion, looking for something to better herself, to make her mark? No, Suzy and Mark needed her. *She* needed her. She was confident, strong, intelligent and better than this. She was a damn sight better than The Grave. Fuck The Grave. Fuck the Deathless. And fuck President Agnew for letting them rot here. Fuck him for having the audacity to play this game of chicken with death. She looked at her feet on the cold concrete of the warehouse, covered in her own vomit. Still scared? Kelly wanted off this island. She wanted Agnew to pay.

"Mark, Suzy, get up." Kelly hauled Mark up and took hold of his shoulders. "It's up to us now. We are not dying here. We're leaving now. There's nothing more we can do for them. There's nothing to be gained by staying any longer." She leaned in closer and spoke in a hushed voice. "Look out for Suzy. She's going to be hit hard by this. I need to know you're with me, Mark."

He nodded and Kelly turned to Roach who had already opened the door. He was peering out into the gloomy alley. It was covered in puddles, but the dead had gone. Drawn by something else, the alley was clear. It smelt of stagnant water, yet the air was cool and crisp. The storm had abated and the early morning sun was casting shadows down the long alley.

"Roach, you said you could help us. So, what have you got?"

Roach dropped his pack and began taking out the items, recounting them as he did so. "A hatchet, two pig-hunting knives, one more gun, two cartridges of ammo, three cans of food, one bottle of water, one torch with spare batteries, and some matches."

Kelly picked up the hatchet and spare gun. "I'll take these. I've done a little target practice in my time." She handed one of the knives to Mark. "Take this, Mark, you're going to need it." Kelly then picked up the other knife and strode over to Suzy. "Take it."

Suzy looked down at the knife and then up at Kelly. Her arms hung limply by her side. She shook her head. "I can't. I can't do this...I..."

Kelly slapped her across the face. Not too hard, but enough to know she meant business. Kelly held the knife out again. "*Take it*." She grabbed Suzy's arm and firmly put the knife in her hand, so Suzy had no option, other than to take hold of it. "Cry all you want later, Suzy, but today we're going home. I'll be *damned* if we're going to be left behind to rot on this island. So get your shit together, and move it."

Startled, Suzy followed Kelly to the doorway. Her cheek fizzed where Kelly had slapped her and she could feel it reddening. She began to move instinctively, not really knowing or caring where they were headed. Her lips could still taste the salty kiss she had shared with Will two days ago. Dead. Why had she run from that kiss they had shared that night? She had not stopped to think about it before, but now that she did, she knew why. She had been scared. She had kissed men before, but Will was different. Kissing him was like kissing someone she had known for a thousand years. It had been exciting and reliable, sexy and comfortable, all at the same time. She had known he was her future then. Will. Was he not running after them now? He was pretending, wasn't he? He just wanted to make sure the others got out safely. Any minute, he would come loping through that doorway, his big grin making her stomach turn as it always did. Suzy looked back at the open doorway to the mall behind her looking for Will. He didn't appear. The mall was absent of life now. She waited, but Will did not come.

Roach had thrown his pack on and held the door open. "Ready?"

Kelly glanced at Mark and Suzy. She felt so many things, so many emotions trying to control her head that it was hard to block them all out, but the over-riding sensation she felt now was anger. Will had been right when he'd said there was no rescue coming for them. They had been left to die. Her eyes blazed, determined that not one more soul would die here, not while she was still around. "What are you waiting for? Let's get out there."

In the shadows of the alley, Roach crept along with his back to the wall and his gun pointed to the ground. His feet splashed through dirty pools of water and he took a breath. He hoped the streets were truly clear of the dead, because he did not want to go back inside the mall. It had been his home for about four years, but it was gone now. Yes, he could go back and make it home again, but what for? To live a subsistence diet alone until one of the Deathless finally found their way in and killed him in his sleep? No, that was no life. This was his chance. Perhaps these people would make it off The Grave and perhaps he could go with them. It was a chance worth taking.

Roach peered carefully around the edge of the building. The street was clear. The shops and stores that flanked the open road were empty and quiet. He stepped quickly into the street and looked back at Kelly, nodding for her to follow. Suzy and Mark followed her, their eyes wide and white, betraying their fear. Roach could not blame them. They didn't know these streets like he did. Their friends had died and they expected to die too.

"Just stay close behind me and try not to make any sound," whispered Roach. "We might encounter one or two drifters, but don't engage them unless you have to. We can outrun them and there's no point wasting ammo. I expect whatever has drawn them all away is either in some other building or back up in the hills. I don't tend to get crowds like last night around much. I can have us on the highway toward the city in five minutes. So keep your eyes open and your heads down. When we're in the clear, I'll let you know and you can breathe out."

Roach tightened his backpack and took off. He could hear the footsteps of the other three behind him as he skirted off around the corner of an old post office. He knew precisely where to go, and as long as the Deathless were occupied elsewhere, they were going to be fine. At least until they reached the capital.

Mark tried to ignore the fear that was threatening to burst out of his guts. They were out in the open now, on the very same roads where only last night, he had seen countless of the dead. He passed the doorway where he had seen the woman's stomach explode and he couldn't help but glance at the putrid bloody stain on the pavement. Roach had better be right about this and know where he was going. Mark leant against a shop window full of nude mannequins, waiting as Roach checked the next street. Mark looked around, desperately hoping they were alone. Then he saw movement back where they had come from in the alley. He watched as a figure emerged into the thin sunlight, stumbling and groaning. The head was hanging to one side as if straining to hear something. Mark looked closer at the tall man. It was Will.

Mark squeezed the knife in his hands. Will had died, hadn't he? It couldn't be. A bubble of hope sprang up inside Mark's brain. Roach hadn't locked the door after they'd left the mall. Maybe Will had made it out? Mark stood up and opened his mouth to call out, to let Will know where they were.

"W..." Mark didn't bother finishing the first word out of his mouth. The bubble burst. It was Will, but it wasn't him; not the real Will. This thing was dead. There was no soul behind the glassy eyes. Mark wanted to hit something, shout, jump up and down, and scream until his throat was sore. It wasn't fair. Will was looking straight at him now.

Mark looked away. Roach was moving on, Kelly and Suzy too. Mark knew Will was trying to follow, but he had to forget him. Nothing could be done for him now. Mark knew if he looked back, he was likely to see Tricia and Claire too. He couldn't face it, the thought of seeing them standing like that, so ghastly and ghoulish, blood covering them. No, he knew he would be seeing them in his future nightmares and he didn't need to see them now.

Mark ran after the others, not telling them what he had seen. It was better that they didn't know. He ran as fast as it took to keep up with them, ignoring where they were going and what they passed. Every second on the island was a second closer to death. He didn't want to be a part of The Grave. He ran away from Will, away from death, away from all he had seen; he ran for his future.

FIFTEEN

Cars, bicycles, dead bodies and mountains of garbage lined the streets. They passed burnt out buildings, petrol stations that had been reduced to rubble, and charred pits in the earth where something or *things* had been torched. The sun was behind them, warming their backs. With a mixture of fear and adrenalin, sorrow and regret, hope and courage, they managed to wind their way through the deserted streets without encountering any of the Deathless. After a little over five minutes, the road flattened out and they were on an off-ramp to the main highway that led directly to the capital of this old island. The homes and shops gradually disappeared, only showing themselves in the near distance between the thick bushes and tall grass.

Roach took them across the flyover and down the ramp onto the four-lane highway that stretched out ahead of them. "You can breathe now," he said putting his gun into his belt. "We should be okay for a while now. It's going to take us a few hours to get to the city from here. With the sun, it's going to be slow, hot work too. I'm not saying we can relax completely, but if any of them are around, we'll have ample time to see them coming. Now, we just follow the yellow brick road."

Kelly muttered thanks to Roach and kept the gun in her hand ready. She didn't want to be caught unprepared again. She let Roach take the lead for now, but if the road did indeed take them to the city, she wasn't going to have to follow him all the way. She had let him take them this far and in truth, it was probably further than they would have gotten had he not been around. She looked over at Suzy who was complying with everything. There was still a faint red mark on her cheek the size of Kelly's hand and the guilt stung her. Kelly threw the guilt off her shoulder quickly. Suzy could deal with it. Right now, they had to keep moving.

"Suzy, Mark, stay behind me and Roach and watch your backs. No more surprises, please." Kelly pulled her shirt out of her jeans and let the cool air sweep up her body. She wished she could wash the smell of death away, but for now, knew it was going to linger over her, probably for a very long time.

She noticed the road was flanked on both sides by vast expanses of green; Taraire and Matai rubbed rough shoulders with Nikau trees above thick Kohekohe, whilst lower to the ground, she saw Spinnifex and the unmistakable orange flowers of the Turepo. There was a certain admiration for how nature was reclaiming this land. Whilst they walked, she thought she spotted a Poroporo shrub with just a hint of some budding yellow berries; something she thought had been wiped out many years ago. It was impressive how quickly the land was being taken back. The edges of the road were slowly being covered; the low-lying bushes and plants, weeds and grass trying to find cracks in the tarmac. Of course, once she got back to New York, she would do everything in her power to make sure the island was destroyed. She would bring a firestorm down on this island and kill everything on it. What good was it now? She had been wrong when she'd told Mark the Deathless had a right to exist; there was no purpose to them. They weren't animals. They weren't people like Suzy thought either. They were death. At least a shark or a snake only killed to feed. A shark had an impulse to live, mate and have young. What part did the dead play in the circle of life? None, except to end it.

An hour passed and the road began to creep uphill rising over undulating hills and sweeping through fields of overgrown vegetation. The ocean had disappeared from sight altogether. They walked past a variety of vehicles: driverless trucks, smashed cars, pickups and delivery vans. All abandoned, all useless. Occasionally, Kelly would peer through a window or a door, but there was nothing inside. She didn't need a map or a cigarette, so she kept walking. Only once did she reach inside a battered old station wagon and take a Blackberry off the passenger side seat. Any hope of getting a signal was dashed when she realised there was no power left. The battery was dead, just like the batteries in all the vehicles that cluttered the highway.

Roach had stayed up front. He never spoke and he began to tire after an hour of walking in the sun. Kelly strode on ahead of him. She was determined not to falter and told him not to lag too far behind as she passed him. He acknowledged her with a brief nod.

Suzy followed at a constant six feet behind Kelly. Nobody spoke to her, and she spoke to nobody. That was how she wanted it right now. She felt better not having to talk and was pleased they were leaving her alone. She had so much to consider, and so much to solve in her mind that, any attempt at conversation with her would have been pointless. She could barely put one foot in front of the other. She walked and she thought. She thought and she walked.

Mark purposefully hung back as Roach slowed. He wanted to speak to him while he could. He had no idea what to say to either Kelly or Suzy now, so he used the opportunity to pick Roach's mind. "You think they've gone? The Deathless?"

Roach shook his head. "They're out there somewhere. Just far enough away from us for now. Let's not tempt fate. I'd rather talk about something else, if you don't mind."

"Sure, sure...so...how did you survive? I mean, really, did you spend the whole time in that mall with...Min was it?"

"Well, not at first. Min and I moved from house to house. After we got out of the city, we ransacked a garden centre and found plenty to defend ourselves with; shovels, pitchforks, crowbars...eventually though we lost them. They either got embedded in some poor sap's skull or we dropped them when we had to run. The mall was sheer luck. We didn't plan too far ahead. We were barely getting by day to day. Min wasn't around for too long with me anyhow. After I lost her, I just decided the best thing to do was see it out. I set up home there, made it as secure as I could and stayed put. You can get by without much food when you have to. You get used to it. The only thing I truly missed was my family. Of course, I still do, but I expect they've moved on. My wife and son will have been fed the same lies as everyone else. I'm a murderer, a terrorist and an anarchist. I hope they were able to move on and Agnew left them alone. I hope..."

A faint squawk came from above and Mark looked up just in time to see an eagle swoop up from a field adjacent to them. The bird's wingspan looked as if it easily reached six feet and in its grasp was a hare, struggling to free itself from the bird's sharp talons. Mark whipped out his camera and took as many shots of the titanic struggle as he could.

Kelly saw it too. The hare was twice as big as it should have been. The eagle was powerful, but it was losing the battle to carry the weight of the hapless creature up into the air. The eagle managed to get twenty feet up before it dropped the doomed hare. Kelly winced as she heard the whump of the body hitting the ground. The animals were growing larger too, as was the island's flora. Whether it was because man had left, or because of the Aqua-Gene, she wasn't sure. She also wasn't sure she cared anymore. She turned and carried on down the road toward the city.

Roach watched Mark sling his camera around to his back. Once the hare had been dropped, the eagle swooped down behind the bushes and they could see no more. What would have been a marvellous spectacle on another trip was now just a passing curiosity. Their focus was on other things - like survival. They resumed walking and Roach carried on talking.

"Where we're going...you know in reality, there are no boxes of food. The complex is there and once a month the helicopter lands so four or five well-armed soldiers can get out. But they are not off-loading food and water. There are no scientists there. There are no living people on The Grave. No, the cargo is much more than just a few crates of supplies. I should know because I was once dumped here.

"The military comes in under the guise of releasing prisoners. In reality, they are escorting people to their death. I saw them on our second day here. Min and I were barricaded in an apartment and we watched them. The chopper landed on the embassy rooftop and I counted six men before the helicopter left. The men were dressed in plain dark clothes. One had shackles around his ankles and his wrists were handcuffed. As the helicopter left, the six men waved at it, shouting for it to return. I heard them begging and pleading not to be left here, but the soldiers either didn't hear them, or more likely, chose to ignore them. The chopper hovered in the air and then the six men were shot where they stood. The soldiers were just taking pot shots at them, like target practise. Two of the men scrambled down into the yard, but the Deathless were there waiting for them. I suppose I should be thankful that I was given a chance. The soldiers don't care what happens. They know there's no retribution for them.

"Look, Mark, I have not exaggerated anything or been untruthful. I have to tell you the whole truth so you are ready. When we get to the city, you'll see there's no base, no experiments, no scientists; nothing. The embassy story is a trick. You understand, we can't risk flagging the military down. Min tried that and they didn't hesitate. Shoot first and ask questions later; that's the way it is. We have to get to the embassy and ambush them. *Force* them to take us back. When you're on that chopper, make sure you get your story out before you get back to the naval ship. If they get hold of you, they'll just bury it. Don't let them cover this up."

Mark rested a hand on Roach's shoulder and they stopped walking. "Not to be morbid, but I want proof and if you don't make it...at least I'll have documented this. I need a picture of you here, with us. I'll have cast iron proof then that you're not living it up in South America, but stranded here. It might not be enough to convince everyone, but it should get questions asked and will put Agnew under pressure. The Grave will be re-examined and then the truth will come out. He's finished. We owe it to everyone who has died here."

Roach nodded and stood as Mark took a photo of him. In the background was a sign indicating Wellington City was ahead. Mark then stood next to Roach and held his camera at length, taking a photo of both of them. When Mark was done, Roach held out his hand and Mark shook it.

"Thank you. Thank you for believing me."

"Come on," said Mark, "Let's get a move on. We've a helicopter to catch."

They picked up the pace and caught up with Suzy and Kelly. The road just seemed to go on and on. The elements had crumbled the tarmac and frequent deep cracks appeared, splitting up the road markings. Weeds grew in the cracks and between slits in the walls of nearby buildings. A black cumbersome rat squeezed out from underneath a red and yellow courier van. Its body was matted with jet black hair and its pink tail left a greasy trail of slime as the rat waddled across the street. Its entire left side had rotted away, exposing its small ribcage. It moved slowly, inelegantly, dragging its bloated body on weak legs over the asphalt toward Kelly. It had heard them coming and ventured out from its resting place. The rat was dead, but its teeth still sharp and its jaw raised and ready to bite them.

Kelly swung her hatchet down on the rat's head and the iron blade crushed its tiny brain on the tarmac. Fragile bones and blood squirted out over the road and Kelly swung again, making sure the rat was dead. She carried on walking, leaving the kill on the road behind her. Suzy, Mark and Roach skipped around the mess, leaving the rat's decomposing, fetid carcass to fester in the heat. Nobody said a word about it.

Kelly was forced to walk along the side of the road, closer to the vegetation to avoid a multiple car crash. Between two tall Nikau palms stood a large leafy tree with tiny clutches of yellow seedpods hanging off the low branches, looking like the swollen fingers of a baby. Kelly shuddered as she walked beneath them, trying to shut out the image. Every time a pod brushed against her hair, she would imagine a dead child above trying to grab at her, its pudgy fingers wispily sweeping through her greasy hair. The part of her brain that knew it was a member of the Kowhai family had switched off. Now every bush, every tree and every blade of grass was an enemy. She could not trust anything she saw. A pool of water, a fallen apple, a bird, a rat, everything and anything might be contaminated with the Aqua-Gene. It had tricked them all. Claire had succumbed, and with it, death had taken Tricia and Will.

Kelly looked over at Suzy. She was morose. Her eyes were vacant, looking around but seeing nothing. Kelly daren't say anything or touch her for fear of setting her off. It was better to let her grieve in peace for a while. She had stopped crying, but she looked pathetic. Her eyes were bloodshot and her smooth cheeks carried the tracks of her tears, staining her smooth skin with the raw emotion of death. Her arms swung loosely as if controlled by the breeze. She almost looked like one of the Deathless.

What could Kelly say? She knew what Suzy was feeling. Will had been one of them. She had thought he would be around forever. Everyone at the museum loved him. She remembered how he had bumbled his way through the job interview. Yet, she had taken a chance on him and boy had he impressed her. The more

Kelly thought about it, the more she wondered if she did know how Suzy felt. Suzy and Will were close; closer than anyone else on this trip was. Kelly had lost a colleague, and yes, a friend. However, Suzy had lost something more than that. Other than her parents, Kelly had never gotten close to anyone else and had never really experienced the death of a loved one or a lover. She glanced over at Mark, but he was lost in his own thoughts. Kelly really didn't know what to say anyway. She couldn't put herself in Suzy's shoes and decided it was best to let Suzy deal with it in her own way. If she wanted to talk, she would.

Their feet walked in rhythm like a military procession. Kelly and Suzy, Mark and Roach, all striding down the highway toward the city, side by side as if in a funeral procession. The air was hot, musky, and smelt of the sea. Kelly noticed the hillside to their left was steep and covered in gorse, and to the right just more decayed houses. She knew over the hill lay the open expanse of the ocean. She wished they could just sail away, as Mark had suggested, but she knew it was impossible. If Roach was being honest, then Min had tried and she had paid the price. The land and the ocean were separated by a thick chain-link fence that muzzled the sun and kept a harsh, mesh screen between the island's inhabitants and freedom.

They passed a slip road and Kelly felt the ground become soft and spongy. Her sneakers were soaking in water and she skipped off the grass back onto the road. There was a large overflowing pond, covered in scum and flies. Whether it was a natural pond or merely the result of a blocked drain she couldn't tell, but a creek ran away to the east, the water sluggish and dirty. Skeletal arms, femurs and scraps of undeterminable organic matter broke the surface of the pond. Human arms and legs poked above the surface, breaking through the algae and flotsam. Kelly gasped as she saw movement. A hand reached up from the long grass nearby.

"Shit," said Mark racing ahead of Kelly brandishing his knife. Nothing raced out of the undergrowth though, so he slowly crept forward to see what it was. Kelly, Suzy and Roach were right behind him.

A woman, her body almost entirely obscured form the road by the tall grass, was pinned to the ground by a road sign. A rusted metal pole with a circular head showing the number eighty protruded from the dead woman's abdomen. Unable to get up, the Deathless woman had lain there for years. Someone had deliberately left it there, deliberately skewering the woman to the ground. The body had wasted away and the skin had peeled back from its face. The woman's jaw was twitching, teeth clacking together as they stepped closer.

"Jesus," whispered Mark. The woman's arms and legs flailed uselessly and she looked like an upturned beetle trying to get on its legs again. The ravaged fingers clawed at the ground and even its own guts to get free, but the dead woman was too weak.

"Look at the bird feathers and bones around its neck. I guess it must have eaten anything that got too inquisitive." Kelly had overcome her shock and stood beside Mark. "Leave it. Take it as a warning to watch your step. All of you."

As Kelly and Roach walked off down the road, Suzy peered over Mark's shoulder and turned her nose up at the foulness permeating the air. "I hope she was dead before she got stuck with that sign in her guts," she said coldly.

Mark left the woman as he'd found her, just another husk littering the roadside. He had to believe she had already turned before she was trapped in the ground like that. Self-defence; that was all it had been. He had been to many dangerous parts of the world and seen some terrible things, and this was right up there with the worst of them.

Suzy waited, staring into the murky water as the others walked on ahead. She fumbled in her pockets and pulled out a small plastic bottle. She unclicked the cap and threw two of the paracetamol into her mouth, remembering how she had given some to Claire last night. There were still four left and she rattled them around their lonely container. Suzy looked around, making sure the others were not watching her and then bent down, scooping the plastic tub through the infected pond water. She sloshed it around, letting the bloody water and Aqua-Gene soak into the tablets. Then she drained the water out, replaced the cap, and shoved it back into her pocket.

Suzy smiled as she hurried to catch the others up. No one else would understand. Nobody needed to know. She had felt so helpless watching Will die. Now she felt bolder. She fingered the rattling tub in her jacket pocket, making sure it was tucked down deep. When she got back to New York, she planned on meeting up with President Agnew. One way or another, he deserved a little present for what he'd done to them, her and to Will.

As they made their way onward, the road edged uphill slightly. Mark looked across to the west as they rounded a bend and the houses that had grown to be such a familiar sight receded. Fertile pasture gave way to a muddy patch of land where nothing grew. Almost a straight line had been carved into the earth dividing the two. On one side, the grass was thick and dark green, growing freely and in abundance. He thought he could see patches of colour where roses grew and ferns reached up from the rich soil. On the other side of the line, a barren stretch ran for miles, utterly devoid of life as far as he could see. It was littered with the bones of the weak and the dead. Aphids and musk-flies danced deliriously over the ruinous, desolate graveyard. The atrophied land was cold and dark despite the glorious sunshine overhead.

"What is that?" said Mark to Kelly as they walked. She pointed at the line in the earth.

"You really want to know?" Kelly kicked a gigantic beetle off her shoe that had crept up unnoticed. It could be infected and she couldn't take any chances. She ground it beneath her feet leaving nothing but a black sticky splodge on the tarmac and two feebly twitching antennae.

Mark nodded and Kelly explained. "This is one of those places I read about, I'm sure of it. Before The Grave became what it is today, the infected were put down. There was no cure, no way of dealing with them, and no one else wanted them. So they were...executed is the best word, I guess. A hundred thousand people had been slain in the first week and they were buried in massive pits outside the city's boundaries. They just scooped them up, dropped them in, and covered them up. There were rumours that some of the Deathless were put in the pits as they were. Just rounded up and buried alive. Now the land is as dead as the people buried beneath it are. Nothing grows on it, not a tree, a plant; not even a solitary weed. Technically, there's no reason why the ground shouldn't be able to support life."

"It's in mourning," said Suzy. "If you ask me the earth knows of the dead in its bowels and the terrible things that went on here. I doubt anything will ever grow there again. Who knows how many people are buried beneath the surface. Their bones and tissue would've meshed with the dirt now, making it soiled, barren, and infected. Even the weeds that sprouted there have died. You can't even see moss growing on the rocks. Nothing could take purchase in such poisonous *filth*." Suzy spat out the last word, as if the earth's very presence offended her.

Kelly was as surprised at Suzy's outburst as much as the fact she was speaking at all. "That's one version certainly. But even weeds need something viable to put their roots into. Maybe the ground was already barren and cannot stimulate or support growth. The soil might have been disturbed and just lost its minerals and nutrients. Don't dwell on it, Suzy. We should keep moving."

"Have you taken everything in, really?" Suzy stared straight ahead as she spoke. "The wild weather, the houses that are just derelict shells now, homes and belongings forgotten, photos and family heirlooms left behind in the rush to leave. The Grave has claimed everything. It has assumed an identity of its own now. I think it has an aura of death and devastation. There is a strange conflict going on, I'll give you that. There is bountiful vegetation in places and certainly, some exotic plants are thriving. Yet alongside this, all evidence that man once lived here is dying. Only corpses and death remain. The Grave pulls you in, doesn't it? You try and you try but you can't escape." Suzy saw Will in her mind, spewing blood, and walked away.

Mark felt hollow. Suzy had cut right through the bullshit. The Grave was pulling them all in, slowly and inexorably. "We're going to die here, aren't we." He didn't mean it as a genuine question; he was just thinking aloud.

"Fuck that," said Kelly, turning away from the desolate vista and resuming her path toward the city. "Suzy has her own issues right now, but don't fall apart on me too, Mark."

He hurried to keep up with Kelly, keeping Suzy and Roach in sight just up ahead. He admired Kelly's spirit, even though he was finding it hard to find that same resolution to keep going.

Kelly wiped the sweat from her face. The heat was becoming unbearable. There was no breeze or wind to offer any respite, no shade from the intense sun. "You ever head of the Brugmansia flower? It has beautiful, fragrant flowers, yet it is also very toxic. You wouldn't know it to look at it, but it contains hyoscyamine, potentially lethal to animal life. You eat some of the leaves and you are going to be ill. You might feel like dying, you might *want* to die, but it's not a given. There is no certainty, Mark. You can live. We can live. Understand? But you have to want it. Suzy is suffering right now, but she'll pull through. She can't see much of a future I suppose. She's thinking about the here and now. But I'm not giving up. The Grave hasn't beaten us yet."

As the sun beat down on them, they passed more signs for the city's suburbs and the heat began to take its toll. They had exhausted their limited water supply and the walk became monotonous and dreary. They had not seen any sign of life since passing the woman pinned down by the road sign a few miles back. There were no Deathless, no birds, no bugs, nothing, and even the vegetation was thinning out. Tall trees and thick bushes were replaced by low-lying scrub and weeds. The heat was merciless and their pace slowed without intention. Resolute, they trudged on. The city was still not in sight. Occasional rusted signs told them they were headed in the right direction, but the highway was slow going. The heat bounced off the hot tarmac and they frequently had to navigate their way past crashed cars and broken down trucks.

Roach began to wonder if Stella would welcome him home. They had been married for ten years before he had been whisked away from her by Agnew's men that terrible night. Had she believed the lies? Had Agnew convinced her that her husband had been a terrorist who had fled the country, sullying the family name and abandoning his family? Of his son, Bobby, he couldn't begin to think how it had affected him. He had grown up without a father. If he came face to face with him again, would they even recognise each other now? Roach knew he had a lot of bridges to mend when he got home. As much as he wanted to face Agnew, Roach knew he could leave the others to get the truth out about him, he didn't doubt that. Only he could try to repair his relationship with his family.

Kelly, Suzy and Mark tried to ignore the oppressive air by entertaining themselves with their own thoughts.

Mark kept planning his story and how he was going to break the news to the world that The Grave was not what they thought it was; that their president was at the heart of this rotten corrupted fabrication.

Kelly tried not to plan too far ahead. If Roach was telling them the truth, then Agnew had to pay. Everyone who collaborated with him to cover this up should pay. The truth *had* to get out. She began thinking about what they would do when they reached the embassy. Would they find countless undead blocking their way to safety or would luck be on their side for once? Would they manage to get to the helicopter or would they be shot down in cold blood by a ruthless military? She tried to picture herself back in New York and she couldn't do it. All she could picture was her dead friends and colleagues, Tricia and Will in particular. She would fight with her last breath to get off this island. There had been enough dying in the last couple of days.

Suzy wallowed in pity, not looking for sympathy, but unable to lift her thoughts above the gloom of seeing Will dead. How could she have a future without him? His death had been so pointless. She could tell Kelly was on a mission now, a crusade to avenge his death and all the deaths their expedition had suffered. Kelly was stronger than she was, no doubt about it. Suzy had always considered herself strong and tough. She told everyone she had been raised by her streetwise brothers in Brooklyn and whilst that was true, she really used it as a cover story to hide how scared she felt sometimes. Now look at her; the truth was that when the shit hit the fan, she crumbled. She hadn't had to deal with death in a long time. Her grandmother had passed when she was small, and since then, she had managed to avoid it. No friends or family had passed, and she had certainly never lost a loved one before. Her relationship with Will was in its infancy, but she knew it was headed for long term. He had been special and now when she remembered that kiss they had shared, it was tainted with the image of his dead body walking toward her.

Maybe Kelly was right. She knew she had to get back and expose Agnew. However, right now, she didn't have the energy for anything. Not even tears. One minute at a time. One day after another. Eventually, something would figure itself out. She fingered the small plastic bottle in her pocket. She would just wait.

SIXTEEN

A smell of rotting flesh wafted over the gentle breeze and made Mark's eyes water. He held his hand over his mouth. "Where is *that* coming from?"

They had recently passed a turnoff to a place called Johnsonville and the road was veering on a downward gradient, still winding through green hills adorned with houses. Power lines ran along the length of the road and there were assorted bird's nests clogging the now defunct wires. In the middle of the road up ahead were several abandoned diggers and trucks forming a roadblock. A swarm of flies like a dirty cloud hung low over them. The air was thick, hot and stifling.

The smell of meat clung to their sweaty, sticky skin. They all put their hands over their mouths and noses, trying to avoid the nasty smell as it enveloped them. As they passed the roadblock, the direction of the wind changed and the smell dissipated. They paused to look back but they all wished they hadn't.

A pile of bodies was in the centre of the road, hidden behind the excavation trucks. It was at least fifty deep and spilled out to the far side of the road, over the median strip and into grassland beyond. There was no way to tell if the pile of bodies had been amassed with any clear intention in mind and it was impossible to see if the people had been eaten or killed.

"Do you think they were infected?" asked Mark.

"I'd forgotten about this," said Roach. "It was so many years ago. I passed this on my way out of the city. I've no idea if they were killed before they turned or not. I didn't take much interest. It doesn't matter now, I suppose."

"We should move on quickly. Dead bodies can carry a lot of diseases we really don't want to be exposed to." Kelly trudged on, leading them all away from the pile of rancid, decomposing bodies.

Five minutes later and Kelly paused. There was a small building ahead, an old warehouse of some sort. The frontage was made of glass and she could see inside to the empty reception. They had been walking for several hours and needed a break. She was so hot that she could feel beads of sweat trickling down her back. She walked over to the open door and stepped inside. The air was dusty, but cool.

"Good idea," said Roach. "We need a pit stop. This heat is getting a bit much."

Roach and Mark shuffled into the reception behind Kelly, and Suzy closed the door behind them. The room had a desk and a plastic plant, a road map of the island on the wall and a calendar that had faded from prolonged exposure to the sunlight. Its corners were curling up and it was coated in a fine layer of dust. The building was shaded and secure, and they slumped to the floor, grateful to have some respite from the sun.

"It must be nearly midday," said Mark squinting up through the window to the sun high above. "How much farther, Roach?"

Roach drew in a long breath and whistled it out. "An hour? Two? We're almost there. It just depends on whether we get a clear run." Roach took his backpack off, the sweat having soaked through his shirt to the pack, and he let it cool off. He took the three cans of food he had with him and pulled back the ring-pulls before offering them around. He shared his with Mark, whilst Kelly and Suzy ate one apiece. "I'm afraid that cold beans are all I have left, but it will give us some energy."

"Shame there's nothing to drink," said Mark, wiping away the last of the beans from the bottom of the can. As they sat there, Mark unhooked his camera strap and took a shot of the room, Kelly and Suzy sitting on the floor, and Roach fiddling with the backpack.

"What the hell, Mark?" Kelly flung her empty can at him and he ducked as it ricocheted off the door and rolled away.

"What? If I'm going to report on what's happening here, it's going to be warts and all. This right here is real and people are going to want to see it. I'm just capturing what I see."

"I know you've been to Bosnia, Somalia, whatever, but this is not a photo shoot anymore, get it? This expedition that we brought you on is not exactly going well, is it? You might want to lay off the photos. I'm sick of it."

Mark clicked the lens cover back on and let the camera hang around his neck. He knew Kelly had a point. "Yeah, okay, I get it. I can't help it. I just see everything through a lens."

"Mark, I think you've got everything you need. It's time you dumped the camera. You really think the military are going to let you bring it back with you?" Roach stared into his backpack. The food and water was gone. The weapons in their hands and a torch were now the only things left.

"Heck, I'm not giving this up, not with what I've got on here," said Mark. He looked around the room and he was met with icy stares. Even Suzy had perked up and was looking at him disdainfully. "Fine, fine, here look." Mark popped open the casing to the memory card, took it out, and snapped it firmly into a clear casing. He held it out for everyone to see and then tucked it into his lapel pocket, buttoning it down, once it was securely inside. "This is a record of everything we've been through, everything we've seen. I guess you're right. I can't see me hopping onto that chopper and taking this back with me." He looked at his camera and threw it over the desk out of sight. "Feels weird not having a camera around my neck. I feel...naked almost."

"You did the right thing," said Kelly appreciatively.

"You have any family, Mark? Anyone waiting back home for you?" asked Roach.

"Well, I've a flatmate, but there's really only Inca. My parents died a few years back and I never had any brothers or sisters. A few friends sure, and people at work I hang out with when I'm not out in the field, but nobody special. Heck, I'm not ready to settle down yet." Mark felt like he was being apologetic, as if it was terrible he didn't have anyone close. He just hadn't met anyone yet and he knew he had plenty of time.

"Who's Inca?" said Kelly absently, drawing a line in the dust on the floor with her finger.

Mark smiled. "She's my best friend. A spaniel I picked up from the pound a couple of years back. My flatmate looks after her when I'm away."

Kelly listened as Mark and Roach chatted some more, but wasn't really taking much notice. She knew they weren't going to get away from The Grave easily and idle chit-chat wasn't taking her mind off it. It seemed to be helping Suzy though, who was starting to re-join the group and leave her sombre mood behind.

Kelly felt the weakness slipping over her again, and couldn't let it take her, not like it had Suzy. She dug up anger from inside her, something that would spur her on. She thought back to yesterday and the hatred she had felt for Will when he let Tug go. She had blamed him in that moment for everything, but it wasn't his fault. Looking back, she knew the second Tug had been attacked that he was dead. Will had saved her. If she had run out to help Tug, she would be dead too, or worse, shuffling around undead. Will deserved better than being left like that: Roach, Claire and Tricia too, in fact all of them. Kelly had taken the opportunity to leave and it had been mostly through self-preservation and fear. She wanted to run. She wanted to get as far away from that tomb as possible. She had been too scared to contemplate going back inside the mall to finish Will, Claire and Tricia off. What was she going to say to their families when she got back? Why should she have to? Ultimately, she had been placed in an impossible situation. The man to blame for all this was Agnew.

Suzy sat staring at the floor, wondering how much longer it was going to take. Occasionally she would slip a comment or a question into Mark and Roach's conversation, but all she was really thinking about was how long the Aqua-Gene would last in a plastic bottle; how long would it take to get to Agnew?

The conversation tailed off and Mark wondered if he would ever get his story published. There was no doubt that if he got off this island, his photographs would be worth a fortune. It wouldn't just be the National Geographic who would want them. His pictures would sell around the world. The fame and money could go hang for all he cared. This time, he just wanted his story out.

Most reports he undertook because he loved the colour and richness of life that he found travelling the world. Every country was different. Whether he was in the middle of a civil war or bunking with the navy patrolling the African seas, there was always something fascinating to be seen through his camera. Nobody had ever been on The Grave before; much less photographed it. He could tell a real story now. He was not just reporting on something but he was living it, experiencing it, facing it head on; *he* was the story. He almost felt proud when he thought about it like that.

It struck him then that there were only four of them sitting in this little room. There had been ten of them aboard the plane, if you didn't count the pilots; so many were dead. Mark realised he wasn't actually the story; they *all* were. Of course, if they didn't get off this hell hole there would be no more story and no more Mark. He could feel the memory card against his chest, just above his heart. He couldn't afford to lose it.

Kelly got up and brushed herself off. "One thing before we go. We need to know how we get into the embassy and onto the helicopter. I don't think we can just stroll in there and ask for a ride."

Roach got up too and cleared his throat. "I've been thinking about that. Getting to the embassy itself is fairly straightforward. It's on this side of the city, just off the highway. We won't have to go through the city itself, so just follow me and I can take us straight there. I can't say for sure, but when I left the embassy, there was an old uprooted tree leaning up against the fence. If it's still there, we'll have to climb in. If not, I guess we look around for another way in."

"And the chopper?" asked Mark, getting up and patting his lapel pocket firmly, checking to be sure the small case was still inside. "How do we get onto it?"

Roach pulled the gun from his pocket. "Shoot first and ask nicely later."

"We have the element of surprise." Kelly pulled the gun from her pocket and checked it over before replacing it. "Once it lands, we get out there and take them down before they even know what's hit them."

"I hope you're as good a shot as you think you are with that then," said Suzy leaving the warehouse.

Leaving their refuge behind them, they began the trek into the city once more. Back on the road, the sun was still strong and after the cramped reception room where they had rested, it felt refreshing to have the warmth of the sun on their faces. They left together a better unit now, aware of what was coming up. The road was on an incline now, and it was also uneven. It had been unattended for years and the ground had started to break up. A deep fissure ran through the road caused by earthquakes and erosion. The stress the land was under was starting to show. They trudged on and at one point had to jump across a gap in the road of three feet. The hillside had slipped, and rocks and stones were strewn across the road.

"Hey, look!" Suzy saw something and jogged over to a bank of trees.

Kelly saw another pile of dead bodies, approximately thirty of them all pushed up against a bank, arms and legs protruding from a bony mound. Most of them were no more than skeletons, just thin scraps of tissue on bones. The Deathless had rotted away or been eaten by something else. A riot of coloured flowers, orchids and Tororaro shrubs had erupted from the pile of rotting bodies. A small tree with huge yellow buds hanging from its branches towered over the pile. Beside it was what Suzy had spotted.

Thick, juicy, red and black berries hung in clusters overhead in the canopy alongside olive coloured leaves. Clots of them made the branches droop low to the ground. It was unsettling to see life springing forth so abundantly from near such death and Kelly wondered if the tree's roots had suckled on the fluids that must have seeped into the ground from the corpses. Had their infected blood helped this tree? Had the Aqua-Gene injected it with a thirst for life?

She watched as Suzy reached up and grabbed a branch. Suzy lowered it and plucked a handful of crimson berries from the branch before letting it ping back up into the air. She handed some of the red fruit to Mark and he popped one in his mouth just as Suzy prepared to do the same.

A shiver ran up Kelly's spine. "No, don't eat them, they're infected!" she shouted, running to Mark. He spat the berry out onto the grass and Suzy looked at her, shocked.

"What? They're just berries, aren't they?" Suzy's face was puzzled, her brow furrowed.

"Kelly's right," said Mark. "Fuck, and I nearly swallowed some too." Mark spat on the ground again and rubbed his fingers around inside his mouth. He wiped them on his trousers and spat once more, getting rid of any trace of the deadly berry. Thankfully, Kelly had reached him in time and he had not ingested any.

Roach kicked at the soft ground. "These bodies have been here for quite some time. Judging by the decomposition, I would say a couple of years at least. These berries are a summer fruit and any matter from these dead bodies would have inevitably found their way into the tree's ecosystem. Its trunk, leaves, and roots. Every inch of it is infected."

Suzy threw her handful of berries down and stomped on them with her boots. "What was I thinking? God, I'm so stupid. I'm sorry, Mark. I just saw them and thought they looked so good. I know we're all thirsty and...fuck, they don't *look* infected, do they."

"Let's go," said Kelly, turning away from the deadly temptation. "This is a kingdom of barbarians and barbarity; a land of the dead and the dying," she said quietly.

As they dejectedly walked down the hot road, Mark looked back at where they had come from. Way back, at least a mile, he saw a lone figure. It was stumbling down the road, arms reaching out forlornly. Another figure appeared, and then another. Had they been followed?

"Um, Kelly, Roach, how much farther?" Mark looked at the knife in his hand and knew it would not do much good if they were attacked. He needed something bigger and stronger. He also suspected the figures following them might be Will and Tricia, but he didn't want to think about it. That would be too much.

Roach was looking back at the figures too. "Too far. They're probably going to struggle to reach us, but the closer we get, the more of them we'll find. In fact..."

Suzy screamed as a man came out of the bushes only feet away. His face was horribly mutilated, his lower jaw missing, and he was naked. His body was covered in sores and pus-filled spots, his skin a sickly shade of green.

"Get the fuck away from me," shouted Suzy as she waved a knife in front of the man's face.

Ignoring her, the Deathless man staggered over the road and reached for Suzy. Two loud cracks splintered the air and the man collapsed, two bullet holes having exploded his skull. Suzy was sprayed with blood and gore.

"Jesus!" Suzy whirled around, shaking. She wiped the dead man's blood from her face, wiping her hands on her thighs.

Roach lowered the gun. "Now, we really need to get a move on. That noise will have alerted more of..."

"Way ahead of you," said Kelly as she fired her gun at a corpse that had appeared behind Roach.

Mark jumped as Kelly fired, putting a hole into an old woman's chest. The Deathless woman stopped and looked down at the gaping hole where her heart had once been. Then she looked up and resumed her advance on Roach.

Kelly fired again and put a bullet in the dead woman's forehead. The walking corpse fell down onto the road, finally dead.

"Roach, we're not going to make it. Is there a quicker way?" said Kelly scanning the surrounding vegetation for more unwelcome surprises, her gun trained on the roadside.

"This is the only road in or out. We have no choice but to keep walking..."

"Fuck that," said Mark running over to a nearby school bus. Its yellow paint had faded and the windows were caked in dirt and grime, but the wheels were intact and it was in better condition than most vehicles. "This road goes *down* into the city, right?"

Roach nodded. "Yeah, it's downhill for quite a way now. It levels out once we get nearer, but..."

"Then give me a goddamn hand." Mark grunted, trying to push the bus doors open. They were already showing signs of movement and Roach and Kelly rushed over to help him.

"What are you thinking, Mark?" asked Suzy. She was trembling, still shocked from nearly being taken out only a moment ago. "It's not going to work. The battery's going to be dead. The engine probably hasn't been turned over in a decade."

"Doesn't have to," said Mark as they finally wrenched the doors open. He stepped up onto the footplate and inside the bus. "The gradient is steep enough that gravity will do us a favour. As long as the axle isn't broken, we should be able to get enough impetus to get down this damn hill. It sure beats walking." Mark turned and slid slowly into the driver's seat behind the wheel. He peered out the front window, which was smeared with dirt and cracked in one corner. In the road ahead were a few of the Deathless wandering aimlessly, scuffing along the tarmac and bumping into other stationary vehicles. Clearly, the gunfire had drawn them out and they were looking for the source of the noise.

Mark looked in the rear-view mirror and scanned the bus – it was empty. The seats were covered by a fine coat of dust and the interior of the bus was gloomy. He could see a few discarded bags and plenty of bird droppings on the seats. The air actually didn't smell too bad, considering. He looked back out through the open door and told Suzy to join him. He got out of the driver's seat and put Suzy behind the wheel.

"Right, Suzy, you're the driver. We're going to give it a push and you're going to stay here and drive. It looks like it's been left in gear, so with any luck we'll be off in a minute." Mark jumped down the step and back onto the road where Roach and Kelly were waiting.

"Okay," Mark said, "let's go around the back and give it a push. As soon as it starts moving, we run like hell for the doors."

"You think this will really work? What if the suspension is gone or the tyres puncture or..." Kelly tucked the gun back into her pocket, aware she was going to need to get both hands dirty if they were going to move the bus.

"Don't worry," said Mark quietly. "It'll work. All she has to do is let gravity take over. It'll save us a lot of time and a lot of hard work trying to avoid *them*."

They rounded the back end of the bus and an arm stretched out in front of Mark's face. The fingers on the end of it brushed his face and he leapt back. One of the dead had come out of the undergrowth and heard the voices. The dead person was not recognisable as either male or female. It looked as if they had been shredded. Skin and sinew hung off the frail frame of the corpse and it barely had the strength to reach for them.

Mark heard Roach cock his gun. "No, save your bullets." Mark took his knife and plunged it into the skull of the dead thing, plunging it right through the brittle skull and penetrating its diseased brain. It slowly sank to the floor as Mark kept the knife pressed in, forcing it down. Once it was down and not moving, Mark twisted the knife to make sure it would not get up again. He spat on the dead person and left the knife where it was. The handle stuck up out the corpse's head like some sort of bizarre ceremonial crown.

Kelly looked on, impressed. She was reminded of how Tug had once saved Mark by doing something similar. It seemed Mark had learnt a few things in the last few days. She handed him the hatchet she had been carrying.

Mark took it and pushed the weapon inside his belt buckle so it hung within his reach. "Push!" Mark shouted. He stepped over the dead body and placed his hands against the warm metal of the bus.

Together, with Roach and Kelly, they all put their full weight on the rear of the school bus. Instantly it began to move, its body creaking and groaning, and its wheels turning slowly as they found purchase on the road.

"Quickly," said Kelly, leading the chase around to the doors as the bus began to pick up speed.

One by one, they jumped onto the bus and sat down in the nearest seats behind Suzy. It seemed sluggish at first, but soon picked up speed.

"How is it?" said Kelly crouching next to Suzy. Navigating their way through the dead would've taken a long time and she had to admit Mark had come up with a good plan. She realised she had some admiration for him too. When he came out from behind the camera, he was a decent man.

"It feels heavy and it wants to pull to the left all the time," said Suzy yanking the wheel to the right as she manoeuvred around another car. "I think we've probably got a flat at the back." She kept her eyes glued to the road, skilfully weaving between the abandoned cars and forsaken bodies of the dead, worried that if she looked away for one second, they would plough into the back of another vehicle. The bus was picking up speed now as it sped down the highway and there were no brakes. She hoped that Roach was right and that the road did level out soon, otherwise they were going to have a very painful, abrupt stop.

Kelly stayed beside Suzy, more for moral support than anything. She could do nothing now but wait and she looked through the streaky glass as they swept past derelict houses and burnt out shells of trucks and vans. The road took them through a gorge and the road was flanked by tall, green hills. A road sign flashed above them, indicating the city was near. Fleeting glimpses of the dead whirled by in a blurry haze, their forms mingling with the bushes, signposts and buildings. They appeared like ghosts, pale human shadows flitting in and out of vision, just vague echoes of what they were. Kelly couldn't help but wonder what awaited them deeper into the city. How many more of these ghouls would there be?

The road curved to the right and Suzy gripped the steering wheel as the bus tried to take them left. As they rounded a bend, the road dipped upward slightly and all of a sudden, they were in the open. The blue sky appeared as if from nowhere and the vast sea opened up before them, the clear blue water shimmering in the afternoon sunlight. The capital city stretched out before them, the tall skyscrapers and buildings that hugged the harbour glistening and sparkling.

"Wow," said Kelly. "It's so beautiful." She could hardly tell where the deep blue of the ocean met the sky. The water was crystal clear and the sky a deep hazy blue. She was reminded of brilliant summer days in New York and she felt a pang of homesickness for her own country.

The bus scraped alongside a row of cars as Suzy swerved into the emergency lane and the shrieking metal jarred in Kelly's ears. She brought her attention back to the highway and noticed how much busier it was. There was no sign of the Deathless, but there were a lot more vehicles now. The bus was slowing down, but still coasting along. Just as Roach had said, the road was levelling out.

"I'm not sure how much further I can get us," said Suzy quickly wiping the sweat away from her eyes. "The road looks pretty blocked up ahead and we're running out of steam here."

"That's okay," said Roach wiping his glasses on his shirttails. "We're almost there." He carefully stepped up behind Kelly and pointed out of the window. "See the tall cream coloured building?

That's a block of flats and there's an off-ramp just beside it. The embassy is right opposite."

Suzy let the wheel go as the bus finally rolled to a stop and it nudged into a metal barrier. Her arms ached and her palms were thick with sweat. She followed Kelly out of the bus, and waited for Roach and Mark to follow, breathing out a sigh of relief that she had been able to get them there in one piece. They had come to a stop just half a mile away from where they needed to be.

"Good job we didn't take the ferry," said Mark jumping out of the bus. He looked over at the harbour where an enormous passenger ferry was capsized. It was on its side and huge mounds of dead bodies lined the dock around it. There were police cars and ambulances with their doors open, and it looked like a scene from a war movie. The dock was a good hundred feet away and the highway was elevated so they could look down on the scene from safety.

Kelly peered over the edge of the barrier, down onto the dock below. She saw dozens of the Deathless walking between the piles of bodies. "They know we're here, but they can't get up to us."

"Well, let's not hang about until they figure it out. I don't like being out in the open like this." Suzy tapped her knife on the side of the bus and began walking toward the flats. The embassy was within reach now.

SEVENTEEN

Fizzy, frothy warm liquid spilled down his chin as Mark drank. He held the heated can to his lips and drank it down.

The liquid tasted foul, but right now, it was all they had and it quenched their thirst. Dodging between the abandoned, rusting cars of the highway, they had stumbled across an overturned truck. Hundreds of cans of cola had spilled over the road.

Mark finished a can and let out a long belch. He saw Suzy looking at him. "No time for pleasantries now." Mark smiled as Suzy followed suit and let out a bellowing belch too.

"True," she said, tossing the can aside.

"Alright guys, keep it down." Roach had led them to the off ramp and they were now approaching the block of flats he had pointed out. The city was strangely quiet and Roach was worried.

"It's so peaceful," said Kelly next to him. Worried about their lack of supplies, she had also drank a can of cola and picked up a tyre iron in the process from an adjacent vehicle. She didn't want to rely solely on her gun.

"I know. That's what worries me." Roach pushed his glasses up his nose.

With the heat of the sun still beating down, his skin was oily and greasy. They all were. Their clothes were soaked in sweat and it was almost impossible to remember how much it had been raining in just the last couple of days.

"So what now?" asked Mark. "That it?"

He pointed up to a looming grey structure that poked above the treetops. Beyond the off ramp to the highway, they could clearly see the tower block. Over the road from it, almost hidden by a bank of trees, was the embassy. From where they stood, they could only see the uppermost floors and grey blocks of concrete.

"Yep." Roach scanned the sky, but there was nothing to be seen. Just a vast expanse of blue.

"You think they're coming?" asked Suzy. "You think the chopper might be here soon?"

Roach looked at her. Suzy's face was a mixture of fear and anxiousness. "*If* they're coming today, they'll be here anytime.

They always come at the same time of day. I heard them flying over the mall nearly every afternoon. We need to get inside and up to the roof as quickly as possible. If they don't turn up today, we'll wait it out in there, as long as it takes. I didn't come all this way to turn back now. I miss Stella. I miss her and my Bobby real bad. I'd tried to forget about them, knowing I'd never see them again, but now that I'm here..." Roach trailed off, his memories of home resurfacing. Being back here, so close to where it all began was also bringing back a lot of unwanted memories: Min, Sergeant Warwick and everything that had happened to him.

Mark put a gentle hand on Roach's shoulder. "Roach, show us. Take us."

Roach looked at Mark, Suzy and Kelly. They were all relying on him now and he knew it. These people were scientists and office workers; just ordinary people in an extraordinary place. He was going to have to go back in there. He pulled the gun from his pocket and cocked it ready. He had four bullets left. He saw Kelly gripping the tyre-iron, Mark the hatchet and Suzy a knife. He scanned the road quickly and saw a road sign that had been knocked over and ripped from the ground by an SUV. He picked it up and held it out for Suzy.

"Take this. You're going to need more than that thing," he said looking at her knife.

Suzy took the signpost and threw the knife away. The paintwork had been scraped off and scuffed, and the sign at the top was rusted away. She held the metal pole with both hands, weighing it up. It was almost six feet in length and heavy. It felt perfect for bashing a few heads in.

Roach raised his index finger to his lips and then began the walk up the road to the embassy. Off the main highway, fewer cars were around, but still plenty of places where the Deathless might be hidden from sight. As he neared the top of the off ramp, he heard a scuffling noise behind him and turned around.

One of the dead had risen from behind a thorn bush, but he had no need to call out to warn the others. Mark had seen it already and without uttering a word had stabbed the creature in the head with his hatchet. Mark withdrew the blade and watched the dead slump to the ground. He nodded briefly to Roach and they carried on walking.

There was an empty coffee shop at the base of the flats and Roach remembered how he had hidden inside with Min once they'd escaped the embassy. In the last four years, nothing had changed. It was surreal. The chairs and tables were still in the same place, the open till still sat askew on the workbench and there were coffee beans all over the tiled floor. Roach remembered the smell as he and Min had ran over them, crunching them underfoot as they ran from the dead.

"Roach," hissed Kelly. "Roach."

Startled, he stopped and realised he had almost gone past the entrance. He saw Kelly crouched down behind a station wagon, Suzy and Mark stooped low behind her.

"Is this it?" whispered Kelly, pointing at the tall fence the other side of the car.

Roach looked at the embassy and felt his heart surge. There it was. Like the coffee shop, very little had changed. The outer edge of the building had changed little; the ferns had turned brown and wilted. The grass and bushes had grown longer and bigger. Beyond them, he recognised the low building and flat roof where he had been dropped by the helicopter so long ago. He recognised the gates surrounding the perimeter of the building, and he recognised the fallen tree that he had escaped over. Unfortunately, he also saw how the tree had rotted and crashed through the perimeter, leaving a gaping hole in the fence. He even saw the ladder on the ground where it had been left. He wondered what the military did with their prisoners now. Did they push them off the roof or let them fend for themselves? It seemed more likely they were just shot and dumped over the side to be eaten.

With the fence no longer there to contain them, the Deathless had spread out. There were still a lot in the yard, roaming the grounds, but just as many had left, probably to scavenge the city for fresh meat.

Kelly peeked through the car windows and saw dismembered limbs lying in crimson pools. She didn't want to think how many people must have been killed in this place. Roach had been lucky to get away. At the corner of the building was a small hut, no doubt the entrance to the embassy. On it were some faded, gold letters:

EMBASSY OF THE UNITED STATES OF AMERICA

Kelly felt ashamed that her country's name had been tarnished by Agnew. He had used one of the most unfortunate events in the history of the world, an event that had killed billions, and warped it, bending it to serve his own perverted needs. She was disgusted.

Roach scurried back to Kelly and hid beside the station wagon. "Yeah, that's it. But the fence is down. We can't get straight up to the roof like I'd hoped now. We're going to have to find another way in or...shit, do you hear that?"

Kelly saw Roach's eyes widen and he cocked his head to one side, intently listening to something. She couldn't hear anything but the faint moans of the dead the other side of their hiding place.

"I hear it," said Mark. "They're coming."

Kelly blocked out all other sounds and listened. She heard it; the unmistakeable throb of an engine and the repetitive whumping sound of helicopter blades approaching fast from the east.

"There's no time. We have to get up there, *now*," said Suzy standing up. She didn't care if the Deathless saw her.

"Suzy, wait..." Roach stood too, exposing himself to the dead, but it was too late. The Deathless has seen Suzy and were now heading toward the car.

"Go!" screamed Kelly and they all ran toward the embassy.

Suzy was first, hopping over the fallen tree and into the yard. She swung the metal pole and knocked two of the dead over. Another lunged at her from the side and before she could swing again, its head exploded. Suzy heard Roach shoot again and a dead woman in front of her went down, half of her face missing. Suzy ran.

Kelly and Mark caught up with her, fending off the dead as best they could. Kelly whirled the tyre-iron like a baton, bringing it crashing down onto reaching hands and arms, shoving the dead away as they swarmed through the yard.

Mark hacked his way through the dead, showering himself with dried blood and limbs, separating shoulders from sockets and heads from shoulders. He slashed at anything in his way, lopping off bones and fingers as if he were pruning an overgrown walking hedge.

Roach skirted around the worst of the carnage, firing until his gun chamber was empty. He could hear the rapidly approaching helicopter and knew they had to make it inside unseen. If the military saw them, they would lose their advantage of surprise.

Suzy reached a door first and pulled on the handle. Nothing happened. She pulled and pushed, but it refused to budge. There was an entry keypad to the side and no place for a key.

"Damn it," she said and turned around just as Kelly reached her. "The door's locked, I can't open it," said Suzy breathlessly.

"That way," said Kelly, spying another door ten feet away. They ran past a brick wall to the door as Mark caught up. Roach was sprinting behind them, sticking to the path they had cleared through the walking dead.

There was another keypad and despite their best efforts, the second door wouldn't open either. Suzy pounded on it in frustration and screamed.

"Leave it," said Kelly. There was a small glass window in the wall nearby, just big enough to squeeze through. She aimed her tyre iron and threw it at the window. The glass shattered instantly and she shouted to the others to get inside.

Suzy cleared away the broken fragments of glass with the metal post that was now smeared with blood. She discarded it and crawled inside, swiftly followed by Mark. Kelly took her gun out and ordered Roach through. As the Deathless advanced upon her, she fired off two more rounds, taking down the closest of the Deathless. The rest were far enough away for her to make a break for it, so she clambered through the small window, letting Mark and Roach pull her in.

Kelly's head hit the floor hard as she was dragged through the open window. No sooner had she gotten inside than arms and hands reached through trying to grab her. She stood up in the dark room and fired off one more round as one of the Deathless threatened to get inside. With the dead body now slumped over the windowsill, it was blocking the rest from getting in. The moaning from outside only grew louder though and it was only a matter of time before they got in. The dead body acted as a buffer between the inside and outside of the embassy, but it would only stay in place for so long with the dead pushing against it.

"Where the fuck now, Roach?" said Kelly annoyed, remembering she had dropped the tyre-iron outside. She now only had one bullet left.

Roach looked around the dark room, which was a small office containing nothing but a shelf full of files, an empty desk and a clock on the wall that had stopped ticking years ago. "I...I don't know...I think..."

"Where the fuck now, Roach?" Kelly screamed at him. "Where the fuck do we go now?" She brought her gun around to face him, pointing it at his chest. "Well?" she screamed.

"Kelly," said Mark, "I don't think..."

"Shut up, Mark. I know what I'm doing." Kelly had no intention of shooting Roach, but she needed him to start thinking. They had just fought their way through a bloodbath and the helicopter could be landing any minute. She didn't have time for Roach to lose it now and she knew a gun trained on him would do wonders for kick-starting his brain.

Roach looked around the room frantically. He had never actually been inside the embassy, so he was going to have to go by gut instinct. He had an impression of the building as to where the roof was; he just needed to find the way up. There was a solitary door in the gloomy room and he prayed it would be unlocked. If they could find some stairs, they would be able to get to the roof.

"There. That way." Roach pointed at the door.

Kelly moved first, holding the gun out in front of her. She tried the door handle and the door pushed open easily. She walked into a small carpeted corridor. There was very little light inside, despite the bright sunlight outside. There were various doors lining the corridor, with a lift at one end and a reception desk at the other. Next to the lift, she could just make out a staircase.

"Kelly, be careful," said Mark behind her in a low voice. "We don't know for sure that this place is empty."

Kelly regained her composure and crept forward. She wanted to run, to run as hard as she could up the steps and find the roof. However, she knew she had to take it slowly. One false move, one bite or scratch, and she would be dead.

Last out of the room, Roach closed the door behind him, but he heard thumping sounds as the Deathless made it in. He could hear them barging around the room, looking for the way out. It would only take them a moment to find the unlocked door.

Up ahead, Kelly found the building horribly quiet. She half expected one of the Deathless to jump out at her at any time. The potted artificial plant, the doorways, and the lifts all offered a place to hide. Stealthily, she continued down the corridor to the stairway.

There was a steady dripping coming from a loose pipe somewhere in the distance, a regular plopping noise that echoed around the corridor to them.

"You think we're alone in here? You really think they're all gone?" asked Mark nervously. He kept his voice to a whisper, not wanting to give away their position.

"Seems like it, but I'm not counting my chickens just yet," said Kelly. She reached the stairs and looked up. They were empty and so she proceeded up them. At the top was another corridor, this one lined with pale blue tiles and whitewashed walls. She glanced up and down the corridor but still couldn't see any sign of life, or death, inside. To her right there was a blank wall and a door with a glass partition. The other way stretched for about fifty feet and then there was another door. This one had bright sunlight streaming through a small glass in the top and she could see blue sky. The roof was within sight at last. She motioned for the others to come on up.

"That it?" Kelly asked Roach.

He saw the doorway ahead and nodded silently.

Mark looked through the closest door and whistled. "This must have been the original place. It looks like a mad scientist's lair." He could see row after row of medicine cabinets, desks cluttered with papers and binders, and test tubes. On one wall, he saw hundreds of photos of bodies in varying states of decomposition and a gurney in the centre of the room with skeletal remains still tethered to it. There were white coats hanging on a stand just inside the room and blood splatter was on the other wall.

"I guess they didn't try to work it out for too long," said Mark. He wished he had his camera on him right then, but patted his pocket, reassured he had everything he needed on the memory card that was still stowed away securely.

"Holy cow," said Suzy looking over Mark's shoulder.

"Um guys, we need to move," said Roach uneasily. "They're in downstairs. I heard them. They're all over the place and they'll be up in here in a minute. Can't you hear them?"

Kelly smiled. "Yeah, but they're downstairs and we're up here. Don't worry, we've made it. That door leads to the roof, doesn't it?"

Roach looked at the blue sky outside through the door's small window. He saw the chopper coming down to land, hovering twenty feet above the roof, and he saw the vague, dark green outfit of a soldier who was sat in the cockpit. He smiled back at Kelly. "Ready?"

Kelly opened her mouth to speak, but Roach never heard her reply. A loud boom echoed around the building as another earthquake began to shake the embassy violently. The quake was tearing through the whole city and the vibrations were causing the building to sway so much they could no longer stand up.

Suzy screamed as Kelly shouted at them to run for the roof. It was impossible to run, walk, or crawl though, as the shaking got worse. The quake was much larger than they had experienced before and the longer it went on, the stronger it seemed to get. The rolling and jolting of the building increased as the massive earthquake rippled through the city.

Mark was thrown backwards as Kelly and Suzy tried to get to the doorway. They ran a few steps down through the corridor before they were thrown off their feet and catapulted against a wall. Roach almost fell back down the stairs, but managed to grab the handrail before flinging himself to the undulating floor.

Ruptures appeared in the walls ahead of them as the shaking continued. A three-foot crack appeared in the floor and rapidly shot up the wall halfway down the corridor. Tiles and plaster began to crumble away, exposing the wiring and pipes behind. A brown sludge spurted from a broken pipe above spraying Mark with slime and gloop. He wiped the noxious substance quickly from his face, careful not to let any into his mouth. He stood to help Kelly and then the earthquake cranked up another notch, shaking the embassy to its foundations. The laboratory door shook off its hinges and fell away, just as Mark was thrown back against it. He skidded to a halt beneath the gurney and everything went black.

A fluorescent strip light back in the corridor jolted free from its joints and swung down, smashing into Kelly's side. She was winded as the floor rippled and bucked beneath her and she lost sight of Suzy. The earthquake refused to die down and if anything, it seemed to be still growing. Overhead tiles rained down, striking them and leaving cuts all over their faces and scalps.

Kelly tried to get up and heard a tremendous tearing sound as the floor was ripped away from under her feet. She felt hands grab her waist and Suzy tried to pull her back from the cavern opening up where the floor had been. Kelly fell and found herself lying on a mass of under-floor pipes. She felt Suzy's hands slip down to her feet and heard the shouting and screams, but she couldn't focus on what Suzy was saying. Through the pipes on which she lay, on the level beneath them, were the Deathless. On the ground floor, the dead were waiting, oblivious to the earthquake and the damage being wrought upon the building. Kelly could see them being thrown around, but they were all looking up at her. She felt hands upon her arms and screamed.

"Kelly, Kelly, it's me."

Electrical wires twisted around Roach and pulled him down, entwining themselves around his arms rapidly, looping around him leaving him as if a fly caught in a giant web. An ocean of the dead crested beneath him, clamouring for him and trying to grab his feet. He had been sucked into the collapsed floor too and if it were not for the wires holding him up, he would already have fallen.

"Kelly, you've got to get out of here," he shouted. The moaning of the Deathless below and the building collapsing around them meant he had to shout to be heard. "Focus on my eyes, Kelly. Look at me."

Kelly let out a scream and then looked at him. He had lost his glasses when the quake struck and he was looking at her with those beady eyes of his. Kelly was gasping for breath, the adrenalin surging through her body. Not like this, she thought, please not like this.

"It's subsiding, but you haven't long. The helicopter is going to leave. *Get out.* Get out now while..." Roach slipped further as the shaking continued and he held onto Kelly. He knew if he let go, there was nothing to support him and he wasn't going to make it.

"Tell Stella I love her. Tell Bobby I'm sorry."

The building was still shaking, but not as violently as before. Roach slipped and Kelly looked at him helplessly.

"Get Agnew for me."

Kelly understood Roach was stuck and she nodded. Roach slipped a few inches down and he screamed. There was a sickening crunch as one of the Deathless snapped their teeth around his ankle, stripping it of flesh and scraping their teeth along the bone.

Roach screamed again as he felt more teeth sinking through his flesh, ripping open his legs and snapping tendons. Sharp incisors sheared the skin from his shinbones and his toes were broken off as his feet were savaged. Blood spurted from his mouth and he grabbed Kelly.

"Please..." His eyes widened as he slipped once more, pulling Kelly with him.

Kelly fought back the tears and shouted for help. Roach was right. They had to hurry. With the earthquake rocking the building like this, the military weren't going to hang around.

"Mark? Suzy, help!" The weight of Roach was dragging Kelly down now and she could see the terror in his face. She could feel his helplessness and his agony as the Deathless began to devour him. She couldn't bear to watch and forced herself to look down through the mass of tangled wires, tiles and plasterboard. Another tile fell away and the hole in the floor widened. Kelly could see the Deathless thronging below as the earthquake continued to expose them, their hands reaching up, and their eyes all upturned and boring through Kelly's. She could see them beyond Roach's twisted body, clawing at his legs, and she knew that she would swiftly follow him down of she stayed there much longer. The building was still gently shaking and the floor was giving way.

"I can't pull you back, you're stuck," shouted Suzy.

Kelly tried to shuffle herself backwards, but it was useless. She realized her arms were wound around some cables and she would have to free herself so Suzy could pull her back. The only way to do that would be to let go of Roach. Kelly rested her forehead on the water pipe that was holding her up and closed her eyes. He had been so close. He had survived The Grave for years before they had come along. It wasn't fair, none of it was. She looked up at him. He had stopped screaming and writhing and she realized he was dead. His eyes were closed and he actually looked peaceful. At some point in the last minute, when she had turned away from him, he had died, probably from shock or blood loss. She looked down and his feet were gone. Now his legs were just bloody stumps that ended at the knee.

"Sorry, Roach." Kelly freed her left arm and let go so she only held him by her right hand. He dangled there, caught up in the broken ceiling and Kelly let go of him with her other hand, expecting him to drop into the sea of dead below. Instead, she found his hand suddenly gripping her arm and she looked up at him, confused. He had reanimated already and his hand became firmer around her arm.

Roach's eyes were open, but lifeless. His body began to writhe and squirm again as his dead body tried to pull Kelly closer. Blood spurted from his mouth and cascaded over Kelly's face. She tried to turn away and closed her mouth, making sure she didn't get any inside her. She briskly wiped her eyes and saw Roach's mouth open wide, exposing his bloody tongue and throat. Roach had joined the Deathless. One scratch or bite from him and Kelly would be dead too.

EIGHTEEN

Kelly recoiled as Roach's grip tightened and she felt herself slipping toward him. The rocking of the building had slowed, but had not ceased entirely.

"Suzy, quick, where the hell is Mark? Fuck." Kelly tried to swat Roach away with her one free hand, but he had a strong grip on her. She reached over for a pipe and tugged on it, hoping it might come loose so she could push him away, but it was stuck fast. Thinking quickly, she used it to force herself backwards. She could feel Suzy pulling on her legs and with Roach still fiercely holding her arm, it felt as if she was being torn in two.

To be so close only to die like this was unbearable. She knew the helicopter was just feet away on the other side of the wall. The thought of giving up and just letting herself fall didn't even occur to her. The more Roach's dead body pulled her down, the instinct to fight and live only grew stronger. Kelly struggled with him, trying to ignore the baying mob of dead below who were waiting to eat her alive. Kelly couldn't release herself from his grip and screamed at him to let go. It did no good though. Her face was only inches away from his and if anything, his grip only tightened as she tried to free herself.

"Watch out," shouted Mark, suddenly appearing beside Kelly.

A fire extinguisher swung down, barely millimetres in front of her face, and the blunt base crashed down onto Roach's head. Instantly, Roach lost his grip on Kelly and swung away from her. Roach dangled there like a deranged angel stuck in a Christmas tree wrapped in coloured wires and cables. Now released from Kelly, the wiring refused to take Roach's weight any longer and he sank beneath the waves of Deathless beneath him. His body was engulfed by the dead and Kelly lost sight of him.

Mark grabbed Kelly's arm as she felt the room open up below. "Climb up," grunted Mark as he dropped the fire extinguisher.

Now free of Roach's death grip, Kelly swiftly disentangled herself from the cables and wires and pulled herself up. Mark dragged her away from the growing hole in the floor and they collapsed back at the end of the hallway.

"Are you all right?" asked Suzy, looking at Kelly. Suzy's face was red from the exertion of trying to pull Kelly back. Her arms were trembling and she sank back against Kelly gratefully.

Kelly just nodded. "What the hell happened to you, Mark?"

"It just knocked me off my feet. One minute you were there and the next...I fell and hit my head and when I woke up, I heard you screaming. I jumped up and that fucking skeleton in the lab was trying to grab me. I just kicked the trolley away and grabbed the first thing I could. I saw Roach had...turned."

As the earthquake subsided, and the shaking of the building decreased to a calm rolling motion, they heard shouts and gunfire coming from the roof.

Kelly got up and wiped Roach's blood from her face. She pulled the gun out of her pocket and knew she had only one bullet left. She would make it count and was grateful it was still there and hadn't fallen out when she had been fighting Roach. "Let's go. Just stay behind me and don't hesitate."

The walls stopped shaking, but Suzy's hands did not. She had no weapon anymore, no gun, no knife, nothing. The Deathless were still below them, waiting for the floor to give way completely, and offer them up fresh meat. Suzy carefully stood. "We need to get out of here."

Kelly barged into the door at the end of the corridor feeling sick and it blew wide open. She rushed out onto the rooftop and was dazzled by the sunlight. The oppressive heat struck her and she tried to take everything in. The sight that confronted her threatened to overwhelm her senses and she found herself holding her breath as her mind reeled. It was like doomsday and at first, she missed sight of the soldiers and helicopter.

A plume of smoke was billowing out as the tall block of flats opposite crumbled. Each floor collapsed onto the one beneath as if it was made of cards. Glass fanned out in all directions and a tumultuous fire raged on the ground. Further afield, she could see other skyscrapers in the city doing the same, falling like a stack of dominos. Massive clouds of black smoke were drifting up into the sky and it felt like the world was imploding.

She saw two soldiers sitting in the cockpit of the helicopter and the blades were speeding up. They were clearly getting ready to take off. Three bodies lay in the middle of the roof. Their bodies were riddled with bullets and bright red blood lay pooling around them. There was one soldier looking over the side of the building, down into the yard, shaking his head. Another man wearing an orange jumpsuit was on his knees sobbing. A soldier was standing behind him, holding a gun to the back of his head. The soldier looked up in surprise as Kelly burst through the door.

"Who are…"

The soldier failed to finish his sentence as Kelly fired her last bullet into the soldier's head. She raced past the prisoner and reached the other soldier who turned just in time to find himself staring down the barrel of Kelly's raised gun.

"What the fuck are you?" asked the soldier as he tried to raise his rifle.

Kelly smashed her gun onto the bridge of the soldier's nose and he crumpled to his knees, blood pouring between his fingers.

"Shut the fuck up," shouted Kelly. She grabbed the soldier's collar and pointed her empty gun at the back of his head. The soldier began whining and pleading for mercy, but Kelly ignored him. "You in the helicopter - put your hands up, now!" she shouted.

Mark had witnessed what Kelly had done and he was impressed. She had taken charge of the situation quickly. There had been no hesitation and she hadn't waited to see how things developed. She was a natural leader and Mark felt his confidence growing. He ran over to the prisoner and prised the gun from the dead soldier's hand who was lying on the rooftop. The prisoner looked up at Mark.

"Thank you, thank you. They just shot them all. Oh, sweet Lord, thank you."

Mark smiled casually at the man and then walked over to the helicopter, holding the rifle out in front of him and training it on the pilot. He could see the shock on the soldier's faces. Finally, they had the upper hand. Mark watched as Suzy walked over to the man in the jumpsuit and helped him to his feet. It was his lucky day.

Responding to Kelly's demands and seeing their colleague held at gunpoint, the two soldiers raised their hands. Mark went over to them and pulled open the cockpit door.

"Afternoon, gents. Fancy taking us for a spin?" Mark said, pointing the rifle at the pilot's face.

"Who are you? What the hell do you think you're doing?" asked the pilot. "You just shot Sergeant Brooks. We're U.S. soldiers, you can't do this."

"It's done. Just hand over your weapons and do it slowly. I would hate to have to fill you full of lead."

Mark waited as the two men slowly unholstered their weapons and threw them out onto the roof. Mark picked up the magnum the co-pilot had discarded and swapped it for his rifle. It was much easier to hold and was more practical. Even though the soldiers were unarmed now, he didn't trust them not to try something. Satisfied they were of little threat now they had no guns, Mark called Kelly and Suzy over. Kelly came dragging the bleeding Sergeant Brooks with her, whilst Suzy brought the chained prisoner. Mark hopped into the back of the helicopter, keeping the gun trained on the co-pilot at all times.

"Right, here's what's going to happen," said Kelly talking to the pilot. She stood outside the chopper, her gun still pointed at the Sergeant. She asked Suzy to pick up the soldier's discarded guns up whilst she spoke. "You're going to take us out of here, back to your base. All of us. No questions, no radio contact with anyone, just fly. Got that?"

"Don't do it," said Brooks, "Remember what Warwick told us? Nothing ever gets off this island. They're infected. They're..."

Kelly smashed the butt of the gun down on his already broken nose and he screamed out in pain as more blood spurted from his face. "You fucking bitch," yelled Brooks.

"Okay, okay," said the pilot. "Just get in and..."

A deep rumble interrupted him and then the violent shaking started again as a huge aftershock tore through the city, threatening to bring down any buildings that were still standing. As Kelly struggled to remain standing, Brooks seized his chance and pushed her over. He grabbed a rifle from the floor and pointed it at Kelly.

Brooks leered at her from the shaking roof. "There's no way I'm letting you off this island. We've never returned to base with anyone and I'm not starting now. You're dead, you hear me, dead."

A single shot rang out and Kelly stumbled backwards. She looked down at her chest, looking for the blood. She hadn't felt any pain, but knew he couldn't have missed from that range. She frowned as she patted herself down, unable to find any blood or wound.

Brooks' body keeled over, dead, and behind him stood Suzy. She lowered the gun she had picked up and calmly walked over to Kelly. "You wanted this?"

Suzy walked back to the surprised prisoner and hustled him into the back of the chopper, before settling inside herself.

Kelly raised the gun at the pilot "Any questions?"

"No. I'll take us up now." The pilot was pale and wanted off the roof as badly as anyone. The helicopter was trembling as the roof shook.

Kelly clambered in behind the pilots and sat down next to Mark. Her stomach lurched as the roof started to give way and the embassy succumbed to the immense aftershock. A corner of the roof gave way, bricks and masonry shattering in the yard below. A deep crack ran across the whole of the roof.

Kelly watched as a segment of the embassy disappeared into the ground, swallowed up by flames that danced in the sunlight.

"Get us up now!"

As the roof collapsed, the helicopter glided up into the air, rising faster than the billowing smoke chasing it. The pilot took them up swiftly, away from the destroyed city and the Deathless. Away from The Grave.

* * *

When they were safely out above the ocean, well away from the island, Kelly reached over and gave Mark a hug. "Thank you," she whispered in his ear. He had saved her from Roach. She was surprised at herself. She had thought little of Mark at the beginning of the expedition, but he had come through for her when it had mattered. He was only a year or two younger than she was and she found herself looking up at him as he looked at the cockpit. His short blond hair made him appear younger than he really was. He hadn't pushed her away so she stayed there, nestled in the curve of his neck and shoulder.

Mark let Kelly rest on his shoulder and said nothing. He knew what they had all gone through in escaping The Grave. They had all played their part. It was a relief to be able to sit down and not have to look over your shoulder. They stayed that way for a couple of hours, not talking, not even noticing the time, but just letting the pilot take them back to civilisation. Mark turned to check on Suzy in the back a couple of times, but she was fine. Quiet, but fine.

Mark knew that now they were clear of the island, they had one more mission. They had to make sure someone knew where they were. If they got pulled in by the military, they would disappear just as Roach had. He kept his gun trained on the co-pilot and made sure nobody tried to signal or radio base.

"Hey, does one of you have a mobile?" Mark prodded the co-pilot with his gun and heard a grunting as the man bent down. A moment later and a mobile appeared. Mark took it and handed his gun to Kelly. "Keep an eye on them for me?"

As Kelly reluctantly pulled herself away from Mark and took the gun, he pulled the memory card from his pocket and examined the mobile. "Perfect," he muttered.

Kelly watched as he ejected the phone's memory card and slid in his own. He turned the phone on and quickly found the images file. Kelly saw a smile spread across his face and she saw brief images flash up on the mobile's screen: the mob at Judgeford, a smiling Will holding the Weta, Roach on the road into the city and more. She watched as he began typing in an email address to send them.

"What are you doing?" asked the pilot. "You can't communicate with anyone without official permission. You're got a lot of questions to answer. Let us get you back to base and..."

Kelly pressed the muzzle of the gun into the back of his neck. "Stop talking, fly-boy. We're not the ones who have to answer to what's happening. You're finished and you know it."

"Shit," said the pilot to his co-pilot. "Commander Warwick is *not* going to like this."

Kelly chuckled, not caring about Sergeants, Commanders, or anything these men had to say. She saw Mark holding the phone aloft and the screen flashed up a message:

EMAILS SENT SUCCESSFULLY

"My boss has everything now. I copied in my flatmate and some buddies too, so we're covered. I sent a few words about what had happened. You want to call anyone?" Mark held the phone out to her.

Kelly looked at it. She couldn't think of anyone she wanted to call right now and shook her head. "I don't really feel like talking to anyone at the moment. Can you just text Freddie Taylor? I'll give you the number. He's the Director at the museum back in New York. Just let him know that I'm alive. Just tell him I'll update him when we land." She prodded the pilot again. "Where are we heading?"

"USS Enterprise, South Pacific. We'll be there in approximately thirty minutes now."

Kelly gave Mark the number and waited for him to send the text.

"You know, I'm just going to call and make sure he spreads the word. I don't want to go missing again." Mark called his boss back in New York and spent a few minutes explaining where they were, what had happened, and where they were heading. He made sure to ask him to contact Freddie Taylor at the Museum of Natural History too.

"Our story is going to be all over the front page tomorrow," said Mark as he tucked the phone away in his pocket. "Apparently, we were missing, presumed dead. Our plane came down somewhere over the ocean. My boss was about to run an obituary for me. Can you believe that?"

Kelly was pensive and wanted to relax, but she still couldn't find it in her to relax just yet. "You think Suzy's all right back there? She's been awfully quiet. I should go check on her."

Mark pulled back the khaki curtain separating the fore of the helicopter from the rear. The prisoner was curled up on the floor, hands still bound. Suzy was sitting, looking out of the window with the gun cradled in her lap. Her look was distant, as if she was thinking about something else and not seated in reality.

Mark looked at the gun in Kelly's hand. It was trembling. He decided it might be best if he went to Suzy. "I'll go." He went back and crouched down beside Suzy, resting a hand on her arm.

Suzy looked at him, withdrawing it quickly. "What?" she said coldly.

"I just wanted to make sure you're okay? We both did. Kelly's worried about you. We'll be at the base soon and there's going to be a million questions to answer. I've sent some emails and texts though, so we'll be fine. They know we're coming home now. Did you want to call anyone?"

"We'll be fine?" Suzy snorted. "It's a bit late for *fine*, Mark. No, I don't need to call anyone. I'll deal with it when we're back in New York. I heard you talking up there. Look at us. We're covered in blood. We've hardly eaten for three days. People are dead. Our friends are dead. No offence, it's not you I'm angry with. I want to make damn sure the world knows what's going on. After all that's happened...I have no idea if anyone even knows about us or if it's been covered up like everything else. We were left to die, Mark. Just left...three days ago we were headed on a scientific journey and now only three of us are still alive. Only three of us are going home. I am *so* not *fine*."

Mark was taken aback. He had half-expected Suzy to cry or to clam up, but not this. "Well look, we're in this together now. Kelly is..."

"Kelly can go fuck herself," said Suzy. "She left him behind. Will, Claire, Rasmus...all of them. Will was...oh what does it matter now? Once this nightmare is over, I'm done. I quit. I don't want anything to do with her again." She stared out of the window as Mark got up.

Mark waited silently, but Suzy said nothing more. "Whatever happens, Suzy, if you need anything, you can count on me."

Unable to say anything else, Mark returned to his seat. As he sat down beside Kelly, he saw her wipe a tear away. "Kelly, I..."

Kelly waved Mark away, embarrassed. "Don't, Mark, just don't. I heard. Just don't."

Mark took her hand and held it tightly. He brushed her dark brown hair behind her ear and wiped away another tear rolling down her cheek. They looked at each other, their eyes saying everything.

They all sat silently for the rest of the journey, waiting for the ship to appear. Twenty minutes later, the helicopter began its descent to the USS Enterprise. At first, it was just a dark speck in the ocean until it revealed itself as a colossal ship, its deck full of sailors and fighter jets. The pilots finally radioed ahead that they were landing and had unexpected guests. The days ahead were going to be revealing for everyone.

EPILOGUE

"Look, I think I've said all I can say on the matter. With the Senate hearing soon, it would be wrong of me to say more at this stage. The pictures you've seen printed in the papers over the last twenty-four hours are amazing, disturbing and undoubtedly warrant further investigation. You know as much as I do about Franklin Roach. However, they are not evidence of some cover up. I mean, come on, guys. This isn't Roswell."

The reporters chuckled nervously in the White House media room as Agnew attempted to wrap things up. None of them believed a word he said, but they all knew better than to question him. The seasoned reporters, both sitting and standing in the crowded room, knew you would only get honest information from sources. They were preparing President Agnew's obituary before he'd finished his speech.

"I think we should finish up now, sir," said Verity Dawson, leaning over and whispering into Agnew's ear.

Agnew stood tall over the podium and looked out over the microphones and cameras. "Gentlemen, I know we've had some banter and we joke about things, but the truth is that people have lost their lives. All this conspiracy talk is insulting to the families and the memories of those who unfortunately died in that plane crash. I am going to do all I can to support the museum in its hour of need, as I'm sure we all will. My wife and I have invited the Associate director, Kelly Munroe, and Suzy Collins up to the White House for dinner tonight, so that we can personally assure them of our support.

"Now before I go, don't forget the memorial in San Francisco Bay on Sunday. See you all there."

Verity took the stage and President Agnew exited swiftly before any more questions were fired at him. He knew he had handled it well, but questions were starting to be asked from the Senate. It was easy to deflect the reporters away, but he was coming under intense pressure in Washington. Commander Warwick should have taken care of it as soon as he knew those people on The Grave had survived. This was not how it was supposed to have gone down. Warwick had let those damn photos of Roach out and now they were splashed across every broadsheet in the country. Agnew was not impressed at being left to clear up the whole sorry mess. As he walked back to the Oval Office, flanked by his security, he squeezed the bridge of his nose. With the ridiculous service for the Golden Gate bombings coming up, he was already under enough pressure.

"Migraine, sir?" Mr White strolled alongside Agnew, always at his side, always looking out for him, and impeccably dressed of course.

"Almost," said Agnew sighing. "Those goddamn fuckers, who do they think they are? My goddamn wife has invited them over for dinner tonight too. The journalist Mark something-or-other, the one responsible for those photographs? He's too busy apparently. *Too busy* to meet the President? He's too busy being an asshole. The other two, well I'd just as soon bury them as share dinner with them. They are going be a major problem, White, a *major* problem."

White opened the Oval office door as Agnew stormed through. The other security guards took up their usual positions outside.

"What do you want to do about them?" asked White. He took a seat on a decorative armchair beside Agnew's desk. "The photos are damaging enough, but if they testify, it's going to be hard to sweep that under the rug. We could take care of them. I could take good care of them. You know next year is a re-election year. The opposition will pounce on any weaknesses."

Agnew swivelled his plush, black leather chair around to face White. He rubbed his eyes, looking pale and tired. He knew it, but there was so much to be done. "Not this time, White. They're too high profile and it would look a little too convenient. Rubbing them out would only make things look more suspicious. I'm heading over to meet them now. I think a little sweetness might be in order. The museum has been crying out for funding for years now. Sophie attended their last fundraiser a few weeks back and they need another five million this year alone. I think if Dr Munroe were to find her fundraising days over, she might be more receptive to forgetting about The Grave, don't you?"

"Keep your friends close, but your enemies closer." White cuckolded his hands, forming a point with his fingers, and leaned over, his eyes studying the carpet as if deep in thought. He nodded, silently agreeing with Agnew. "What about the reporter?"

Agnew got up and walked over to the full-length mirror. He pulled his tie up and smoothed down his slick brown hair, then walked over to the exit. He turned to White and smiled. "Remember how Senator Collins had that car accident last week? Terrible business. You sent my flowers to his wife, didn't you?" Agnew turned the door handle. "I would hate for our reporter friend to suffer a similar accident. That would be very...unfortunate."

Agnew winked and left the room, knowing White would carry out his instructions without need for further elaboration. He strode down the corridor, trying to push back the headache that was ploughing its way through his brain. He had to put on his game face. Kelly Munroe and Suzy Walker were now VIPs and he had to step carefully around them; they knew far too much. Sophie was so naive that she didn't know the truth behind anything that went on and he knew she would be entertaining them now, warming them up for him. Agnew had wined and dined with the most powerful men in the world. A girl from the Bronx and a museum director would be a breeze.

Agnew walked into his private chambers and could almost feel his teeth grind as he saw Sophie and Suzy chatting. They were sitting on the bed. Sophie had her arm around Suzy who was dabbing at her eyes with a tissue.

"Evening ladies, how are we?" he said cheerfully. He didn't give a damn how they were, but he had to start with the pleasantries.

They got up and Suzy rummaged around in her handbag for a tissue.

"Richard, don't be so insensitive, honestly." Sophie gave him a stern look.

Agnew put on his best concerned face and took Suzy's hand. "My dear, I am so sorry for what you have gone through. Your whole ordeal must have been just horrible. I can't even imagine what you experienced."

Suzy looked at the President. He looked a lot younger than his fifty-one years. He still had a full head of dark hair and had an athletic build. He was slightly taller than she was too, so she had to look up to him, even though she was wearing new high heels for the occasion. Agnew was holding her hand firmly and when he spoke to her, it was with a soft tone, his voice soothing and comforting. Yet his brown eyes gave him away. She could tell he wasn't sorry. Like every good politician, he was practised in manipulation and Suzy was going to play along with him.

"It was unbelievable. I was just talking to Sophie about it. I'm trying to deal with a lot of things, you know? I'm here, alive and well, yet so many of us didn't make it back. Josef, Wilfred, Rasmus, Claire, Will, Tricia, Tug...Franklin Roach." She stared intently at him as she lingered over the last name. If he felt uncomfortable hearing Roach's name, he didn't show it. Suzy felt him squeeze her hand just a fraction more and wondered if he was squirming inside. She hoped so.

"Yes, all your colleagues and friends, I know, it was such a terrible accident. Because of the crash site, I'm afraid retrieving the wreckage is quite impossible, so unfortunately we may never know what brought your plane down. Suzy, I am going to make sure your friends are remembered. With God as my witness, we will not let them be forgotten. They paid a terrible price, the ultimate price really. We will work something out, won't we, Sophie."

Agnew never even flinched as he spoke to Suzy. The lies and deception came easily, flowing off his tongue like fish swimming downstream. He ignored the mention of Roach completely and kept his brown eyes boring into Suzy's. Both knew the other was hiding something, keeping their true thoughts buried, yet neither was prepared to show their hand.

"Absolutely," said Sophie. "I was saying to Suzy how I want to be more involved with the museum. There's a vacancy opening up on the board now that Professor Rasmus...well, you know, I just think it would be a great opportunity for me to help out. I mentioned it to Kelly too."

Agnew dropped Suzy's hand and turned to his wife. "Where is Dr Munroe? I assumed she would be here tonight too?"

Sophie could read her husband's mannerisms better than he knew and she could see an icy glint in his eye. The way he said Kelly's name made Sophie feel unsure of herself. It was as if Dr Munroe had insulted him.

"She's waiting for us in the dining room. She got a call from the museum, so Suzy here asked for a whistle-stop tour of the White House. We were just about to head back." Sophie glanced at her watch. "Dinner will be ready soon. What do you say we go to the dining room now, Richard? Perhaps we can open that gin you've been saving for a special occasion?"

Agnew put on a perfect smile and flashed Suzy with his perfectly white teeth. "A wonderful idea, Sophie."

He walked over to the door and his wife followed him. Suzy stayed standing by the bed.

"I'm sorry, but would you mind if I had a moment? I just need to compose myself. I didn't mean to start crying like that, I must look awful." Suzy sniffed and dabbed at her puffy eyes with a tissue.

Agnew's smile faltered momentarily as he watched Suzy wipe away her mascara. "Well, we really should..."

"Of course you can, Suzy," said Sophie. "Honestly, Richard, we can give the poor girl a moment. Suzy, I'll wait right outside. You can use the en-suite bathroom to freshen up. Just go through the door to the right there. Take as long as you need, all right? Richard can go keep Kelly company."

Sophie bundled her husband through the door, ignoring his protestations about leaving Suzy alone in their bedroom. Suzy stopped sniffing and stuffed her tissue back into a pocket. They had bought her sob story and she knew she didn't have long. They probably had hidden cameras everywhere too so she had to be discreet. She sat down on the bed and pretended to rummage around in her handbag for something. She had already scoped out the room with Sophie earlier and worked out whose side of the bed was whose. She was in no doubt as one bedside table was covered in jewellery and an e-book reader; the other table had an A4 file, cufflinks and a wooden bowl containing an assortment of pens, clips and lapel badges.

Her fingers wrapped around the small bottle of headache pills in her bag and she seized her moment. Suzy got up from the bed and knocked the A4 file off with her handbag so that the papers flew out onto the carpet. She bent down and pushed the papers back into the file before putting it back onto Agnew's bedside table. At the same time, she casually dropped the bottle next to the file, so smoothly and discreetly that nothing would have looked out of place. She pulled the tissue from her pocket, dabbed at her eyes once more, then walked over to the bathroom. She spent no more than a minute in there fixing her hair and makeup, feeling flushed with excitement. She knew it was a longshot, but she also knew the President suffered from constant headaches and the chances of him reaching for a bottle in the next few hours were high. There was no way she would be suspected of anything and highly doubted that anything would've been picked up on camera. Agnew deserved his fate. Even when he was on his deathbed, Suzy knew he would probably have round the clock care.

Suzy went back into the corridor to Sophie, beaming. "Thank you, Sophie, I'm feeling much better now. Shall we go find Kelly?"

Sophie gave Suzy a warm smile. "Let's go eat. Please ignore my husband. He can be a bit insensitive sometimes, but he means well."

"Oh, it's nothing, honestly, I'm sure he does. I believe in karma myself. You know, what you give out, you get back. I'm sure the President will get his rewards for everything he has achieved."

Sophie led Suzy down the corridor to the dining room where Kelly was waiting. As they entered the room, Suzy saw the security outside. There was a man she thought she recognised. He had short cropped blond hair and she could see him watching her as she walked into the room. His gaze made her feel uncomfortable, but she couldn't place his face.

"There you are, Suzy," said Kelly sipping a glass of red wine, "I was wondering where you'd gotten to."

Kelly was wearing a grey suit, flat black shoes and little makeup. Since the quarantine, the interviews, and the funeral services, she had not had time even to think about shopping. Every day since arriving back into the U.S. had been a blur. Dinner with the President was another long line of commitments she had to attend, except she was looking forward to this one. She wanted to challenge Agnew about The Grave and about what was really going on. A lot of what had been reported had been subjected to ridicule. Mark's photographs were in the newspapers daily and the broadsheets were full of comment and speculation. So far, everything they had thrown at Agnew had slid off him. Kelly wanted to get some answers tonight. She wanted him to know that he wasn't going to get away with what he'd done.

Suzy offered Kelly a false smile. "I was just talking to Sophie. Problem?"

The animosity in Suzy's tone was obvious. Kelly had hardly seen her since they had left The Grave. It was evident that Suzy wanted nothing more to do with her or Mark, and had handed in her notice on her first day back in New York.

"Richard, let's give Kelly and Suzy a minute, shall we?"

Sophie pulled her husband to one side, leaving the two women standing facing each other, as if they were about to duel.

"Suzy, look, can we just keep things courteous for now? Please?" suggested Kelly quietly. She didn't want to argue in front of the President of the United States, she wanted to get him on her side. She thought if she was pleasant and polite, he might be more inclined to be honest with her. Every word he said was going to be repeated later. She had arranged an interview tomorrow via Mark's flatmate who worked at the Daily Post. Tonight was her best shot at exposing Agnew.

"Sure," said Suzy shrugging her shoulders and taking a glass of wine offered to her by a waiter. "I'm going to get drunk. I really don't care much for these people. Once tonight is over, it won't matter anyway."

Kelly grabbed Suzy's shoulder as she attempted to turn away. "What do you mean, it won't matter," she hissed. "What's going on in that head of yours? You and me...we were like best friends. I know what happened was tragic, but you have to know it wasn't my fault. We should be working together, not against each other."

Suzy put her mouth against Kelly's ear and lowered her voice. "You really think Agnew is going to spill his guts to you? You're deluded, Kelly. Leave it to me and stay out of my life."

"Suzy. Suzy, please." Kelly watched as Suzy walked away.

It was too late. Suzy ignored Kelly, knocked back her wine, took another from the waiter, and sat down at the dining table.

"Shall we eat?"

* * *

Two days later, New York was gripped in the early onset of winter. The temperature had dropped to just above zero, which was unseasonably cold for November, but not unheard of. The pavements were covered in an icy sheen and the wind blew through Central Park making the tourists shiver.

Mark hurried back to his apartment, the newspaper tucked right under his duffel coat. He took the stairs up to his third floor apartment on the Lower East side, preferring the exercise to the old lift that frequently broke down.

He locked the door behind him, sliding the two latches across and brushed off the cold air on his coat. He slung his coat over the back of an old suede sofa, turned the coffee machine on in the kitchen, and settled down on the sofa. He scanned the front-page news; it was all about the war in Yemen, with smaller articles around the outside of the main feature, full of tales of homicides, rapes and murders. He flicked through the paper as the coffee machine began its familiar chugging noise, permeating the kitchen with the sweet smell of his favourite blend.

A door banged shut in the distance and Mark looked up toward his bedroom. The door swung open and he could see the outline of a figure in the darkness. He put the paper down and watched as the figure walked slowly out of his room, over to the sofa.

"Sorry, did I wake you up?" he said to Kelly as she leant down and gave him a kiss. She was wearing one of his old Mets shirts and old pyjama pants.

"No, I was only dozing. I don't sleep too good these days." Kelly made two cups of fresh coffee and then settled onto the couch besides Mark. "Still nothing?" she said looking at the newspaper.

Mark yawned. "No. I haven't found anything. I can't believe how quiet it's gone. With all the stuff I put out there, you would've thought someone would be asking Agnew some pretty tough questions by now."

Kelly sipped her coffee and nestled in closer to Mark. "Powerful people have powerful friends."

They sat in silence for a moment, drinking their coffee.

"Is your flatmate back today?" Kelly yawned, feeling the pins in her eyes. She was going to have to take the medication that she had been subscribed and get a good night's sleep. It was either that or drink a ridiculous amount of coffee to get through the day.

"Yeah, Joel should be back later," said Mark. "I said I'd pick him up from Newark. His flight gets in this afternoon."

"Sweet. So we still have a few hours together?" said Kelly playfully. She gently rubbed Mark's cold head, tenderly stroking the back of his neck.

Mark laughed. "We can find something to do, I'm sure..." He hesitated before carrying on, knowing he had to say something, but unsure of what Kelly's reaction would be. They hadn't talked about Suzy at all since she'd come back from the White House a couple of days ago.

"I was thinking that maybe we should check on Suzy later today? We could ask her round for dinner. What do you say? I can call her." Mark looked at Kelly and was not surprised when she stiffened up and stopped rubbing his neck.

"I don't think so," she said. "Suzy and me...let's just say she needs some time to deal with things. I don't think now is the right time." Kelly shook her head sadly. "I don't know what to do or say to her anymore. She hardly spoke to me at all at the dinner the other night. She was acting strange too. As if she knew something that I didn't. I don't know. I guess we should give her some space to come to terms with what happened."

Mark murmured in agreement. "Okay, well I was thinking of showing my face at work today. You can come in with me if you want?"

"Thanks, but another day. I'm shattered. I might just go back to bed for a while."

"Now that's what I'm talking about," said Mark grinning and taking Kelly's hand. He led her back to the bedroom and Kelly didn't sleep again for a few more hours.

* * *

Kelly looked at herself in her pocket mirror and then flipped the case shut. She had tried to cover up the bags under her eyes, but she thought she still looked terrible. She was sitting in a Starbucks close to the museum, drawing down her third coffee of the day. She had walked past the museum four times, trying to pluck up the courage to go in, but chickening out each time. There were too many memories, too many reminders of what she'd lost. The last few days had been a whirlwind. Each of her former colleague's memorial services were blurring into one. There were no bodies to bury and too many people to comfort.

There was a television in the coffee shop and she had ignored it, preferring to focus on what she was going to do about her work at the museum, than the latest reality show. Someone turned up the volume just as she looked up and she saw Mark walking toward her. He had his duffel coat on and Inca was trotting obediently beside him on a red leash. She watched Mark walk, finding herself falling for him more every day. She had certainly not expected to meet anyone and had not felt herself drawn to him at first. But now there was something that connected them, something nobody else would understand. Mark was an assured, honest man and she already felt comfortable in his presence. She watched him tie up Inca outside and then the coffee shop bell jangled as he strode in.

"Not late, am I?" he said frowning.

"No, no, I'm early. I ordered you a latte. Then we can pick out some food. I'm famished."

"Must be all that energy you're using," said Mark winking as he sat down.

Kelly smiled back, still not sure how to acknowledge their relationship. As good as it was, it was still early days and she didn't want to put pressure on him for anything. She didn't have the experience either and so she tended to deflect attention away from herself when she could with a smile, a kiss, or something more.

Mark could see Kelly was distracted and he reached over the table for her hand. "What's up?"

"Oh, nothing really. Just lots on my mind." She leant over and gave Mark a quick kiss. "What's with the television? With that and the coffee grinder, I can barely hear myself think in here. You want to go somewhere else?"

Mark looked up at the television and realised why it had been turned up. "It's the memorial service in California. See?"

Kelly turned to see the screen positioned high up in an alcove above the counter. Whilst they waited for Mark's latte, they watched some footage of the newly built Golden Gate Bridge before the TV station cut to President Agnew. He was stood on a semi-permanent platform, somewhere in downtown San Francisco. He was flanked by his security and Kelly was sure she recognised some of them from the White House. A man with cropped white hair was there and behind him, she could just see Sophie. President Agnew stepped up to a multitude of microphones to begin his speech.

"Let's just listen to what the prick has to say," said Mark. He was curious to know if Agnew would make any reference to The Grave. He felt sure the media would have a barrage of questions lined up. He watched as Agnew slicked back his hair and brushed away the first question.

"...given Senator Collins' untimely passing, I am deeply honoured to be here today. I was not going to let a slight cold bar me from remembering those who lost their lives in this magnificent American city. The terrorists will never win. I know the American people stand shoulder to shoulder, united in defeating our enemy whoever and wherever they are."

Kelly heard Agnew say he had a cold, but he looked fine. Probably another tactic to gain some sympathy, she thought. There was a smattering of applause and some audible coughing that grew louder.

"Someone's too close to the mike," said Mark to Kelly. "They should..." Mark stopped as he realised something was wrong. Agnew was looking backwards and not at the camera. Agnew looked puzzled by something.

Kelly stood up, knocking her coffee over. She ignored it as a shiver ran down her back. "Mark. You don't think…"

"What?" said Mark frowning. "What's wrong?"

Kelly watched the screen, unable to tear her eyes away and unable to believe what she was seeing. Behind the President, people were gathering around something or someone. The white-haired man crouched down and Kelly was sure she saw Sophie collapse. Agnew appeared unsure if he should carry on with the speech or stop and attend to his wife. A young blonde woman rushed up and said something to the President before stepping back out of the camera's view.

"Ladies and gentlemen, it's nothing to worry about. Unfortunately, my wife seems to have caught the cold I managed to shake off. I'm assured she will be back up on her feet any moment and we can carry on with the service." Agnew glanced over his shoulder uncomfortably as various people ran back and forth behind him.

A scream echoed through the television signal to every home in America. Kelly heard something shatter, some shouting and then saw the group of people behind Agnew scatter. They ran in all directions, leaving Agnew standing alone on the stage. One man clutched his arm to his chest with blood clearly pouring from a fresh wound. Somebody threw up as they ran in front of the camera and the white-haired man Kelly vaguely recognised was staggering away whilst pressing something against his neck. The cloth, or whatever he held, was turning a dark crimson, and he was helped off stage by two other men in suits.

The cameraman appeared to be unsure of what to do as the images on the screen blurred in and out, until he finally zoomed in on the chaos behind the President.

Sophie Agnew had blood dripping down her front. She was chewing on something ragged that looked like strips of bacon and her eyes were glassy. They settled on her husband, and the cameraman panned back as Sophie staggered toward the podium.

Abruptly, the television screen turned black. There was a faint electronic whistle as the power died and Kelly became aware of the gasps of the people around her. The cafe was silent, apart from the coffee machine gurgling away on the counter. Kelly could hear sirens wailing in the background and Inca barking. She turned to the glass doors. A female jogger ran past outside, a crumpled newspaper flitted by and a yellow cab pulled up quickly. For New York, it was another ordinary autumn day and yet she had a horrible feeling in the pit of her stomach.

Mark stood up as the atmosphere in the café became tense. People were shouting for the TV to be turned back on and others were leaving quickly. "What the hell was that?" he said to Kelly.

Kelly broke out in a cold sweat. Images flashed to her of Will, Claire and Tug. Roach's hands gripped her and she was rooted to the spot. She couldn't hear Mark's insistent voice, telling her they had to leave, and only turned to him when the TV was turned back on. The screen had an emergency broadcast signal on, announcing they hoped to be back on the air momentarily. "Oh, Suzy, what have you done?" said Kelly.

Mark grabbed her and they ran outside into the cold New York wind.

THE END

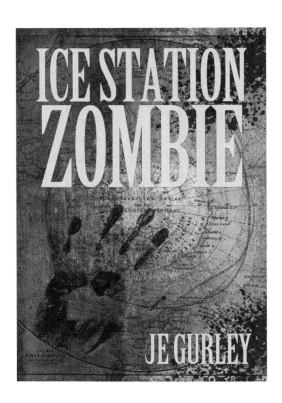

ICE STATION ZOMBIE
JE GURLEY

For most of the long, cold winter, Antarctica is a frozen wasteland. Now, the ice is melting and the zombies are thawing. Arctic explorers Val Marino and Elliot Anson race against time and death to reach Australia, but the Demise has preceded them and zombies stalk the streets of Adelaide and Coober Pedy.

The Coalition

When the dead rose to destroy the living, Ron Cutter learned to survive. While so many others died, he thrived. His life is a constant battle against the living dead. As he casts his own bullets and packs his shotgun shells, his humanity slowly melts away.

Then he encounters a lost boy and a woman searching for a place of refuge. Can they help him recover the emotions he set aside to live? And if he does recover them, will those feelings be an asset in his struggles, or a danger to him?

THE STATE OF EXTINCTION: the first installment in the **COALITON OF THE LIVING** trilogy of Mankind's battle against the plague of the Living Dead. As recounted by author **Robert Mathis Kurtz.**

www.severedpress.com

RANCID

Nothing ever happens in the middle of nowhere or in Virginia for that matter. This is why Noel and her friends found themselves on cloud nine when one of their favorite hardcore bands happened to be playing a show in their small hometown. Between the meteor shower and the short trip to the cemetery outside of town after the show, this crazy group of friends instantly plummet from those clouds into a frenzied nightmare of putrefied horror.

Is this sudden nightmare related to the showering meteors or does this small town hold even darker secrets than the rotting corpses that are surfacing?

"Zombies in small town America, a corporate conspiracy, fast paced action and a satisfying body count- what's not to like? Just don't get too attached to any character; they may die or turn zombie soon enough!" - Mainak Dhar, bestselling author of Alice in Deadland and Zombiestan

www.severedpress.com

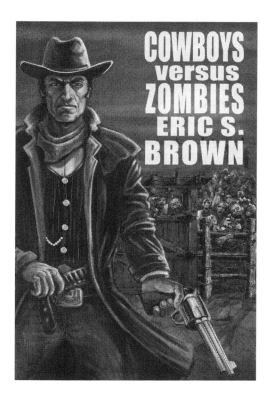

COWBOYS VS ZOMBIES

Dilouie is a killer. He's always made his way in life by the speed of his gun hand and the coldness of his remorseless heart. Life never meant much to him until the world fell apart and they awoke. Overnight, the dead stopped being dead. Hungry corpses rose from blood splattered streets and graves. Their numbers were unimaginable and their need for the flesh of the living insatiable.

The United States is no more. Washed away in a tide of gnashing teeth and rotting, clawing hands. Dilouie no longer kills for money and pleasure but to simply keep breathing and to see the sunrise of the next dawn. . . And he is beginning to wonder if even men like him can survive in a world that now belongs to the dead?

TIMOTHY
MARK TUFO

Timothy was not a good man in life and being
undead did little to improve his disposition.
Find out what a man trapped in his own mind
will do to survive when he wakes up to find
himself a zombie controlled by a self-aware
virus.

www.severedpress.com

4902388R00140

Printed in Great Britain
by Amazon.co.uk, Ltd.,
Marston Gate.